Someone Else's Shoes

Someone Else's Shoes

JOJO MOYES

MICHAEL  JOSEPH

PENGUIN MICHAEL JOSEPH

UK | USA | Canada | Ireland | Australia
India | New Zealand | South Africa

Penguin Michael Joseph is part of the Penguin Random House group of companies
whose addresses can be found at global.penguinrandomhouse.com

First published 2023

006

Copyright © Jojo's Mojo Ltd, 2023

This novel was inspired by the short story 'Crocodile Shoes'
from *Paris for One and Other Stories* by Jojo Moyes,
published by Penguin Michael Joseph in 2016

The moral right of the author has been asserted

Set in Garamond MT

Typeset by Couper Street Type Co.

Printed in Great Britain by Clays Ltd, Elcograf S.p.A.

The authorized representative in the EEA is Penguin Random House Ireland,
Morrison Chambers, 32 Nassau Street, Dublin D02 YH68

A CIP catalogue record for this book is available from the British Library

HARDBACK ISBN: 978–0–241–41553–5
OPEN MARKET PAPERBACK ISBN: 978–0–241–41554–2

www.greenpenguin.co.uk

For JWH

I

Sam stares up at the slowly lightening ceiling and practises her breathing, like the doctor advised her, as she tries to stop her 5 a.m. thoughts congealing into one enormous dark cloud above her head.

In for six, hold for three, out for seven.

I am healthy, she recites silently. My family is healthy. The dog has stopped that weeing-in-the-hall thing. There is food in the fridge and I still have a job. She slightly regrets putting in that *still* because the thought of her job makes her stomach clench again.

In for six, hold for three, out for seven.

Her parents are still alive. Although admittedly it can be hard to justify including that in a mental gratitude diary. Oh, Jesus. Her mother is going to make some pointed comment on Sunday about how they always visit Phil's mother, isn't she? It will come at some point between the small sherry and the over-heavy pudding, as inevitable as death, taxes and these random chin hairs. She imagines fending her off with a polite smile: *Well, Mum, Nancy has just lost her husband of fifty years. She's a bit lonely just now.*

But you visited her all the time when he was still alive, didn't you? she hears her mother's response.

Yes, but her husband was dying. Phil wanted to see his dad as much as possible before he shuffled off this mortal coil. We weren't having a bloody knees-up.

She realizes she is having another imaginary argument with her mother, and pulls it back, trying to put the thought into a mental box, like she read in an article, and place an imaginary mental lid on it. The lid fails resolutely to shut. She finds she has a lot of imaginary arguments, these days: with Simon at work, with her mother, with that woman who pushed in front of her at the checkout yesterday. None of these arguments ever leave her lips in real life. She just grits her teeth. And tries to breathe.

In for six, hold for three, out for seven.

I am not living in an actual war zone, she thinks. There is clean water in the taps and food on the shelves. No explosions, no guns. No famine. That's got to be something. But thinking about those poor children in war zones makes her eyes prickle with tears. Her eyes are always prickling with tears. Cat keeps telling her to go and get HRT but she still has periods and occasional hormonal spots (how is that fair?) and, anyway, there is no time to book a doctor's appointment. The last time she rang they didn't have a single one available for two weeks. *What if I was dying?* she had thought. And had an imaginary argument with the doctor's receptionist.

In real life, she simply said: 'Oh, that's a bit far off. I'm sure I'll be fine. Thanks anyway.'

She glances to her right. Phil is slumbering, his face troubled even in sleep. She wants to reach over and stroke his hair, but lately when she does that he jumps awake, looking startled and unhappy, as if she has done something cruel.

She folds her hands in front of her instead and tries to adopt a relaxed, even pose. Rest is as good as sleep, someone once told her. Just clear your thoughts, and let your body relax. Let your limbs release any tension they're holding, from the toes up. Let your feet grow heavy. Let that feeling travel slowly up to your ankles, your knees, your hips, your stom—

Ah, fuck it, says the inside of her head. It's a quarter to six. I might as well get up.

'There's no milk,' says Cat. She is staring accusingly at the interior of the fridge, as if waiting for some to materialize.

'You could run to the shop?'

'I haven't got *time*,' Cat says. 'I have to do my hair.'

'Well, I'm afraid I haven't got time either.'

'Why?'

'Because I'm going to that gym and spa you bought me a day pass for. Bodyworks. It expires tomorrow.'

'But I gave you that a year ago! And surely you'll only get a couple of hours in there if you're going to work.'

'I've arranged to go in a bit late. At least it's right near the office. I just haven't had any time.' She never has any time. She says it like a mantra, along with 'I'm so tired'. But nobody has any time. Everybody is tired.

Cat raises her eyebrows. For her, self-care is a necessity, coming before the more prosaic needs of money, housing and nutrition.

'I keep telling you, Mum, use it or lose it,' says Cat, who eyes her mother's increasingly indistinct hip-to-waist ratio with barely concealed horror. She closes the fridge. 'Ugh. I just don't know why Dad can't even buy a carton of milk.'

'Leave him a note,' she says, gathering her things. 'Maybe he'll be feeling better today.'

'And maybe monkeys will fly out of my butt.'

Cat stalks out of the kitchen in the way that only a nineteen-year-old young woman can. A few seconds later Sam can hear the furious roar of her hairdryer and knows that it will be left in Cat's room until she retrieves it.

'I thought you didn't drink cow's milk any more, anyway,' she shouts up the stairs.

The hairdryer stops briefly. 'Now you're just being annoying,' comes the response.

She locates her swimsuit at the back of the drawer and shoves it into her black kitbag.

She is peeling off her wet swimsuit when the yummy mummies arrive. Glossy and stick thin, they swiftly surround her, talking loudly and across each other, their voices filling the fuggy silence of the changing room, completely oblivious to her presence. Sam feels the brief equilibrium gained by her twenty-length swim evaporating like mist. It has taken her an hour here to remember that she hates these places: the apartheid of hard bodies, the corners where she and the other lumpy people try to hide. She has walked by this place a million times and wondered whether to go in. She realizes that these are the kind of women who leave her feeling worse than if she'd never come in at all.

'Are you going to have time for coffee afterwards, Nina? I thought we could go to that lovely café that opened up behind Space NK. The one with the poke bowls.'

'Love to. Got to be away by eleven, though. I'm taking Leonie to the orthodontist. Ems?'

'Oh, God, yes. I need some girl time!'

These are women with designer athleisure, perfectly cut hair, and time for coffee. These are women whose gym bags bear designer labels, rather than her fake Marc Jacobs knock-off, and have husbands called Rupe or Tris, who carelessly toss envelopes containing hefty bonuses onto shining Conran Shop kitchen tables. These women drive huge off-roaders that never get muddy, double-park their way through their day and demand babyccinos for querulous children from harassed baristas, tutting when they are not made to their exact specification. They do not lie awake until 4 a.m. worrying about electricity bills, or feel sick about greeting their new boss with his shiny suit and his barely disguised disdain each morning.

They do not have husbands who stay in their pyjama bottoms till midday and look hunted whenever their wives mention maybe having another go at that job application.

Sam is at that age, the age where all the wrong things seem somehow to stick, fat, the groove between her eyebrows, anxiety, while everything else – job security, marital happiness, dreams – seems to slip effortlessly away.

'You have no idea how much they've put up the prices at Le Méridien this year,' one of the women is saying. She is bent over, towelling her expensively tinted hair. Sam has to wiggle sideways to avoid touching her.

'I know! I tried to book Mauritius for Christmas – our usual villa's gone up by forty per cent.'

'It's a scandal.'

Yes, it's a scandal, she thinks. How awful for you all. She thinks of the camper-van that Phil bought two years ago to do up. 'We can spend weekends by the coast,' he had said cheerfully, eyeing the huge van now blocking their driveway with its giant sunflower on the side. He never got beyond replacing the back bumper. Since his Year of Carnage, it has sat in front of their house, a nagging, daily reminder of what they have lost.

Sam wriggles into her knickers, trying to hide her pale flesh under the towel. Today she has four meetings with important clients. In half an hour she will meet Ted and Joel from Print and Transport, and they will try to win their company some vital business. And she will try to save her job. Maybe all their jobs.

No pressure there, then.

'I think we're going to do the Maldives this year. You know, before they sink.'

'Oh, good idea. We loved it. Such a shame, the whole sinking thing.'

Another woman pushes past Sam to open her locker. She is dark-haired, like Sam, maybe a few years younger, but her body has the toned look of someone for whom hard exercise, moisturizing and buffing are daily occurrences. She smells expensive, like it actually oozes from her pores.

Sam pulls her towel tighter around her pale, dimply skin and disappears around the corner to dry her hair. When she returns, they have all gone. She breathes a sigh of relief and slumps onto the damp wooden bench. She thinks she might just go and lie down on one of the heated marble beds in the corner for half an hour. The thought fills her with sudden pleasure: a half-hour of just lying there in blissful silence.

Her phone buzzes in her jacket, hanging in the locker behind her. She reaches into her pocket and pulls it out.

You ready? We're outside.

What? she types. We're not due at Framptons till this afternoon.

Didn't Simon tell you? It got moved up to 10. Come on – we need to leave.

She glances at her phone in horror. This means she is apparently due at the first meeting in twenty-three minutes. She groans, wriggles into her trousers, sweeps the black kit-bag from the bench, and stomps off towards the car park.

The dirty white van with GRAYSIDE PRINT SOLUTIONS on the side is waiting by the loading doors, engine idling. She half runs, half shuffles towards it in the gym flip-flops. She will return them tomorrow but already feels guilty, as if she's committed some major transgression. Her hair is still damp and she is puffing slightly.

6

'I think Simon's gunning for you, sweetheart,' says Ted, as she climbs into the van. He shuffles up the front bench seat to make room for her. He smells of cigarette smoke and Old Spice.

'You think?'

'You want to watch him. Double-check all the meeting times with Genevieve,' says Joel, wrenching the steering wheel around. His dreadlocks are pulled back into a neat ponytail, as if in deference to the day ahead.

'It's just not the same since they took over, is it?' says Ted, as they pull onto the main road. 'Feels like we're walking on eggshells every day.'

There are two empty, sugar-strewn paper bags on the dashboard, and Ted hands her a third, containing a huge, still-warm jam doughnut.

'There you go,' he says. 'Breakfast of champions.'

She should not eat it. It contains at least twice as many calories as she has just burned off swimming. She can hear Cat's sigh of disapproval from here. But she hesitates, then stuffs it into her mouth and closes her eyes at the warm, sugary comfort. These days, Sam takes her pleasures where she can.

'Genevieve heard him talking on the phone about redundancies again,' says Joel. 'She says when she walked into his office he changed the subject.'

Every time she hears 'redundancy', a word that now flutters around the office like a trapped moth, her stomach clenches. She doesn't know what they will do if she loses her job too. Phil is refusing to take the anti-depressants the doctor prescribed. He says they make him sleepy, as if he doesn't sleep most days till eleven anyway.

'It won't come to that,' says Ted, unconvincingly. 'Sam's going to bring in the business today, aren't you?'

She realizes they're both looking at her. 'Yes,' she says. And then, more positively, 'Yes!'

She does her makeup in the small vanity mirror, cursing quietly every time Joel goes over a bump, and rubbing off the resulting smudges with a licked finger. She checks her hair, which has not dried too badly, all things considered. She flicks through the file of paperwork, making sure she has all the figures at her fingertips. She has a vague memory of when she felt confident about all this stuff, when she could walk into a room and know that she was good at her job. *Come on, Sam, just try to be that person again*, she tells herself silently. And then she slips her feet out of the flip-flops and reaches into her kitbag for her shoes.

'Five minutes away,' says Joel.

It is only then she realizes that although the kitbag looks like hers it is not hers. This bag does not contain her comfortable black pumps, suitable for pounding pavements and negotiating print deals. This bag contains a pair of vertiginous red crocodile-skin Christian Louboutin slingbacks.

She pulls out a shoe and stares at it, its strappy, unfamiliar weight dangling in her hand.

'Blimey,' says Ted. 'Is the first meeting at Stringfellows?'

Sam bends down and rifles through the bag, coming up with the other shoe, a pair of jeans and then a neatly folded pale Chanel jacket.

'Oh, my God,' she says. 'This isn't mine. I've picked up the wrong bag. We have to go back.'

'No time,' says Joel, staring straight ahead at the road. 'We're pushing it already.'

'But I need my bag.'

'Sorry, Sam,' he says. 'We'll go back later. Wear what you wore to the gym?'

'I can't wear flip-flops to a business meeting.'

'Wear the shoes that are in there?'

'You're kidding me.'

Ted takes the shoe from her. 'She has a point, Joel. Those shoes aren't very . . . Sam.'

'Why? What's very "me"?'

'Well. Plain. You like plain stuff.' He pauses. 'Sensible stuff.'

'You know what they say about shoes like that,' says Joel.

'What?'

'They're not for standing up in.'

They nudge each other, chuckling.

Sam snatches the shoe back from him. It's half a size too small. She eases her foot into it and fastens the strap.

'Great,' she says, looking at her foot. 'I get to pitch to Framptons looking like a call-girl.'

'At least it's an expensive call-girl,' says Ted.

'What?'

'You know. Rather than the five-quid-no-teeth-blowjob kind . . .'

Sam waits for Joel's laughter to die down. 'Well, thanks, Ted,' she says, staring out of the window. 'I feel so much better now.'

The meeting isn't in an office, as she had expected. There is a problem in Transport, and they will have to pitch in the loading area, where Michael Frampton is going to be overseeing some issue with a botched hydraulic system. Sam tries to walk in the heels, feeling the cold air on her feet. She wishes she had had a pedicure, maybe some time since 2009. Her ankles keep wobbling, as if they're made of rubber, and she wonders how on earth anyone is expected to walk normally in footwear like this. Joel was right. These are not shoes for standing up in.

'You okay?' says Ted, as they draw closer to the group of men.

'No,' she mutters. 'I feel like I'm walking on chopsticks.'

A forklift truck carries a huge bale of paper in front of them, causing them to swerve, and her to stumble, its beep a warning that sounds almost deafening in the cavernous space. She watches as every man around the lorry swivels his head to look at her. And then down at her shoes.

'Thought you weren't coming.'

Michael Frampton is a dour Yorkshireman, the kind who will let you know how hard he's had it, and simultaneously imply that you haven't, in any conversational exchange.

Sam musters a smile. 'So sorry,' she says, her voice bright. 'We had another meeting which —'

'Traffic,' says Joel, simultaneously, and they glance awkwardly at each other.

'Sam Kemp. We met at —'

'I remember you,' he says, and looks down. He spends an uncomfortable two minutes talking through the contents of a clipboard with a young man in overalls, and Sam stands helplessly, conscious of the casual curious glances of the men around him. Her inappropriate shoes glow like radioactive beacons on her feet.

'Right,' says Michael, when he finally finishes. 'I have to tell you before we start that Printex have offered us very competitive terms.'

'Well, we —' Sam begins.

'And they say you won't have the flexibility now Grayside has been swallowed up by a bigger company.'

'Well, that's not entirely true. What we have now is volume, quality and — reliability.'

She feels faintly stupid as she speaks, as if everyone is looking at her, as if it is obvious that she is a middle-aged woman in somebody else's shoes. She stammers her way through the meeting, stumbling over her answers and flushing, feeling everyone's eyes on her feet.

Finally she pulls a folder from her bag. It contains the quote she has spent hours refining and laying out. She makes to walk across to hand it to Michael, but her heel catches on something. She stumbles and twists her ankle, sending a sharp pain up her leg. She turns her grimace into a smile, and hands him the file. He glances down at it, flicking through the pages, not looking at her. Eventually she walks away, slowly, trying not to wobble.

Finally, Michael looks up. 'We're looking at serious numbers for this next order. So we need to make sure we're with a firm that can definitely deliver.'

'We've delivered for you before, Mr Frampton. And last month we worked with Greenlight on a similar run of catalogues. They were very impressed with the quality.'

His whole face is an extended frown. 'Can I take a look at what you did for them?'

'Sure.'

She flicks through her folder and remembers suddenly that the Greenlight catalogue is in the blue folder on the dashboard of the van, the one she had thought she wouldn't need. And that that involves walking out of this loading area and across the car park, in full view of all the men. She looks meaningfully at Joel.

'Why don't I go and get it?' says Joel.

'What other samples have you got in the van?' says Frampton.

'Well, we did a similar run for Clarks Office Supplies. In fact, we have quite a few different catalogues from last month. Joel, could you –'

'Nah. I'll take a look myself.' Frampton starts to walk. This means she has to. She sets off, a little more stiffly, alongside him.

'What we need,' he says, thrusting his hands into his pockets, 'is a print partner who is fast-moving, someone flexible. Fleet-footed, if you like.'

He is striding too briskly. It is at this point that she turns her ankle again on the uneven surface, and lets out a yelp. Joel thrusts out an arm just as her knees buckle and she's forced to grab it to stay upright. She smiles awkwardly as Frampton looks at them, his face unreadable.

Later, she will recall, her ears hot with embarrassment, his muttered words to Joel. The last words he will utter to Grayside Print.

Is she drunk?

2

Nisha Cantor is running furiously on a treadmill. Music pumps in her ears and her legs are pounding like pistons. She always runs furiously. The first mile is the worst, fired by a choleric mix of resentment and lactic acid; the second makes her really, really angry; and the third is where her head finally starts to clear, when she feels suddenly like her body is oiled, like she can run for ever, and then she's angry again because she has to stop and do something else just at the point when she's started to enjoy it. She hates the run, and she needs it for her sanity. She hates visiting this damn city, where there are people all over the sidewalks, meandering slowly, so the only place she can run properly is this crappy gym, to which the hotel has siphoned its guests while its own superior facilities are apparently being renovated.

The machine informs her that it's time for her to cool down, and she turns it off abruptly, unwilling to be told what to do by a freaking machine. *No, I will not cool down*, she thinks. As she pulls out one of her earphones she becomes aware of a ringing sound. Nisha reaches over to pick up her phone. It's Carl.

'Darling –'

'Excuse me.'

Nisha looks up.

'You need to turn your phone off,' says a young woman. 'This is a quiet area.'

'Then stop talking at me. You're very loud. And please don't stand so close. I might be absorbing droplets of your sweat.'

The woman's jaw drops slightly and Nisha presses her phone to her ear.

'Nisha, darling. What are you up to?'

'Just at the gym, my love. Are we still meeting for lunch?'

Carl's voice, as smooth as butter, one of the things she has always loved about him. 'Yes, but perhaps we could have it at the hotel. I have to come back to pick up some papers.'

'Of course,' says Nisha, automatically. 'What would you like me to order for you?'

'Oh, anything.'

She freezes. Carl never says 'anything'.

'You want Michel's special white-truffle omelette? Or the seared tuna?'

'Sure. That will be lovely.'

Nisha swallows. She tries to keep her voice level. 'What time would you like it?'

Carl pauses and she hears the muffled sound of him talking to someone else in the room. Her heart has started to pound.

'Midday would be wonderful. But take your time. I don't want to rush you.'

'Of course,' says Nisha. 'Love you.'

'You too, darling,' says Carl, and the line goes dead.

Nisha stands very still, her blood pumping in her ears in a way that has nothing to do with running. She thinks briefly that her head may actually explode. She takes two deep breaths. Then she punches another number into the phone. It goes straight to voicemail. She curses the time difference with New York.

'Magda?' she says, her hand raking through her sweaty hair. 'It's Mrs Cantor. You need to get on to your man, NOW.'

When she looks up, a gym attendant, in a polo shirt and cheap shorts, has appeared. 'Ma'am, you cannot use a phone in here, I'm afraid. It's against –'

'Just back off,' says Nisha. 'Go clean a floor or something. This place is a goddamn Petri dish.' She pushes past him towards the changing room, snatching a towel from another attendant as she goes.

The changing rooms are packed, but she sees nobody. She is running through the telephone conversation in her head, over and over, her heart thumping. So this is it. She needs to clear her head, to be ready to respond, but her body has gone into a weird stasis and nothing is working as it should. She sits down on the bench briefly, staring blankly in front of her. *I can do this,* she tells herself, gazing at her trembling hands. *I have survived worse.* She presses her face into the towel, breathing in until she's sure she's got the shakes under control, and straightens, pushing her shoulders back.

Finally she stands and opens her locker, pulling out her Marc Jacobs kitbag. Someone has placed their bag on the bench beside her locker and she shoves it onto the floor, putting her own in its place. Shower. She must shower before she does anything. Appearances are everything. And then her phone rings again. A couple of women look over but she ignores them and picks it up from the bench beside her. Raymond.

'Mom? Did you see the picture of my eyebrows?'

'What, darling?'

'My eyebrows. I sent a picture. Did you look?'

Nisha holds out her phone and flicks through her messages until she finds the picture he has sent. 'You have beautiful eyebrows, sweetheart,' she says reassuringly, putting the phone back to her ear.

'They're terrible. I just feel really down. I saw this programme on, like, the dolphin trade and there were all these dolphins just being made to do tricks and stuff and I felt so guilty because we went to that place and swam with them in

Mexico, remember? I felt so bad I couldn't leave my room and then I thought I'd tidy up my eyebrows and it was a disaster because now I look like mid-nineties Madonna.'

A woman has started drying her hair nearby and Nisha briefly considers wrenching the hairdryer out of her hand and clubbing her to death with it. 'Sweetheart, I can't hear you in here. Hold on.'

She walks out into the corridor. Takes a deep breath. 'They look perfect,' she says, into the muffled silence. 'Gorgeous. And mid-nineties Madonna is a totally hot look.'

She can picture him, cross-legged on his bed back in Westchester, the way he has sat since he was tiny.

'They don't look gorgeous, Mom. It's a *disaster*.'

A woman comes out of the changing area and passes her, her feet slopping in flip-flops, her head down as she hurries past in her cheap jacket. Why don't women stand up straight? The woman's shoulders are slumped, her head dipped into her neck like a turtle's, and Nisha is immediately irritated. If you look like a victim, why are you surprised when people treat you badly? 'Then we'll get them microbladed when you come home.'

'So they *do* look terrible.'

'No! No, you look gorgeous. But, sweetheart, I really need to go. I'm right in the middle of something. I'll call you.'

'Not until three my time, earliest. I have to sleep and then we have self-care. It's so dumb. They make you do all this mindfulness stuff like it wasn't being stuck in my head that got me here in the first place.'

'I know, darling. I'll call you after that. I love you.'

Nisha ends the call and dials again. 'Magda? Magda? Did you get my message? Call me as soon as you get this. Okay?'

She is ending the call when the door opens. A gym attendant walks in and spies her holding her phone.

'Ma'am, I'm sorry but –'

'Don't. Even,' she snarls, and he closes his mouth over the words. There are some advantages to being an American woman over forty who no longer has any fucks left on the shelf, and he can see it. It is the first thing she has felt glad about all week.

Nisha showers, moisturizes her limbs with the gym's inferior products (she will smell like an Amtrak restroom all day), ties her wet hair into a knot and then, her feet safely on a towel (changing-room floors make her nauseous – the skin cells! The verrucas!), checks her phone for the eighteenth time to see if Magda has responded.

Trying to suppress the giant ball of fury and anxiety that is swelling in her chest is getting harder. She takes her silk blouse off the hanger, feeling the liquid fall of it sticking to her warm damp skin as she pulls it over her head. *Where is Magda, for God's sake?* She sits and glances at her phone again, reaching absent-mindedly into her kitbag for jeans and shoes. She feels around and finally pulls out a very tired, ugly, block-heeled black pump. She turns and blinks at her hand for a moment before dropping the shoe with a little gasp of horror. She wipes her fingers on a towel, then slowly opens the bag with a corner of it, peering inside. It takes her a moment to grasp what she is looking at. This bag is not her bag. This is fake leather, its plastic covering already peeling at the seams, and what should be a brass 'Marc Jacobs' tag has tarnished its way to a dull silver.

Nisha peers under the bench. Then behind her. Most of the annoying women have gone now, and there are no other bags, just a few gaping lockers. There are no other bags. This bag looks like her bag – same size, same colour, similar handles – but it definitely isn't hers.

17

'Who took my bag?' she says aloud, to nobody in particular. '*Who the hell took my bag?*' The few women in the changing room glance over at her but look blank.

'No,' she says. '*No no no no no*. Not today. Not now.'

The girl at the desk doesn't blink.

'Where's the CCTV?'

'Madam, there's no CCTV in the ladies' changing room. It would be against the law.'

'So how am I meant to find out who stole my bag?'

'I don't think it's been stolen, madam. From what you said, it seems like an accidental switch, if the bags were so similar –'

'You really think anyone would "accidentally" pick up my Chanel jacket and custom-made Louboutin heels made by Christian himself when they dress themselves normally in . . .' she peers into the bag, grimaces '. . . *Primark?*'

The receptionist's face doesn't shift a muscle.

'We can go through the CCTV at the entrance but we'll have to get clearance from head office.'

'I haven't got time. Who was the last person out of here?'

'We don't hold those records, madam. It's all automated. If you hold on I'll call the manager and he can come over.'

'Finally! Where is he?'

'He's staff training in Pinner.'

'Oh, for God's sake. Give me some track shoes. Do you have track shoes here? I just need to get to my car.'

Nisha peers out of the window. 'Where is my car? Where's the car?'

She turns away from the desk and punches a number into her phone. No answer. The receptionist pulls out a plastic packet from under the counter. She looks as bored as if she has just had to listen to a two-hour TED talk on the Drying of Paint. She plonks them on the counter. 'We have flip-flops.'

Nisha looks at the girl, then at the shoes, then at the girl again. The girl's face is a blank. Finally, she snatches them off the counter and, with a low growl of frustration, wrenches them onto her feet. She hears the muttered '*Americans!*' as she leaves.

3

'Never mind, love. Still three to go,' says Ted, kindly.

They have driven in silence to the next meeting. Sam has spent the past twenty minutes in the van under a cloud of crushing misery, guilt seeping into every cell that once contained what remained of her confidence. What must they have thought of her? She could still feel the disbelieving stares of those men, the barely concealed smirks as she wobbled back into the van. Joel had clapped her on the shoulder and told her Frampton was a wanker and everyone knew he was a late payer anyway so it was probably the best thing all round, but even as he spoke all she could see was the distant curl of Simon's lip as she had to tell him that she had lost a valuable contract.

In for six, hold for three, out for seven.

Joel pulls up in the car park and switches off the ignition. They sit for a moment, listening to the engine tick down and looking up at the glossy-fronted building. Her stomach is somewhere in the footwell of the van.

'Would it be really bad to go into this meeting in flip-flops?' she says, finally.

'Yes,' say Ted and Joel, at the same time.

'But —'

'Babe.' Joel leans forward over the steering wheel and turns to face her. 'You wear those shoes, you've got to style it out.'

'What do you mean?'

'Well, you looked . . . embarrassed back there. You still look embarrassed. You've got to look like you own them.'

'I don't own them.'

'You've got to look confident. Like you just threw them on, you know, while you were thinking about all those big-bucks deals you already signed today.'

Ted compresses his mouth into a fleshy line and nods. He nudges her with a ham-like arm. 'He's right. Come on, sweetheart. Chin up, tits out, big smile. You can do it.'

Sam reaches for her bag. 'You wouldn't say that to Simon.'

Ted shrugs. 'I would if he was wearing those shoes.'

'So the lowest we can do on that job is . . . forty-two thousand. But if you switch the page numbers and change the title page to mono, we could shave eight hundred off that price.'

She is outlining their print strategy when she observes that the managing director is not listening to her. For a minute she feels the flush of embarrassment again, and stammers the rest of her words. 'So – so how do those figures sound?'

He doesn't say anything. He rubs a spot on his forehead and makes a noncommittal *mmm* sound, like she used to when Cat was little and she was listening to her endless babble with only half an ear.

Oh, God, I'm losing him. She looks up from her notes, and realizes the managing director is staring at her foot. Mortified, she almost loses the thread of what she is saying. But then she looks again, registers his glazed expression: it is him who is distracted. 'And, of course, we could do that on an eight-day turnaround, as discussed,' she says.

'Good!' he exclaims, as if hauled from a daydream. 'Yes. Good.'

He is still staring at her foot. She watches, then tilts it slightly to the left and extends her ankle. He gazes at it, rapt. She glances across the table and sees Joel and Ted exchange a look.

'So would those terms be acceptable to you?'

The managing director steeples his fingers, briefly meets her eye. She smiles encouragingly.

'Uh . . . yes. Sounds good.' He can't stop looking. His gaze slides from her face downwards, back to the shoe.

She pulls a contract from her briefcase. She tilts her foot and lets the heel strap slide slowly down her heel. 'So, shall we agree terms?'

'Sure,' he says. He takes the pen and signs the document without looking at it.

'Don't say anything,' she tells Ted, her gaze fixed straight ahead, as they walk out through Reception.

'I'm saying nothing. You get us another deal like that, you can wear a pair of flippers for all I care.'

At the next meeting she makes sure her feet are on display the whole time. Although John Edgmont doesn't stare, she sees that the mere fact of the shoes makes him reassess his version of who she is. Weirdly, it makes her reassess her version of herself. She walks into his office with her head high. She charms. She stands firm on terms. She wins another contract.

'You're on it, Sam,' says Joel, as they climb back into the van.

They take an actual lunch break – something they haven't dared do since Simon was put in charge – and sit outside at a coffee shop. The sun comes out. Joel tells them about a date he went on the previous week where the woman asked him what he thought of a wedding-dress picture she had cut from a magazine – 'She said, "It's okay, I only show people I really like"' – and Ted spits his coffee through his nostrils and she laughs until her sides hurt and realizes she has no idea when she last laughed at anything.

Nisha is pacing up and down the chilly sidewalk outside the gym, the bathrobe over her blouse and flip-flops. She has left nine messages on Peter's cellphone and he is not picking up. This is not a good sign. Not a good sign at all.

'Peter? Peter? Where are you? I told you to be outside by eleven fifteen! I need you here *right now*!'

The final time she calls, a tinny, automated voice tells her this number is unobtainable. She checks the time, curses loudly, reaches into her pocket and pulls out her room-key card. She stares at it for a moment then stomps back into the gym.

The bag outside her locker is still sitting on the bench. Of course it is. Who would want that? She rifles through it, grimacing at the thought of touching clothes that aren't hers. She pulls out a damp swimsuit in a plastic bag, winces, and dumps it on the bench. Then she reaches tentatively into the side pockets, emerging with three damp ten-pound notes, which she holds up. She can't remember the last time she held actual money in her hand. It's the most unsanitary thing, worse than lavatory brushes, if some article she read was right. She shudders and puts them into her pocket. She rips one of the plastic bags from the dispenser above the costume spinner and wraps it around her hand. Then she picks up the kitbag by its handles and walks out through Reception.

'Madam, you can't take the bathrobe –'

'Yeah, well, this country is freezing and you've lost my clothes.' Nisha pulls the robe tighter around her, knots the belt, and walks out.

They can moan incessantly about how much trade Uber has cost them but it turns out no fewer than six taxi drivers will still ignore a woman in a bathrobe trying to hail a cab before one stops. He winds down his window and opens his mouth to say something about what she is wearing but she holds up a hand. 'The Bentley Hotel,' she says. 'And just don't. Thank you.'

The taxi journey costs £9.80, even though it took barely five minutes. She walks into the hotel, without acknowledging the perplexed glance of the doorman, and straight across the foyer to the elevator, ignoring the swivelled heads of the guests around her. A couple, middle-aged, him in a suit jacket and slacks, her in a badly cut dress that reveals two oysters of armpit fat – probably down from somewhere provincial for a 'treat' – are already inside as she sticks out an arm and stops the door closing. She walks in, stands in front of them and turns to face the doors. Nothing happens. She glances behind her.

'Penthouse,' she says.

When they stare at her, she flicks a hand at them. Then flicks it again.

'Penthouse. The button,' she says, finally adding, 'please,' and the woman reaches over tentatively to push it. The lift hums upwards, and Nisha feels the tension clawing at her stomach. *Come on, Nisha*, she tells herself. *You can fix this*. And then the lift shudders to a halt and the doors slide open.

She is about to step out into the penthouse suite but collides instead with a broad chest. Three men are standing in her way. She recoils, disbelieving. Ari, who is in the middle, is holding out an A5-sized envelope.

'What –' she begins, making to push past him, but he steps sideways, blocking her.

'I have instructions not to let you in.'

'Don't be ridiculous, Ari,' she says, batting at him. 'I need to get my clothes.'

His face wears an expression she has never seen before. 'Mr Cantor says you are not to enter.'

She tries a smile. 'Don't be silly. I need my things. Look at me.'

He's like someone she's never met. Nothing in his expression registers that he has known her, protected her for fifteen years. This is a man she has shared jokes with. Jesus Christ, she's even remembered to ask about his annoying wife occasionally.

'I'm sorry.'

He stoops and places the envelope on the floor of the elevator behind her, then steps back to press the button to send her down again. She feels the world tilting around her, and wonders briefly if she might pass out.

'Ari! Ari! You can't do this. Ari! This is insane! What am I supposed to do?'

The lift doors begin to close. She sees him turn and exchange a look with the man beside him. It is a look he has never before allowed himself to use in front of her, a look she has been familiar with her whole life: *Women*.

'Just give me my handbag . . . for God's sake!' she yells, as the doors close against her.

'I can*not* get over the way you nailed that, babe,' Joel says, banging the steering wheel for emphasis. 'Absolutely nailed it. The way you walked in there, like a *boss*. Edgmont was going to sign before you even sat down.'

'He couldn't stop staring at your legs,' says Ted, slurping at a can of Coke, then belching discreetly. 'Didn't hear a word I said about batch production.'

'He would have signed over his missus if you'd said the word.' Joel shakes his head. 'His firstborn. Anything.'

'You know, I could have sworn you said we were going to do that job for eighty-two,' says Ted.

'I did,' says Sam. 'But when I saw how it was going I just had this sudden urge to push it to ninety.'

'And he just nodded!' Joel exclaims. 'He just nodded! Didn't even look at the small print! Wait till Simon sees that!'

'Brenda's been going on about getting a new Peugeot for months. If we bag this last one, I'm going to put down a deposit.' Ted takes a last swig from his can and crushes it in a fat hand.

'Sam'll get it. She's *en fuego*, man.'

'You what?'

'On fire.'

'She's that, all right. Who have we got next?' Ted scans the folder. 'Oh. It's the new one. A – uh – a Mr Price. This is the big one, sweetheart. This is the big bucks. This is the missus's new 205.'

Sam is reapplying her makeup. She purses her lips in the mirror, then thinks for a minute. She reaches down into the kitbag and carefully pulls out the Chanel jacket. She holds it up, admiring the cream wool, the immaculate silk lining, breathing in the distant smell of some expensive scent. Then, briefly releasing herself from the seatbelt, she slides into it. It's a little tight but the weight and feel of it are delicious. Who knew expensive clothes could actually feel different? She adjusts the mirror so she can see the way it hugs her shoulders, the way the structured collar frames her neck.

'Too much?' she says, turning to the men.

Joel glances over. 'Never too much. You're freaking owning it. You look good, Sam.'

'He's not going to know what hit him,' says Ted. 'Do that thing where you dangle the strap off your heel again. They totally lose focus when you do that.'

Sam gazes at her reflection and preens a little. It's an un-familiar feeling and she is warming to it. She looks like someone she doesn't even recognize. Then, abruptly, she stops and turns to the others, her smile suddenly fading. 'Am I . . . letting down the sisterhood?'

'What?'

'By out-negotiating a bunch of men in suits?' says Ted.

'By – you know – using sex as a weapon. They are basically sex, these shoes, right?'

'My sister says she has period pains to cut short staff meetings that go on too long. Says the men can't get out of there fast enough.'

'My wife once showed a bouncer her bra to get into a club,' says Ted. 'I was actually quite proud.'

Joel shrugs. 'Far as I can see, you use the weapons at your disposal.'

'Forget the sisterhood,' says Ted. 'Think of my new car.'

They have arrived. Sam steps out of the van one leg at a time. She stands a little straighter. She is more confident in the shoes now, has worked out a more deliberate way of walking so that her ankles don't wobble. She checks her hair in the wing mirror. Then gazes down at her feet.

'Do I look okay?'

The two men beam at her. Ted gives her a wink. 'Like a boss. Mr Price doesn't stand a ruddy chance.'

Sam enjoys the brisk click of the heels on the marble floor as they walk to the reception desk. She sees the girl check out her jacket and shoes and observes the way she tilts her chin, as if she is about to be just that little bit more receptive to whatever Sam wants. Imagine being the kind of woman who wears these shoes every day, she thinks. Imagine living the kind of life where you only ever walk short distances across marble floors. Imagine having nothing to worry about except whether your pedicure matches your expensive shoes.

'Hello,' she says, and she registers distantly that her voice has a new tone, a confidence and ease that she didn't have at the beginning of the day. 'Grayside Print Solutions to meet Mr M. Price. Thank you.' She is that woman. She is going to nail this.

The receptionist scans a screen. She taps at her keyboard, expertly slips three name cards into see-through plastic fobs and hands them over. 'If you could just wait over there, I'll call upstairs.'

'Thank you so much.'

Thank you so much. Like she's royalty or something. Sam sits, carefully, on the lobby sofa, her ankles together, then quickly checks her lipstick and smooths her hair. She is going to get this deal, she can feel it. Joel and Ted exchange smiles behind her.

She hears footsteps on the marble. She looks up to see a petite, brown-skinned woman in her fifties approaching the sofa. Her black hair is shaped into a neat bob and she is wearing an unflamboyant, beautifully cut navy suit with a cream silk T-shirt and flat pumps. Sam looks up and glances behind her. The woman holds out a hand.

'Hello – Grayside Print? I'm Miriam Price. Shall we go up?'

It takes a second before she realizes her mistake. She glances behind her at Ted and Joel, whose expressions have frozen. Then they all stand abruptly with smiles and gabbled hellos. And follow Miriam Price across the lobby to the lifts.

It takes ten minutes to discover Miriam Price plays hardball, and an hour to discover quite how hard those balls are. If they go ahead with what she's insisting on, their margins will be sliced to almost nothing. Miriam is small, serene, implacable.

Sam feels hope draining away as Joel and Ted slump in their chairs.

'If you want the fourteen-day turnaround I can't go higher than six sixty,' Miriam says again. 'Our transport costs get higher the closer we are to deadline.'

'I explained earlier why six sixty makes it very difficult for us. If you want the high-gloss finish, it takes longer because we have to use a separate press.'

'Whether or not you have all the presses you need shouldn't be my problem.'

'It's not a problem. Just a question of logistics.'

Miriam Price smiles every time she entrenches. A small, not unfriendly smile. But one that says she is in complete control of this negotiation. 'And, as I said, my logistics require a more expensive transport because of the reduced travel time. Look, if this job is problematic for you I'd rather know now while we have the time to find alternative providers.'

'It's not problematic. I'm just explaining that the print processes of that size of order require a longer lead time.'

'And I'm just explaining why I need that reflected in the price.'

It feels impossible. They have hit a wall. Sam is sweating inside the Chanel jacket and feels a faint anxiety that she will leave marks in that beautiful pale lining.

'I just need a word with my team,' she says, rising from the table.

'Take your time,' says Miriam, leaning back in her chair. She smiles.

Ted has lit a cigarette and is smoking it in short, hungry drags. Sam folds her arms in front of her, unfolds them, and folds them again, staring at a Renault van that is reversing repeatedly and pointlessly into a too-small space.

'If I go back with margins that small Simon is going to blow his top,' she says.

Ted grinds the cigarette butt with his heel. 'If you don't go back with a deal Simon is going to blow his top.'

'This is impossible.' Sam shifts her weight. 'Ugh. These shoes are killing me.'

They stand in silence for a moment. Nobody seems to know what to say. Nobody wants to be responsible for either course of action. The Renault van finally turns off the engine and they watch as the driver discovers he has no space to open the driver's door. Finally Sam says, 'I really need a wee. I'll meet you back in there.'

In the Ladies, Sam sits in the cubicle and takes out her phone. She texts:

Hey love. How's your day? Have you been outside yet?

She waits, and after a moment a response comes back.

Not yet. Bit tired. X

She can picture him in a T-shirt and tracksuit bottoms, barely rousing himself from the sofa to pick up his phone. Sometimes, she hates to admit it, it's almost a relief when he isn't in the house, as if someone has suddenly opened all the curtains, letting in the light.

She wipes, and flushes, and adjusts her clothes, feeling suddenly guilty and stupid for using the shoes and the jacket. Could you be prosecuted for wearing someone else's clothes? She washes her hands and gazes at her reflection. All the confidence of earlier seems to have drained away. She sees a woman of forty-five, the past year's sadness, anxieties and sleeplessness etched onto her face. *Come on, old girl,* she tells herself, after a minute. *Push on through.* She wonders when she started calling herself *old girl.*

The door of one of the cubicles opens and Miriam Price steps out behind her. They nod politely at each other's reflection while washing their hands, Sam trying not to betray her sudden feeling of awkwardness. Miriam Price smooths imaginary stray hairs from her face, and Sam reapplies her lipstick, mostly just for something to do. She keeps trying to think of something to say, something that will convince Miriam Price to work with them, some magic few words that will casually betray what a great and professional company they are, and stretch those tiny price margins. Miriam smiles that small, serene smile. She is clearly not trying to think of something to say. Sam wonders if she has ever felt so inadequate in a Ladies loo before.

And then Miriam Price looks down. 'Oh, my God, I love your shoes,' she exclaims.

Sam follows Miriam's gaze down to her feet.

'They are absolutely gorgeous.'

'Actually they're n–' Sam stops. 'They're great, aren't they?'

'Can I see?' Miriam points at them. She holds the shoe that Sam removes, lifts it up under the lights and examines it from all angles with the reverence one would apply to a work of art, or a fine bottle of wine. 'Louboutin, right?'

'Y-yes.'

'Is it vintage? He's made nothing like this for at least five years. In fact, I'm not sure I've seen anything like it at all.'

'Uh . . . uh, yes. Yes, it is.'

Miriam runs her finger down the heel. 'He's such a craftsman. You know, I once queued for four hours just to buy a pair of his shoes. How crazy is that?'

'Oh . . . not crazy at all,' says Sam. 'Not where I'm concerned.'

Miriam weighs it in her hands, examines it a moment longer, then hands it back almost reluctantly. 'You can always tell a proper shoe. My daughter doesn't believe me, but you can tell so much about someone from what they wear on their feet. I always dress from the ground up. These old things are Prada. I just felt like I needed an on-the-ground kind of a day so I'm wearing flats but, honestly, looking at those I'm overcome with heel envy.'

'I tell my daughter the exact same thing!' The words are out of Sam's mouth before she even knows what she's saying.

'Mine just wears trainers the whole time. I don't think they understand the totemic power of shoes.'

'Oh, mine too. Enormous Dr Marten's boots. And they really don't,' says Sam, who is not sure she understands the meaning of 'totemic'.

'I tell you what, Sam. Can I call you Sam? I hate negotiating like this. Shall we speak next week? Let's the two of us thrash something out away from the boys. I'm sure we can reach a deal that works for both of us.'

'That would be great,' Sam says. She wrestles the shoe back onto her foot, and takes a breath. 'So . . . can I say we have an agreement in principle?'

'Oh, I think so.' Miriam's smile is warm, conspiratorial. 'I have to ask . . . is that jacket Chanel?'

4

Nisha sits in the depths of a plush rose-coloured sofa in the foyer of the Bentley Hotel, a towering arrangement of birds of paradise in a torso-sized vase beside her, her cellphone pressed to her ear. Around her a few guests cast glances at the woman in the dressing-gown when her voice lifts over the sound of the chatter.

'Carl, this is ridiculous. I'm in the foyer. Come down and let's talk.' The message ends. She redials immediately. 'Carl, I'm going to keep calling until you pick up. This is not the way to treat your wife of eighteen years.' The message ends and she redials again.

'Nisha?'

'Carl! I – Charlotte? Charlotte? No. He's forwarding his calls. I want to talk to Carl. Please put him on.'

'I'm so sorry, but I can't do that, Nisha.'

Charlotte's voice is as calm as if she featured on a meditation app. There is something new in her tone that makes Nisha bristle too, a faint air of superiority. And then she registers: *Oh, my God, she called me Nisha.*

'Mr Cantor is in a meeting and has issued direct instructions that he can't be disturbed.'

'No. You get him out of the meeting. I don't care if he doesn't want to be disturbed. I'm his *wife*. Do you hear me? Charlotte? . . . Charlotte?'

The line has gone dead. The girl actually put the phone down on her.

When she looks up, the people on nearby sofas are staring at her. She stares back, until their heads swivel away, in a flurry of raised eyebrows and murmurs. Her whole body is suddenly flooded with cortisol, and she might actually want to kill someone, or run somewhere, or scream. She is not entirely sure which. Nisha looks down and realizes she cannot get through this wearing a cheap robe and flip-flops. She thinks of her clothes upstairs in the penthouse and feels an almost maternal anxiety that she cannot get to them. *Her clothes.*

She glances around and sees a concession store across the foyer. She shoves her phone into her pocket and walks over. The clothes are predictably awful and hideously overpriced. Nisha rifles quickly through the rails, pulling off the least gaudy jacket and shoes she can find, trying to ignore the awful muzak being piped through the tiny store. She looks at the shoes in their size-delineated boxes and grabs a pair of plain beige pumps in a size seven. She piles them onto the checkout desk where a young woman is watching her with a faint air of anxiety.

'Charge those to the penthouse, please,' she says.

'Certainly, Mrs Cantor,' the girl says, and starts ringing them up.

'I need to try the shoes. With a stocking. A new one.'

'I'll just check if we've got —' She stops abruptly. Nisha glances up at her, then follows her gaze and turns. Frederik, the hotel manager, has entered the concession. He smiles at her and stops, several feet away.

'I'm sorry, Mrs Cantor. We have instructions not to charge anything to Mr Cantor's account.'

'What?'

'Mr Cantor says you are no longer authorized to charge anything to his account.'

'Our account,' she says, icily. 'It's *our* account.'

'I'm sorry.'

Frederik stands completely still, his eyes never leaving her face. His manner is unruffled, his tone completely implacable. It is as if everything is crumbling around her. An unfamiliar feeling of panic is rising in her chest.

'We are married, as you know. That means his account is my account.'

He says nothing.

'Frederik, how long have I been coming here?' She takes two steps towards him, resists the urge to grab his sleeve. 'My husband is clearly in the grip of some kind of episode. He won't even let me get my clothes. My clothes! Look at me! The least you can do is let me get something to wear, surely.'

The manager's expression softens very slightly. There is a faint wince when he speaks, as if it pains him to do so. 'He has given very . . . emphatic instructions. I'm so sorry. It's not up to me.'

Nisha lifts her hands to her face. 'I don't believe this is happening.'

'And I'm afraid . . .' he says '. . . I'm also going to have to ask you to leave. The bathrobe, it's . . . The other guests are . . .'

They stare at each other. Some distant part of Nisha registers that the checkout girl takes advantage of this moment to sweep everything swiftly off the counter. 'Eighteen years, Frederik,' she says slowly. 'Eighteen years we've known each other.'

There is a long silence. It is the first time he has looked properly embarrassed. 'Look,' he says finally. 'I'll organize a car for you. Where do you want to go?'

Nisha looks at him, opens her mouth a little, then gives a small shake of her head. She feels suddenly swamped by an unfamiliar sensation, something huge and dark and ominous, like quicksand sucking at her feet. 'I don't . . . I don't have anywhere *to* go.'

And then it is gone. She will not have this. She will not tolerate it. She crosses her arms and sits down firmly on a small wicker chair beside the shoe area.

'No, Frederik. I'm not going anywhere. I'm sure you'll understand, but I'm just going to sit here until Carl comes down to talk to me. Please go and fetch him. This whole thing is ridiculous.'

Nobody speaks.

'I'll stay here all night if I have to. Please go and get him, we'll sort this out, and then we'll work out where – or *if* – I go anywhere.'

Frederik gazes at her for a moment, then lets out a small sigh. He looks behind him and, as he does, two security men walk into the concession and stand there, waiting. All eyes are on her. 'I'd really rather there wasn't a scene, Mrs Cantor.'

Nisha stares. The two security men move forward. One step each. The neat choreography of it is almost impressive.

'As I said,' Frederik continues, 'Mr Cantor was very emphatic.'

5

'Nice one today,' says Marina, lifting her hand for a high-five as they pass in the corridor. 'Joel says you played a blinder.'

Sam is back in the flip-flops, had put them on in the van, as her toes had begun to go numb, and the balls of her feet ache in a way that tells her she will be hobbling in trainers tomorrow. But she is still buoyant, an unfamiliar smile creeping into the corners of her mouth with every conversation. She feels a strange mixture of invincibility and slightly limp relief. *I did it. I brought in the business. Maybe this is the turning point. Maybe now everything will be okay.* She meets Marina's palm with a slap that is only mildly self-conscious. She is not normally a high-five sort of person.

'Ted says everyone's going for a drink later. He said we haven't had that much business in at once since he was in thirty-six-inch-waist trousers. You are coming, right?'

'Uh . . . sure! Why not? I've just got to call home first. White Horse, is it?'

Sam gets back to her cubicle and dials home. It takes Phil six rings to answer, even though she knows the phone will be on the coffee-table in front of him.

'How are you doing, love?'

'I'm okay.' Just for once she had hoped she wouldn't hear that defeated, resigned tone. She forces a smile. 'Listen. I had a really good day today. Brought in a lot of business. A few of us are going to the pub after work to celebrate and I thought maybe you could come down and meet us. Ted will be there. You like Ted. And Marina. You and she did that X-rated "Islands in the Stream" at the karaoke night, remember?'

There is a short silence on the other end, as if he is considering it.

'Just a drink or two? We haven't been out together for ages, have we? It would be nice to have something to celebrate for a change.'

Say yes, she urges him into the silence. Cat says her dad looks like he's on standby mode, these days. Sam keeps thinking that there will be one thing that unlocks this, a night out or an event that will suddenly switch Phil on again.

'I'm a bit tired, love. Think I'll stay here.'

But you haven't done anything!

Sam closes her eyes. Tries to disguise the sound of her sigh. 'Okay. I'll be home once I've done these figures.'

Less than a minute after she's ended the call, her phone rings again. It's Cat. 'So how did it go?'

She feels a surge of love for her daughter, who has remembered how important this day was. 'It went really well, thanks, lovely. I got three deals out of four, and they're all big ones.'

'Yay! That rocks. Well done, Mum. It must have been the trip to the gym that did it!' She lowers her voice. 'What was Dad saying?'

'Oh, I invited him to the pub but he's not really feeling up to it. I'll get some food on the way back and I'll be home at about . . . seven fifteen? I've got to pop to the gym first and hand something back.'

'Why are you coming home?'

'To cook dinner?'

'Mum. Go to the pub. You haven't been out in months and you just pulled in a massive deal. What are you, a Stepford Wife?'

'I don't know. I don't like leaving your dad when –'

'Go on. Let your hair down for once. You don't have to look after everything.'

She reassures her mother that, yes, she is sure, yes, it's all fine, yes, she can make sure her father eats something. She is nineteen, not twelve. Dad is more than capable of making himself beans on toast! Women do not have to do all the emotional labour! she tells Sam emphatically, with the assurance of someone who has never had to do any. And Sam puts down the phone and thinks suddenly that it might be quite nice to have an evening somewhere other than her front room with her sad husband staring at nothing beside her.

Sam finishes her paperwork, enters the figures into the software, and tots up the zeros with satisfaction. She pulls a little face to herself as she does it, wrinkling her nose and nodding. This morphs into a little dance, her head bobbing on her neck as she bounces in her chair. *Oh, yes. Ninety-two in that column. Tot up those totals. There's another zero. And another. And another.* 'I am going to the pub. To the pub. To the pub.' She lets out a little 'Oooh, yeah.'

She turns to reach for a pen and yelps. Simon is standing in the entrance of the cubicle. She does not know how long he has been standing there, but from the studied insouciance of his expression, probably long enough to see her pulling her victory chair-dance.

'Simon,' she says, when she's recovered herself. 'I was just entering today's figures.'

'Mm-hmm.' He gazes at her impassively. 'I heard we got Piltons and Bettacare,' he says.

That smile again. She can't help herself. 'Harlon and Lewis, too. Yes,' she says, turning to face him fully. 'And on better margins than last time.' It is only as she speaks that she registers his use of the word 'we'. As if he'd had anything to do with any of it. Swallow it, she tells herself. Everyone knows who brought these deals in. And the numbers do not lie.

'I've also managed to extend the deadline on the –'

'What happened to Framptons?'

'I'm sorry?'

'Why didn't we get Framptons?'

She has just brought in nearly a quarter of a million pounds' worth of business and he wants to talk about the small one that got away? She feels winded, stumbles over her words, and he leans back against the door frame. He sighs. 'I think we need to talk.'

'What? Why?'

'Because I had a call from Michael Frampton's office. He said you turned up to the meeting drunk.'

She stares at him in disbelief. 'Are you serious? Oh, for goodness' sake.'

Simon puts his hands in his pockets and tilts his groin forward slightly. He does that a lot when he's talking to women.

'Oh, God, that man. I wasn't drunk in the slightest. There was a mix-up before work and I had to wear high heels that weren't mine and there was an uneven surface in the loading area and I –'

'What are those?' She is interrupted by his finger pointing towards her feet. 'What have you got on your feet?'

She follows the line of his finger. 'Oh . . . flip-flops?'

'I hope you didn't go to the meetings in those. They're hardly professional footwear.' His shoes, she notices, are perfectly shiny lace-ups. Slightly pointed at the ends, in a nod to fashion. She thinks about what Miriam Price said: something about Simon's shoes tells her everything she has ever needed to know about him.

'Of course I didn't, Simon. I was just telling you that –'

'I mean if you're meant to be representing our company

– and I would remind you that it is a very different matter now you're representing Uberprint too – then you need to be doing it in the utmost professional manner. At all times. Not slopping about wearing bloody flip-flops.'

'Simon, if you let me finish, I told you I –'

'I haven't got time for this, Sam. It's not just Grayside now. I hope you can conduct yourself in a more professional manner in future. I can't be worrying about whether I'm going to have more clients calling up to complain about you being drunk, or whatever it is you're wearing on your feet. You've put me in a very awkward position today.'

'But I – I wasn't . . .' she begins, but he has already turned and left the cubicle.

Sam stares at the space where he had been, her mouth hanging slightly open.

Then she shuts it abruptly. Knowing Simon, he will suddenly reappear and accuse her of wearing an unprofessional facial expression.

'He's a grade-A wanker,' says Ted, shaking his head so that his jowls wobble. 'A proper waste of skin.'

She had been so shaken by the exchange that she had nearly gone home. She should stop off at the gym after all. But Marina had come past just as she was packing the cream Chanel jacket into her bag and told her there was no way she was letting her go straight home tonight. She was the one who had brought in all the money. She could drop off the bag in the morning. 'Don't let that little scrote ruin your day. Don't give him what he wants. C'mon, Sam. Just for one drink.'

So she has come next door to the White Horse, surrounded by the workmates she has known for more than a decade, a family of sorts. She knows the names of their partners and children, the various pets of the child-free, and often, these days, people's ailments. She used to bake birthday cakes and bring them in, but the first time she had done that after Uber-print took over, Simon had walked into the breakout area as they gathered round to sing 'Happy Birthday' and said he really couldn't believe they thought they had time for this. What was it? A kindergarten?

'How's Phil?' Marina puts another glass of white wine on the table in front of her and settles in. 'Has he found another job yet?'

She does not want to talk about Phil tonight so she utters a bright 'Not yet!', the kind that suggests she has every confidence that this is the most temporary state of affairs, and changes the subject swiftly. 'Hey, you'll never guess what happened to me this morning.'

Marina is agog. 'Show me,' she demands, as Sam tells the story, and Sam reaches under the bench and pulls out the kitbag, unzipping it to show her one of the shoes.

'I should really have taken them back instead of coming here,' she says. 'I'll have to do it tomorrow.'

But Marina isn't listening. 'Oh, my God. You did a whole day in these? I wouldn't have been able to walk five steps.'

'I nearly didn't. But, Marina, by the end of the day I was *working* it. I swear it was wearing them that got me the deals.'

'Well, what are you doing?'

Sam looks at her blankly.

'You're not celebrating in those bloody awful flip-flops. Put them on! I want to see!'

Marina is exclaiming about the beauty of the shoes ('I bet they cost the same as my mortgage!') when Lenny from Accounts asks what they're talking about, and before she knows it, Joel is telling the other end of the table, and her workmates are demanding that she parade up and down in the shoes. She is three glasses of wine in now, and despite the acid

42

warning in her stomach that she will pay for this, especially on an empty stomach, she finds herself doing a fake catwalk-type strut up and down in front of her colleagues, while they hoot and clap approvingly.

'You should wear heels every day!' says Ted.

'Yeah, we will if you boys do, too,' says Marina, and throws a peanut at him.

Someone has put on music and the pub is now packed with people competing for space on the little square dance-floor, office workers marking their survival through the stress of another week, those with quiet crushes on colleagues looking to alcohol to ease their way forward, those unwilling immediately to embrace the responsibilities, the dread silences, of a weekend at home. Marina grabs her hand and they are suddenly in the throng, arms up, clapping to the music, dancing in the way that middle-aged people do, badly, but with the confidence that comes from the fact that they no longer care, that sometimes just the act of dancing, letting go in a room of people while a beat thumps through your veins, is an act of rebellion against the dark, against the tough times that will inevitably come tomorrow. Sam dances, closes her eyes and enjoys the clench of her thighs, the feel of the heels on the hard floor. She feels powerful, defiant, sexy. She dances until her hair sticks in strands to her face, and sweat runs into the small of her back. She feels Joel's hand around her waist, and he takes hers and lifts it so that she twirls under his arm. 'You looked absolutely gorgeous in those shoes today,' he murmurs into her ear, as she spins. She laughs and blushes.

She has just sat down, still pink and giddy, when the man appears.

'Blimey, you've pulled,' Marina mutters, as he stops in front of her. Tall, wearing the kind of dark uniform and muscular bulk that shows this is a person who takes themselves very seriously indeed. He looks her up and down.

'Um . . . hello?' she says, half laughing, when he does not speak. She wonders briefly if the shoes have gifted her some strange new sexual potency.

'This is what you want.' He hands her a Jiffy bag. And before she can say anything, he turns and is gone, swallowed by the throng of sweaty, extravagantly gyrating bodies.

6

The problem with having more than one home is that the thing you want at any given time is nearly always in another place. Likewise, the problem with only having rich people as friends is that they are always in the wrong damn country. Nisha has three friends living in London – if you can call them friends – Olivia, who, her answering service tells her, is currently at her house in Bermuda, and Karin, who is back in the US, visiting family. She calls both but is put onto voicemail. It's a time-zone thing. She asks, in as casual a tone as she can manage, whether they might call her back when they get this message. When she puts the phone down she realizes she is not entirely sure what she will say to either of them when or if they do.

Angeline Mercer has been divorced twice, the second time after she caught her husband sleeping with the nanny. She at least might be sympathetic to Nisha's situation. Angeline greets her charmingly, listens while Nisha explains insouciantly that there has been a little situation with Carl – all rather embarrassing – and could she possibly just see her way to wiring her a small sum while she sorts it all out? Angeline's voice is just as smooth when she tells her that, yes, Carl had explained the situation to James, and she is very sorry but they don't really feel they can get involved. 'It would be like taking sides,' she says sweetly, making it quite clear which side they have taken.

Nisha wants to ask what the 'situation' was that Carl had described, but some last vestige of pride will not allow her to. 'I quite understand. So sorry to have troubled you,' she says calmly. And then lets out three curses so bald and extreme that they would have sent her grandmother racing for the emergency Bible.

She does not try anyone else. Nisha is not big on female friends. School had left her with a deep distrust of the subtly volatile dynamics that form when girls get together. Female friendships were febrile, prone to little explosions, frequently leaving you feeling like the ground was shifting under your feet in ways you couldn't quite fathom. After she left home and started her new life in the city, she was too nervous of betraying herself to feel she could truly unburden herself to anyone, except Juliana. And she doesn't think about Juliana any more. Some things are just too painful. No, women trade compliments or troubles like currency. Women smile understandingly at your confidences, then use them against you like weapons. Men she finds predictable, and Nisha likes predictability. You behave a certain way, a man responds in a way that is *manageable*. She understands the rules of this game.

And then, of course, as the wife of any wealthy man knows, other women become competitors, threats to a hard-won status quo. When she was newly married to Carl, there were the women who eyed her with disdain – *team Carol* – who couldn't believe Carl had been so disappointingly predictable, so *obvious*. But Nisha didn't put a foot wrong as Carl's wife. She educated herself into his world so comprehensively that there was no tiny crack in which weakness could be exposed. She had watched Carl's friends' marriages implode around her in stages, just as his first had, and she understood exactly what was going on with the new wives, their careful, blank faces and honeyed words, that each was loyal only unto her husband and her own position.

Yes, that had served her very well indeed, until she reached forty and learned there was a whole new threat. The younger women. The ones who would sniff out a sell-by date, and decide, like a targeted missile, to home in. Tight young bodies, willing to please, pleased to be willing, with nothing to lose and not yet weighed down by disappointment or anger or just plain exhaustion at trying to be all the things all the time. Nisha, in response, learned just to be better. She was a good-looking woman, her hair lustrous, her skin the constant recipient of whatever top-of-the-range serums and moisturizers hit the market, so that she frequently passed for someone ten years younger. She worked out every day, had her nails done weekly, her waxes done fortnightly, her hair extensions refreshed every four weeks, Botox every twelve. She was there, ready for him in La Perla, fresh flowers in his room, his favourite wine in the cellar. She laughed at his jokes, applauded his speeches, flattered his colleagues and emphasized his superiority and virility in infinite subtle ways, in public and private. She replaced his shirts and pants, booked his barber's appointments before the assistant knew they were even due, made sure every property was ready for his arrival with his favourite food and wines. She allowed no domestic stresses to impede his path. She let nothing drop. She was all over this being-female thing.

And it turns out even that isn't fucking enough.

Nisha has walked to four different cashpoints in the vicinity and each one has either swallowed her remaining array of cards or spat them out, telling her in bald digital terms to contact bank staff. But she doesn't have to contact bank staff to know what is going on here. She had walked to Mangal, the exclusive boutique she had used for the past five years whenever she was in London, and before she had even tried on the thick Alexander McQueen coat, Nigella, the manager, had come out to explain that she was very sorry but Mr Cantor had closed their account that morning and without a credit

47

card they were not going to be able to help. She had peered surreptitiously at the towelling robe as she said the words, as if trying to assess if this was some new-season fashion-forward item she hadn't been aware of.

Nisha sits in the coffee shop, ignoring the curious stares of the other customers, and tries to think. She needs something to wear, she needs somewhere to stay and she needs a lawyer. Without money she can access none of these things. She could ask Ray to wire some, but then this will be out there, irrevers-ible, and she does not want to drag her son into it. Not just yet. Not with everything else he has gone through this year.

'Hello?' She snatches up the phone.

'It's me. I'm so sorry, Mrs Cantor.' Magda's voice is hushed. 'I had to use my husband's phone because mine was cut off.'

'Did you speak to your guy?'

'Yes. He's got it. He's going to call me shortly and tell me where to meet you. He doesn't want to call you directly . . . in case. This is why it's taken me so long to get back to you.'

She sounds genuinely apologetic.

'When is he going to call? I need help here, Magda. I've got nothing.'

'He says within the next hour or so.'

'I am literally wearing a bathrobe. Carl won't let me get my things. Can you send some clothes? And I'm going to need my jewellery FedExed, and some cash. And, oh, my laptop –'

'This is the other thing, Mrs Cantor.' Magda sniffs noisily down the phone and Nisha shudders slightly. 'Mr Cantor fired me. I didn't do anything and they say he fired me.'

Nisha knows she should say something comforting. But all she can think is *fuck fuck fuck*.

'The housekeeper shut me out of the house and they said he's paid me off with immediate effect. I don't know what we're going to do because Laney's medical bills –'

'You can't even get in the house?'

'No! I had to get the subway all the way to Janos's work to use his phone because they took the phone off me before I left. I got there seven a.m. as usual and they threw me out by seven fifteen. Luckily I knew your number by heart so I could still call you.'

She must write down every number in her phone book, she thinks suddenly. He will cancel her phone, too, as soon as he remembers to.

'I need money, Magda. I need a lawyer.'

But Magda has started to cry. 'I'm so sorry, Mrs Cantor. I couldn't get any of your jewellery, your photographs, anything. They said they would get the cops if I tried to remove anything, it would be theft, and they would get Immigration involved. They literally pushed me out of the door! I tried to get your –'

'Yes, yes. Look, call me as soon as you hear back. I need to know where to meet him. This is really important.'

'I will, Mrs Cantor. I'm so sorry.' She is sobbing now. A ringing sound has started in Nisha's head. She has to get off the phone.

'Don't worry. Okay? Don't worry. We'll fix this and then I'll rehire you. Okay?' She has no idea if this is possible, but it makes Magda stop crying. She ends the call with Magda's grateful exclamations still echoing over the line.

The stares of the people around her are becoming unbearable. Nisha is used to being looked at – she has always drawn attention – but it is for being fit and beautiful and privileged. These looks, she sees, are suffused with pity, or wariness, or even revulsion. *What is that crazy lady doing in her robe?* She has to get hold of some clothes.

She has avoided looking at the shop across the road the

49

whole time she has sat here nursing her soy latte, but now she knows she has little choice. She gets up, tucks her phone into the pocket of her dressing-gown, and makes her way across the road to the Global Cat Foundation goodwill store.

The smell. Dear God, the smell. The very air in the shop is a stale perfume of scraping by, of a singular lack of beauty, and of despair. She walks in, turns on her heel and walks straight out again, standing on the roadside breathing gulps of the relative freshness of traffic-filled Brompton Road. She waits a minute, composes herself, then turns and walks back in. 'It's only for a few hours,' she mutters, under her breath. She just needs something that will get her through a few hours.

The barrel-shaped woman with turquoise hair looks at her as she walks in and she ignores her slightly challenging 'Hello.' Everything in here looks and feels cheap. She doesn't even want to touch the blouses on their rails, the nylon shirts and market-stall jumpers. There is an old woman two rails away looking at the shoes, her face screwed up in concentration as she examines each for size and condition. She is going to have to wear the kind of clothes a woman like *this* is buying.

Just for a few hours, she tells herself. *You can do this.*

She picks through the rails with the tips of her fingernails until she finds a jacket that looks barely worn, a pair of trousers that look like they might be a US 4. The jacket is seven pounds and fifty pence, and the trousers eleven.

'Get locked out, did you?'

She doesn't want to speak to this woman with her blue hair, but she forces a half-smile. 'Something like that.'

'Do you want to try them on?'

'No,' she says, curtly. *No, I do not want to try them on. No, I do not want to go into your horrible, reeking, curtained-off corner cubicle. I do not want to be in the same zip code as these cheap, stale-smelling clothes that have been worn by God knows who, but my husband is having some kind of mid-life crisis and trying to destroy me so that he can get a divorce, and I cannot fight him in a bathrobe.*

'Would you like to fill out a Gift Aid form?'

'Gift Aid?'

'That way the charity gets to claim back tax. You just put down your name and address.'

'I . . . I don't have an address just now.' The truth hits her like a punch. She recovers herself. 'Actually, I do. My address is in New York. Fifth Avenue.'

'If you say so.' The woman lets out a quiet snigger.

She pays for the items, waving away the change, then changes her mind and demands it, a move that makes the assistant *hmph* audibly. Then Nisha pulls the tags from the clothes, hauls on the trousers, grabs the jacket from the counter, and walks out, dropping the towelling bathrobe in a heap on the floor of the shop.

Magda books her a hotel she says is not far from the Bentley. The Tower Primavera. 'I told them to tell the front desk you couldn't give your credit card for security as your purse was stolen and they finally agreed.'

'Oh, thank God.' The used scent of these clothes has somehow lodged in the back of her throat, and she thinks she may be coming out in hives. She once read that if you smell something you're absorbing actual molecules of it into your body. The thought makes her retch. She keeps plucking at her sleeves to try to keep the fabric from touching her skin.

'But I'm afraid they say without a card you cannot have a minibar.'

'I don't care. I just need to shower and make some calls.'

There is a long pause.

'I . . . have to tell you something else, Mrs Cantor.'

Nisha checks the map on her phone and starts walking. 'What?'

'It's not ... the kind of hotel you and Mr Cantor are used to.'

Magda rambles on about how she was sorry but they had no credit on their card this month, something to do with her medical insurance blah-blah-blah. 'It was one hundred and forty dollars. But there is a kettle in the room to make a drink. And maybe cookies. I asked for extra cookies for you. I was thinking you must be hungry.'

She is too distracted to be mad about it. Whatever. She thanks Magda and ends the call, thinking at least now Magda will be able to reach her, if – or when – he cuts her phone.

The walk is interminable. Magda is clearly useless at judging distances on a map. Nisha slaps along the grey pavement in the too-large flip-flops, as the skies darken and lower and eventually it starts to spit with the kind of chill, malevolent rain that you seem to get only in London. Nisha stops briefly and, admitting defeat, takes out the shoes from the bag. There is, at least, a clean pair of socks in there. She puts them on and then, wincing, puts on the black clumpy, tired-looking shoes. They fit reasonably well, but possess the unnerving contours of someone else's long-term use. *I will not think about them*, she tells herself. *These are not me.* Then she puts on the jacket, feeling the cheap fabric weld to her shoulders, and pushes away feelings that suddenly threaten to swamp her. Her walk becomes something like a stomp, the unfamiliar flat heels changing the way even her hips move. There has always been a car waiting like a shadow outside whichever building she happened to be in, and to be out here without one in a city that is suddenly unfamiliar makes her feel untethered, as if she is just floating wildly in the atmosphere. 'Keep it together,' she mutters to herself, as she powers on, scowling at anyone who has the temerity to look at her. She will get what she needs and she will be back in the penthouse by this evening. Or some other penthouse. Either way, Carl will pay for this.

The hotel is a squat, modern building in cheap burgundy brick, with a plasticky illuminated sign over the sliding doors and when she finally reaches the street she pauses, double-checking that she has the name right. As she gazes up, a man in a football shirt walks out holding a can of beer. He stops to shout something at his companion, who is eating from a packet of potato chips held high up to her nose, like a pig in a trough. She watches as they veer off, yelling about needing a Big Mac.

The receptionist has a note against her room, and repeats several times that she will not be able to have the minibar, so sorry, given that they are not able to take a card.

'We wouldn't even normally accept the booking,' she says. 'But we're not that busy today, and your friend was so sweet and worried about you. I'm sorry about your stolen bag.'

'Thank you. I won't be staying long.'

She hesitates before pressing the elevator button to the fourth floor, not wanting to touch the button. She jabs at it once, twice when it fails to register, then wipes her finger several times on her sleeve. When she arrives at Room 414, having navigated a long stretch of bright swirling carpet clearly designed by someone who wanted an entire customer base to pass out from nausea, she opens the door and stops. The room is small, with a double bed facing a tired fake-wood sideboard on which a flat-screen television sits. The carpet and the drapes are turquoise and brown. It smells of cigarettes and synthetic air-freshener, with notes of something sour and Clorox-like underneath, like the aftermath of a crime scene clean-up. What terrible thing has happened in here? The bathroom, while apparently clean, houses its shampoo and conditioner in locked canisters on the wall, as if its clientele cannot be trusted even with that.

She takes off the jacket and tosses it onto the bed, then washes her face and arms thoroughly with the cheap soap. She checks the thin, slightly rough towels – apparently laundered – then dries off with them. She sees herself in the mirror, her hair still scraped back in the ponytail from her shower at the gym, her face free of makeup. She looks ten years older, furious, exhausted. She sits on the edge of the bed (hotel bedspreads make her shudder. Have you *seen* what shows up under ultraviolet light?) and waits for Magda to call.

'He says somewhere low key and busy so that he doesn't attract attention. He is worried about Ari finding out. He wants to meet in a British pub.'

'A pub. Okay.' She remembers a pub she had stopped outside to refasten the awful shoes. 'The White Horse. Tell him to meet me at the White Horse. How will I know who he is?'

'He knows what you look like. He will find you. He says you must be there from eight p.m.'

'Eight o'clock tonight? That's four hours away. Can't he get here sooner?'

'He says eight o'clock. He will be there with what you want. Wait inside. He will find you.'

Nisha stares at the carpet. Her voice, when it emerges, is less confident. 'Can I trust him, Magda? Do we know what he has?'

There is a short silence.

'He says he will be there, Mrs Cantor. I just tell you what he told me.'

*

54

It takes sixteen paces to go fully backwards and forwards around the bed in the little room. It is thirteen hundred and forty-eight paces before she finally stops. Her heart is racing, a Rolodex of thoughts spinning as she registers what Carl has done, what he has tried to do to her. She has witnessed Carl's ruthlessness with his business enemies, the way he would summarily bring down a guillotine on even long-standing relationships without turning a hair. One minute they were embedded in the inner circle, lunched handsomely, lent a driver or consulted over late-night cognac with jokes and bonhomie, the next it was as if they had simply been erased. He would pick up and drop people as they suited him, and it was as if he could barely remember their names afterwards. Carl has never worried about parking tickets, legal problems or employment tribunals. He always says that's why he employs other people, to sort out life's 'messes'.

She realizes that she, his wife, has suddenly morphed into one of his messes.

There is a tight knot in Nisha's stomach that just keeps getting tighter, as if someone were pulling a cord around her waist. Every time she stops walking, she feels as if she can't breathe properly, as if the air won't reach the bottom of her lungs. She needs a drink, but she doesn't want to drink the water (what might be lurking in those pipes?), and she doesn't want to leave the room to get a bottled water in case Magda calls, so she deliberates and finally makes herself an instant coffee, boiling the kettle three times with fresh water before she feels safe drinking it. (She had once watched a *Morning Show* item when they said some guests had used kettles to *boil-wash their underwear*. It had actually given her nightmares.)

And what was she going to tell Ray? He'd have to know eventually, of course. They would concoct some mealy-mouthed statement about people changing, not being able to live together any more, but Mummy and Daddy still loved each other blah-blah-blah. Carl would probably get a lawyer to write his. And she would have to put on a brave face, pretend that this was what she had wanted too. Make it as easy and light as possible so that Ray could cope with it.

Who was it? That's the question, a drumbeat running through her head underneath every new thought. She runs through a mental list of eligible women who had raised her internal red flag in the past months: a little too much attention, a casual hand on an arm at a fundraising dinner, a whispered joke through heavily glossed lips. There were always women, and she has watched them carefully, always closely monitoring the vibrations in the atmosphere. She had known something was off, but she couldn't think who might be behind it. Or that Carl, reliably – sometimes annoyingly – libidinous, was suddenly tired more often than he was not. It wasn't that she enjoyed the morning attentions she was obliged to give him, but it unnerved her more when they stopped. She never asked him what was wrong – she was not the kind of woman to be *needy* – but she'd bought new, outrageous, lingerie, and taken charge of matters when he got back from his last trip, using tricks she knew he couldn't resist. He was less tired then. Of course he was. But even as she held him in the sweaty aftermath there was something different, a discordant note humming away in the background. She had known, *oh, she had known*, and that was what had finally persuaded her to seek insurance.

Well, thank God she had.

She's hungry. That's not unusual: Nisha has been hungry her whole adult life (you think you could maintain a figure like hers otherwise?). But she thinks back and realizes suddenly that she has eaten nothing at all today. She goes to the tray with the plastic kettle and there, in a brightly coloured wrapper, are two packets of cheap cookies with something unidentifiable and creamy in them. She scans one of the little packets suspiciously. Carbs have been the enemy for so many decades that it requires a huge mental leap to persuade herself that on this occasion she needs to consume them. God, what she really wants is a cigarette. She hasn't wanted a cigarette for five years, but she would actually kill for one right now.

To distract herself, she boils the kettle three times again, makes a black tea and drinks that. And finally, when she can take the clawing hunger pains no longer, she rips open the little packet and puts a cookie into her mouth. The pale cookie manages to be both dry and claggy at the same time. But it might be one of the most delicious things she has ever tasted. Oh, God, it's so good. So full of crap and so damn good. Nisha closes her eyes and savours every mouthful of the two small cookies, letting out little noises of pleasure. Then she eats the second packet. She shakes it onto her palm, to retrieve the last few tiny crumbs, rips it open and licks the inside. Then, when there is definitely nothing left, she throws it into the bin.

Nisha sits, and checks her watch.

And she waits.

She has been to an English pub once before, in the Cotswolds, with one of Carl's associates who owned a sprawling shooting estate and thought it would be fun for them to partake in the English tradition of 'sinking a pint'. The building had been straight out of the history books, full of beams and wonky ceilings, suffused with the smell of woodsmoke, with a cute hand-painted antique sign outside and the door surrounded by roses. The landlord had known everyone by name, and had even allowed entry to dogs, which lay at the feet of men in tweed with bad teeth and braying voices, the car park a mix of mud-spattered old four-wheel drives and the immaculate Porsches and Mercedes of weekenders.

A bar girl served up little plates of cubed cheese (you wanted to see the lab bacterial results on shared plates – ugh) and small brown pies with unidentifiable meat that she had pretended to nibble at. The bottled water was lukewarm. She smiled at the raucous jokes, and wished she had stayed back at the house. But she had made it a habit to be at Carl's side at all times.

This is not that kind of pub. This is like the bars in roadside joints several miles off the highway where she had grown up, where girls wore vest tops and short shorts and men wished they were in a branch of Hooters and behaved as if they were. She walks into the White Horse and is instantly enveloped in a sea of bodies and noise, groups of people yelling beery fumes at each other over thumping music that is just a few decibels too loud. She pushes her way through the crowd, trying to shrink to avoid the men who are lurching around aimlessly, apparently already drunk at seven thirty in the evening.

She had hoped to sit quietly in a corner somewhere, but all the seats are taken, people elbowing their way in as soon as a table vacated, like some kind of muscular game of musical chairs. She waits instead in a porch area by a door, as if she were thinking of going for a smoke, and shaking her head at the guys who asked her if she 'has a spare fag'. All the while she scans the crowd, waiting for a man who will give her a nod of recognition.

He has come via a friend of a friend of Magda's husband, who knew people, and has contacts in every country. She had made the arrangements directly on a burner phone six weeks ago so that Magda was involved as little as possible. (She had pleaded to be kept out of it, *It is better if I know nothing, Mrs Cantor, I do not want to get into any trouble.*) And when the guy had reported back last week, he said the surveillance job had been embarrassingly easy and that she 'would not be disappointed'. She had sent him cash, and a Patek Philippe watch that Carl had decided he needed two years ago at the airport in Dubai and had been too drunk to remember buying afterwards.

There was no point in her trying to identify this guy by his looks. They were all the same, these goons, anyhow, with their military haircuts and their thick necks. She'd know him because he'd be the only guy here who wasn't drunk and spraying saliva halfway around the room.

'Got a fag, darling?' A young man appears in front of her. He wears a white polo shirt, and track pants, whose crotch sags down to his knees, and he has a glassy flush to his cheeks that says he has been drinking for some time.

'No,' she says.

'Waiting for someone, are you?'

She looks him up and down. 'Yes. Waiting for you to get lost.'

'*Whooooh!*' She sees then that a group of other young men are with him, equally well lubricated, nudging each other and howling.

'You're sassy. I love a sassy lass,' he says, and raises his eyebrows suggestively, like she might find that a compliment. 'American, are you?'

She ignores him and shifts slightly, so that she is facing away from them all.

'Aww, don't be arsy. C'mon. Let me buy you a drink, darling. What do you drink? Vodka tonic?'

'Let him buy you a drink, Yankee Doodle.'

She keeps her face turned away. She can smell his aftershave, something cheap and pungent. 'I don't want one. Please go right ahead and enjoy your night.'

'I won't enjoy it without you . . . Come on, darling. Let me buy you a drink. You're all on your . . .'

He puts a hand on her arm, and she whips around and hisses, 'Fuck off, and leave me alone.'

This time the *whooooh!* from his friends has a slightly harder tone. They are getting annoying. She needs to focus, to make sure she doesn't miss her guy.

The young man's face has flushed and hardened to a blank stare. 'No need to be rude,' he says.

'Yeah. There is, apparently,' she responds. And then as they shuffle off back into the pub with a couple of sulky backward glances, she walks over to a portly middle-aged guy in a rumpled jacket talking to a friend, leaning against one of the windows.

'Excuse me, would you happen to have a spare cigarette?' She smiles sweetly at the man, and he is disarmed immediately. Doesn't even speak as he rummages hurriedly for his packet. He lights the cigarette, like a gentleman, keeping his hands from hers, and she rewards him with another smile. 'Actually, you couldn't give me a couple for later, could you? I've left mine at home.' He gives her the packet, insisting she take them, that he can buy some more. 'You're a doll,' she says, and his ears go pink.

She smokes the cigarette in short, angry puffs, relishing the acrid taste of the smoke, the chance to do something for a few minutes. Where the hell is he? She stubs the last of the cigarette out with her heel. *Just hurry up*, she wills him. She cannot remember the last time she was on her own in a public bar at night. She is normally insulated from people like this. That snotty kid wouldn't have approached her if she was in her normal clothes. This is what she's spent her whole life getting away from.

She checks her watch, then shoves her hands into her pockets, and pulls them out again quickly with an audible *ugh* when she remembers what she is wearing.

At a quarter past nine she makes her third circuit of the pub, pushing through the groups of increasingly raucous customers, her head dipping and bobbing as she tries to make out who is there. A young woman no longer wearing any shoes offers her a cigarette outside and tells her her hair is beautiful. She says thank you nicely because she wants the cigarette. She suspects the nicotine will give her a headache tomorrow.

Nisha waits as the hours pass and the bar takes a more Bacchanalian turn around her, the voices louder, the glasses sloshing alcohol as people push past her. A group of office workers starts dancing on the tiny, sticky dance-floor and she stares at them, marvelling at people's willingness to humiliate themselves. The side door is locked at a quarter to eleven, and people begin to spill out of the main doors, laughing, stumbling, stopping to smoke or kiss messily, or wait for taxis. He does not come.

'Is it closing time?' she asks a young Asian man, part of the office celebration.

'Yes, babe,' he says, saluting. 'Nearly eleven, innit?' He slings an arm around the shoulders of a ginger-haired man in an ill-fitting T-shirt and they walk off singing.

She cannot believe it. She turns and peers inside: the place is emptying, barmen wiping tables and stacking chairs. Could she have missed him? He couldn't have been here without her knowing. He just couldn't. She curses under her breath, preparing to walk back to the hotel.

She is only a few minutes away from the pub when she hears them behind her, catcalling, their footsteps echoing on the wet pavement. *Oi! Yankee Doodle!* She turns and recognizes him immediately, pushing forward, like a pustulent boil, from the surface of their little gang. *Oh, great.*

She picks up her pace, but they pick up theirs too and she knows they are gaining on her. Her heart thumps in her ears with a sudden surge of adrenalin. She runs through the calculations that every woman knows as standard: this street is too dark; there are no other people nearby; the main street, with its strip lights and traffic, is still a hundred, two hundred paces away. She has no Ari, no personal alarm, not even any keys to wedge between her fingers. He is coming. She knows it in her gut.

Three strides, two strides. She hears his approach, feels the hot breath on her neck. Just as his arms surround her in a clumsy bear hug, Nisha squats and drops abruptly, shifts her weight onto her back foot, turns and swings her right forearm up hard between his legs. Just as her Krav Maga tutor had shown her. She hears his high-pitched cry as he collapses onto the pavement behind her, the shocked exclamations of his friends as they reach for him. The curses. The *what the f-*

But they are drunk, and before they can fully grasp what has happened, she is sprinting away down the unlit back road, all the power of a thousand tedious daily sessions on a treadmill in her feet, suddenly grateful that, for this day in her life at least, she is not wearing a pair of beautifully handmade couture high heels, but a pair of cheap and nasty perfectly flat pumps.

She is almost at the hotel, her brain still fizzing, before she discovers that during the scuffle her phone has fallen out of the too-shallow pocket of the second-hand jacket.

She curses, then doubles back and runs the route she has come, ignoring the drunks weaving their way along the street. She scans the sidewalk but there is nothing. Of course there isn't. How long does a cellphone last on an inner-city street? Nisha stands under the flickering sodium light, closes her eyes and wonders how much worse this day can get.

*

'Magda! There are six different White Horses in London! Why didn't you tell me? I just looked them up! He must have gone to a different one!'

She has borrowed the phone of the soft-voiced Nigerian man on Reception, and as Magda answers, she is standing in the corner by the vending machine, ignoring the anxious glances he is sending in her direction.

'What? But he called me!'

'What do you mean he called you?'

'He said he handed it to you two hours ago. He got held up so he was late and he called me.'

'He did not give it to me. He went to the wrong bar!'

'No. No, Mrs Cantor. The White Horse. I told him what you would be wearing. I knew this was Friday's outfit, because I have them all on the chart. He said he recognized you by your shoes.'

'What?'

'The Louboutins. He said there are too many women your age with dark hair, five foot six. So I said this would be the best way to recognize you. Because there's only one pair in the world, right? Very distinctive shoes. I even sent him a picture of them just to be sure. I knew you'd be wearing them because you said Friday you were going to get your hair done after the gym and then straight to Hakkasan for dinner and you said Mr Cantor wanted you to wear them.'

'But . . . my shoes were stolen. They were stolen this morning.'

There is a silence at the other end of the line.

' . . . You weren't wearing the shoes?'

Nisha stands up, her hand gripping the phone as she realizes what Magda is saying.

'Oh, my God. Who the hell has he given it to?'

7

There is a particularly vindictive tenor to the kind of hang-over that occurs in your forties, as if the body, not content with acting as if it has been poisoned, also decides to send furious signals across all nerve endings: *How old do you think you are? Was that really a sensible idea? Hmm? Think you're still young enough to play hard? WELL, TRY THIS.* Sam, her eyes screwed shut against the light, and the terrifyingly loud noises coming from the kitchen, observes she is now having imaginary arguments with her nervous system. She knows she'll have to embrace the day. Or at least touch it gingerly with her fingertips and possibly weep a little.

'Good night, was it?'

Cat appears in front of her in a satin bomber jacket and huge clumpy black boots, and places a mug of coffee on the table with what feels like a malicious level of enthusiasm.

'I – I think so.'

'Sit up. Or it'll dribble down your chin.'

Sam pushes herself upright, groaning softly at the pain in her head. 'Where's Dad?'

'Still asleep.'

'What time is it?'

'Half nine.'

'Oh, God, the dog –'

'I've walked him. And I bought some more milk. And I washed up Dad's stuff from last night. Can I borrow your gold stud earrings? I'm going to a fur-farm protest after work and I worry that my hoop ones will get ripped out if there's trouble.'

Sam's gaze slides towards her daughter. 'The ones I said you couldn't borrow under any circumstances? Hang on. "Ripped out"? What?'

'Fake gold ones make my ears itch. Here. Drink your coffee.'

Sam takes a sip. It tastes like a lifeline. 'Nice negotiating. Get her while she's vulnerable.'

'I learned from the best.' Cat beams. 'Thanks, Mum. I promise I'll look after them.'

Sam has a sudden memory of Joel, the weight of his hands on her waist, smiling at her in that way he does. Marina's voice in her ear: *He's sweet on you.* She flushes and is not sure whether the prickling heat in her face is alcohol, embarrassment, or something hormonal. Either way, she pushes herself up from the sofa. 'Have a lovely time at . . . Wait, did you say *protest*? What – what are you doing?'

'Protesting! Just winding up the police a bit! Have a nice day, Mum!'

'Wait – is that a tattoo?'

She hears the door slam and her daughter is gone.

Phil is curled up in the duvet, like a human sausage roll, and does not stir as she enters the bedroom. The air in the room seems peculiarly still and weighty, as if it sits more heavily in here. She stands for a moment and observes him, his brow furrowed even in sleep, his hands close to his chin, as if unconsciously braced to defend. Sometimes she wants to scream at him: *You think I wouldn't like to lie around all day and let someone else take over? Let someone else worry about the bills and my awful boss and walk the dog and do the shopping and vacuum the bit on the stairs that always gets covered with hair? You think I wouldn't like to abdicate responsibility for everything?* Other times she feels a terrible sadness for him, her once cheerful, motivated husband who used to sing tunelessly in the shower and kiss her when she wasn't expecting it and who now looks hunched and haunted all the time, buffeted by the double-whammy of losing his beloved job and even more beloved father in the same six months. *I couldn't help him, Sam*, he would say, chalk white when he returned home, night after night. He had told her a few weeks ago that being this age was like walking among snipers, that people he cared about were being picked off and there was nothing you could do and no way of telling who was next.

'That's a bit of a gloomy way to look at it,' she had said. It had sounded feeble even as it fell out of her mouth, and he hadn't said anything after that.

Unlike Sam's house, outside which the rusting camper-van is now host to a growing fortress of weeds and thistles, and shelter to a collection of takeaway cartons thrown from passing cars, the frontage of Andrea's little railway cottage is always immaculate. No weeds sprout in the cobbled front-age, and the row of terracotta pots is dutifully tended, bright blooms switched according to the seasons, fed and watered daily with almost maternal care.

She knocks on the door – the special knock that tells Andrea this is neither a weirdo stalker nor a double-glazing salesman – and after a moment it swings open in front of her.

'Ooh, you look like shit,' Andrea says cheerfully, and Sam raises her eyebrows, faced with Andrea's missing ones, the still ghostly pallor of her skin. 'Come in, come in. You'll have to make the coffee. For some reason milk keeps making me gag.'

They sit knees up, end to end on Andrea's sofa, which is always covered with a selection of crocheted blankets and soft wraps, as she gets cold easily. They are in bold colours, because she likes things to be upbeat and cheery, and as they sit, Mugs, Andrea's beloved battered ginger cat, climbs

66

between them and kneads a cushion rapturously, sending out hoarse purrs of pleasure.

'So what happened to you?' says Andrea. She has placed a soft wrap on her head, which matches the blue of her eyes. 'Tell me all the goss.'

'I brought in three big deals, got accused by my new boss of being drunk, and got very, very drunk,' she says.

'Excellent. Any bad behaviour?'

She thinks about Joel and pushes away the memory. 'No. Beyond dancing so much in high heels that my feet looked like unbaked bread this morning.'

'Ugh. I dream of bad behaviour. Sometimes I dream about going out and getting slaughtered, and it's almost a disappointment when I wake up and there's no hangover.'

'You can have this one. Honest. It's on me.'

They had met on the first day of secondary school and Andrea had shown Sam her impression of an orange (it involved pursing her entire face and was oddly convincing), then revealed the love bite she had got from the PE teacher's son. In all the years they have been friends Sam can remember only one falling-out, over a holiday Andrea had taken without her when they were eighteen, and after which they had tacitly agreed never to argue again. Andrea knows her to her bones. Every crush, every sadness, every passing thought: she is a constant conversation running through Sam's life, and every time Sam leaves her she feels restored in some subliminal way she never quite understands.

'Is Phil up?'

'Not yet.'

'Have you talked to him about the meds again?'

Sam groans. 'He won't do it. It's like he's decided that the moment he takes anti-depressants he's officially mentally ill.'

'It's just depression, Sam. It's ridiculous. Everyone needs

help sometimes. It's like – it's like this. But in his brain instead of his tits.'

Andrea is the only person she feels able to tell the truth to about Phil's illness. How sometimes she hates him. How she is afraid he'll never get better. How she is afraid that one day he will be better and she will hate him for this so much that she won't be able to feel the same way again about him. How what has happened to him – and to Andrea – has left her feeling like the earth can shift under your feet without a moment's notice so that nothing in the world, no happiness, feels secure.

'How are you feeling?' Sam says, to change the subject.

'Oh, just tired, mostly. I've watched the whole of *ER* this week on one of the streaming channels, just because it makes me feel better when people die and it isn't me.'

'The last scan was still good, though, right? You're on the mend?'

'Yep. One more to go before I can breathe again. Hey – my hair's started to grow back.' She lifts the wrap from her head, revealing a hint of fuzz.

Sam leans across and runs her hand over it. 'Nice. You look like Furiosa in *Mad Max*.'

'Well, people *are* always mistaking me for Charlize Theron.'

There is a brief silence in the little room. Mugs has fallen asleep, his back legs in the air like a rabbit's, and they pause to stroke him gently.

'Oh, and I was let go from work.' Andrea doesn't look up from the cat.

It takes a moment for Sam to register what she said. 'What?'

'Nothing to do with *this*, of course, just a restructuring of the department so that my position no longer exists.'

'They can't do that! Not after what you've just been through!'

68

'Well, they did. I get a small payoff, so there's that.'

'But – but how will you get by?'

Andrea shrugs. 'No idea. I thought I might sell my body.' She smiles weakly at Sam. 'I'll go to the benefits office next week and see what I'm entitled to. You'd think being half dead would entitle me to *something*.'

'Don't,' says Sam. 'Don't even joke about it.' She reaches across and takes Andrea's hand. She squeezes it gently.

'It'll be all right,' says Andrea. 'Something will happen.'

'I'll help you.'

'I've got savings.'

'You told me you'd burned through most of them.'

'Your memory is way too good,' says Andrea. 'Anyway, you're as skint as I am.'

'Seriously, can I do something? Can we sue them? Get a lawyer involved?'

'It's a huge corporation with whole legal departments devoted to squishing people – and honestly? I haven't got the energy to fight anything else just now.' Andrea keeps her eyes on the cat as she speaks, and the conversation is apparently closed. They sit in silence for a while, both lost in their thoughts, still both stroking the cat until he decides this is way too much human contact and stalks off the sofa.

'Oh. I have a fun thing to tell you.'

Andrea lifts her head. 'About time, Sam. Jesus. You've been about as much use as a wet weekend in Grimsby for half an hour and *now* you have something positive to tell me?'

She tells Andrea the story of the high-heeled Louboutin shoes, from Frampton to Miriam Price, and then the story of the handsome man with the Jiffy bag.

'Well, where is it? The thing the guy gave you.'

'Uh . . . I think it's in my bag?' She rifles through it and brings out the Jiffy bag. In it is a small memory stick.

'What are you doing? It might be something exciting. Details of Swiss bank accounts. Pentagon codes that I can use to bomb my HR department. Riches from a long-lost Nigerian royal family. Let me have a look. Come on.' Andrea raises herself from the sofa and reaches behind her for the laptop on the desk.

'What if it's got malware or something on it? I don't want to put bugs on your computer.'

Andrea rolls her eyes. 'Do I look like bugs on my computer even registers on my list of things to worry about right now?' She takes the memory stick from Sam and slots it into her laptop. They settle beside each other so that both can see the screen.

'If it's Pentagon codes I'm targeting my ex-mother-in-law first,' says Andrea, gleefully. 'Just a small guided missile. Maybe radioactive. Nothing too dramatic.'

The screen flickers into life, and they are suddenly silent. It is Andrea who speaks first, after a few seconds of watching the two grainy bodies writhe furiously.

'Uh . . . Sam? I'm not sure what this is, but I'm pretty sure that's not . . . legal.'

'Or it shouldn't be.'

They watch in silence for a few moments longer, transfixed and horrified, unable to look away. Their mouths drop open.

'He shouldn't do . . . Oh, no. Oh, no no no.'

'Is that . . . is that the guy who gave it to you?'

'No! He was much younger. And not . . . Ew.'

'What is she *doing* to him? Turn it off. Turn it off! I feel ill.'

They slam the laptop shut and sit there in silence for a moment. Andrea looks at Sam and shakes her head.

'Is this a thing now? If you fancy someone, instead of sending a dick pic you hand them niche porn in a Jiffy bag?' Andrea shudders. 'Jesus. I'm almost glad I'm too ill to date.'

Few people are wearing smart dark suits in this scruffy residential neighbourhood, but this is a part of London described as 'lively' or 'up and coming' by estate agents, a place where it would not be unusual to see a man dressed as a goat, or a member of the Hare Krishna group dressed in flowing orange robes and waving a tambourine, so the few people who do pass Ari Peretz pay him little attention. He would not have noticed if they had: he is focusing intently on his phone, the screen of which is showing a pulsing blue dot that is growing ever closer to the travelling red one. He stops by a postbox, takes a step forward, then glances around his feet, as if he's looking for something. He ducks, peers under a nearby hedge, then over a low brick wall, still scanning his phone. He gets down on his hands and knees, and squints under a parked car, using his phone as a torch. He edges closer, then reaches under the car and pulls out another phone, which he dusts off. He stands up, brushing down his trousers, and gazes around him. He lets out a heavy sigh, the kind one emits when one knows one is going to have to make a call that will likely not end well. Finally he dials.

'I found it. She's nowhere. We may have a problem.'

8

It had come to her in the small hours: the Chelsea house. Carl has bought and sold property compulsively during their marriage, and because this one had been under constant renovation, they hadn't actually stayed there yet. In the chaos of the previous day, she had almost forgotten its existence. But she needs a base, while this is sorted out, and whatever state it's in, it will be better than the Tower Primavera. The sudden recollection of it, at 2.14 a.m., had made her almost giddy with relief.

She has no key, but if the builders are still working there they will let her in. And if they aren't, she will break in. No policeman in the world is going to object to a homeowner breaking into their own house. Nisha lies awake, planning her next move. Install herself in the house, get a lawyer, recover her bag, then kick Carl's butt. It is this last thought that consoles her into a fitful sleep until seven, when she showers, climbs into yesterday's clothes, and heads down to the dining area to eat the all-inclusive breakfast.

'What do you mean, there's no à la carte?'

Nisha stares at the server, who blinks at her and turns away. There are a million reasons why Nisha hasn't eaten a buffet breakfast in two decades: the food is always the cheapest; greasy eggs sitting under hot lights, pallid sausages sliding in metal trays. Strangers lean over the stainless-steel containers, shedding hair or skin cells as they loom. It has always been her worst nightmare.

Until she was hungry.

This is not Nisha's habitual hunger, low-grade, ever present, but a new variety that leaves her shaky and a little faint, unable to think about anything but food. She stands in the busy breakfast room, a gaudy yellow conference hall where the chairs are covered with plastic and the walls bear translations for 'Good morning!' in a dozen different languages. Despite her revulsion, her stomach growls and claws, like an animal about to loose itself.

She takes two tomatoes, something that describes itself as scrambled egg, and two hash browns. She adds a banana – at least nobody can get into those – and places some sealed rectangles of cheese in her pocket. A man to her right gives her a pointed look, and she glares at him until he colours slightly and turns away. She carries her plate to the furthest point of the room, sits and studies one of the free newspapers, though she barely takes anything in.

While she eats, she goes over and over the plan in her head. Once she has secured her base, she will need money. She will have to borrow some, just till a lawyer comes through. She wonders who she might possibly be able to borrow money from. Pretty much all her friends, these days, she recalls, with a creeping sense of dismay, are Carl's friends. She thinks briefly about Juliana, but they have not spoken in more than fifteen years, and Juliana never had any money anyway. The man Magda had spoken to, the one who was supposed to provide her with insurance, has disappeared.

As she sips her coffee, she starts to feel a rising sense of panic: *how has she ended up here?* She forces herself to close her eyes and breathe deeply. She thinks of Carl's bloated, self-satisfied face. He's probably eating his eggs Benedict in the suite right now. She thinks of how it will feel to turn the tables on him. She has survived worse, she tells herself, murmuring under her breath. She will survive this.

When she opens them again a bored-looking kitchen worker is standing by the table. 'You need to clear your tray into the bins when you've finished.'

Nisha stares at the woman for a full three seconds, some furious internal struggle just visible in her features. She takes a long breath, then picks up the tray and walks, stiff-backed, past the woman to the bins.

Using the last of her loose change, Nisha catches a bus and sits near the front, refusing to acknowledge the scattering of passengers around her. She gets off by Chelsea Bridge and walks the ten minutes to the little square. It seems acceptable: white stucco buildings, pretty boutiques and decent coffee shops. A florist sells exquisite arrangements of blue hydrangeas and she pictures a display of them on a dining-table once she's in, and plans what she will book at the nearby beauty salon. Right now she would kill for a massage. But it's fine. She will survive here for the foreseeable. She finally enters the little square, quietly satisfied at the evident peace of it, the sight of the nanny walking past with well-dressed children, the elderly woman with her dachshund. This at least is a place that understands how things are done, a million miles from the grease and noise and bustle of the hotel.

And there it is. Number 57. She stops in front of the gate and looks up, vaguely recalling its frontage from the real-estate agent details. It's a fairly modest house by Carl's standards, but he had chosen it for the location, and she remembers nodding and smiling and saying it was lovely, as she did with all his property purchases. He is a light sleeper and insists on living on roads where there is no through traffic or, preferably, surrounded by acres of their own land. The building work's finished, she thinks, pleased, noting the neutral blinds, the carefully tended roses around the front garden.

74

She is just wondering if she can remember the name of the construction firm – Barrington? Ballingham? – when the front door of her house opens and a woman steps out. The interior designer, Nisha thinks, and steps forward, but almost immediately the woman shepherds out two small children. She looks up when she sees Nisha standing at the gate, and half waits. The two women stare at each other for a moment, blank, confused smiles on their faces.

The woman breaks first. 'Can I help you?' she says, when Nisha doesn't move. She is whippet thin, her hair a straight curtain of natural hazel and blonde, clad in the expensive casual wear of the wealthy non-working mother.

Nisha is taken aback by her brazenness. 'Uh . . . you can tell me what you're doing in my house.'

The woman blinks. Half laughs.

'This is . . . my house?'

'It is not. We bought this house three years ago. I have the documents to prove it.'

The woman stiffens. 'We bought it four months ago. I also have the solicitor's emails to prove it.'

They stare at each other. The children gaze, wide-eyed, then look up at their mother.

'This is ridiculous,' says the woman, moving them behind her, as if she is dealing with a crazy person. 'I'm afraid you must have the wrong address. Please leave us alone.'

'Number fifty-seven,' says Nisha. 'That's my house.'

'It's not your house.'

'It is.'

Both women half laugh without humour, as if aware of the absurdity of the conversation. Nisha sees the woman take in her cheap clothes, the low-quality shoes, and she observes a flicker pass across her face, as if Nisha might be dangerous, perhaps recently released from a mental facility.

'Who are you?' says the woman, her voice tense.

'My name is Nisha Cantor.'

'Oh!' says the woman, suddenly relieved. 'Cantor! Yes! You are the people we bought it from!'

'But – but we haven't sold it,' says Nisha. 'He would have needed my signature. He would have –'

She realizes with a jolt what Carl has done. 'Oh, God.'

The street starts to buck and spin around her.

'Are you . . . are you okay?' The woman's demeanour has softened slightly. She steps forward and makes to touch Nisha's arm. Nisha immediately snaps it away. She does not like to be touched at the best of times, least of all by someone showing visible *sympathy*.

'Four months ago.' She shakes her head. 'Of course.'

'Look, I think you'd better speak to your solicitor. But this house is very definitely ours. I have the solicitors' and land registry papers to prove it. I can get them from inside if you –'

'Oh. No. I – I believe you,' Nisha says. She feels winded. He must have been planning this for months. She lets out a small sound that might have been a groan, and tries to steady herself before she pushes herself upright.

'Are you okay? Would you like me to –'

She turns before the woman can say anything else, and sets off at a brisk walk back towards the bus stop, feeling three pairs of eyes burn into her until she is out of sight.

'Mom? Why are you calling so early? And why are you calling collect?'

'I knew you'd be up, darling. I know you're a night owl. How are you doing?'

'Fine.'

She winces. 'Fine', in teenager-speak, can cover anything

from ecstatic to 'Just been scrolling through a dozen You-Tube videos about the best way to kill myself.'

'How was your day?'

'Fine.'

She hesitates. But this cannot wait. 'Baby, I have a little favour to ask.'

She can hear a screen burbling in the background. He is probably playing one of those online games that involve wearing earphones and screeching at distant team-mates.

'I need you to wire me some money.'

'What?' He says it twice, clearly perplexed.

'I . . . I want to buy Daddy a birthday present and I don't want him to see it come out of the joint account,' she says smoothly. 'You know how he is about watching all the financial stuff.'

'Can't you use your card?' He sounds distracted. She hears the sound of distant explosions, followed by gunfire.

'I – I had my bag stolen yesterday. I've lost my phone and all my cards.'

'Oh, no! Which bag?' says Ray, his attention suddenly drawn from the game. 'Not the Bottega Veneta?'

'No, no. Just – just an old one. I'm not sure you even know it.'

'Oh. Cool. Well . . . how do I do that? I don't know how to wire money. Sasha! Shooter! On your left!'

She talks him through the process and he does it online as they speak. He seems to find the idea of wiring her some money almost akin to an adventure, and she realizes with a faint sense of guilt that they have so seldom asked him to do anything practical. He arranges to wire five hundred dollars, the most she feels she can ask for without prompting suspicion.

'What are you going to buy?'

77

It takes her a second. 'For Daddy? I – I don't know. I'm – uh – looking at options.'

'No, what *bag*. To replace yours.' His voice lowers. 'The new Autumn/Winter YSL is cute. Mid-size cross-body with kind of diagonal cushioning. It's in the newest *Vogue*, page forty-six. You'd rock that, Mom.'

She smiles, delighted at his sudden animation. 'I'll take a look, sweetheart. It sounds fabulous. Thank you. And I'll pay you back as soon as I've got everything straight this end.'

There is a short silence.

'So . . . when are you coming home?'

'Soon, darling, soon.'

'Sasha's leaving on the eighth. I can't be here once he's gone. He's the only good one left. Everyone else is just . . .'

'I know. I'll fix it. I promise. I love you.'

He heads back to his game and she ends the call and breathes a long sigh of relief. That's three more nights taken care of and her food. It will buy her time to breathe at least. She sits on the bed and feels the softness that always envelops her when she talks to Ray gradually harden as she considers her day. Right. She'll brush her teeth in the hideous bathroom. Next stop: the gym to see whether her bag has been returned. And then a damn good lawyer.

'Nobody's handed in any bags.'

It has taken Nisha fifty-two minutes to walk here. She is cross and sweaty, the jacket is making her neck itch and there is definitely something off about the way this girl is talking to her.

'Well, what are you going to do about it? There's a Chanel jacket and Christian Louboutin shoes in that bag. The bag itself is Marc Jacobs, for God's sake.'

The girl gives her the kind of pleasantly blank look that

says, *Boy, am I going to talk shit about you as soon as you're out of here.* She raises a smile that isn't a smile.

'I'm so sorry, madam, but there *are* signs on the wall saying we cannot be liable for items that go missing in the changing rooms. We *do* advise all clients to lock their lockers and keep an eye on their belongings.' Her peculiar patronizing intonation makes Nisha want to hurl herself over the counter fists first.

'I'll be happy to put it in the incident book,' the girl adds.

'Incident book?'

'Well, it's usually for minor injuries. But I'm happy to put it in there so that *if* and when your bag is returned, whoever is staffing Reception is aware that it belongs to you. If you'd like to give me your details I'll make sure someone contacts you in the event of it reappearing.'

The way she says 'reappearing' makes it clear to Nisha that she doesn't expect it to 'reappear' any time soon.

'Well, you have been *immensely* helpful,' she says. 'I'll be in touch. Maybe to get a recommendation for whoever is in charge of your customer-service training.' She sweeps out, thanking God that she hadn't bothered to bring the other bag with her.

She picks up Ray's money from the wire service, buys a cheap pay-as-you-go phone from a pawnshop, some top-up vouchers from the supermarket, and at 3 p.m. she uses the hotel Wi-Fi to call Leonie Whitman. After a modicum of small-talk and fake admiration for her latest Instagram posts (Leonie is so thirsty for attention – like a woman with her ass should be posing in a bikini, even if it is on her husband's yacht), Nisha asks her if she can recommend a good divorce lawyer. 'It's my assistant,' she says, lowering her voice. 'She's in a dreadful situation and I'd like to help if I can. She's such a sweet woman and I want to protect her.'

'Oh, you're so kind to your staff,' says Leonie. 'I couldn't *bear* Maria when her husband left. She was so moody and I kept finding her weeping in closets. Honestly, I was *that* close to firing her. It just affected the whole mood of the house.'

'Well, you know, a good assistant is worth looking after.' Nisha smiles, thinking guiltily of Magda. She jots down the number and ends the call as swiftly as she can. She doesn't think she heard anything in Leonie's voice that suggested Angeline Mercer had told her what was going on, but Leonie is a one-woman broadcasting service, and she needs to act quickly.

Saul Lowenstein, esteemed New York divorce lawyer, takes the call. She suspected he might, despite it being a weekend, given her name. He is unctuous, charming on the phone, his mellifluous, confidential tone that of someone who has listened to a wealth of furious soon-to-be-ex-wives.

'And how can I help you, Mrs Cantor?'

She explains the situation in as bald and emotionless a manner as she can manage. But even as she does, hearing the words out loud, she feels an unexpected prickling behind her eyes, the fury and the unfairness of it catching like a plum stone in her throat.

'Take your time, take your time,' he says gently, and even this makes her furious: the fact that Carl has turned her into one of *those* women; the women who wail that their husband has left them and how can he do this to her blah-blah-blah.

'But he can't do this to me,' she finishes. 'I mean, I'm pretty sure he can't do this to me. We were *married*. For almost two decades! He can't just shut me out without a dollar. I mean, I'm his wife!'

He asks the extent of their assets, and she tells him what she can remember: the duplex in New York, the house in Los Angeles, the estate in the Hamptons, the yacht, the cars, the private jet, the office buildings. She is not sure what his business is worth, or even what exactly he does, but she explains it as best she can.

Saul Lowenstein takes a moment before he speaks. He speaks reassuringly, as if this is all just a minor inconvenience that can be sorted. The prospect of his fee for such a case, she thinks, eases the most reticent of minds.

'Right. Well, the first thing we can do to help your immediate situation is to send a letter demanding access to the joint account. Luckily for you, Mrs Cantor, London's divorce laws are some of the most equitable in the world. You will get, if not half, then a very decent proportion of his earnings for the last eighteen years.'

Nisha drops her face into her hand. 'It is such a relief to talk to you, Mr Lowenstein. You have no idea how stressful this has been.'

'I'm sure. And then we need to find you a base while we sort this unfortunate business out. Now, do you own any property in England?'

'We did,' she says. 'He appears to have sold it.'

'Ah. A pity. Most judges are reluctant to turn a woman out of a marital home.' She can hear him scribbling notes as he speaks, the rude blare of a New York siren somewhere in the background. It makes her oddly homesick.

'Now, the divorce papers you say your husband's security man gave you. Can you read the first page to me?'

She does as he says and sits, almost in a dream, while he digests it. As he takes notes, she thinks about what she will do once this is sorted. She will fetch Ray. She might even bring him back to stay in London for a bit. She has no desire to head back to the US and all those rubberneckers who, when the news gets out, will suddenly find an excuse to call her, just to be able to report back the gossip to each other.

No, she and Ray will get a place here while they work out how to proceed.

'Mrs Cantor?'

She is pulled back from her reverie.

'These are the papers he handed you?'

'Yes,' she says. 'I don't have any other sets of divorce papers.'

He sighs. 'These appear to be American divorce papers. He must have drawn them up in the US. Unfortunately, American divorce law is quite different.'

'Meaning what?'

'It is going to be difficult to challenge your access to the bank accounts. You don't seem to have enough links to the UK to employ Part Three of the Matrimonial Causes Act 1984 as I might otherwise have suggested. Transatlantic enforcement of divorce rulings is notoriously tricky. We could potentially try for a court order but it cannot be enforced, especially if he decides to fly back to the United States. We can send him a legal letter, but –'

'Carl has never paid any attention to a legal letter in his life. You don't understand, Mr Lowenstein. Carl does not believe rules apply to him. I have watched him at close quarters for twenty years and he does what he wants. Always. It's like . . . a point of pride for him. He cannot ever be seen to lose.'

Saul Lowenstein lets out a heavy sigh. 'Then I'm afraid this does not bode well. I see a lot of high-net-worth clients, Mrs Cantor, and it usually goes like this: the husband – because I'm afraid it usually is the husband – divests himself of all assets into offshore holdings in the Caymans or Liechtenstein, and the wife is left trying to claim half of something that no longer officially exists, while chasing him around the globe. And there is the other problem . . .'

'What?' says Nisha, her head spinning. 'What other problem?'

'Well, without any money, Mrs Cantor, you cannot pay me.'

Nisha freezes. 'I'm a very wealthy woman. You'll get your money.'

'I can only operate on cases at this level with a sizeable cash retainer.'

'But I haven't got anything right now. He's shut everything down. I told you.'

'I'm very sorry, Mrs Cantor. I really can't do anything without a retainer. If you could sort things out at that end I'd be very happy to take on your case. Beyond that, I'm afraid there's little I can do at this time. I'm not sure of any lawyers worth their salt who could.'

She is speechless. She thinks, for one horrific moment, that she might burst into tears. He waits a few seconds before he breaks the silence.

'It's not an unusual modus operandi among those of your income bracket, Mrs Cantor. He thinks, I'm going to screw her, grind her down, until she's just glad to agree to anything. And that appears to be what's happening here. You could, if you're in desperate need, approach the police perhaps. Or the American Embassy.'

'I don't want the police involved!' She drops her head into her hand. 'I don't understand,' she whispers. 'I don't understand why he's done this.'

He sighs, then says, his voice low and confidential, 'In my experience, it's worth looking at the assistant.'

'His assistant?' she says, her skin prickling. 'But –'

'Young, pretty?'

She thinks of Charlotte with her glowing skin and immaculate, sleeked-back ponytail. Her bland smile whenever Nisha walked into the office.

'The assistant knows the husband's every need, every want, and every movement. They also know where the money goes.

I am very sorry to say, Mrs Cantor, but in the vast majority of cases that's where you'll find your explanation. I hope very much that you're able to sort this out, and of course I'm always here for you.'

'If I can get a retainer,' she says.

'If you can get a retainer.'

He ends the call abruptly, as someone who charges eight hundred dollars an hour but isn't getting paid for this particular communication is wont to do. And Nisha is left sitting on the flammable bedspread breathing heavily into the silence.

9

Sam arrives home at 3.30 p.m., her headache resolutely refusing to lift. The dog greets her with the slightly pained and bug-eyed demeanour of a creature who desperately needs to empty his bladder. As she clips the lead to Kevin's collar, without even removing her coat, she hears the television in the living room and feels a flash of irritation. Would it really be so hard for him just to get up and walk the dog for fifteen minutes? Would it? God knows he does nothing else to help around the house these days.

'Has Kevin been out?' she says carefully, although she knows the answer.

'Oh,' Phil says, turning to look at her like the dog's needs are a surprise. 'No.'

She waits for a moment.

'How's Andrea?' he says.

'On the mend. Please God.'

He sighs heavily, as if Andrea's woes merely add to his own burden, and gives her a small, unconvincing smile before turning back to the television. Sometimes this smile makes her sad. Today it makes her want to scream.

'I'll take Kevin, shall I?' she says, when his gaze returns to the television.

'Sure,' he says, as if that were the only sensible option. 'You've got your coat on.'

She leaves the house with a low hum of rage ringing in her ears. *You shouldn't leave him alone so much*, her mother had told her the previous week. *I mean, it's hard for a man not being the main breadwinner. He's bound to feel sorry for himself.*

Men of that age are surprisingly fragile, their GP had said. *I do believe women are the much tougher of the species.* He had said it like he expected her to take it as a compliment.

You're a bit moody these days, Mum, her daughter had said. *Shouldn't you think about taking HRT or something?*

No, I'm not tougher. I'm not moodier, she wanted to yell at them. *I'm just bloody tired. But if I give up and lie on the sofa all day the whole damn thing will fall apart at the seams.*

She scolds Kevin, who dawdles outside the neighbours' house, sniffing endlessly at the base of their privet. Then she feels guilty because none of this is poor Kevin's fault, crouches down and throws her hands around his fat neck, whispering, 'Sorry, darling, I'm so sorry,' until she looks up and sees Jed from number 72 staring at her like she's finally lost her marbles.

She walks all the way to the canal because she cannot think what to do if she's at home, ignoring the couples who walk arm in arm, scowling at the cyclists who force her onto the side of the path. Cat is working this afternoon. She seems to have a portfolio of part-time jobs – barista, delivery girl, waitress ('It's making the gig economy work for you, Mum. You don't want to be dependent on just one job.') – and Sam knows that if she stays at home she will either have to sit with Phil in the dead-aired, enervating living room, or start one of the 148 tasks that need doing in the house that everyone else seems to believe are her responsibility. If she does this, she will be seething, her rage barely suppressed, within minutes. And then she will hate herself for it, because depression is no one's fault. As she has never had it, she reminds herself, she cannot fully understand the compulsion to do nothing. Or perhaps the lack of compulsion to do anything. Either way, at least if she's walking Kevin she can feel like she's done something – and boosted her step count while she's at it.

She recalls a philosophy teacher asking her class, 'How many of the decisions you make each day are because you actually want to do something, and how many are to avoid the consequences of not doing it?' Nearly everything she does these days is just to stop something else happening. If she doesn't keep her steps up she will get fat. If she doesn't walk the dog he will wee in the hall. Sometimes Sam feels she has been so conditioned to be useful every minute of every day that there is almost nothing she does in which she is not simultaneously keeping a subconscious tally.

Do men hear this constant inner voice, telling them constantly to strive to be better, to be productive, to be useful? Even when Phil was happier he was mostly oblivious to the towel rail that had half come out of the bathroom wall, the pile of socks that needed sorting on the washing-machine, the crumbs on the floor, the fridge that really needed its shelves wiped before they all died of penicillin poisoning.

She finds herself wondering absently if Joel does things. She pictures him changing a toilet roll without being asked, his expression cheery, no hint of *I changed the toilet roll for you, babe* on his lips. Like some kind of fantasy man. And then she thinks of dancing with him the previous night, the heat of his hands on her waist, and flushes with guilty pleasure. *He's sweet on you*, Marina had said, and she finds herself mentally counting all the nice things he has said to her before deciding she's being ridiculous and pushes the thought of him away.

She pulls Kevin out of the path of another rampaging cyclist who rings his bell and swears as he whooshes past (she wants to yell at him but she once read a newspaper story about a woman who was pushed into the canal after protesting to a cyclist so she stays quiet). She remembers, with a jolt, she hasn't taken that kitbag back to the fancy gym. Will the owner have alerted the police about the missing designer clothes? She thinks about the list of things she has to get through in the rest of her day: pick up her father's prescription and drop it round to her parents, stopping for a cup of tea so they don't complain that they never see her, sort out the pile of washing on the upstairs landing, defrost the freezer because the door has stopped closing, go through the pile of bills on the side that she has put off all week. She checks her watch. She'll take the bag back before work on Monday. Another job to squeeze into her already packed day.

Then she thinks about Andrea, who has nothing in her day except time in which to contemplate the abyss she has been staring into for months. And then she feels guilty for complaining about anything.

I need a holiday, she thinks. And that thought makes her think of the camper-van. She puts her head down and trudges towards home.

The camper-van. Sam lets out an involuntary sigh every time she sees it, staring at the giant yellow sunflower painted on its side. Phil had bought it two years ago from a friend at work – back when he was still in work – and had arrived home full of enthusiasm and visions of their future trips together. 'It just needs a bit of TLC. I'll respray it, replace the bumper and update the interior. The engine's in pretty good shape. It's always the roof on these things that you need to watch. Water seepage,' he had added knowledgeably, as if he had any more experience of a camper-van than a week-long family holiday in Tenby when he was ten years old.

She had been quietly furious at first – how could he splurge three thousand pounds of their savings without consulting her? – but gradually she had allowed herself to be carried along by the picture he painted of holidays around the south coast – 'Maybe even the continent. Wouldn't that be great, Sammy? Lying out in the South of France? Sleeping under the stars?' He had hugged her to him, murmuring into her ear. Sam had remembered a holiday in the South of France where being bitten by mosquitoes and the horror of the pit-like campsite toilet you had to squat over had reduced them to hysterical laughter. They had been good at adventures. Even the ones that involved having to wash your shoelaces after you'd been to the bathroom.

Phil had serviced the engine, got it through the MOT, and removed the rear bumper, ready to find a replacement on his online auction site. But then his father had received his diagnosis, and there was no time to do anything, aside from work, but look after Rich and Nancy. Three months after the awful toxic mix of chemotherapy and suppressed emotion, Phil had been made redundant, and the camper-van had apparently been forgotten.

'Why don't you spend some time this afternoon working on the van?' she would suggest every few weeks, hoping that the mixture of practical problem-solving and fresh air would make him feel more himself. And at first he would nod and say, sure, definitely, if he had time. But as the weeks passed he would look hunted if she mentioned it, and after a while it was easier never to mention it at all. Now the van sits, its innards three-quarters removed, its bumper still missing, silently rusting in their driveway until it's taxed again, its unmoving bulk a rebuke to her dreams of holidays, and a better way of living, and also to the idea that they might be able to park the car somewhere other than three streets away from their own house.

Kevin sniffs its rear tyre, which is as deflated as she feels, then abruptly cocks his leg, letting out a thin stream of urine against it. She has a sudden urge to do the same thing, just lowering her pants and cocking her leg against the wheel, a bald expression of her disgust at the whole damn thing. She pictures the neighbours, appalled, staring out of their windows and conferring as she crouches, and smiles. And as she tells Kevin he is a good dog, a very good dog, and makes her way inside, she realizes this is the first thing that has made her laugh all day.

'How was the pub?' Phil has raised himself to a sitting position on the sofa. Kevin bounds up to him, giddy and delighted to see the man he hasn't seen for a whole forty-five minutes, completely free of resentment for his stretched bladder. Phil fondles the dog's ears.

'The pub? Oh. Fine. It was fine.'

He looks at her for a moment and, briefly, something sad and self-aware passes across his face. 'I'm sorry I didn't make it. I was just . . . really tired and . . .' His voice tails away.

'I know.'

'I'm sorry,' he says again, quietly, looking down. And Sam, parking her mental list of jobs, sits down beside him, takes his hand and lets her head rest, just for a while, on his shoulder.

10

Nisha has located two more White Horse pubs, walking miles through insalubrious London streets in the awful shoes, in both cases to be told, no, they had no idea about any stolen shoes, and none of the bar staff at the one pub with CCTV knew how to work the playback. 'You can come back when the manager is here.' The girl had shrugged in a way that told her he was likely to be even less interested than she was. Nisha has barely slept these two nights, her thoughts twisting and congealing as she considers what Carl has done to her, her fury mounting, along with her determination to reclaim what is hers.

She was at the breakfast buffet when it opened at 6.30 a.m., her hair damp and scraped into a ponytail, and downed two swift coffees, ignoring the growling of her stomach.

She finally slows her pace as the Bentley Hotel comes into view. She sees the top-hatted doorman greeting a weary traveller, whose suitcases are being unloaded from a taxi, and wonders briefly whether Frederik will have briefed him not to let her in. She doesn't care, she tells herself. She will walk straight past him, sit down in the lobby and this time she will refuse to move.

She straightens the awful jacket, and checks her watch. Seven thirty-seven. Carl will be dressed by now, up in the suite, sitting at his desk and checking the financial pages while waiting for his coffee: black, two sugars. Who is bringing him that coffee? she thinks suddenly. Is it Charlotte? Nisha's favourite black silk dressing-gown draped around her body? A smile of post-coital satisfaction on that tight, young, duplicitous face? She pauses, her jaw setting, and runs through what she plans to say to him: *You can have your divorce, Carl. I just want what's mine. I want simply what you owe me.* She will do it with dignity, with pride. Or maybe she will just kick him in the nuts.

She takes a deep breath, walks two steps towards the door, and it is then that she spies Ari standing a short distance from the doorman, his earpiece in, his mouth barely moving as he conducts some discreet conversation with one of his men. Ari, whom she once watched knock a man to the ground with a single swift jab to the neck. That can only mean one thing: that they half expect her to try to come back. Before he can see her, she ducks into the side alley that runs alongside the hotel, her heart pounding in her chest. Outside a door, halfway down, two kitchen workers are sitting on a step, smoking and drinking coffee. She stands close to them and lights a cigarette, turning her back to the road and trying not to breathe in the scents of urine and stale food.

She might get past the doorman, but she will not get past Ari. And there is somehow a greater humiliation involved in being blocked and removed by the man who had been paid for the last decade to protect her. She takes short, jittery drags on the cigarette while she considers her options, oblivious to the two men who glance at her with incurious eyes, then continue their conversation. A woman in an anorak with a bowed head walks past and steps into the doorway beside them. And then another, talking animatedly in a foreign language on her cellphone. A third, with braided hair and a long, padded coat, stops in front of her. 'You waiting to go in, darling?'

Nisha looks up.

'You don't want to go in smelling of ciggies. Frederik hates it. Here.' The woman pulls a spray from her handbag and before Nisha can protest has blasted her with a cloud of cheap musk. Nisha screws up her eyes at the chemical smell and coughs. Tucking the spray back into her bag, the woman says, 'C'mon. You new? Follow me.'

Ari appears at the end of the alley, still looking the other way. Nisha makes a split-second decision and follows the woman into the back entrance of the hotel, walking along a narrow corridor, past hurrying waiters and someone pushing a large trolley of laundry. She backs against the wall to let it pass, not wanting to touch any of the pile of germ-ridden sheets.

'Your first time here?'

Nisha nods, gazing behind her.

'You got papers?'

'Papers?'

'National Insurance number?'

Nisha shakes her head.

'Don't worry. Just say you're waiting on a replacement passport. They never ask too much – how the hell else are they going to get anyone in on these wages?' She laughs drily, as if she has amused herself. 'What's your name?'

'Nisha.'

'I'm Jasmine. Don't look so worried! They don't bite here! C'mon. Let's get you kitted out and I'll take you over to Sandra. She's in charge of rotas.'

Nisha finds herself in a room full of lockers, the air heavy with the leftover scents of food and overworked bodies. 'Oi! Gilberto! Take your trash out, man! I'm not paid to clear up after you lot as well as the guests.'

A short, wiry man with nicotine-stained skin lurches in and picks up a polystyrene box from which a strong smell of fish seeps. 'He's put me on doubles till Thursday. I swear, Jas, I'm going to drop if this carries on.'

Jasmine lets out a noise that sounds like a growl, and Gilberto leaves. 'They're short-staffed at the moment,' she says,

93

opening a locker and putting her bag inside. 'It's been a nightmare. Since Brexit the hotel has lost forty per cent of the staff. Forty per cent! Where are you from?'

'New York.'

'New York! Don't get many Americans here. Only the paying kind. Here. What size are you? Eight? Ten? You're just a little skinny thing.' She rifles through a pile of uniforms until she hauls out a black tunic and trousers. 'We can wear our own stuff but it's better to wear theirs. Some days I am *too glad* to leave the filth of this place behind and put my own clothes on again, you know? You don't want to take that shit home with you.'

While she stands, holding the folded pile of clothes, Jasmine peels her way unselfconsciously out of her elasticated dress, then hauls on a pair of black trousers and a tunic. She checks her appearance in the small mirror on the back of the door, then glances back at Nisha.

'C'mon! Don't hang around! If we get upstairs by quarter to there'll still be some breakfast.'

She has no idea what she's doing. But staying close to Jasmine seems as good a plan as any right now. Nisha wriggles into the clothes (thank God they smell of laundry service), rams her stuff into an empty locker, and follows Jasmine out and along the corridor.

Nisha is not hungry, but in past days she has learned to eat when food is available, and she follows Jasmine mutely through the kitchens, watching as the younger woman greets her fellow workers. 'What's going on, Nigel? Your mum out of hospital yet? Glad to hear it, babe . . . Katya! I watched that thing you told me! I nearly crapped myself, man! What business have you got making me watch horror? You know I don't have a man to protect me!' Jasmine laughs easily, and pushes

94

through doorways like she expects the world to fall away and clear her path. Nisha's mind races. She scans each room they enter, half waiting for Ari's figure to appear in front of her. But, no, there are just these brisk, sometimes shuffling, figures hurrying past, their faces etched with exhaustion, clearly focused on their jobs.

'Here. What do you like? This is the one perk to starting early: Minette's pastries. Oh, my God, I swear I was seven stone till I started working here.' Jasmine hands her a plate, and motions to a large tray on which a selection of *pains aux raisins*, *pains au chocolat* and croissants are laid out. Nisha takes a *pain au raisin* and bites into it. In less than a nanosecond she recognizes that this is the best thing she has eaten in three days: light and moist and delicately buttery, genuine French patisserie, still warm from the oven. For the first time in days her brain stops spinning and she is lost in pleasure.

'Good, right?' Jasmine takes two and closes her eyes in bliss as she eats. 'My day from five thirty is mental. I have to get my daughter up and dressed, make her packed lunch if it's a school day, then take her to my mum's in Peckham, then two more buses to come here, and I swear the only thing that keeps me going is the thought of these beauties waiting for me.'

'Oh, that's good,' says Nisha, through a mouthful of crumbs.

'Minette's a goddamn genius. Almost as good as you, Aleks!' Over by the flaming stove a lean man in chef's whites turns from his pans and nods at Jasmine. 'You done?'

Nisha nods.

'Okay. Let's go.' Jasmine wipes her mouth with a paper napkin and heads towards the door on the far side of the kitchen, pausing only to tell Nisha to 'Straighten up your hair a bit', reaching over to tighten her ponytail before Nisha can stop her. Jasmine pushes through the double doors, walks briskly down a corridor and turns left into a small office.

'We've got Nisha starting today. Papers are in the post.'

'Oh, thank God,' says a red-haired woman, who is scrubbing names out on a rota and doesn't look up. 'I've had four call in sick today. She need training?'

'Do you need training?' Jasmine says to her.

'Uh – yes?' says Nisha.

'Can't be helped,' says Red-hair. 'Okay, Jas, you'll have to show her the ropes. I'm going to up your rooms as you're two-handed. We've got sixteen to do by two and two early check-ins. Here's the list. What's your name again?'

Nisha is about to speak, then says: 'Anita.'

'Okay, Anita. Come back and pick your badge up at twelve. No illnesses, injuries or allergies? Fill this out when you return. We haven't got time for you to do it now.'

'I thought you said your name was Nisha?'

The two women look at her.

She has a sudden memory of Juliana. And swallows. 'I find . . . Anita is easier for guests to pronounce.'

Red-hair shrugs. 'Anita it is. Okay – go get your stuff. Jas, we're really low on bleach. Sorry about that. Elbow grease only wherever possible today. We'll need to save it for the bad stuff.'

'Elbow grease. The one thing they know we'll never be out of,' Jasmine grumbles, and they head off towards the store cupboard.

Ten minutes later Nisha is following Jasmine as she pushes the housekeeping trolley along the carpeted corridor of the third floor. She feels electrified, visible, as if every guest who looks at her will guess what she's doing, and know she's an imposter. She finds herself ducking her head as they pass, not wanting anyone to notice her.

'What are you doing?' Jasmine turns, as the third guest walks by.

'What do you mean?'

'We have to say good morning to all guests. It's company policy. You have to make them feel like they're part of the Bentley family. On the sixth and seventh floor we have to say their names too.'

She and Carl had occupied the suite on the seventh floor. Nisha was so used to staff knowing who she was that it had never occurred to her these greetings were part of any kind of policy. She mutters, 'Good morning,' as they pass the next guests, a German couple, who return a formal greeting and continue to the elevators.

Jasmine brings the trolley to a halt outside Room 339 and knocks twice, flicking through her clipboard as she waits for a response. 'Housekeeping!'

When nobody responds, she uses her key card, pushes the door and waits until Nisha is behind her. The room is one-tenth the size of the suite. An unmade bed is in the centre, the sheets covered with crumbs and leftover food from the breakfast tray that is lying on the covers. A television blares the news. An empty wine bottle and two glasses stand on the side.

Jasmine bustles round and turns off the television. 'Okay. You start on the bathroom, I'll strip the bed. We normally have around twenty minutes to do these rooms or we'll get written up, and this morning we've got extra so you'll have to get a wiggle on.'

Until then, Nisha realized afterwards, she hadn't really thought she was going to be asked to *do* anything. She had thought perhaps she could just don the uniform and dis-appear into the bowels of the building, work out how she could make her way into her suite.

But now Jasmine is staring at her, one hand holding a blue cloth, her face slightly quizzical. 'It ain't brain surgery. Just clean it like your own bathroom, babe. But better!' Jasmine lets out a hearty laugh and dons her latex gloves before pulling off the coverlet briskly like she knows what germs it might contain.

Nisha stands in the bathroom, frozen. There are unidentified short hairs in the basin, the toilet seat is wet and there are two damp towels on the floor, one bearing a pale brown mark that she hopes very much is makeup. She thinks about walking straight out, but this is her one opportunity to remain in the hotel, for the time being, anyway. She takes two deep breaths, pulls on the gloves, and starts to clean the basin, trying not to look as she wipes.

She is almost halfway through when Jasmine appears at the door. 'Babe! You're going to have to switch it up! Have you done the bog roll? Fold the corners when you put it on. Half-used ones go back on the trolley. Here. I'll do your bottles.'

Jasmine sweeps all the half-empty mini-bottles of shampoo and body lotion into a bin bag and disappears into the corridor. It is at that point that Nisha turns to the lavatory. It has yellow splashes dried onto the seat, and a clear brown mark in the pan. She feels the remains of her breakfast rise ominously into the back of her mouth. *Oh, God, this cannot be happening.*

'C'mon, girl!' She hears Jasmine's voice in the other room. 'We've got seven more minutes.' Nisha takes hold of the toilet brush and, looking away, starts to scrub vaguely at the inside of the bowl. She heaves twice, involuntarily, and has to pause to let her eyes stop watering. She allows herself a brief look down into the bowl – the brown mark is still there. She places the toilet brush against it and pushes, yelping involuntarily when water splashes upwards. *I will kill you, Carl,* she says silently. *I could just about forgive you the money and the stupid assistant, but I will never, ever forgive you for this.*

Nisha gags again as she lifts the toilet seat and wipes it, then pauses and wipes her face. Her eyes are streaming. She has never hated humanity as much as she does in that moment. And for Nisha, that's saying something.

She is nineteen-year-old Anita, just off a Greyhound bus at the Port Authority Bus Terminal, who blinked, gritty-eyed, at the towering buildings around her, and asked for a job at the first place she came to, a narrow, tired-looking three-star hotel near 42nd Street. It had taken her ten weeks of cleaning hotel rooms to get a better housekeeping job working for a wealthy family. Ten interminable weeks of disgusting bathrooms, leering male guests, who decided to stay in their room while she cleaned, ten weeks of bedbugs and stained linen and foul spillages and chemicals so strong they stripped all the moisture from her hands. After eighteen months with the family, she got a job working reception at the Soho gallery of a friend of that family, and the moment she had donned her anonymous uniform of black sweater and trousers, and greeted the first slightly distracted customer, Anita had become Nisha and swore that she was never going to clean again.

They do eleven more rooms in the next two hours. It is back-breaking work, lifting mattresses to make the beds, replacing furniture (why do guests move tables and armchairs?) and vacuuming. There is a used condom in one room, and blood-stained sheets in another. Both make her gag, and her eyes water almost constantly. 'People are animals,' Jasmine mutters, ripping the undersheet from the mattress. 'They come in here and from the moment they check in it's like they turn into savages.' She harrumphs as she heads off to find a new protector.

As Jasmine chats and occasionally hums alongside her, Nisha tells herself repeatedly just to get through it. That this will soon be over. She thinks of the many ways in which she will make Carl pay, only a few of which involve a swift and merciful death. At eleven they are allowed a tea break, and take their place in the tiny locker room, where a heavily made-up receptionist called Tiffany and a bell-boy sit and vape on the little wooden benches. Nearly everyone she meets smokes, either cigarettes outside or gulping thirstily from vapes. Nisha accepts a cigarette from the bell-boy, grateful that the acrid smell of smoke briefly makes her forget the worse human scents she has just left behind.

'You okay, Nisha? You've gone a bit quiet.' Jasmine refills her tea and hands it over to her.

'Just . . . I've not done this for a while.'

'You don't say.' Jasmine's laugh bursts into the room. 'You're doing fine, babe. You're going to have to speed up a little but you're all good.' She looks up. 'Those nails ain't going to last long. I stopped getting normal manicures some time around 2005. They've got to be armour-plated to survive this.'

Nisha looks down at her nails, the beautiful dark red edges now chipped from the endless scrubbing and rubbing, even with the latex gloves they are given. She can feel the sweat drying on her skin. Just a day, she thinks, and then she will work out how to get into the suite and never have to do this again.

In the meantime she finds herself listening to the workers chat around her. Jasmine, she observes, is a life force, sunny and opinionated. She laughs often, as if almost everything is amusing, and although in normal life Nisha might have found this irritating, today she is grateful for it. She has had so little human contact in the last forty-eight hours that listening to normal conversation is almost pleasurable. The workers chat about bus routes, about cancelled benefits and dysfunctional families. She says little, because what can she say? To these people she is just Anita, another temporary worker, who may or may not be here tomorrow.

At lunchtime – which takes place at two – they are given sandwiches by Aleks, the man who was in the kitchen at breakfast. She had suspected they would be the same kind of cheap bread and filling that she has seen at the Tower Primavera, but they are beautiful soft sourdough bread filled with cheese, cured meats and butterhead lettuce. He hands them over with exaggerated politesse, as if they are cherished guests. She would normally ask for salad, but she is so hungry after the morning's physical work that she just puts her head down and eats, taking huge, indelicate bites.

'Aleks says food is for the soul, so he ignores the management and does us the same he would do for the guests,' says Jasmine, chewing. 'I worship that man.' As she takes another huge soft mouthful, Nisha thinks she probably worships him too.

'Jasmine? When . . . when will we be doing the penthouse?'

'The penthouse? Oh, no, babes. They're picky up there, so it's got to be senior housekeepers like me, people the hotel knows they can rely on. Mind you, those arseholes never tip. It's not a gig you want.'

Nisha blinks, and focuses extra hard on her sandwich.

And then, at six, as her lower back twinges and the ache in her shoulders switches from intermittent to a non-stop, pulsing protest, the day is over. Jasmine calls her daughter, tells her she is on her way, asks her to tell Nana to leave her some stew, and hopes the buses will sort themselves out this evening. Her gait is a little wearier now, her laugh a little less ready. Nisha can barely move. She has pains in muscles she didn't know she had. She puts on the horrible jacket and sits slumped on the wooden bench, wondering how she'll pluck up the energy to walk back to the hotel. She'll get a taxi, she thinks, then remembers she has no cash for a taxi.

'How far you got to go, babe?' says Jasmine, who is checking her appearance in the small speckled mirror on the back of the door, reapplying lipstick with a connoisseur's slow, sure hand.

'Uh . . . Tower Hill,' she says.

'Not too bad. Though the Highway is nuts this time of night, even on a Sunday. Aleks lives over that way and sometimes it takes him an hour on the bus just to get that far.'

'I'm walking,' she says.

'The whole way? Good on you. That's why you're such a little bitty thing! See you tomorrow?'

Tomorrow. What is she going to do tomorrow? Her brain is so tired she can barely think. 'Sure,' she answers, because it's the easiest thing to do. 'Hang on,' she says, as Jasmine makes to leave. 'What about my money?'

'Money?'

'For today.'

Jasmine pulls a face. 'You don't get paid by the day, babe. What do they do where you come from? Agency and temp workers get paid at the end of the week. Just talk to Sandra and she'll sort it for you. I'm guessing you're cash in hand?'

She must have caught Nisha's look of horror, because her face softens. 'You really short, huh?'

Nisha nods, dumbly. Jasmine stops and reaches into her bag.

Nisha stares at her. She does not want to take money from this woman, with her catalogue-quality jacket and cheap trainers. She does not want to think of herself as *poorer than this*.

Jasmine gives her a steady look, as if assessing her, then pulls out twenty pounds and holds it towards her. 'I wouldn't normally do this but . . . I like you. You worked hard today. Make sure you get yourself something good to eat – if you haven't done this for a while, today will have taken it out of you.' Nisha takes the notes and stares at them.

Jasmine lets out a small *hmm*.

'I'll see you tomorrow then,' she says eventually. And smiles. 'I'm trusting you. And don't you come in smelling of cigarettes again, okay?'

She hoists her bag over her shoulder, and she is gone, her phone already pressed to her ear, her free hand spraying clouds of the perfume around her shoulders.

She tries the White Horse on Bailey Street before she goes back to the hotel. It is almost empty, just a handful of red-faced elderly men punctuating the corners, and the carpet sticks slightly to the soles of her feet. When she explains that she's looking for a missing pair of high-heeled shoes the barman actually laughs in her face.

11

Company gone into liquidation. Closed until further notice. Sam looks at the sign, the kitbag slung over her shoulder, then peers through the glass door that has already been covered with newspaper, as if to stop the outside world looking in at a financial murder scene.

A young man, his tanned, rippling arm muscles visible through his vest, even though the air is chilly, arrives beside her and lets out a loud curse. 'I just joined!' he protests at Sam, as though it is her fault. 'I just paid them a year in advance!'

Sam watches him stride back across the car park, still cursing, wondering what she's supposed to do now about returning the bag to its owner. She feels briefly cross at the thought that she will now have to lug it to the office and home again afterwards and work out what on earth to do about it. This makes her think about Simon, no doubt checking his watch already, waiting to see if she is even a minute late to add to his checklist of things she has done wrong. She hauls the bag more tightly over her shoulder and heads for the Tube station.

There was a time, not that long ago, when Sam enjoyed her job. She didn't spring out of bed every morning whistling, or come home feeling like she had particularly added to the joy of the world, but there had been a quiet satisfaction in being with people whose company she enjoyed every day, and knowing she could do the job she had done for twelve years pretty well. There were Sams in every office, the people who quietly, and without drama, kept everything running smoothly, willing to step in if extra hours were required, satisfied enough by what they did not to require ego-stroking or excessive praise. She had received three salary increases in that time, none of which had been huge, but enough to make her feel like a valued member of staff.

That had changed the day that Simon had arrived. He had stalked his way coldly around the offices of Grayside Print with thinly veiled disappointment, as if the desks themselves were a let-down. He had repeatedly interrupted Sam during her first meeting with him, and even shaken his head a couple of times while she was speaking, as if everything she said was in some way wrong.

You're going to have to explain more clearly what you mean.
But why are you taking ten days on jobs that could be done in seven?
You're aware that Uberprint strives for excellence in every single job?
And your boss was happy with the way you run things here, was he?

Everything he said seemed calculated to imply some deficit on her part, her attention levels, her schedules, even her punctuality (Sam was never late).

At first she tried to brazen it out. Joel told her not to take it personally, there was one like Simon wherever you went – 'He's just dick-waving, babe, trying to make his mark' – but the relentlessness of it had started to chip away at her so that she became all fingers and thumbs in his presence when trying to flick through her desk diary, or stammered pre-emptively, waiting for him to cut in over her in meetings. Now, as she left the house in the morning, a heavy, sickly feeling would settle in Sam's stomach. She had taken to listening to podcasts or ambient music on her journey to work, just so that she didn't have to think about what was likely to happen when she arrived. Every day, when she walked in, Simon, visible in his glass-walled office, would look ostentatiously at the office clock and raise an eyebrow, even if she was five minutes early. He would text her late into the evening asking what had been done about improving the margins on the Carling job, or whether she had double-checked the pages weren't stuck together on the garden-furniture catalogues (this had happened once, while she was away on a week's holiday and Hardeep was meant to be covering, though this fact seemed irrelevant to Simon).

It took her two months to realize that he never did it to the men. He would chat with them, his face wreathed in smiles, any suggestion that there was a problem covered with matey caveats, a suggestion that they go for a drink later and sort it out. He would stand too close to the younger women, his hands half submerged at angles in his pockets as if he were perennially pointing to his genitals, and smile and stare at their chests. Some – like Dee – would smile back and flirt with him, then bitch about him in the Ladies: 'That slime-ball. He gives me the ick.' But aside from Betty in Accounts, who never spoke to anyone but had a mathematical brain that could work faster than a desk calculator, and Marina, who didn't give a monkey's what anybody thought about her, and would say as much without prompting, Sam was now the oldest woman in the office and, Simon had apparently decided, not worthy of any attention that wasn't entirely negative in tone. It was exhausting.

Once, she could have confided all this to Phil, and he would have calmed her, commiserated, offered strategies to help deal with it. She had mentioned it one evening after a particularly bad day but instead of sitting her down and pouring her a glass of wine he had put his head into his hands and told her he was sorry, he couldn't deal with anything else. She had been so alarmed at his apparent fragility that she had immediately reassured him it was nothing, nothing at all. Just a bad day. And never mentioned it again.

Ted, Joel and Marina kept her going, day to day, but nobody ever stepped in, or stood up to Simon when he was haranguing her. Of course, Simon would save his most negative comments for when they were alone, or murmur them as he passed her cubicle – *Jesus, I don't know how you get any work done with a desk like that*. Most of the time, if there was an audience, he would simply ignore her. But what could she do? With Phil out of work, and their savings depleted, they were reliant on her salary. She kept her head down, did her best, ignored the ever-present knot in her stomach, and hoped that at some point he would grow bored and decide to pick on someone else.

'Simon's headed your way.' Marina puts a coffee on her desk furtively, like she's imparting classified information, and her expression as she turns away fills Sam with dread.

'What now?' she says, but Marina has already gone.

She slides the kitbag under her desk and hangs her handbag on the back of the chair, sits down and logs on to her screen.

He is there within seconds, wearing a pair of slightly too tight suit trousers and a belt with a high shine. His demeanour is that of a headmaster who has been dragged out of an important meeting to deal with a recalcitrant child.

'Why did you not warn Fishers about the look of the colours on the uncoated paper?'

'I'm sorry?'

She turns too quickly, and almost knocks her coffee from the table with her elbow.

'Four thousand copies of their new property brochure and they're on the phone yelling because of the colour quality on the uncoated paper.'

'They said they wanted uncoated paper. They were keeping costs down. Ted and I did warn them it would look different from what they were used to.'

Simon pulls a face, as if there is no way this could be true. 'Mark Fisher says you didn't tell them anything. Now he wants us to redo the whole job at cost. They say nobody is going to buy houses with everything looking so flat and colourless on the page.'

'I sat down with Mr Fisher specifically at our last meeting and told him it would be a very different look. I showed him examples of the Clearsills catalogue. He dismissed it and said that would be fine.'

'So Mr Fisher is lying, is he?' Simon's voice is scornful.

'He – he might be misremembering. But I remember it clearly. I even took notes. He said cutting costs was their main concern. It's not our fault, Simon, if he's changed his mind. Besides, it's the designer's job to communicate these things to the client. I – I only stepped in because I wasn't convinced they understood what they were asking for.'

'Well, Samantha, you stepping in has been pretty unhelpful because they are now convinced it's all Uberprint's responsibility. And you need to work out how you're going to put this mess right before it has very serious ramifications indeed.'

He spins on his heel and is gone before she can protest. She has not even had time to take her coat off. She lets out a long sigh and slumps slightly in her chair.

An email pings as she slides her left arm out of the sleeve, and she leans forward to open it.

Chin up, babe. Don't let him get you down x

She looks up and over at Joel, whose face has appeared above the side of the Logistics cubicle ten feet away. When he smiles at her she can't work out whether she wants to blush or burst into tears.

*

At lunchtime the builder who has ignored Sam's increasingly frantic messages for the best part of four months calls without warning and announces they will be starting work the following week on rebuilding the front wall, which had been irrevocably damaged in June by a pensioner no longer able to see their reversing mirrors. It's an insurance job, for which Sam breathes a sigh of relief: who knew a small wall could be so expensive?

She calls home while sitting in the staff eating area, one of the few places Simon never visits (he seems to see it as beneath him, with its carefully demarcated coffee-mug ownership and microwave oven). She is eating a tuna and sweetcorn sandwich made with two-day-old bread. It is claggy in her mouth, or maybe today's altercation with Simon is making it feel like that.

'Hi, love,' she says, forcing brightness into her voice. 'How are you doing?'

'Okay,' Phil says flatly.

She can hear the burble of the television down the phone, and pictures him staring blankly at the overly made-up women discussing current affairs on the screen.

'Well . . . Des Parry finally got back to me. They're going to start work on the wall next Monday – finally! – so you'll need to move the camper-van.'

'The camper-van? To where?'

'I don't know. Onto the road?'

'But it's got no tax.'

'Well, we'll have to tax it. He can't get to the wall if it's parked where it is. Or maybe one of your friends with a garage could look after it.'

'Oh, I don't think I can ask the boys.'

She closes her eyes for a moment.

'We haven't really spoken in a while. It would feel . . .' His voice tails away.

'Phil. Love. We need to move the van, whatever. It would be great if you could work out how to do that. I'm pretty stretched here.'

There is a long pause.

'Can't we put them off for a bit? I don't think I'm up to that right now.'

It is then that she feels the anger boil up inside her. 'Up to what? Moving a van six feet?'

'The whole tax and MOT thing. And . . . I don't know where we would put it. I can't really handle it right now.'

'Well, you'll have to work something out. Because the builder is coming.'

'Just put him off a week. I'll think about it.'

'No, Phil.' She can hear her voice becoming high and shrill. 'I will not put him off. It's taken me months to get him in the first place, and I can't risk him going to another job. And that wall is dangerous. You know it is. If someone climbs on it and it collapses, they'll be seriously hurt. And we'll be liable. So just sort out the bloody van and move it. Then we can both get on with our lives, okay?'

There is a long silence on the other end of the phone.

'You don't have to be aggressive about it,' he says grimly. 'I'm doing my best.'

'Are you, though? Are you really?' Something has unlocked in Sam and she can't help it: words pour out of her mouth like hard pebbles. 'I'm working flat out and running the house and trying to look after Andrea and Cat and the incontinent dog and dealing with bloody Simon and you are lying on your arse on the sofa for sixteen hours a day, and in bed the other six. When did you last do a supermarket shop? Or walk Kevin? Or – or sweep the kitchen floor? Or anything at all other than feel sorry for yourself? You're not doing anything! Just wallowing! You do nothing but wallow!'

Silence. And then he says: 'Eight. It's eight hours in bed.'

'What?'

'There are twenty-four hours in a day. Sixteen hours on the sofa. That leaves eight.'

'Oh, for Christ's sake, Phil. You know what I'm saying. Just *do* something, okay? I know you're sad and I know you feel like life is hard, and it is. My God, I know it is. But sometimes you just have to get up and bloody get on with it. That's exactly what I've been doing for months and I can't do it on my own any more. Okay? I just can't!'

This time she doesn't wait to see how he will respond. She ends the call, and stares at the wall, her heart pounding in her chest.

It is then that she turns and jumps at Simon standing in the doorway.

'"Dealing with bloody Simon",' he says slowly, nodding, a peculiar half-smile on his face. 'Interesting. I was just coming to tell you that you need to renegotiate the figures on the Billson job. Head Office says the margins aren't good enough.'

Sam stares, as he turns and walks away. She looks at the clingfilm-wrapped sandwich on her lap, her blood pumping in her ears, and without even really knowing what she's doing, she hurls it across the room so that it explodes soggily against the wall.

Seven minutes later Sam straightens her jacket, gets up and, using squares of kitchen towel, picks up every bit of sweet-corn from the carpet, wipes the mayo and butter from the wall with a damp cloth, then puts the whole thing carefully into the bin.

12

'So what . . . do I do?'

'What do you want to do?'

Phil looks at the man, and wonders if this is a trick question. If he sits on the seat closest to him will it look needy? Or weird? But he doesn't know about lying on that bed thing. Plus he's a little worried that if he lies down he will immediately fall asleep. He falls asleep all the time, these days. If he does, will he look like a crazy person?

It's as if he can hear his thoughts. 'Some people find it more comfortable to sit. Some lie down. It's really just about what's most comfortable for you.'

Phil hesitates, then sits on the edge of the rattan sofa, leaving an empty seat between them. The man gazes at him and waits. Phil wonders whether he could get up and leave now. There is nothing keeping him here, after all. But Cat had been adamant, and his daughter is surprisingly hard to contradict.

'Do I talk? Or do you talk?'

'You can start. And then we'll talk together.'

'I don't know what to say.'

A long silence.

'So what brings you here, Philip?'

'Phil. It's Phil.'

'Okay, Phil.'

Phil stares at the floor. 'My doctor. Well, he didn't actually bring me here. But he said if I wouldn't take the anti-depressants I needed to try talking therapy.' He scratches his head. 'And my daughter. She's . . . concerned about me. Silly, really.'

'And you were reluctant to come?'

'I'm British.' Phil attempts a smile. 'We're not big on feelings.'

'Oh, I'd disagree,' says Dr Kovitz. 'I think British people are very big on feelings. Expressing them comfortably, perhaps not so much.' He smiles.

Phil smiles back awkwardly. It seems to be expected.

'Do you want to talk me through what took you to the doctor in the first place?'

Phil feels his chest tighten, as it does reflexively whenever anyone demands he discuss the events of the past year.

'Let's keep it simple to begin with. You said your father died. Was it unexpected?'

There are things that are almost too much to put into words. And the months leading up to Dad's death are so huge and so dark in his mind that he is afraid that if he revisits them he will be a small planet sucked into a black hole. A vast, terrifying vacuum he will not be able to claw his way out of.

He lets out a small cough. 'Well, yes and no,' he says, and shifts in his chair. 'Yes, in that he was fit and healthy for a seventy-five-year-old. No, in that once we knew, we had months to see what was coming down the line.'

'Cancer?'

'Yes.'

'Were you close?'

'Uh . . . yes.'

'I'm sorry. That must have been very hard for you.'

'Oh, I'm fine. He had a good life. It's . . . you know, my mum. They were married fifty years. She's the one I worried about.'

'And how is she doing?'

That was the thing. Nancy was doing fine. For the first six months after Dad died he would brace himself for the evening call. She would start every conversation in a tremulous, brave voice, talking about the small things she had achieved: the emptying of a drawer, moving some things from the shed, then, inevitably, she would crumble. *I just miss him so much, love.* He had learned to dread those moments, his feelings of impotence and sadness, his inability to lift any of that weight. He and Sam would head over every Sunday and either take her for a pub lunch or help her prepare a roast, and chat to her as they all washed up afterwards. She had seemed so diminished, as if she couldn't survive physically without him. She had never paid a bill on her own, never had the car serviced, never eaten a meal in a public place without him by her side. She lost her interest in food, in going out. She would revisit memories like worry beads, going over and over the past months and wondering aloud if they should have done things differently, if there had been something she had missed. He had wondered occasionally whether they would need to ask her to live with them. She seemed fundamentally unsuited to being alone. It was only the fact that they had no actual bedroom to put her in that had stopped them.

And then, abruptly, everything changed. His mother had grieved, and grieved, and then one day he had turned up and her hair was blow-dried and she was wearing lipstick. 'I had a big think about it and I decided Rich wouldn't want me sitting around weeping and wailing. I think he would have got quite cross with me. Can you show me where I put oil into the car?'

And that was it. Two months ago she had started volunteering with refugees at the community centre, giving baking classes every Tuesday. Phil wasn't sure how many of them really needed to learn how to make a Victoria Sandwich, but she said it wasn't about the food: 'It's just getting them to do something, being in a group. And everyone feels better after cake, don't they? It's a fact.'

She said it made her feel better, being useful. Listening to their stories, she felt grateful that she'd had such a peaceful life, so much love. She – a woman who had shunned garlic for years as 'too foreign' – even started to enjoy the food they brought in for her. 'It was so spicy, Phil, honestly. My face went as red as a beetroot. But it was actually rather good.'

He was glad for her, but also oddly troubled by his mother's ability just to get on with her life. Because he couldn't. At night he dreamed of sitting beside his father's bed, his bony, translucent hand gripping Phil's with surprisingly strong fingers as he struggled for breath, his eyes furious as he gazed at Phil over his oxygen mask. The way he looked as if he actually hated his son. He saw those eyes boring into his every time he closed his own.

'She's doing well,' he says. 'You know. Considering.'

'So we have that,' says Dr Kovitz. 'That's a major life event. A lot to cope with. Is there anything else you're navigating?'

Well, I lost my job, and with that my wife lost all respect for me, and my daughter thinks I'm a dud and I can't see the point in getting dressed, or even washing most days. I don't see my friends any more, because who wants to be around a miserable person?

I'm too tired to go out. And home just reminds me of all the things I haven't done. I can't even put the recycling out because I wash up a plastic tray and it seems ridiculous. What is the point in us washing out the trays that the chicken thighs came in when China is pumping out a billion tonnes of carbon dioxide a minute? I can't watch the news because it makes me want to bury my head under the duvet, and the sight of the floods and the fires makes me anxious for grandchildren I haven't even had yet so I just stay on the sofa where it's safe and watch shows where people buy and resell antique boot-pulls to make two pounds' profit, or women in brightly coloured dresses discuss diets and soap operas, and the only reason I watch those shows is because I cannot bear the silence. I cannot bear the silence.

And I know my wife is exhausted and fed up with me but every time I try to do something to help her she sighs and tuts under her breath because I do it wrong. And she used to love me but now she just wears this expression that tells me I'm useless. So I mostly just pretend to be asleep to stay out of her way, and then my daughter, who is smarter than either of us, comes in and says, *Dad. You need to get up now.* Like she's the mother of a teenager, or a carer in a home. But I can't explain it to her: that I just want to sleep. At least once a day I realize that the only thing I can think about is my bed, waiting for me to crawl into it, and all I'm doing is waiting till everyone goes out so that I can head upstairs and sink into oblivion for a few more hours.

And the doctor told me to improve my diet, but the truth is I have no energy to put together nutritionally beneficial meals. So I eat biscuits, toast with butter. And I watch my waistline soften and enlarge and despise myself for that too.

'Navigating?' he says. 'Um. Bits and bobs. Normal stuff.'

Dr Kovitz looks at him over his notepad. Phil notices then the two boxes of tissues on the table. He wonders absently how many people cry in this office every day. He wonders if Dr Kovitz empties the bin between sessions so it won't look like the saddest room in the world. He wonders what this man would do if he just lay down on the sofa and cried and cried. But the thing is, if he let himself do that he would probably never stop.

'Normal stuff,' Dr Kovitz repeats thoughtfully. 'That's an interesting concept. Do you think there's such a thing as normal stuff?'

'Well. What have I got to complain about, really?'

He smiles at Dr Kovitz. What has he got to complain about? It's all pathetic. Compared with most people Phil has a lot. He has a body that works pretty well. He has a house, even if there is a weighty mortgage attached to it. He has a wife. He has a daughter. He will probably get a job again at some point. He is not running from armed terrorists or walking forty miles to fetch water. He is not counting his ribs, or trying to comfort a starving child. And what the hell can this man here do anyway, with his rattan furniture and his boxes of tissues? What good will talking do? It's not going to rewrite his dad's ending. It's not going to lift the burden on Sam. It's not going to get him a new job, or stop his daughter eyeing him as if he's become some weird, deformed creature at a zoo.

It feels ridiculous. It's all ridiculous.

'I should probably go,' he says, rising to his feet.

'Go?'

'You – you have people far more in need of help than me. I – I don't think this is for me. Sorry.'

Dr Kovitz doesn't try to stop him. He just watches him. 'Okay, Phil,' he says. 'Well. I'm going to keep your session open next week and hope that you come back.'

'There's really no need.'

'Oh, I think there is.'

He stands before Phil can tell him not to and steps past him to open the door for him. He holds it open, and says quietly, 'I hope I'll see you next week.'

It takes Phil twenty-three minutes to walk home. When he gets in he closes the door behind him, pats the dog and climbs the stairs heavily towards bed.

13

The gym was closed until further notice. Nisha had walked there on her way home the previous evening and stared at the sign, letting herself absorb the fact that that was it. Her clothes, the things that made her feel like her, were never going to be returned to her. She is not sure why the shoes bother her so much – perhaps because they had been her last gift from him, an emblem of their marriage. Carl had presented them with a huge flourish, admired her in them, wanted her to wear them on their most important trips. It had not been unusual for Carl to dictate her wardrobe. 'I like to see you in them. I like everyone to see you in them.' What had been the point when all this time he had been busy planning to eject her and install Charlotte in her place? It all adds to the growing feeling that she has been played, and that in turn makes her so angry she feels like her veins are permanently fizzing with it.

'Girl, you've speeded up!' Jasmine puts her head around the bathroom door and pulls an admiring face. Anger seems to fuel Nisha now. She is awake before her alarm, attacks stains and marks as if she is rubbing out Carl's face. She obliterates dirt as if she is obliterating the past week.

'You ready for your break? Or will I just leave you to do the other twelve rooms while I have a coffee?'

Nisha straightens up as Jasmine laughs, wipes her warm brow with the back of her arm. 'Sure.'

It's her fifth day at the hotel. Five days in which she has arrived at the narrow alleyway at 8 a.m., changed into the hotel-issue black clothes, eaten good pastries and cleaned disgusting rooms, all the while her mind humming with resentment. Today she will be paid, and she is not sure what she will do beyond that. The locker-room chat is full of stories of Immigration raids, of cancelled Leave to Remain. People come for one shift and are never seen again. Some stay weeks but never speak to another soul, their eyes darting away from contact as if they would prefer to be invisible. She sees a whole army of people who remain under the radar, living hand-to-mouth as they, like her, try to work out what to do next.

And Nisha has not yet worked out what to do next. She does not want this job, but it brings her daily proximity to her suite, and is still the best chance she has of recovering her things. Every floor that carries them closer she feels her heart beat faster as she tries to work out how she can get in. But undocumented maids do not get to work on the sixth and seventh floors. They are restricted to the cheaper rooms, the ones where business travellers and people who have booked on discount internet sites tend to spend one night. Jasmine says housekeeping staff need to be there for at least a few months before they are considered experienced or trustworthy enough to be allowed to the more exclusive floors.

She will get in there, she knows. But until she works out how, she must play a waiting game.

'Hey, baby.' She logs on to the hotel Wi-Fi (everyone does it) and calls Ray at two; she and Jasmine are on a late lunch break and she knows it will wake him far earlier than he's used to, but she's on her last night's paid-for stay and she cannot work out what to do next.

'Mom? Why are you calling so early?' His voice is thick with sleep.

She tries to smile reassuringly as she speaks. 'Darling – I need a favour. I need to borrow some more money. It's a little complicated but I'll explain everything when I'm home.'

'More money?' She hears him shift in his bed.

'Yes. Another five hundred. Do you think you could wire it to me today? The same place as last time would be great.'

'I can't, Mom.'

'You don't have to do it right now. I just wanted to call early so that you could plan your day around it.'

'No, I literally can't. Dad has frozen my account. Apparently there's been fraudulent activity on it. Didn't he tell you?'

'What?'

'I can't buy *anything*. Not clothes, not games, not even deodorant. He says I have to put any requests in an email to Charlotte. They pay with his card and have it sent to me.'

Oh, God. Carl had worked it out.

'Don't you have anything you can use?' she says desperately. 'Your savings card? What happened to your savings account?'

'Ugh. Frozen too. He's so mean. I literally have no access to my *own money* just now. Can you talk to him about it, Mom? He only speaks to me through Charlotte.'

'I will, darling. I'll do that. I'm so sorry. I'll – I'll speak to you later.'

She ends the call, lets out a low groan and slumps on the bench. Across the room Jasmine is chatting in low tones to Viktor. When Nisha looks up she is staring at her. 'You okay, Nish?'

'My – my ex has frozen our bank accounts. It's . . . it's a mess.'

Jasmine raises her eyebrows. 'Your ex? What is he? A deadbeat dad? Don't tell me, has he cleared you out?'

'Something like that.'

'Ugh!' she exclaims. 'I *knew* something like that was going on. You know what my mum once said to me? "Never marry a man you wouldn't want to be divorced from." My ex, he's good as gold. Pays his share on the fifteenth regular as. Shows up for Gracie. Always speaks respectfully. Mind you, I do wonder if it's because he's still soft on me.' She shrugs, gestures to her face. 'I am a *lot* to get over.' She laughs suddenly, so that Nisha is unsure whether she's joking. 'He got a job? Your bloke?'

'Carl? Kind of.'

'What does he do?'

'Um. Import-export. That kind of thing.'

'Oh, like my friend Sanjay. He runs a warehouse out near Southall. Buys up stuff on the docks that's fallen out of containers and sells it to the market traders. One minute he's living high, next he doesn't have a pot to piss in. What about your folks?'

'I don't – I don't speak to my family.'

'Oh, mate. You got kids?'

'One boy. But he's in New York. He's – he's fine.'

'Well, that's something, I guess. Though you must miss him. How are you getting by?'

'Payday today, right?'

Jasmine pulls a face. 'It is, babe, but you won't be getting a taxi to Louis Vuitton. You know what I'm saying?'

She's not wrong. At the end of the day Nisha receives an envelope with a barely comprehensible handwritten payslip and £425 for her week of ten-hour shifts. The undocumented maids get eight pounds fifty an hour. Fifty has been deducted for the use of the uniform. She stares at it, unable to believe this paltry amount is the result of all those hours of work. It takes her a moment to calculate that at that rate she will not be able to afford to stay at the Tower Primavera while she waits to reclaim her life, cheap as it is. In a matter of days she will have nowhere left to go.

Jasmine tells her she wants to be glad they didn't put her on the books – 'Because then they're taking off National

Insurance and putting you on emergency tax codes and all that crap, and honestly? You might as well just go back on the dole.'

'Oh.' Nisha rifles in her pocket, suddenly remembering. 'Here. Sorry, I forgot.' She holds out the twenty-pound note.

Jasmine looks at it. Then back at Nisha. She pats Nisha's hand. 'You're all right, babes. Give it back to me when you're sorted.'

And somehow that makes Nisha feel even worse.

She has just taken extra supplies of hair conditioner and body lotion to the fifth floor when she sees him. She is walking back to the elevator, feeling mulish at the way the over-made-up young girl who opened the bedroom door snatched the little bottles from her, slamming the door in her face without even a thank-you, when a familiar figure comes towards her along the corridor.

Ari.

Her heart stops. She fights the urge to duck into a doorway, but her keys do not give her access to rooms on this floor and there is nowhere to go. He is distracted, talking on a telephone, his black suit immaculate, his eyes fixed on the middle distance in front of him as he strides silently along the plush carpet.

'No, he doesn't want to. Bring the car round to the front and wait. I don't care. Go round the block if you have to. He has to be in – where the hell is it? – Piccadilly, by two fifteen. Charlotte has the address.'

She feels every part of her go rigid as he approaches. Her breath lodges in her chest. She curses her decision not to bring the trolley up with her. She could have crouched behind it, pretended to be looking for something, rammed him with it if he came for her. But it's just him and her in this corridor and there is no escape. She closes her eyes as he comes close, closer, turns her face towards a door, waiting for his meaty grip on her arm, his threatening growl. *What the fuck do you think you're doing here?*

Her breath stops briefly in her chest. And then . . . nothing. The sound of his footfall continues past her. A brief curse into his phone, and then a burst of laughter. She waits a second, opens her eyes, turns her head slowly. He continues down the corridor, gesturing with his free hand as he speaks.

He hasn't even seen her. She's the only person in the whole corridor and he hasn't seen her. And then it hits her: in this uniform she is invisible.

Nisha Cantor, a woman used to turning heads for twenty-five years, has donned a cheap black top and nylon trousers and, in her service apron, completely disappeared.

14

Her brain is still humming with the encounter, her heart racing when she gets back to the locker room. And then something equally unexpected happens: Jasmine announces she has stomach-ache and asks if Nisha could give her a break and finish Room 420 while she has a lie-down. 'I wouldn't ask, babe, but it's killing me. I just need to stretch out.' Nisha tells her it's no problem, she'll do 422 too, and she cannot hear Jasmine's grateful response over the sound of something sparking inside her head. Jasmine removes her apron, groaning and sighing as she moves, hangs it on her peg, and heads off to lie down on the daybed the reception staff use in the quiet room next to the laundry.

Nisha waits until she is sure she has gone, then rifles through Jasmine's pocket until she finds the all-access room key. She shoves it quickly into the front of her apron, and leaves.

Nisha cleans Room 420 at double speed, her mind racing as she strips and remakes the bed, empties the bins and runs the disinfectant-soaked cloth over the remote control. She does 422, thanking God for single women who barely touch the room during their stay. With fifteen minutes to spare she pushes the trolley into the elevator, hesitates just a moment, touches the card to the security pad, then presses the button to the seventh floor, her stomach tightening as she ascends the floors.

'Housekeeping!' She hesitates as the doors open, half braced for a harsh voice, a sound that will send her scurrying back inside. But the suite carries the heavy silence of non-occupation. She stands for a moment, taking in the rooms that had been hers, the belongings scattered around that suddenly feel strangely alien: Carl's files, his slippers, neatly placed on a cotton square by the door, the fruit bowl with only grapes and peaches, his favourites. She heads for the desk, to get her passport, but it's not in the drawer. She opens the cupboard which holds the safe, and punches in his birth-date, but the machine bleeps obstinately and will not let her in. She tries two other variations, her own birth-date, and then Ray's but neither opens the door. She curses, and straightens up. And then she heads through to the bedroom.

The bed has already been made and she feels a brief surge of gratitude that she has not had to see further evidence of his betrayal in tangled sheets, leftover bottles of Ruinart, perhaps a scattering of sex toys. She looks away, heads past it to the dressing room and opens the double doors. And there they are: her clothes, all neatly lined up on perfectly aligned hangers, exactly as they were when she left. She stands staring for a moment, then lets out a low moan of longing and presses her face to a Chloé shearling jacket, like a mother reunited with her children, breathing in their scent. Her scent! She has felt naked without it. She turns, scans the dressing-table and sees the familiar bottle, places it swiftly in her pocket. And it is then that she sees it: a woman's makeup. Not hers. She stares at the oversized half-unzipped bag, at the large compact of eye-shadows, the foundation too pale for Nisha's skin. The curling tongs resting by her brushes. She feels something in her turn to stone, and then a thought occurs – she turns back to the wardrobe. And there it is: a dress that is not hers, nestling among her suits and dresses. She pulls it out: Stella McCartney; black, overtly sexy, flashy, her black stole slung over the back of it. She feels a ball of rage. He is letting this woman use her clothes? Place these flashy interloper garments among her own? She sees a trouser suit, a pair of Jimmy Choo heels in a size 41. Nisha has not until this point been entirely sure what she would do when she was in the penthouse again, but now, with a barely suppressed roar of rage, she begins to pull her clothes from the rail: her Chanel suits, her brightly-coloured Roland Mouret dresses, her Valentino skirt. She takes an armful of her favourite things, ripping them from their hangers, knowing there is no way she can stomach Charlotte (it must be Charlotte! That bitch has clown-sized feet) wearing *her things*. She can help herself to Carl all day long, if she must, but there is no way she is sliding that treacherous body into Nisha's *clothes*. Nisha slings them over the trolley in a heap, then runs back and adds her full-length shearling coat and the Yves Saint Laurent black velvet suit with the high padded shoulders. And then, her face still contorted with rage, she pushes the trolley back across the penthouse suite, into the elevator and presses the down button, for once forgetting to cover her finger with her sleeve as she hits it.

She is halfway along the laundry corridor with her haul when Jasmine appears in front of her. She stands, does a double-take at the pile of clothes, as if she can't believe what she's seeing, and then folds her arms. 'What the – ?'

'Get out of my way.'

'Nisha?'

'She was wearing *my clothes*.' Nisha is wild now, as if some stopper has been released, letting out all the anger and frustration of the last week. 'She is not having *my damn clothes*.'

'What are you talking about? Where did you get these?'

Nisha makes to push past her, but Jasmine blocks her way. 'The penthouse,' Nisha hisses.

'You've been in the penthouse!' She blinks, then adds, 'You stole *clothes* from the penthouse?'

'It's not stealing if they're mine.'

'What are you saying, girl? Have you gone crazy?'

Nisha drops the trolley handle. She walks up to Jasmine. 'I'm Nisha Cantor. Married to Carl Cantor. He has locked me out of the penthouse since last week and blocked all my money. I'm just taking back what is mine.'

Jasmine stares at her, as if trying to register what she has just said. '*You* are married to the guy in the penthouse?'

'Yes. For more than eighteen damn years. Until last week when he pulled a number on me.'

Jasmine is shaking her head, tiny shakes, her palms raised, as if she cannot digest this. 'You went in there to get your clothes? But how did you –'

'I've had nothing. *Nothing*. I've had to wear clothes that *aren't even mine*!' Nisha scrabbles in her pocket for the all-access pass and hands it back to her. 'Here. Take this. I've got what I came for.'

'You can't do this.'

'It's not stealing. They're my clothes.'

'Nisha. This is a bad idea. You have to stop.'

'I'm sorry, Jas. It's been lovely meeting you. You are a good, good person. I like you. And I don't like anyone. But I'm taking my things.'

Jasmine stares at the little card. 'No no no no no. You just went in on my pass. It's all registered to me. If you steal all those clothes they're going to pin it on me.'

'I'll tell them it isn't you. I'll call them. Whatever.'

'Nisha. I'm a Black single mother from Peckham. You just used my all-access housekeeping card to get into a room where – what? – ten thousand pounds' worth of clothes have just been removed.'

'More like thirty thousand actually,' says Nisha, affronted.

'We have to get these back in the room. We can sort it, babe. But not like this.'

'No!' Nisha protests, but Jasmine grips her arm.

'Don't do this to me. You know we'll all be in trouble if you do this. I need this job, Nish. I need it. And I've worked bloody hard to get to where I am. Twice as hard as most people have to work. You have no idea, okay? You have no idea. Don't you ruin this for me.'

There is a steely tone to Jasmine's voice, but genuine anxiety too. Nisha feels a flicker of uncertainty. She thinks about Jasmine handing her twenty pounds when she had barely known her.

She lets out a low moan. 'Please, Jas. You have no idea what it's been like. He's taken everything. I need my things. I *need* them.'

'If this is how you say it is, we will fix it,' says Jasmine, quietly. 'But not like this.'

The two women lock eyes. And suddenly it's over. Nisha knows she cannot do this to the one person who has treated her decently.

'Arrrrgh. *Dammit!*' she yells.

'I know, darling. I know. C'mon,' says Jasmine, suddenly brisk. 'Come with me. We have to get these back before they realize they're gone. Jesus Christ, my stomach. What are you doing to me?'

They say nothing to each other in the elevator but Jasmine keeps stealing glances at her, as if she is totally reassessing everything she has believed. They reach the seventh floor and exchange a look. But as the elevator stops, they hear voices. Loud, male voices. Somebody is back in the room. Without missing a beat, Jasmine slams the down button with her palm.

The elevator hesitates as the doors begin to open, as if not sure about this change in instruction. And then they close again and it lurches suddenly downwards.

They exit on the sixth floor. Nisha's head is spinning. 'What do we do now?'

Jas holds up a finger as if she has already worked it out. She presses a button on her walkie-talkie. 'Viktor? Do me a favour, babe? I need . . . fifteen, twenty hangers. With plastic. Yes. Yes. Fast as you can. Thanks, babe. I'm outside six twenty-two. I owe you.'

Less than two minutes later Viktor, a tall Lithuanian with sad eyes, arrives at a half-run bearing the hangers.

'Put the clothes in these. Quickly. Give us a hand, Vik, will you?'

Nisha does as she's told, threading each outfit up through the plastic. The three of them work in silence, Nisha's fingers turning to thumbs as she tries to straighten collars on hangers, to push the wire frames through the tiny clear plastic holes. When they are done, a huge pile of clothes is lying over the trolley. Jas wheels it back into the elevator and motions to Nisha. 'Put your mask on. And keep your head down.'

The doors open at the seventh floor. Jasmine motions at Nisha to stay in the elevator.

'Housekeeping!' she calls.

A man – is it Steve? – she can't tell with her head down – appears at the doors.

'What's this?'

'I have your dry cleaning, sir.' Jasmine sweeps an armful of the plastic-covered clothes off the trolley.

'Dry cleaning,' Steve yells behind him.

She hears Carl's voice from the study area.

'What dry cleaning? I didn't order any.'

Nisha's heart stops.

But Jasmine steps out. 'Your wife scheduled for her clothes to be collected for dry cleaning, sir? We're just returning them. *Stay here,*' she murmurs to Nisha.

'My wife? I told Frederik she wasn't to charge anything on my room.'

'This was arranged some time ago, I believe, sir. I'm just bringing the clothes now.'

Carl's voice is angry. 'I told him she was to charge nothing. Nothing. He should have cancelled any scheduled orders.'

Jasmine has disappeared. Nisha can hear the swish of hangers being returned to a rail. Their voices are muffled.

'I'm so sorry, sir,' Jasmine says calmly. 'There must have been an error in communication with the laundry. I'll make sure all these are comped to your room.'

She steps into the elevator, sweeps up the second armful of clothes and exits again.

'Did you say all of them?'

'Clearly an error on the hotel's part, sir. I will ensure that these items have all been cleaned free of charge.'

Nisha hears a shift in tone. Carl loves getting stuff for free. It's like he feels it's his due, like the universe has suddenly seen him for what he deserves. He is worth millions and yet if someone comps him something he's like a child given a free lollipop in a sweet shop.

'Okay. Put a note on my file so that anything else she fixed up before she left is cancelled. Okay? I don't want anything else like this happening.'

'Of course. Consider it done. Thank you for your understanding, sir. Again, I'm so sorry.'

Jasmine walks into the elevator and Nisha turns away in case Carl materializes. But Jasmine has hit the button and the lift is already juddering downwards.

*

Afterwards Jasmine does not say a word. They complete their room allocation in mutual silence. Nisha feels numb with shock. All these days spent working out what would happen when she got back into the room, and what was the result? They had handed every single item back. Back into the hands of that witch. And she had been so blindsided by rage at the sight of the clothes that she had completely forgotten to get anything more useful – her jewellery, money from the desk.

She is owed a rest break, but she does not want to go into the locker room. She does not want to have to endure the questions from Jasmine and anybody else, or to have to think about what has just happened. She walks instead along the corridor to the kitchens. They are near-empty mid-afternoon, the chefs and sous-chefs grabbing a precious breather between the lunch and evening shifts, some napping, some sneaking cigarettes outside. She has eaten nothing all day, and goes to check on the table where the sandwiches are usually left. It is empty, just a platter with a few crumbs.

Crumbs. That is what remains of her life. She picks up the stainless-steel platter, stares at it, and then almost before she knows what she is doing, hurls it to the floor so that it clatters with a smash on the hard surface. She reaches round and picks up a pile of newly laundered aprons and throws them onto the floor too. Then the plastic mixing bowls. They bounce off the stainless-steel surfaces.

'Fucking fucking fuck! What the fucking fuck has happened to my life?' She closes her eyes, clenches her fists and roars. Her scream is primal, erupts from the core of her. She curls over her stomach and sinks to her knees, clutching herself as if she is in pain.

When she finally opens her eyes, still panting from the effort, she becomes aware that someone is watching her. She turns and sees a tall man standing by the stoves. Aleks.

He's leaning against one, his arms folded in front of him, his checkered chef's trousers flecked with small stains from the morning shift.

'What?' she says defiantly. 'What?'

She looks down at the mess she has created. She climbs to her feet and, after a moment, starts picking up the aprons, folding them and placing them back on the side, whacking them down with displeasure. Still grimacing with fury, she picks up the mixing bowls, stacking them as she goes, and the steel tray. Her hair has come loose from its tie and she pulls it back off her face, wrenching it into a knot.

When she glances behind her, he is still watching. 'What?' she says, pulling a face. 'You never seen someone get mad? I'm picking up your damn things. Okay? I'm doing it.'

His expression does not change. He waits a moment, then says calmly, in heavily accented English: 'You are very beautiful woman.' He adds: 'Very angry. But very beautiful.'

Nisha's mouth opens. He turns away from her to the stove and reaches up for a small pan. He swipes some oil around its innards, then breaks two eggs expertly into it. He goes to the enormous refrigerator in the corner and returns with an armful of ingredients.

She stands, unsure what she is watching. He turns his head, nods towards the chair in the corner. 'Sit,' he says.

She walks over, a little tentatively, and sits, still holding the steel tray to her chest. Aleks doesn't speak again. He mixes something in a bowl, whisking with the speed and efficacy of someone for whom this is a daily task, the muscles clearly demarcated on his tattooed forearm. He chops herbs briskly with a sharp blade and tosses them in, then reaches over to the toaster and pulls out two perfectly done slices of toast, which he slathers in butter. He takes a plate from the low oven, his back to her, and rearranges something on it. Then he walks over, and hands her the plate. On it is eggs Benedict, crowned with glossy yellow Hollandaise sauce, on two pieces of lightly browned brioche.

'Eat,' he says, handing it to her, then turning to get her a napkin. He doesn't wait for thanks, but walks quietly back to his work station, wiping it down with brisk strokes and clearing the pans, which he takes to the wash-up area. He is there, unseen for a few minutes, clattering pans and running water. He reappears as she is halfway through the second piece.

The eggs Benedict is the best she has ever eaten. She is weak with pleasure. She can't even speak. She just looks up at him, still chewing, and he gives a small nod, as if in acknowledgement. 'It is hard to be so angry if you have eaten good food,' he says.

And then he waits until she has finished and wordlessly takes the plate from her. He has turned and disappeared before she can speak again.

15

Sam enters to find her mother and father on their hands and knees, surrounded by newspaper. Her father is putting his full weight on some kind of compression device, trying to squeeze water out of a rectangle of papier-mâché gloop. Their living room has always been cluttered with books and piles of papers, every surface covered with items they insist cannot be moved as they know where everything is. But now her mother is feeding newspapers through a shredder in the corner, while her father sends jets of water running over the top of the old baby bath with every grunt and push. The whirring sound of the shredder means that they don't hear her initially, and Sam picks her way over the piles of newspaper and stoops to wave in her father's face. He is puce, and there are small pieces of paper in his hair. *Hello, darling!* he mouths.

Merryn stops the shredder mid-flow. 'We're making paper logs!' she announces, too loudly given there is no longer any sound in the room, bar the effortful noises of Sam's father. 'Your father saw a thing on YouTube. Saving the planet!'

'You've put the *National Geographic*s in the wrong pile,' exclaims her father, breaking off to point.

'No, I haven't, Tom. Those are over there because they contain the wrong chemicals. We'll die in our beds if we use them, because of the gloss. And the chimney-sweep says it tars up the flue. Newspaper only. Tom, there's too much moisture in that briquette. It will take years to dry out.'

'I *know*.'

'Well, push harder.'

'You push, if you're so good at it.'

'I'll make the tea,' says Sam, and picks her way across the living room to the kitchen.

For years she had been comforted by the ordered chaos of her parents' kitchen, with its pinboards of Greenpeace stickers, its curling photographs of their younger days. Jars and spices jostled for space on the worktops where they had been pulled out and simply left. These days she notes the slackening standards of hygiene, spongy apples and day-old yoghurts on the side. Each one is like a tolling bell, warning her of further responsibilities in days to come. They won't contemplate a cleaner: it goes against their socialist beliefs. But they have no problem with Sam taking time out twice a week to come and clean up after them. She pulls on her mother's rubber gloves and starts piling dirty crockery in the sink, listening vaguely to her parents bicker about briquettes.

I've pushed this one umpteen times. I don't know where all the water is coming from.

'You didn't fill the kettle all the way up, did you? It's not ecological.' Her mother walks in, wiping her hands on her jeans. She is wearing a raspberry-coloured jumper with a grey one over the top. Both have holes in the elbows through which Sam can see two small discs of pale skin.

'No, Mum. I measured out three mugs.'

'We've only managed two briquettes since lunchtime. How we'll keep warm on this I have no idea. Honestly. The shed is so full of old newspaper I keep telling your father it's a fire hazard.'

The irony is clearly lost on her. Sam washes up while her mother makes the tea and lifts the lids of various tins, letting out little ohs of disappointment when the expected cakes or biscuits fail to manifest themselves. From the other room they can hear occasional grunts or curses from Sam's father as he attempts to compress the papier-mâché bricks.

'How's Phil?'

Never *How are you?* Sam thinks resentfully, and smothers the thought. It's good that her parents care about Phil. Lots of people dislike their sons-in-law. She should be grateful.

'Um . . . much the same. Bit tired.'

'Has he got another job yet?'

'No, Mum. I'd tell you.'

'I called the other night. Did Cat say?'

'No. I've barely seen her.'

'Always working, that girl. She'll go far. Anyway, I wanted to tell you about a television show we were watching. I can't remember what it was now. What was it called . . . ? It was on the television. Oh, yes, she said you'd gone out *drinking.*'

Sam takes a long, careful sip of her tea. 'I had a drink with my work colleagues to celebrate bringing in some deals. It was nothing.'

'Well, I'm not sure it's a good idea leaving Phil on his own if he's down in the dumps. I never leave your dad to go drinking at the pub. I'm not sure he'd like that very much.'

You never went to work, Sam wants to say. You never had to earn money just so that your family could keep a roof over its head. You never had to deal with a boss whose every laboured sigh tells you he thinks you're a waste of space. You never lie next to the back of a sleeping man wondering if you've actually become invisible.

'Well,' she says carefully, 'it doesn't happen very often.'

Her mother sits down at the table and sighs. 'It's very hard for a man, you know, losing his job. He doesn't feel like a man any more.'

'That's not very egalitarian of you, Mother. I thought you believed both sexes should be treated equally.'

'Well, it's just common sense. They get – what's the word? – *emasculated*. If you're earning all the money and then going out to the pub in the evening, how's poor old Phil meant to feel?'

'Are you telling me you never go out without Dad?'

'Only to my book group. And that's only because Lina Gupta always wants to talk about her haemorrhoids and that kind of talk makes him go a bit funny. Honestly, how she can shoehorn a reference to Anusol into a discussion about *Anna Karenina* I don't know.'

Sam and her mother chat for a while – or Merryn chats and Sam adopts her well-worn role as tame audience for her mother's concerns about the planet, annoyance at the politicians who are variously self-serving, idiotic or just plain irritating, her neighbours' woes (who is dying, suffering some terrible ailment, or already dead). Sam had observed some years previously that her mother was uninterested in the minutiae of Sam's own life beyond how it might affect her or Phil, whom she considers the finest of sons-in-law ('You're *very* lucky to have him'). Also, while they profess endless public love for each other, her mother and father use every available opportunity to offload on her separately about the maddening qualities, difficulties and frailties of the other. ('He *cannot* read a road map any more. He says he can, but then he goes completely the wrong way'; 'She leaves her glasses everywhere. And then she accuses me of taking them! She's so blind she can't see where she's put them.')

'So what are you going to do about Phil?' her mother says, as Sam puts her coat on to leave. She has cleaned the kitchen and the upstairs bathroom, faintly saddened by the sheer number of unpronounceable pills and other medication her parents now seem to require just to function.

'What do you mean?'

'Well . . . I think maybe you need to give Phil a bit of a boost. Make him feel good about himself.'

'Why should *he* get to feel good about himself? I don't.'

'Don't be facetious, Samantha. He needs your support, even if it is irritating.'

'I'm doing everything I can.' She cannot keep the weariness from her voice.

'Well, sometimes you have to do more. When your father had that problem with his you know what –'

'Mum, I told you, I really don't want to know about Dad's penis troubles.'

'Well, we got him some of those blue pills. And apart from that unfortunate incident in Sainsbury's, after he took too many, they worked a treat. He felt like himself again and that means we're both happy.' She pauses, thinking. 'That said, we do have to use the Tesco over by the bypass now. And the parking spaces are much too narrow for a family car.'

Her mother places a hand on her arm. 'Look, all I'm saying is that it may well be that you're having to do more than your share of the heavy lifting just now, but if you can boost Phil up a bit it'll make you both feel better in the end.'

Her mother's blue eyes are piercing. She gives Sam a re-assuring smile. 'Just have a think about it . . .' Then her gaze swivels. 'Tom, what *are* you doing with that wretched device? I can hear the water sloshing onto the living-room floor from here. Honestly, do I have to do *everything* myself?'

Sam thinks about her mother's words during the short walk home. She and Phil have been, in the language of women's magazines, *disconnected* for months. Without any outings together, there is little for them to discuss beyond the dog (no, he has not walked him), their daughter (no, he's not sure where she is) or her work (he doesn't want to talk about that).

Maybe this is one of those times when she really does have to try a little harder. Maybe if she focused less on how tired she is, and how furious at the deficit of support coming her way, they could see a way through.

She stops for a moment on the pavement and registers this. It's quite a startling thought for Sam, to be taking seriously advice given by her mother. And then she thinks about her father and the blue pills and has to sing loudly to herself all the way to the post office to get the image out of her head.

Phil is on the sofa, watching some programme in which couples bicker about low ceilings and storage space. Sam stops as she hangs her coat on the peg and gazes at the top of his head, where his hair is thinning slightly. She had persuaded him to get a haircut two weeks previously, as he had begun to veer tragically towards Mad Professor, and now at least he looks like somebody she recognizes. She has a sudden memory of the two of them, legs entwined on that sofa, Phil reaching over to kiss the top of her head, and she thinks, *Maybe I could make you feel better.*

She cooks chicken pie, mash and greens, one of Phil's favourites, and sets the table in the kitchen so that he cannot just slide his plate from the work surface and eat it in front of the television. She opens a bottle of wine, and pours them both a glass. He doesn't speak much but he doesn't complain about the seating arrangements and even makes a bit of an effort, telling her about their neighbours' new car. He clams up when, two glasses in, she tries to ask him how he's feeling – she sees his face close over as if someone has drawn a curtain – so she chats on gamely, filling the silence with tales of her parents and the briquette-maker and he does his best to look interested. The kitchen clock ticks loudly.

'Nice wine,' he says.

'It is, isn't it? It was on special offer.'

'Yes. It's . . . nice.'

At one point Cat texts her to ask if either of them have seen her driving licence and there is a brief interlude when they become almost animated discussing the missing licence, how easy it is to lose the little plastic ones, how often Cat loses things she shouldn't. And then it fades and the sound of the kitchen clock takes over and Phil settles back on the sofa to watch the ten o'clock news. She reminds herself that in Phil terms, these days, dinner has been something of a success.

She washes up, hoping that whatever he watches does not depress him again. She eyes the bottle of wine, two inches remaining, and then, abruptly, picks it up and glugs briskly, letting the dark acid warm her throat, wiping her mouth with the back of her hand.

When the kitchen is done she heads upstairs, showers and, after a moment, adds a little spray of scent. She gazes at her reflection in the steamed mirror of the bathroom. She's not too bad for her age. She has a nice neck. Good tits. Nothing too saggy yet. Not hard and lean like those yummy mummies, but not a bad body, given everything. *Think about how you felt in those shoes*, she tells herself firmly. *Think about how you felt in the later meetings, how you felt on the dance-floor: powerful, magnetic, unstoppable.*

She climbs into bed and waits for the sound of his feet on the stairs, thinking of how he used to chase her up those stairs when they first moved in, his hands grabbing at her bottom in his eagerness to get to her.

She watches through the bedroom door as he heads into the bathroom, listens to the sounds of him washing, brushing his teeth, a quick gargle with mouthwash, sounds that are as familiar to her as the boiler clicking on in the morning or the squeak of the gate outside.

And then he is climbing in beside her, the bedsprings creaking slightly under his weight. For some time now they have slept with their backs to each other: Phil snores, so he has learned to sleep on his side.

It is eleven months since they last had sex.

She had calculated it one evening, working back from the last time he had been to the pub. At work, the coffee room is full of women complaining that their husbands are all over them, joking about how they would prefer to read a book. Sam is very tired of reading books. Sex used to be the lubrication of their marriage, the thing that stopped the small irritations mattering – the pants on the floor, the failure to empty the dishwasher, the parking ticket. Sex used to bring them closer. Sex was the thing that made them feel like themselves again, not some desiccated shadow of what once was.

She lies there for a minute, thinking, then turns over silently and slides her arm around him. His skin is warm, and he smells vaguely and pleasingly of soap. When he doesn't move she edges herself closer, so that every bit of her is pressed against him. She kisses the nape of his neck and rests her cheek on him. She has missed him, missed his touch. She wonders why she hadn't done this months ago. He shifts a little and she feels a tiny thrill of desire. Her leg creeps forward and slides between his. She strokes his stomach, feeling the soft hair on his lower belly, and then the thicker hair as she slides her hand lower. *This is going to happen. She is going to make this happen. This will be a new start for them.* She kisses him again, letting her lips trail softly down his spine, pulling at him slightly to make him twist to face her. *I am unstoppable. I am a female force. I am sexy.* She will slide herself on top of him and –

His voice breaks into the darkness. 'Sorry, love. Not really feeling up to it tonight.'

It is as if she has been stung. His words hang there in the dark. Sam grows very still, then lightly removes her hand from her husband's groin. She wiggles her way backwards under the duvet and turns away so that she is lying on her back. She wishes she had put on her nightie. They lie in silence for a minute.

And then he speaks again. 'The chicken pie was very nice, though.'

If Phil acts as if she no longer exists, the other man in her life, Simon, is, as the younger members of staff put it, all up in her grill.

Some of her colleagues have begun noticeably steering clear of her at work, as if whatever bad juju she is carrying could become infectious. Nobody wants to acknowledge what is happening as, you know, a job is a job and they are hard enough to come by just now.

Except for Joel.

She has begun sitting in her car at lunchtimes, as the coffee room makes her feel exposed, and she can no longer eat in her cubicle because Simon will inevitably walk in at the exact moment her mouth is full. So she sits and listens to one of her Calming Classical music downloads and eats her sandwich alone, trying to avoid her thoughts.

'What are you doing out here?'

She jumps as the door opens and Joel climbs in, bringing with him the chill air of outside and a warm scent of citrus. He closes the door and she sees he has his petrol-station cheese sandwiches in his hand. He is wearing his puffy coat and his tiny neat dreadlocks are tied back in a low ponytail.

'At least run the engine and get some heat in here, Sam. Jesus, it's freezing!'

'I just —'

'I couldn't work out where you'd been the last few lunch breaks. Simon sent that idiot Franklin out with us to pitch for the Cameron job. God knows how he brought that in. And I came to see if you wanted to grab a coffee, but they said you weren't in there. And then I saw your car windows had steamed up so –'

Franklin. Young, swaggering Franklin with his shiny suit and his perma-grin. So that was it. She lets out a slow breath. 'I . . . prefer it out here just at the moment.'

His smile fades. He studies her face. 'Want to talk about it?'

'Not really.' If she says a word about it right now she will cry. And not even normal tears: she feels as if she is permanently on the verge of huge, terrifying sobs that will engulf her and leave her red-nosed, snotty and heaving. And Joel witnessing that will be almost the worst part.

'Ah, babe . . .' He shakes his head in disgust. 'Ted said Simon gave you a hard time in yesterday's budget meeting.'

She is so conscious of the proximity of Joel in her little car. Of the smooth skin on the back of his hands, so close to her thigh, of the male scent of him. His wet eyelashes curl up in tiny starry points. She has never seen an adult with eyelashes like that. She feels as if she could touch each one and she would feel its spiky imprint on her fingertip. They have known each other for eight years and she is not sure she has ever noticed his eyelashes before.

She thinks suddenly about Phil rejecting her the previous evening, the way she had viewed her sleepless reflection in the mirror that morning: old, baggy, unwanted. It is too hard to have Joel being nice to her. Because, of course, he is not sweet on her. That was just her getting overexcited in those stupid shoes. He probably sees her as some geriatric auntie figure. *Let's make sure poor old Sam is okay.*

She is suddenly overwhelmed by the certainty that he needs

to leave her car immediately. 'Actually,' she says, 'I'm fine. By myself, I mean.'

She cannot look at him as she says this, doesn't want to see the sympathetic look, the head tilt. She keeps staring at her knees, a peculiar smile on her face. 'Really. I'm just going to listen to some music and chill out for a bit.'

He says, after a moment: 'I could just eat my sandwiches and keep you company.'

'No,' she says, glancing over. 'They're cheese. I don't like cheese.'

They sit in the heavy silence. *I don't like cheese?* she thinks. *Since when?*

'Okay,' he says, after a short pause. 'I was just . . . checking in. Just . . . wanted to make sure you were okay.'

'I'm fine. It's all good. You don't need to check on me. I'm a grown woman!' She looks up then, an awful wonky smile on her face, and she sees something in his expression that makes her stomach turn itself inwards into a tight knot. 'Really. It's very kind of you. But you should go. You should go.' Her voice is harder than she had intended.

He waits a moment longer, and then, without a word, he picks up his unopened sandwiches and climbs out of the car.

16

Jasmine is off. Nisha checks the rota and sees the other woman is owed several days, perhaps because she is working through the weekend. Much as she misses cheerful conversation, she is glad Jasmine isn't there. Anger – and guilt at what she almost cost her – have permeated her so completely she thinks she might combust.

She completes her shifts in a silent fury, powering her way through the filthy bathrooms, scowling at anyone who asks her for an extra roll of toilet paper or hair conditioner. She knows there may be complaints from guests about her attitude, so she pretends she cannot speak English, adopts a half-smile that is faintly threatening and carries in her demeanour at least the vague suggestion that she might return to murder annoying guests in their beds.

Nisha has tried six top divorce lawyers back in New York, only three of whom would take her call, and two who said they had already been retained by Carl. She calls her bank, and Jeff, its relationship manager, promises he will get back to her but doesn't. Four times. *Carl.* She tries to take out a credit card so she can at least live, but the application fails because she does not have a permanent address in the UK, and the US credit-card company will only send it to her home address in New York. Which will clearly not be forwarding her post. *Carl.*

She calls Ray every day and talks to him of trivial things: of what he had for lunch, his conviction that one of his room-mates is secretly a Mormon, his despair at not being able to stop biting his nails, and she knows she has no vocabulary with which to explain to him what has happened to their family. Her boy. Her gorgeous, fragile boy, who makes her heart ache and bleed at a distance of five thousand miles. She will have to tell him soon, but she is afraid of inflicting this wound on him when she cannot be there to comfort him. It is too soon after the Thing.

She hates Carl for this perhaps most of all.

When she hides out in the kitchen for her mid-afternoon breaks, Aleks is there, sometimes prepping for evening service, sometimes sitting in the corner reading a tattered paperback, usually something about food. He doesn't speak to her, but when he sees her he puts his book down, moves to his station and cooks wild mushroom omelettes with *fines herbes*, toasted sandwiches with chicken and truffle mayonnaise. He places these in front of her and leaves her to eat, his manner unobtrusive as if he understands that this is a woman in the middle of a raging inferno, and he merely wishes to leave her a small fire hose. He has hair that always looks as if he has just woken up, and tired eyes, and there does not appear to be an ounce of fat on his body. It's not that she has noticed this particularly, but she has always unconsciously registered people's apparent fitness or body-fat ratios and he looks . . . fit. Tired, like all the chefs (the long hours and inferno-like conditions of the kitchen mean they seem to age at twice the rate of anyone else), but fit.

'I'm not going to sleep with you, you know,' she says, when he hands her a particularly beautifully cooked steak sandwich.

He regards her steadily, and gives a small smile, as if she has said something amusing. 'Okay,' he says, as if the thought hadn't even occurred to him, and she is both embarrassed and furious at his response.

She lies awake in the horrible hotel room, these thoughts whirling around her head in a toxic black cloud, and when she wakes she is so exhausted it is only bleak fury that propels her back to the Bentley Hotel again. Twice in the small hours between 2 a.m. and 4 a.m., when it is just her and the sirens and the sound of the couple fighting in the next room, she has picked up her phone and typed in one of the few numbers she knows by heart: Juliana. And then she stops, gazes at the words, deletes the message and puts down her phone.

She adds up her wages and the money from Ray, and she knows her days at the hotel are numbered. And then it happens: the Tower Primavera tells her she cannot stay another night. She is walking to the breakfast room at six thirty when the receptionist passes her in the hallway. 'Oh, Mrs Cantor. We're fully booked for a conference for the next two weeks. I'm afraid we'll need you to check out tomorrow morning.'

'But where am I supposed to go?' she says, and the receptionist looks at her blankly, as if she has never been asked this question.

As Nisha walks to work, she wonders if she will actually end up on the streets, like the formless, grey-faced men in cardboard boxes she walks past every morning. And not one person returns her calls. Not one of the women she has sat beside at society events for the last eighteen years. Not one of the so-called friends. Carl – or Charlotte – will have told them all and she will now be untouchable. She feels the humiliation of their conversations about her from across the Atlantic.

– *Well, normally I'd say how awful, but she was such a dreadfully cold person I'm really finding it hard to care.*

– *Oh, Melissa! You are a hoot!*

She strides along the river, trying to work out a plan, and she hates this city. She hates the stationary cars with their foggy passengers behind the windscreen wipers. She hates the blank stares of the fellow commuters as she curses at errant bicycles, hates the four-wheel drives with their tight-lipped mothers who ignore their children, hates the catcalling builders and the sly, assessing groups of the younger men who congregate outside bars. She hates that she is no longer insulated from any of it, just a tiny invisible atom freefalling in a universe of drudgery and chaos. She walks, her collar up against the damp, a decent wool scarf she has not yet managed to take to the hotel's lost property room wrapped high around her neck, and although she is not a woman prone to introspection, if she had been, Nisha Cantor would have observed that she had never been unhappier in her life.

'We need to talk.'

Jasmine appears as she finishes her shift. She is in her off-duty uniform of ruby satin padded coat and jogging bottoms, with a chain-link bag crossing her body and her nails have been freshly painted a glittering iridescent blue. 'I swear I've thought of almost nothing but what happened here on Tuesday.'

Nisha rips her jacket out of the locker and slams the door. 'You forcing me to hand back *my own things*, you mean?'

But Jasmine pulls a face. 'Don't give me that. I'm not the enemy.'

Nisha shoots her a questioning look. But Jasmine is already heading down the corridor.

'Hurry up and put your jacket on,' she says. 'You're coming to mine.'

They catch the first of two buses, and as it growls and heaves its way through the traffic, Jasmine asks her about her life and what has happened to it.

You were actually living in the penthouse until recently? The actual penthouse?

Hang on, even though you had a house here? You had a house? More than one house? How many bloody houses did you have?

148

You really just moved around the globe month to month? Well, where was your home? What do you mean all of them?

How come all those clothes were yours? Did he just give you money to spend every week? How much? HOW MUCH? Did you never have a job? That's not a job ... Tccchh.

Literally not one of your friends has been in touch? Not even to help? What kind of women are they? (That one stung.)

What does your son think about it all? (That one stung even more.)

Well, when are you going to tell him? Babe, you can't keep this quiet. Who are you protecting? Your cheating snake-ass husband?

And who the hell is this little witch who's fucking him anyway? Do you know this woman? Huh. Of course. OF COURSE. What are you going to do about it?

Jasmine asks her questions openly and without embarrassment. She does not hold back on her opinions. Nisha is so taken aback by this way of communicating – so different from the coded conversations she had grown accustomed to among Carl's friends' wives, the meaningless smiles and the sliding glances – that the anger she has been carrying begins to dissipate and she finds herself answering honestly, without considering what unwitting nuggets might be harvested from each answer, or later used against her, as she would normally when speaking to another woman.

They have walked ten minutes from the bus stop, still deep in conversation, neither of them apparently conscious of the rain that has started to fall. The housing project they are now walking through – Jasmine calls it an estate – is a huge, sprawling thing traversed by empty walkways and punctuated by the glow of orange streetlights and Nisha stays close, unsure if she lost Jasmine whether she would be able to find her way back out.

'This is unreal,' Jasmine is saying, reaching into her handbag. 'I mean, I've heard some shit but this is next level.'

149

She is opening the door of her apartment by the time Nisha realizes the woman has just taken a two-bus journey across London simply to find her.

The apartment is the smallest Nisha can remember ever being in, every wall and surface stacked with neat plastic boxes stuffed full of clothes, or hanging devices bearing drying washing. There are clothes everywhere, hanging from the backs of doors or folded into neat piles on chairs or chests of drawers.

'Grace?' Jasmine motions Nisha into the little kitchen and walks straight back out again. 'Did you do your homework?'

A voice emerges from another room, over the sound of the television. 'Done it.'

'Done it or actually put some thought and effort into it?'

'Who's with you?'

'Nisha.'

Nisha perches on one of the stools beside the fold-out table and takes off her jacket. The apartment is stuffy with the smells of home cooking and a sweet, musky perfume. On the hob something meaty is stewing gently, obscuring the window pane with a fine, flavoured mist. It makes her realize how accustomed she has become to the nothingy, chemically cleaned smell of the hotel room. Then she remembers that she can no longer stay there after tonight. She has a plan involving the bed beside the laundry rooms at the Bentley but she is not sure how long she will get away with that.

'Well, don't be rude, Grace! Show your face!'

A girl of thirteen or fourteen pops her head around the door. She gazes at Nisha, who gives a hesitant wave.

'Oh! You're quite pretty.'

She hears Jasmine's burst of laughter before she walks back in. 'She's training for the Diplomatic Corps.'

'I meant it nicely! That Greek woman you brought in looked like she'd been run over.'

'Did I bring you up to be this rude to guests in my house?'

'Sorry.' Grace is clearly not sorry at all. 'Do you work with my mum?'

'I do.'

'Are you the one who didn't know how to clean a toilet?'

Nisha thinks for a minute. 'Probably.'

'Did you put on the rice like I asked?' says Jasmine, lifting the lid on one of the pots.

'It's in the bottom oven with the lid on.'

'Thank God. I'm so hungry. Grace, clear your things off the table, please.'

Jasmine busies herself around her, pulling plates from cupboards and bustling past her to the living room where she lays the small table beside the television. Grace fetches cutlery, casting shy glances at Nisha as she sits in the middle of it all, unsure what to do.

'You're American, right?' Grace edges past her. 'Have you been to Disneyland?'

'I took my son when he was your age but he didn't like it much.'

'Why?'

'He doesn't like rides. He prefers movies and computer games.'

'Boys always like computer games. My mum won't let me have them.'

'She's smart. His shrink says they are basically crack cocaine.'

'What's a shrink?'

'A . . . a psychiatrist. A person who helps you with your head.'

'Is your son crazy?'

Nisha hesitates. 'Um. Probably a little. Aren't we all?' She smiles.

'No,' says Grace, and fetches a tea-towel.

There is a small settee in the room and an armchair on which a large pile of bed-linen teeters, its corners pressed with blade-like precision. An ironing-board stands on its end beside it. As Grace brings glasses and a jug of water, Jasmine places the laundry in clear plastic bags Nisha recognizes from the hotel, securing each with a small strip of sticky tape. Jasmine sees her staring at the Bentley monogram.

'They throw them away after one use so I basically think of it as recycling.'

'I thought I had a lot of clothes,' Nisha says.

'Oh, they aren't mine.' Jasmine motions her to sit down at the table. 'Those are ironing and alterations.'

'What?'

'That's what I do when I'm not at the hotel. Ironing and alterations.'

Nisha stares at her. When Nisha finishes her shifts at the Bentley she is so exhausted it's all she can do to walk back and climb into a shower. The idea of starting work again is unthinkable.

Jasmine brings the lamb stew to the table and dishes up. The food, rich and delicious-smelling, steams gently on the plates beside fluffy white rice and greens. It is the first home-cooked meal Nisha has eaten in two weeks. Once she might have picked at it, inwardly calculating protein versus fibre and pushing aside the white rice. But now she mixes them together greedily with her fork, soaking the rice in the delicious gravy, eating in huge, hungry mouthfuls. She eats fast and barely stops to speak. She has finished her plate before the other two are even halfway through theirs.

'Aleks not in today, huh?' Jasmine says, until Nisha looks up and pauses. 'Go on, help yourself.'

She hadn't realized how much she had come to rely on his

daily meals, or that Jasmine had noticed this. Nisha waits just a moment, then spoons more onto her plate. Jasmine chats to her daughter about her homework and what she has to do for school tomorrow and then, when she is sure Nisha has had enough (she has: her stomach is actually hurting), waits while her daughter clears the plates and takes them through to the kitchen. Then she turns to Nisha.

'So where are you living?'

'In a hotel. But . . .' She doesn't want to admit it.

'But what?'

Nisha sighs. Stretches her arms above her head. 'They want the room back. And I can't afford to stay there anyway. I was going to ask you . . . about that little back room at the Bentley. Where you went when you had stomach-ache that time.'

'Oh, no.' Jasmine shakes her head. 'Forget that. They use it for the night-shift workers. There's people in and out of there all night. Two hours is the limit.'

'Well . . . do you think I could use a guest room? Just, you know, sneak in? Like if we checked whether it had occupants that day and – I mean I'd lie on top of the covers. There's nothing I couldn't fix up in five minutes.'

Jasmine's look tells her what she thinks of that idea. 'Seriously,' she says, 'what are you going to do?'

'I have no idea.'

Jasmine pushes herself up from the table. 'Well,' she says eventually, 'I guess you'll have to stay here.' She says it like it's already decided.

'What?'

'Well, where else are you going?'

'But you don't seem to . . . have a lot of room.'

'I don't. But you have none. So there we are. I'm not offering you room service and a five-star massage, Nisha. Just a bed. Till you can get yourself sorted. You can help mind

Grace for me when you're not on shift. Cook some meals. Pay me back that way. Hah! Unless you're going to tell me you had a private chef and you don't know how to cook.'

There is a brief silence. They gaze at each other.

'Oh, no. Oh, no.'

Nisha shakes her head slowly.

Jasmine's eyebrows shoot upwards. And suddenly the mood shifts and Jasmine erupts into fits of laughter. Nisha feels something quite alien. She doesn't know what to say. She doesn't know what to feel. She is in a tiny apartment with a woman she barely knows and she is beyond grateful for a bed she wouldn't have been caught dead in a couple of weeks ago. And this woman is laughing at her.

'Oh, my days. You're unreal, Nisha.' Jasmine is wiping her eyes. 'Seriously. You are *unreal*.'

'I'm going to fix this,' Nisha says seriously. 'I am. I'm going to make a plan and I'm going to make that man pay. For all of it.'

'Oh, I don't doubt it.' Jasmine leans back in her chair. She is still laughing, as if this is the best thing she has ever heard. 'And I am here with the popcorn for when that happens. Front-row seat. Family-sized carton. Ohhh, yes.'

The spare bed sits a full two and a half feet above Grace's. Nisha will be sleeping on the top berth of a chipped blue bunk bed covered with stickers from some previous occupant and under a My Little Pony duvet cover. Nisha stares at the little room, which is dominated by the beds, beside which a wardrobe and a small desk jostle for space under a wall covered with posters of singers she doesn't recognize. Grace turns from her desk to look at her.

'You need to get your stuff off the top bunk, baby,' says Jasmine, pointing.

Grace turns to her mother, and her face is a mute protest.

'I won't be here for long,' Nisha says, trying to sound conciliatory.

She imagines Ray's response if she told him a stranger would be staying in his bedroom. His expression would be a close variation of Grace's. 'I promise I don't snore.'

Grace lets out a low harrumphing sound.

Jasmine hands Nisha a towel. 'She doesn't like being here by herself. So it'll all work out fine.'

Forget Grace. Nisha wonders briefly if she'll be able to tolerate this. She and Carl had their own dressing rooms and bathrooms. She hasn't spent time in such close contact with other people since she was at school.

'Oh,' says Jasmine. 'And I got something for you.' She disappears as Nisha stands there, holding the small yellow beach towel that will be hers. She returns with a plastic supermarket shopping bag and holds it out. 'T-shirt?' Nisha asks. They have discussed the fact that she will stay tonight and return for her things first thing in the morning.

'Open it,' says Jasmine.

Nisha hesitates, then peers into the bag. And slowly pulls out three pairs of her black silk La Perla knickers and her dark blue Carine Gilson lace bra. She stares at them, her fingertips registering that she knows them, that these are her things. Her underwear. She runs her hand across the silk, and looks up at Jasmine.

'Well. A woman can't feel like herself in someone else's undies, right?' And, abruptly, for the first time since this whole stupid mess began, Nisha bursts into tears.

17

'She's acting weird.'

'What do you mean acting weird?'

'Like she's never home. And when she is home she seems to spend as much time as she can away from me. She's always walking the dog or upstairs sorting laundry.'

'Are you sure these aren't just things that she feels she has to do . . . if you're not doing them?'

'Well, maybe. I guess. But normally when she's home she just feels more . . .' Phil scratches his head '. . . present? And there's the makeup.'

Dr Kovitz waits.

'Sam doesn't wear makeup. I mean, a bit of mascara sometimes, yes. But mostly she just can't be arsed. She's not into all that. And I never minded, you know? I think she looks nice whatever. She's, you know, not a bad-looking sort.'

'And now she's wearing it?'

Phil thinks. 'Most days. I mean I'm in the room while she's getting ready in the morning and she's putting on foundation, eye-shadow, that blush stuff.'

'But you don't . . . say anything to her about it?'

'No.' Phil shifts uncomfortably in his seat. 'Well . . . well . . . I've found . . . it's usually just simpler if she thinks I'm asleep.'

'So she doesn't know you know she's putting on makeup.'

'No.' It sounds stupid put like this.

'Phil, do you have specific concerns? I mean, do you understand why this is worrying you so much?'

'It just doesn't feel very . . . Sam.'

There is a long silence.

'Can I ask about the physical side of your marriage?'

'It's fine.'

'"Fine."'

'I mean, it's always been fine. But obviously since I've been . . . well, it's . . . I mean it's only normal that things . . .'

A long silence.

'Are you telling me it's fallen away a bit?'

Phil's ears have started to burn. He nods, wipes at his nose.

'Can you remember when you last had . . . relations with your wife?'

Phil wants to die. He actually wants to die. He is regretting his decision to come back here.

'It's been a while. Like . . . months. Probably . . . well, maybe getting on for a year.'

'And is this a situation you're both comfortable with?'

He cannot tell him. The searing shame he felt when Sam was cuddling up behind him the other night, her obvious need for him. And he just . . . couldn't. He couldn't tell her it wasn't that he didn't want to try, but that he was afraid that if he couldn't make it happen, that was it, the end of everything. That it was easier if they just didn't try at all. Just till he got past this . . . whatever it was. He couldn't say any of it. Not out loud.

Once upon a time she would have made him talk about it, maybe even laugh about it. But the other night she just flopped onto her back and sighed this big sigh, like he was disappointing and irritating, and he wanted to crawl into a little ball and disappear.

'I mean I know she probably feels a bit let down by me at the moment. But – but I can't – I just feel . . .'

'It's too much.'

'Yes,' Phil says, relieved. 'Too much. It's . . . I just can't deal . . .'

There is a long silence. Dr Kovitz is keen on long silences. Eventually he says, 'What do you think would happen if you told Sam how you feel about things just now, Phil?'

Phil isn't sure if he moves physically, but he feels an internal slump at the thought. 'I can't talk to her. She's so angry. I mean, she's not a shouter. She's not walking round yelling at me. But I can feel it. I've let her down. She thinks I leave her to do everything. And I guess she's kind of right. But I can't. I just feel . . . so . . . tired. Like I just want to lie down and let it all drift away around me. And if I tell her how I feel she's just going to think that's one other thing she has to deal with. One more burden.'

'So . . . your strategy is just to wait until it all passes?'

'I guess.'

Dr Kovitz waits again.

'I haven't really got the energy to do anything else.'

'What did you feel when your dad died, Phil?'

The words sound wrong said out loud, even now. 'What do you mean?'

'You said before that when he was dying you felt like you'd let him down.'

'I don't want to talk about that.' The words are thick on his tongue.

'Okay. But I suppose what is coming through from our discussions is that you feel you're letting people down. Is that a fair assessment?'

'It's not what I feel. It's what I know.'

'Has Sam used those words?'

'No. She wouldn't say that.'

'So that's your interpretation.'

'She's my wife. I know her.'

'Fair enough.' A long silence. 'What do you think you'd have to do for her not to feel that way?'

'Well. Well, it's obvious, isn't it? Get a job. Be a man again.'

'You don't think you're a man?'

'A real man.'

'What'a real man, Phil?'

'Oh, now you're being ridiculous.'

Nothing Phil says offends Dr Kovitz. He just keeps watching him, his expression bland, a half-smile on his lips.

'Can you elaborate? What's a real man to you?'

'Just the obvious definition. Someone who has a job. Looks after his family. Does stuff.'

'And you don't think you're a real man if you're not doing those things?'

'Oh, this is just word games.' Phil gets up. 'I've got to go.'

Dr Kovitz doesn't protest. He doesn't say anything. He just waits while Phil puts on his jacket and then, as he walks to the door, calls: 'I'll see you next week, Phil.'

Nisha has spent three nights at Jasmine's flat. Two of those days she rode the buses to work with Jasmine, familiarizing herself with the routes. They do the morning journey in silence, both half asleep from the 5.30 a.m. start and bracing themselves with flasks of coffee for what the day ahead holds. In the evening they sit together in the packed bus and chat companionably about who got the best tips that day, the latest bizarre guest behaviour, what they will eat that night. Nisha is not generally one for small-talk but she knows it is the price for Jasmine's hospitality and does her best not to appear visibly exhausted by it.

They collect Grace from Jasmine's mother and bring her back – she doesn't like being in the flat by herself since it was broken into eighteen months ago ('They took my christening bracelet and Grace's laptop. It took me six months to pay off that thing.'), so on any night that Grace's father cannot pick her up, the evenings contain a long diversion to get her. Jasmine works in the evenings after supper, the apartment filled with the whoosh and hiss of the steam iron and the occasional whirr of her electric sewing machine. Nisha washes the dishes and clears up after dinner, so that Jasmine has one less thing to do.

The most reluctant of hosts, Grace speaks to Nisha when she has to, but it's clear that Nisha's presence in her room bugs the crap out of her. She avoids her eye, sighs heavily when Nisha gets down from the top bunk, and puts her earphones in ostentatiously whenever she is in the little bedroom. Nisha cannot blame her. She very quickly finds living in the tiny apartment with Jasmine and Grace exhausting. There is no room to move. No place to put her things, if she had any. No place to escape to. She cannot even sit in the bathroom without one of them banging on the door and demanding immediate access to hair products, toothbrushes or the loo. There is constant noise: the television, Grace's music, the radio in the kitchen, the washing-machine on spin (it never seems to stop), the doorbell ringing day and night as people come to collect laundry or drop it off. This way of living – the relentless grind, the lack of peace – is clearly normal to them.

And yet she knows she must be grateful. It is still, somehow, so much better than the awful hotel room. It is better, frankly, than anything else she can manage while she waits to work out her plan. And she finds herself in awe of Jasmine, who seems able to raise a smile for almost any occasion, who curses misfortune with a sailor's filthy mouth, then tells herself things could be worse and finds something to laugh about. Jasmine would like to open her own dressmaking business, but she enjoys her job at the Bentley, and is worried she'd get lonely working by herself full-time. 'Really I'd just like more space. A little shop maybe that I could put all this stuff in' – she gestures around the apartment – 'so me and Gracie could have a bit more room to ourselves.' Yes, she would like a boyfriend, but she has zero spare time, is 'picky as hell', 'and me and Gracie come as a package, you know? Anyone who likes me needs to get the Gracie seal of approval first.' (Grace had raised her eyebrows like *that* was unlikely to happen any time soon.) A couple of times Jasmine has begun joking about something – usually men, or sex – and Nisha has unwittingly found herself laughing along with her, once till the tears streamed down her face. For the first time in her life, she glimpses the solidarity of women, and likes it.

Until she sees that Charlotte Willis is wearing her coat. Her $6,700 pale tan and cream only-one-in-her-size Chloé shear-ling coat. Nisha sees the coat coming towards her down the main corridor as she pushes the cleaning trolley and feels a jolt of recognition before she notices who is wearing it. When she sees Charlotte, her face wreathed in that vaguely con-spiratorial smug smile, turning to say something to the young woman beside her, she thinks she might faint with rage. She stops abruptly, so that Jasmine crashes into the back of her, and when Jasmine realizes what she is looking at, she swings Nisha back round by the elbow and steers her briskly down the corridor towards the concession shop, leaving the trolley stranded where it stopped.

'That her?' she says.

'My coat,' says Nisha, who may be hyperventilating. 'She's wearing my coat. Jesus motherfucking Christ. What am I seeing? What am I *seeing*?' They pause by the service elevator and Nisha glances over, turns back to Jasmine, straightens up and shrugs, as if there is no alternative. 'Well, now I have to kill her.'

Jasmine lets out a bark of laughter, then straightens her face and gives her the kind of look she probably gives Grace. 'No, Nish. You are not going to kill anyone.'

'It's my *coat*.'

Nisha has had enough. Some things are too much to be borne. It's *Chloé*, for God's sake.

'Let her go,' Jasmine says firmly. And then, when Nisha protests, 'Let. Her. Go. Nish. Listen to me. Play the long game.'

'What? What the hell is that supposed to mean?' Nisha's voice lifts and Jasmine pushes her back into a doorway, her face fixed with a smile at passing guests as if this is all some glorious joke among the happy staff. 'Long game? I don't have a long game.'

'Babe, that's *all* you've got right now.'

Nisha watches as Charlotte steps into the gold elevator with her friend. She can remember buying that coat in the store in New York, the way it felt the first time she slid it over her shoulders in the private dressing room, the gorgeous cut, the comforting, faintly leathery scent of the shearling. The way the shop assistants smiled at her as she gazed at her reflection in the mirror. The softness. The beautiful, luxurious softness of it.

'I hate you,' she says to Jasmine, as Charlotte disappears behind the sliding gold doors.

'I know,' says Jasmine. 'Come on. Let's get you a sandwich.'

'I feel like fucking Cinderella. Except the Ugly Sister has got my fucking dress, my pumpkins, the fucking blind mice and the whole lot.' Nisha takes a bite from the sandwich that Aleks has prepared, then pushes the plate away.

'I don't think the mice were blind. But okay.' Jasmine sips her tea. 'I hear you, babe. I hear you. Oh. Hang on.' She glances at her phone. 'Sandra wants me in the office. It'll be about that carpet stain in two oh three. You stay here. I'll be back.'

Nisha is so locked into her rant of injustice that it takes her several minutes to notice that Jasmine has disappeared. She eyes the sandwich – it's prawn and mango, delicious – but her stomach has gone into cramps and she doesn't think she can eat any more.

Aleks gets up from his chair slowly. He puts down his book – something about slow cooking in the Nordic highlands – and reaches into his pocket for a packet of cigarettes. He shakes out the package and offers it to her, flipping one into his mouth with an easy gesture.

'I don't smoke,' she says irritably.

'I know,' he says.

He walks out of the back door where the bins are and, after a moment, she follows him. It's not that she wants to be with him, but she doesn't think she can be alone, without someone to witness what she is going through. He has lit his cigarette and is standing by the low wall. There is a vague, cabbagy smell seeping from the huge plastic food bins but, like the other members of staff, she barely notices it.

'My husband,' she says. 'He's turned me over. Stripped everything I own from me. And I have no fucking way of getting my life back.'

'That's not good . . . ' He exhales a long plume of smoke thoughtfully. 'I believe the English expression is: *he has done you up like a kipper.*'

She is so startled by this that she lets out a laugh. 'Are you kidding me? A kipper? What does that even mean?'

He laughs. 'I have no idea. English expressions are very strange. A guest told me last week I was "yanking his chain". I definitely never touched his chain.' His smile is slightly too knowing for him to be completely serious.

He holds out his cigarette packet again and this time she takes one. When he lights it for her he takes care that his scarred hands, cupped around the flame, do not touch hers. She inhales with the guilty nihilistic pleasure that comes with every cigarette she has smoked.

'So what are you going to do?'

She deflates. She takes another drag. Then she shrugs, and suddenly she is speaking, unsure why she feels she must explain. 'I have no clue. I'm staying in Jasmine's tiny apartment. Her kid hates me because I'm in her room, which has barely enough room for her as it is. I'm cleaning toilets. Actual toilets. It's basically all my worst nightmares and I have no idea how I'm going to get out of it.'

'But you haven't spoken to him?'

'Not since the day it happened. He's not taking my calls.'

He nods, as if he understands. They sit and smoke in silence for a while.

'If you cannot fix it,' he says, 'maybe you have to look at it differently.'

She frowns at him. He keeps gazing out at the alleyway. Two pigeons are tussling over a chicken bone, snatching and tossing it, before hobbling after it on deformed claws.

'Maybe you have to think about all the things about your old life that you didn't enjoy and say, "Okay, so here is an opportunity to start again. Perfect freedom. No ties. Maybe this is the dream." Maybe one day you will even be happier than you were.'

'With no money, no home and none of my things? That's the biggest bunch of Hallmark greetings-card self-help crap I've ever heard.' She inhales angrily.

'Perhaps. But if you cannot change your situation, then you have no choice. You can only change how you think about it.'

'And you like working eighteen-hour shifts here, do you? Till you're dead on your feet? Being yelled at by Michel because some guest says you haven't cooked the bacon just right? Catching a bus home in the small hours only to do it all again the next day with a double shift because they didn't pay the last guy properly and he fucked off somewhere else?'

He looks at her then, and his eyes crinkle with amusement. 'I do. Besides, I always cook the bacon perfectly.'

She makes a scoffing sound. 'Don't give me that bullshit.'

'I get to make people happy with my food.'

'These guests wouldn't know happiness if it whacked them in the face with a dumbbell. The people who eat in this hotel eat for fuel, or for status. The women eat with half their brain cells calculating the calorie count of every mouthful. The food is an agony for them as much as a pleasure. It's something they're never allowed to fully enjoy. Which is why half of it gets left on their plates.'

'I wasn't talking about the guests.' He smiles at her, and puts out his cigarette.

She stares at him. 'I should keep calling him, shouldn't I?'

'I think it's the only way you can sort this out.'

'Fuck it. I'm going to do it.' She starts to tap in Carl's number.

'No,' says Aleks. 'Use my phone. You do not want him to know where you are.'

She sees the sense in it, takes his phone and starts to type again.

'You want me to leave?' he says.

Without knowing what she is doing, she grabs his sleeve. 'No. No, please. Stay.' The phone rings. She realizes she is trembling. And then Carl answers.

'Finally,' she says, trying not to let her voice shake.

'Nisha! How are you, my love?' Only the faintest hint of

surprise in his voice. Carl is calm, in control. Like he has just come back from a short business trip.

'Oh, just great. Wonderful . . . How the fuck do you think I am, Carl? You shut down my whole life.'

'That's a little dramatic, darling.'

'It's been pretty fucking dramatic, Carl. What are you doing? What the hell is going on?'

'Darling . . . darling. Let's just have a civilized discussion.'

'Don't "darling" me. You ejected me – your wife – from my house, my clothes, my life. You cut me off without a penny. For all you know I could have been sleeping on the damn streets.'

'Where are you? I'll send Ari to pick you up. I've been trying to reach you.'

She freezes. Aleks is watching her.

'I'm using . . . a friend's phone. Just send me some money. Okay? I'll get a lawyer and we can sort this out.'

'No no no. We should meet.'

'Okay.' She takes a breath. 'Where?'

'I thought we could meet at the warehouse. I have a new building. In Dover, Kent.'

'You want me to come to a warehouse in *Kent*?'

Aleks is shaking his head.

'No,' she says. 'At the hotel. We meet at the hotel. Downstairs in the lobby.'

His tone changes, just infinitesimally. 'If you like.'

'Today,' she adds.

'I'll reschedule my meetings and be there in an hour.'

'Fine.'

He sounds vaguely irritated. He is not used to her dictating terms.

'And no Ari,' she adds. 'No Charlotte. No lawyers. No anyone else. Just you and me.'

166

He ends the call. As she puts down the phone and stares at Aleks, she feels almost dizzy.

'Are you okay?' Aleks is watching her carefully.

'I think I need another cigarette,' she says, looking down at her uniform. 'No. No. What I need is something to wear.'

The walls of the laundry room are obscured by floor-to-ceiling rails with plastic-covered clothes. Viktor and Jasmine stand shoulder to shoulder in the tiny dark chemically infused space and rifle through them, checking sizes or when they are due back in a guest's room, Jasmine shaking her head or holding up hangers for Nisha's approval. They settle on a black suit from Sandro and a pale silk blouse that Viktor says he can re-clean before the guests want it back on Friday. There are no shoes – apparently nobody leaves their shoes out for cleaning any more – which means she will have to wear the terrible pumps she has had to wear since this thing started. It sucks. But, then, compared to everything else in her life that is going on, it isn't the worst. While Viktor gets one of the porters to polish them, she does her hair in the Ladies and Jasmine curls the ends with heated tongs borrowed from one of the executive rooms and lends her some mascara and lipstick. The person Nisha sees in the mirror, for the first time in more than two weeks, looks a little like someone she might actually recognize.

'You look like a boss,' says Jasmine, who has offered to buy her the time by cleaning one of her rooms. 'Ready?'

'Ready,' says Nisha. But she's not sure that she is.

Carl rises to his feet as she crosses the foyer of the hotel. It's strange to look at him at this distance: she notices suddenly how jowly he has become, the way his belly bulges over his belt, like dough bursting out of a bread pan. Everything about him, from his well-cut suit to his perma-tan, his chunky watch, Italian shoes, screams money. He looks, she realizes with a start, like a stranger. How can eighteen years be wiped away so easily? He is smiling warmly, as if he is genuinely pleased to see her, and she is so taken aback when he goes to kiss her cheek that she lets him. He is wearing a cologne she doesn't recognize and she feels a brief, residual flash of anger. *Who is buying you different cologne?*

'Two coffees,' he says to the waiter, who appears out of nowhere as they sit down. 'Double espresso for me, an Americano for the lady. Cream?'

She shakes her head.

She is trying not to tremble. She has imagined this moment so many times over the past days, pictured everything from his abject apology to stoving in his head with a blood-spattered pickaxe. And now here he is, the genuine article, acting, weirdly, as if nothing has happened and this is just another lunchtime coffee together.

'So . . . did you come far?'

'No,' she says.

She sits very still, her ankles folded neatly under her, her eyes trained on his face. This is the man I shared a bed with for almost twenty years, she thinks, whose every need and whim I catered to. This is the man whose head I caressed when he had headaches, whose shoulders I massaged when he complained of stress, whose measurements I knew by heart so that I could order him clothes from any tailor in the world. This is the man whose beloved child I bore, whose tantrums I calmed, whose enemies I watched and reported and undermined for him, whose life I streamlined and smoothed and imbued with as many comforts as much as any human being could.

This is the man who cut me off as if I had never even existed. Who fucked his assistant and lied to me the whole time he was doing it. And the whole thing seems so surreal that she wonders briefly if she is dreaming.

'So how are you?' he says, when the coffees arrive.

'Is that a joke?'

'You look well.'

She stirs her coffee.

'What the fuck is going on, Carl?' she says. And he laughs. He actually laughs, his eyes warm, as if she has said something he finds amusing.

'I'm sorry, darling,' he says finally. 'I . . . I haven't handled the last couple of weeks as diplomatically as I might have done.'

'Diplomatically? Seriously?'

'I was badly advised by my lawyers. I realized that this was not the way. Our way.'

He reaches out a hand to place over hers, and she lets it briefly rest there, shocked by the familiarity of its weight, until she snatches it away. He watches her, settles back in his chair.

'You're hurt. And angry. I can understand that. And I'm here to . . . make things better.'

'I'm not getting back with you.' She throws it down like a gauntlet.

'I know. I think we have probably reached the end of our road. But what a road it's been, uh?' He smiles fondly.

She is frowning at him. Is this Carl? Or has Ari employed some actor to take his place?

'All those good years. Some good times. Fun trips. Our beautiful son. I think we did okay. We should still be able to be friends, yes?'

'You have zero relationship with our son. You haven't spoken to him in eighteen months, except via the staff.'

He rubs a hand over his head. 'What can I say, Nisha? I am a flawed human being. I'm working on it. We . . . we have had contact this last couple of weeks and –'

'You told him what you did?'

'No. No. I thought maybe some of this would be better coming from his mother. You always were better at handling him.'

She shakes her head. Of course it would fall to her to do the emotional heavy-lifting.

He leans forward over the table, his expression earnest. 'Look, Nisha, I'm here to say I'm sorry. I've handled everything very badly. I've not accorded you the respect you were due. But I'd like to change that. I'd like to think we can close this chapter of our lives in peace and harmony.'

She doesn't say a word. She understands instinctively that the best power she has right now is silence.

'I would like to make you a settlement.'

She waits. 'Okay.'

'I will get my lawyer to talk to your lawyer and draw up something that will be fair and equitable.'

'I don't have a lawyer, Carl. You've seen to that.'

'Then I will fix it. And then our lawyers will talk and we will work out a way that you can move forward in comfort.'

She regards him curiously. Is Charlotte behind this? Has he been advised to say these things? He seems genuine. She scans the room surreptitiously and cannot see Ari or Charlotte or anyone else at any of the other tables. She catches sight of Jasmine sweeping the lobby and glancing her way. Jasmine raises an eyebrow, as if to say, *You okay?* And she gives her the slightest of nods. She sits back in her seat and crosses her legs.

'So I thought we should . . .' he continues. Then: 'What – what are those shoes?' Carl is staring at her feet.

'Oh. Those. It's a long story.'

'Where are your Louboutins?'

'Why would you be looking for my Louboutins?' *Don't you*

know her clown feet are too big for them? she wants to say. But she doesn't want him to know that she knows.

He takes a sip of his coffee, doesn't meet her eye. 'Well. Just that they would be part of the settlement.'

She stares at him. 'You want the damn *shoes off my feet?*'

'I bought them, Nisha. Legally speaking, they are . . . my shoes. Along with everything else.'

'Which you gave me. Making them legally mine. Why would you want my *shoes?*' *Go on*, she thinks, *just say it. You want to give them to your clown-footed girlfriend.*

'I had them made specially. They're . . . they're worth money.'

'You're being weird, Carl. You have, like, a gazillion things that are worth more than those shoes.'

'Sentimental reasons, then.'

'You're about as sentimental as the Berlin Wall. Don't give me that.'

'Don't be obstructive, Nisha.' His voice holds a warning. 'I am being very generous here.'

'I'm not being *obstructive*, Carl. And you're not being generous. Yet. For all I know you could be about to offer me a suitcase full of fucking lentils. Anyway. I don't have the shoes.'

'What do you mean you don't have them?'

'They were in my bag. And someone took them.'

'"Took" them? You mean stole them?'

'I don't think so. They picked up the wrong bag. The day you served me with papers.'

'What? Who? Why haven't you got them back?'

'You know what, Carl? In the grand scheme of things, given you left me with no money, no clothes and nowhere to even spend the night, losing a pair of my fucking heels really didn't feel like my biggest problem just then.'

He has always been weirdly possessive about things he bought her, as if they were somehow still his own. She remembers a Gucci handbag she left in a restaurant in the early days of their marriage. He hadn't spoken to her for four days.

'Well, when are you going to get them?'

'Believe it or not, I've been trying to work out how to survive with no money and no roof over my head. You wanted to show me how powerful you can be, well done. You did it. You stripped me of everything in an instant. I got the message loud and clear: that you're the one with all the cards. I'm sorry if I mislaid some of your *stuff* in the process.'

He seems appalled. At his own behaviour maybe?

She waits a moment before she speaks. 'What did you *think* was going to happen to me, Carl?'

He shrugs. 'I don't know. I thought you'd go stay with one of your friends.'

'I don't have any friends in this country.'

'I thought someone would fly you home. Why would you want to stay here?'

'I didn't have a passport, did I? Because it was in the penthouse with all my other belongings.'

'Oh,' he says distractedly. 'Oh, yes.'

It felt kind of stupid. Like the two of them had been locked in a game that, now it was over, seemed weird, and pointless, a prank that had got out of hand.

'Look,' she says. 'You send me the money for a lawyer, we'll sort out our settlement, and you can have any pair of shoes I own. Just let me have my stuff and move on, okay? No fuss. No publicity. I just want what I'm owed.'

But his face suddenly closes over.

'You get nothing without the shoes,' he says. 'Not a dollar.'

'What?'

'You don't just lose my stuff! Okay? You don't lose what I have paid for! Like it's just . . . nothing!'

'What are you talking about? They were stolen! How the hell could I have –'

When he talks now his eyes are cold, his jaw set. 'Get me back those shoes and then we'll talk.'

'*Carl?* What the . . .' She yells: 'What about my money? The lawyer? Carl! I need my clothes, my things – Carl!'

But he has turned and is already walking across the foyer. Ari materializes out of nowhere and they are shoulder to shoulder with their backs to her, already deep in conversation.

18

Sam sits in the waiting room and watches from behind a three-year-old copy of *Woman's Weekly* as the nurse tries for the fifteenth time to explain to the man in the wheelchair that his family, including four bickering women and a gaggle of chaotic children, cannot come into the room with him. She hates this place. Hates the sanitized waiting areas infused with a mixture of fear and defeat. Hates the hushed conversations, the way time slips and stalls. Mostly she hates that she has to be there at all. In an effort to distract herself she has played three games of Words With Friends on her phone with a woman she doesn't know in Ohio, tried to call the gym twice to return the shoes (nobody picks up) and answered fourteen work emails, eight of which are from Simon.

'I'm very sorry, but it's the rules. A lot of our patients are immuno-compromised and we cannot risk infection.'

Sam gazes at the snotty noses of the children and thinks, They are basically just little germ factories in trainers.

But the older of the women, her hair scraped back into a ponytail, isn't having it. 'My dad doesn't want to be in there on his own. He wants his family.'

'I want to go in with my family.'

'I understand that, sir. But it won't be for long.'

'He wants his family with him. You should respect his wishes.'

A child starts rocking the water dispenser beside Sam vigorously. When it looks precarious, and then as if it might fall, she puts out a hand to steady it. The child stops and watches her, dead-eyed. One of the women is staring at her in an unfriendly manner, as if she has committed some grand imposition by failing to allow him to pull it over.

The nurse is still talking, her voice tinged with exhaustion. 'Madam, I don't have any choice here. The hospital has to protect all its patients, and the rules say no one, not friends or family members, is allowed in during the procedure. Perhaps you could wait in the canteen and we will let you know when he's ready.'

'He won't go in by himself.'

'I won't go in by myself.' The old man folds his arms across his chest.

'Then, sir, I'm afraid we cannot give you your medication.'

'He needs his medication! That's what the doctor said!'

'I've explained the rules, madam.'

'No. You're just discriminating. You're meant to respect your patient's wishes and you're just ignoring what he wants. He's not a vegetable, you know.'

'I'm not a vegetable,' affirms the man.

Sam glances at her watch. She has been here an hour and forty minutes and in that time the nurses have had to deal with three no-shows, a hysterical teenager and endless, endless patients who seem to feel the failure of this unit to run to their exact requirements is some kind of personal affront. She meets the nurse's eye, briefly, and tries to raise a smile, but drops it when the ponytailed woman shoots her a look.

'What are you staring at?' she spits at Sam.

'Nothing,' says Sam, blushing.

'You want to mind your own business.'

'Yeah,' says the other woman, who might be her sister. She walks so that she is a couple of feet from Sam, her shoulders square and her chin jutting. 'You want to butt out.'

Sam tries to think of something to say but cannot think of anything, so just lifts up her magazine and tries to hide the uncomfortable flush that has stained her cheeks. As she does this, the boy finally pulls over the water dispenser, which collapses in a gush, soaking her feet. Security is called, there is yelling and an attempt to mop up the water, someone starts to cry, and eventually the man is wheeled out, with his extended family, still cursing, into the corridor. It is at this point that Andrea appears. She is ghost white, her lips pinched together. Sam leaps up and puts on her mask to meet her.

'How was the scan?'

'Bloody marvellous. Can't wait to come back,' she says.

'Well, thank you again for bringing me to all the hot places,' Sam says.

'Don't start shouting about it. Everyone will want to come.'

Andrea threads her arm through Sam's and they walk slowly to the car park.

In the car, Andrea doesn't speak. Sam has done this trip enough times now – and has been friends long enough – to know when to leave her be, and when to try to lift her spirits. Halfway back from the hospital, though, she looks at the whiteness of Andrea's knuckles and reaches behind her for the soft blanket in the rear seat. She waits until they are at the traffic-lights and places it gently over Andrea's lap. Neither of them says a word, but a few minutes later Andrea reaches across and squeezes Sam's hand. She doesn't let go until Sam has to indicate and finds her eyes welling with tears, unsure whether it was just a thank-you or someone reaching for a life raft.

'It will be okay, you know,' she says. 'I have a good feeling about this one.'

She gives Andrea £740 to cover her month's mortgage when she leaves. Andrea doesn't say anything but stares at the cheque, then puts a pale hand over her mouth and shakes her head. She puts the cheque carefully on the sideboard and holds her friend tightly.

They both know that Andrea doesn't have it, that the mortgage company has refused for weeks to confirm whether they will give her a payment holiday, that the benefits do not cover Andrea's meagre outgoings. Only one of them knows that it is nearly all that remains of Sam's savings.

I didn't have a choice, she tells herself, to try to quell the fear that rises in a bubble in her chest as she drives away. She would have done the same for me.

The following morning she is on the phone to the builder about the fact that Phil has still not moved the camper-van when Simon finds her. She turns while she is in the middle of the call, suddenly conscious of someone watching her, and he is standing a few feet away, one finger tapping the face of his oversized watch, his face solemn.

'Well, can you move it?' she murmurs into the phone. 'If he's not answering the door perhaps he's gone out. Look, the key for the ignition is under the wheel arch. It's not locked. I know . . . I know it has a flat tyre. But you only need to back it onto the street . . .'

Simon walks round, his pace slow and deliberate, so that he is standing directly in front of her. She glances up, one hand over the mouthpiece.

'I'm so sorry. I'm at work. There's nothing I can do from here . . . Please don't do that – look, I'll try to reach him and get it moved. Please don't go. I'm sure he can sort it . . . Hello? . . . Hello?'

Simon beckons her to his office and closes the door behind her. His office is made of glass so that everyone can see when you're being dressed down. She looks round and sees a couple of co-workers glance her way awkwardly across the cubicles. They know. They all know.

Simon sits down, sighing as if this very conversation causes him pain. 'Sam, I'm afraid I've reached a point where I can no longer ignore your failure to do your job properly.'

'What?'

He doesn't invite her to sit.

'The thing is, you're not a team player.'

'What? How –'

'I've given you every chance. But you're not up to speed. You're not reliable.'

'Hang on. I'm as good as anyone else here.'

'Well, I don't receive complaints about anyone else.' He sits down, not meeting her eye, and begins to click his stainless-steel ballpoint pen. She notices his initials are engraved on the side of it. Who the hell engraves a ballpoint pen? 'Plus we need energetic people here. Dynamic. You give off a depressed vibe. You need to sharpen up your act.'

'Simon – I just brought in two hundred and ten thousand pounds' worth of business.'

'Your team did. And lost us a valued client in the process.'

'He told us when he got there that he was already going to go with someone else. Nothing we did would have made any difference –'

'I'm not interested in excuses, Sam. I'm interested in results.'

Mortifyingly, she feels tears spring to her eyes. The unfairness of it. She feels like she did when she was ten and a teacher had unfairly blamed her for writing graffiti on the toilet doors. She hadn't even known how to spell 'bollocks'. 'Simon – I've been here twelve years. I never had a complaint about my work before you came. Never.'

He looks briefly sad, and shakes his head. 'Well, perhaps

at Uberprint we simply hold higher standards. I'm trying to help you out here, Sam. I'm trying to let you know that you need to up your game.'

She stares at him. 'Is there an "or" in this conversation?'

'Well, that's up to you. But I have to tell you that we're looking to streamline the organization, to make cuts. And if that happens we will, of course, be looking to retain the more effective members of staff.'

There is a short, weighty silence.

She stares at him. 'Are you telling me I'm about to lose my job?'

He smiles. It is not really a smile at all. 'I would think of it more as an incentive to sort things out. A spur to improve. And if you really can't, Sam, well . . .' he runs his hand through his gelled hair '. . . it will probably be the best thing for both of us if you seek pastures new.'

There is a peculiar quality to the silence that greets you when you emerge from your boss's office and everyone knows you've basically been told you're for the chop. The faintest of lulls and then a quiet hum of industry as if everyone has magically remembered what they were meant to be doing. Sam walks past the backs of people's heads, slides into her cubicle and sits at her chair, her back straight, conscious of the attention of the thirty-odd people who are pretending not to notice her.

She stares at her screen, her mind buzzing, seeing nothing, clicking the mouse purposelessly. What will they do if he sacks her? He is clearly making her out to be useless so that he doesn't have to pay her redundancy. They will lose their house. They will lose everything. She looks up to see Simon motioning Franklin into his office. They sit down opposite each other, Simon's feet up on the desk, and start laughing

179

about something she cannot hear. You don't have to be John le Carré to work out manoeuvrings are going on.

Her email pings and she looks at her screen.

Joel: You okay?
Sam: Not really.
Joel: Want to go out for a sandwich at lunchtime?
Sam: I don't think I dare. He'll probably make that a
    sackable offence too.
Joel: Quick drink after work?

She thinks about the camper-van that she will probably have to move herself.

Sam: I don't think I can.
Sam: But thank you.
Sam: Sorry.
Joel: The offer's there, babe. Chin up and tits out as
    Ted would say.
Joel: And probably shouldn't.
Sam (her eyes filling with tears again): Thank you x
Joel: Always here for you x

She is not sure how she gets through the rest of the day. She hears her voice as if from afar, checking on print schedules and laminated pages. She calls up clients, conscious that her voice sounds weirdly strangled. There is a lump in her throat that never quite goes away. She does not look at Simon's office. When she is conscious of someone glancing over at her she makes sure her face is a perfect blank.

She leaves at six thirty. She walks out through Transport so that she doesn't have to pass his office, and Joel is there going over the week's tachographs with one of the drivers. He looks up as she passes and she tries to smile but she suspects it doesn't reach her eyes. It is raining. Of course it is. She climbs into her car and finally lets out a long shuddering breath. As she starts to drive, tears are sliding unchecked down her cheeks and she hopes that nobody can see through her rain-spattered windscreen. She drives the twenty minutes home, pulls up in the street and stares at the camper-van, which Phil has failed to move so the builders have had to start work round it. The light is on in the living room and the television flickers. She knows she has to tell Phil what has happened but she doesn't know if she can cope with his anxiety on top of hers. Sam sits in her car, not hearing the radio burbling quietly. And she slowly brings her head down to rest on the steering wheel and leaves it there for a while, just trying to remember how to breathe.

Her phone pings.

Joel: Hope you're okay. Here adding anti-freeze for another half-hour if you change your mind x

She watches the three dots pulsing and then:

Everyone needs an ear.

She stares at her phone. She lets her finger rest on the keys, and then, after a moment, starts to type.

Sam: You're kind. But I'm fine. Thank you x

She sits still for another moment. Then she drags her bag from the passenger seat, and, with a weary sigh, climbs out of the driver's door and walks inside.

The house is warm. Too warm, given their electricity bills. Phil used to walk around turning down the thermostats but he no longer seems to notice. She glances in as she passes the living room. He is lying on the sofa staring at the screen. She waits in the doorway briefly but Phil does not appear to notice she is there.

She goes into the kitchen and takes off her coat, leaving it on the back of a chair. Phil's plate from lunchtime sits in the sink, as does a pan encrusted with spaghetti hoops. She gazes at the dried tomato sauce globs on the waxed tablecloth, at the empty tea mug. A scribbled note in his handwriting says: *Your mum rang says can you clean Thursday instead.*

She stands in the middle of the little kitchen, holding it.

No, she thinks suddenly. *No. No, I cannot. None of it.*

She turns and walks back into the narrow hallway, half waiting for Phil to call a greeting. But he is engrossed in the television. She runs nimbly up the stairs and, almost without knowing what she is doing, she puts on the blue trousers she wore to Cousin Sandra's second wedding and a fresh jumper and pulls the Louboutin shoes out from under her bed. She straps them on and stands, feeling immediately taller, more formidable. She puts on some makeup in the mirror, a dark pink lipstick and some mascara, pursing her lips at herself and lifting her chin. She sprays some dry shampoo into her roots to zhuzh her hair up a bit. And then, after a moment, she adds a squirt of scent. Then she walks downstairs, puts her coat back on, grabs her bag and types into her phone:

If you're still there, Coach and Horses 20 minutes.

She waits, and then adds: x

*

182

Joel is already at the pub when she arrives. He has his back to her, standing at the bar as he chats to the barman. Joel seems to know everyone. There is rarely a job they turn up at where he doesn't greet someone warmly. He turns 180 degrees when she opens the door, as if he knows by some internal compass that she has arrived.

'White wine?' he says, and smiles.

'Yes, please.'

She finds a corner seat, suddenly a little self-conscious in her smart clothes in the scruffy pub. Why had she worn the Louboutins? They look out of place among the scuffed boots and trainers. She folds her legs under the table, feeling oddly exposed. When Joel arrives, a drink in each hand, he places them down carefully. 'You look nice. Going some-where?'

'Um . . . no. I – I just . . . needed a lift,' she says, and takes a long sip of the wine. 'Probably a bit silly.'

'Not at all. Good move,' he says. He smiles. 'You brought the big guns out.'

She gazes at the shoes and laughs ruefully. 'They just . . . make me feel like a different version of myself, I guess. I'd wear them every day if I could.' She keeps her eyes on her feet.

'Simon?' says Joel. 'That man . . .'

'It's not just Simon. It's everything,' she says. Now she's embarrassed. 'Oh, God. Listen to me whining already. Bet you're really glad you came, aren't you?'

'Whine away, babe,' he says. 'That's what I'm here for.'

What are you here for? she asks him silently. And then she pulls herself together.

'I think I'd rather just drink, actually,' she says, and after a moment he holds up his glass, they chink them together, and they begin.

*

183

It's the first time she has felt seen, or heard, for ages. They talk and talk and talk, and punctuate the talking with trips to the bar. He tells her about his last break-up. The impossible demands put on him by his ex-girlfriend. 'I just felt like every emotional situation was a trap by the end – do you know what I mean?' She nods, even though she doesn't. She hates this girlfriend, even though she's never met her, and she pities her too. Imagine having a man as lovely as Joel and losing him.

'I mean, she was a nice woman. But, man, I felt shredded. Shredded. Every time I saw her. It just felt like she would look for the worst possible interpretation of anything I did. She asked so many questions about why me and my ex-wife split up that in the end I thought she was looking for deficiencies in my character.'

'I know that feeling,' she says. *I wouldn't do that to you*, she thinks, then shuts the thought down.

'The thing is, I was straight with her. I don't like messing people about. But it's just exhausting, feeling you're not seen for who you are, you know?' He shakes his head, and then smiles. 'Of course you do. You're dealing with it every day. I don't know why Simon can't see how valuable you are.'

Just Simon? she thinks. And something in her constricts.

Joel is so kind, so intimate and conspiratorial. She is trans-fixed by his mouth, so that sometimes she barely hears what he says, and after they get the third round of drinks he moves round so they are side by side on the bench, and she can feel the warmth of his shoulder against her, watch his strong, dark hands. They talk about their parents and he cries laughing when she tells him the story of her father and the little blue pills. 'My dad doesn't need them,' he says. 'Every afternoon at two thirty he taps his watch and tells Mum it's time for their "afternoon nap". Doesn't even care if we're all round watch-ing telly.' He lets out a laugh that is almost a giggle.

184

'You're kidding.' Sam is agog.

'Nope. When me and my sisters were younger we'd be dying of embarrassment. Now, I'm like "Dude, if it's still all working for you, good on you." It's a nice thought, right? That you'd still be that into someone in your seventies?' He gives her a quick sideways look, and she feels her cheeks colour.

They discuss work and he glowers when she says Simon's name, and curls his fists, like it's all he can do to stop himself heading back to work and punching him, and the thought of this makes her warm inside. They talk of his awfulness, how work hasn't been the same since his arrival. She tells him about Simon's personalized engraved ballpoint pen and feels a quiet sense of triumph when Joel bursts out laughing. 'The man has engraved a *ballpoint pen*?' Joel urges her to stand up for herself, not to take Simon's shit, and three glasses in she finds she is saying, *Yes, yes!* as if she actually will, rather than slope off with her head bowed, wishing she was anywhere else in the world.

'What does Phil say about it all?' he says eventually. He looks straight ahead and takes a sip from his glass as he speaks his name.

'We don't really talk about it. Things . . . things are a bit tricky at home.' She feels a stab of disloyalty even as she says this, but she can't help herself. 'We're flat broke. My daughter is pretty much the only person who says anything to me. Phil won't talk – he's depressed – but he won't do anything about it. Won't go to the doctor. Won't sign up for help. Won't take any meds. But it's like living with a ghost. I'm not sure he even notices if I'm there any more. Normally I'd talk to Andrea about it all – she's my best mate – but she's had cancer and I don't want to put anything else on her. Mostly I just muddle on through but today, with the job threat and everything, I just felt like I couldn't . . . cope.' Her voice is suddenly thick with tears and she screws up her face, trying to stop them.

Her eyes are actually closed when Joel puts his arm around her and pulls her into him. He smells of a delicious aniseedy aftershave she hasn't come across before, and warm, clean skin. No man other than Phil has put his arms around her like this, not since they first got together. She stiffens initially, but then it feels so nice to be held, so reassuring, that she slowly softens and lets her head come to rest on his shoulder. *Can I just stay like this for ever?* she thinks.

'I'm here for you, babe,' he says softly, into her ear.

'Sorry,' she says, wiping at her eyes. 'Stupid, isn't it? I should be able to handle this stuff.'

'Nah. It's not easy. You're my friend. I don't like seeing you this low.'

She turns to face him. His lips are inches from hers. His eyes are soft, unreadable. *Are we friends?* she thinks. His eyes search hers. Something gives inside her. It is a moment that seems to last several years. She stands abruptly. 'So . . . shall I get the next round?'

He is leaning back in his chair when she returns. She feels awkward as she walks towards him, as if she has exposed too much of herself. But he smiles as she approaches.

'I've had a thought,' he says.

'Okay,' she says.

'You know what you need?'

She takes a sip of her drink. She realizes she is definitely drunk.

'Boxing.'

'What?'

'Boxing. It's about energy, Sam. Mental strength as well as physical. You need to look more assertive to deal with that prick. You need to look like nobody is going to mess with you. You're walking with your head down just now. Like he's knocked all the stuffing out of you. You need to get your mojo back. Can you throw a punch?'

She finds she is laughing. 'I have no idea. Probably not.'

'Tomorrow night. Come to the gym. Don't look at me like that – there's loads of women do it. They love it. You can pretend the punchbag is Simon's face. I tell you, when I've had a bad day at work I just head down there, put some gloves on, and *doof doof doof doof.*' He mimics throwing punches at speed. 'An hour later I feel *great.*'

But that would mean wearing tight gym clothes in front of you, she thinks. It would mean being sweaty and wearing no makeup. Being hopeless at something while you watch. She remembers suddenly how she'd felt at the awful gym, the yummy mummies making her feel lardy and invisible. 'I don't th–'

He puts his hand over hers and clasps it. His is warm and solid. 'C'mon. You'll enjoy it. I promise.'

There is something about his smile that removes the word 'no' from her vocabulary. She gazes at him.

'Trust me?'

The words stall in her mouth.

'Okay,' she says, when she can speak again.

He leans back, takes a swig of his drink. 'It's a date. Seven o'clock. I'll text you the details.'

19

Over the next two days Nisha thinks constantly about the shoes. She wonders whether they were ever returned to the now-closed gym. She wonders whether the woman who took them did it deliberately. She wonders whether you can legitimately ask the police to investigate a theft when you're wearing the nasty black shoes that belonged to the person who took yours. When she is not thinking about the shoes she is wondering at the oddness of Carl, and if it's one of those things you see clearly only when you're at a distance. He was always a little particular about what she wore – clothes were routinely 'too matronly', 'too whorish' or sometimes 'make you look fat'. He didn't like her in flat shoes as they made her legs look 'dumpy'. She had always assumed it was because he wanted her to look as nice as possible. But was there something about the clothes themselves that had made him want them so dramatically? Some strange fetish? Anything seems possible, these days. Or did he just want them for Charlotte? Had they become some kind of symbol? She remembers, queasily, how he had insisted on her wearing the shoes on the day he gave them to her, the way he seemed to be unusually turned on by the sight of them. And this thought makes her feel so uncomfortable that she pushes it away.

Jasmine is on lates so Nisha mostly works alone and she is relieved: things have started to feel a little tricky in the apartment. Some days the space actually seems to shrink, so that the three of them are forever in each other's way, arguing over bathroom time or inching round each other in the kitchen as they try to get to the fridge or kettle. Jasmine has taken on extra ironing and the hallway is narrowed by even more piles of laundry in huge woven plastic holdalls. Her usual good humour is fraying at the edges under the pressure of it all and the exhaustion. Grace, meanwhile, is furious with Nisha all the time for taking up space in her room. She understands it, but the eye-rolling and heavy sighs are becoming a little hard to bear cheerfully. At least when she and Jasmine are on different shifts there is a good chunk of each day when she can just be herself, when there is no need for her to put on a cheery, accommodating smile she doesn't feel. And she rarely does.

What has happened to the damn shoes? The thought spools and reels in her head as the hours pass. She has to find them: the sooner she gets them back the sooner she can get her money from Carl, leave the tiny apartment and start reclaiming her life. She is sure Ray has worked out that something is going on. On yesterday's call he had been super-quiet and finally said he'd thought she and Dad would be home by now. She'd had to make up some nonsense about Carl having to deal with an unexpected piece of business, and although she'd sounded convincing, Ray is too sensitive to be fobbed off for long. 'I just need to see you, Mom,' he said, at the end of the call, and a huge lump landed in her throat that took several minutes to swallow.

'I know, darling. Me too. It won't be long, I promise.'

In her lunch break she heads to the bin area and, standing by the window where she is sure she can still reach the hotel Wi-Fi, she smokes a cigarette and calls Magda.

'Mrs Cantor! You didn't answer any of my messages? Are you okay? I've been so worried.' In the background Nisha can hear the whine of pneumatic spanners as they separate wheels from car bodies.

189

'I've been busy. Look, I need to ask you something. Do you have any idea why Carl would want my shoes?'

'Your shoes?'

'The Louboutins. Can you ask around? Is there any way you can ask your man if he can describe the woman who was wearing them in that bar? I need them to negotiate with Carl.'

'I'll ask him, Mrs Cantor. As long as he is on the same number – sometimes they change numbers, you know? Please – any news on my job? Turns out I am not so good at fitting tyres . . .'

'I need those shoes back to give you a job, Magda. Okay? It's very important. For both of us.'

'I understand. *No, we do not have any Michelin! Only Goodyear that size!* You can rely on me, Mrs Cantor.'

Wishing that statement gave her more confidence than it did, Nisha ends the call, stubs out her cigarette and walks back through the kitchen. It is the peak of lunch service, and around her flames erupt from gas burners, while curses and yelling surge over the sound of pans and metal whisks. She ducks through the bodies in food-spattered whites, and spies Aleks bent low over a pan of scallops. He sees her and beckons her. He leans over to yell into her ear to make sure he is heard above the racket. 'Come by later. I have something for you.'

She narrows her eyes.

'You will like.'

'What?' she yells. It makes her uncomfortable, this constant giving of things. Like she is somehow becoming indebted to him in a way she has little control over. She does not want to be indebted to anyone ever again.

'It's to eat.'

'What is it? And what do you want? For the food thing?' When he doesn't answer, she adds: 'Like – what do I have to give you?'

He frowns, as if she has said something confusing. Then he shakes his head almost irritably and turns back to his scallops.

It is a duck. Aleks gives her a duck. The suppliers delivered too many, he says, as she gets ready to leave. The management will not notice. He hands her the surprisingly weighty bird wrapped in muslin. It is organic. Very good taste. She can make a nice meal for Jasmine and her daughter.

'You know how to cook duck?' When she looks blank he goes to the larder room and makes up a small package containing star anise, arrowroot, some green herbs and a small jar of orange liqueur, placing them all in a jute bag. He doesn't look at her as he writes out instructions. He has beautiful handwriting. She doesn't know why this surprises her.

'It's not difficult. Most important thing is let the meat rest ten minutes minimum when you have finished roasting, yes? Ten minutes minimum. That way it will be very tender.'

Something about this whole exchange puts her on edge. He definitely wants something. Why would he do all this otherwise? These delicious daily meals and little food gifts. But she doesn't feel she can push him on this again without insulting him. This kind of confusion is new to Nisha, so that she is curt with him when she takes the package, her answers brisk and cursory. And when she heads back to the locker room his quizzical look makes her angry with herself.

Nisha does what she always does when faced with difficult emotions. She ignores them. She works her way through six rooms, like an automaton, fierce and thorough. She finds these days that she is oddly grateful for the distraction of cleaning. In the absence of running, or a gym, she finds the physical effort it involves calms her in some strange undefined way. The undemanding mental involvement of stripping and replacing linen, scanning for dust or dirt eases the whirring of her brain. The physical exhaustion it brings feels necessary. She is just ending the day sitting on the bench with a mug of coffee in the locker room when Jasmine texts her:

> My ex says he can't bring Grace back. Could you swing by and pick her up from my mum's on the way home? I don't like her travelling by herself.

She thinks of the bird in her locker, the mindless following of instructions, the prospect of a good meal this evening. She thinks of being able to offer something to Jasmine, which will make her feel less like the recipient of charity.

> Sure, she types. And don't eat before you come back tonight. I am doing a surprise!

She thinks about going back to the kitchen before she leaves, to thank Aleks properly for the duck. But something stops her: it's too awkward, or maybe it will somehow make her feel even more weirdly indebted if she makes too much of it. It's just a damn duck, she tells herself. What does she care about a duck in the grand scheme of things?

The bus is heaving. Jasmine has sent her a text reminder of which numbers to catch; she thinks she will never get to grips with London's labyrinthine transport system, its huge, sprawling districts, which all look the same to her. She has mastered the art of disappearing into her thoughts while on the bus. They tend to be pretty dark but it's better than listening to the coughs and irritatingly loud cellphone calls of her fellow travellers. So she doesn't notice when the woman speaks to her initially, and only looks up when she is virtually sitting on her lap.

'Excuse me?' she says, as the woman's coat flips over her leg.

'I asked you to move. I need more room.' The woman is tall, dressed in a large patchwork velvet coat and does not look at her as she speaks, as if Nisha is merely an irritation, an obstacle in her way.

'I'm as far over as I can get. Hey. Hey! You're *on* me.'

The woman just lets out a *hmph* sound and pushes further in. She has badly dyed hair and smells of patchouli.

'Lady!' says Nisha. 'You are way over the line. Get back.'

'I asked you politely. You didn't move,' the woman retorts.

'I don't want your damn coat touching me.' Nisha picks it up with two fingers and flicks it off her leg.

'Well, if you moved over I wouldn't be touching you, would I?'

Nisha feels the blood rush to her head. 'Hey. It's not my fault if you're too damn big for this space. But I sure as hell don't have to sit here and take it while you sit on my lap with your stinking coat.'

The woman is actually squashing her into the seat. She is so close Nisha can smell her deodorant and it makes her want to gag. *Oh, my God, she's so close I'll be breathing in little cells of this woman.*

'Move over!' she demands.

They have caught the attention of the other passengers now. Nisha is dimly aware of the low buzz of interest that passes round the seats, the wary glance of the driver in the rear-view mirror.

'You don't like it,' says the woman, impassively, 'you move.'

'I was here *first*.'

'You own this bus, do you? Go back to your own country if you don't like it here.'

'My own *country*? MOVE YOUR ASS.' Nisha cannot believe this woman. The audacity. She is a dead weight, and

Nisha realizes she cannot physically move her. She elbows her hard and the woman elbows her back. When the woman stares mulishly ahead, Nisha reaches down, grabs the woman's handbag from her lap and hurls it towards the front of the bus, where its contents scatter, sending lipsticks and bits of paper reeling under the other seats. The woman stares at her in shock.

'Pick up my bag!'

The two women are standing now. Nisha feels the woman shove her, but can tell despite her heft that she has little real strength and so she pushes back, hard, with both arms. There is a collective *oooh!* on the bus as the woman loses her balance and falls heavily against the seat opposite with a scream. She is scrambling to her feet when the bus stops abruptly. The driver opens the barrier between the driver's area and the aisle and looks at them. 'Oi! You two! Off!'

'I'm not getting off!' says the woman, scrabbling for her bag. 'She pushed me!'

'She sat on me! She was literally suffocating me!'

'Off!' says the driver. 'Or I'm calling the police!'

'I'm not going anywhere,' says Nisha, sitting down firmly. 'I am staying until my stop.'

'You think I'm scared of the police? You got another think coming. This bitch is going to get her head smacked before I –'

Ten minutes later Nisha is standing on the kerb while the bus finally pulls away, her skin burning from the radioactive looks of the delayed passengers still on board. Her ears are ringing with the sound of the warning given to her by the police officers, who didn't seem to care whose fault it was, bored – and possibly a little amused – by the sight of two women going at it over bum space on a bus seat. She is already calculating how long it will be before the next bus arrives and she will be able to pick up Grace. This goddamn country.

It is twenty-two minutes later, as she finally climbs furiously onto the next bus – it's packed, of course, and she has to stand – that she realizes the beautiful organic duck, with all its carefully picked accompaniments and dressings, is still tucked neatly under the seat of the bus she was removed from.

Grace doesn't talk to her the whole way home. Nisha doesn't even try. Grace plugs in her earphones and gets on and off the two buses in silence, so that they walk alongside each other without acknowledging each other's presence. When they finally reach the apartment Grace mumbles that she's not hungry, she had something at Nana's, and disappears into her bedroom with a slammed door.

Nisha has had enough. She makes a cheese sandwich out of the remaining slices of bread in the bread bin, and swallows its two claggy halves, trying not to think about the duck, which is probably still en route to a depot somewhere. There is no hot water, so she puts on the electric immersion heater and twenty minutes later shuts herself into the bathroom, pouring shampoo into the bath in place of decent bath oils or scented bubbles.

She lies there, submerged to her chin, for an hour and a half, her thoughts pinging between errant ducks, Louboutin shoes and the annoying enigma that is Aleks, half trying to suppress the desire to kill the entire world, half working out the various ways in which she could do it. There was barely a time in Nisha's life when she couldn't remember being angry, but now it's as if her eyes have been opened to the myriad ways in which just being female is like being dealt some infinitely crappier hand – a hand nobody else even acknowledges. She thinks of her teens, the endless daily trail of men who tried to touch her or leered at her, the many ways in which she could not go about her daily life without unwanted attention. The man at the feed shop who offered her a dollar when she was twelve if she'd let him put his hand down her top. The guy at the garage who used to make obscene gestures when she bought her gas. The creeps on subways, the men who followed her back to her shared apartment, the subtler, more expensive hands on her ass when she worked at the gallery. She thinks about the ways in which she has been expected to conform to some ideal that takes endless, endless effort just to stay married: keep your figure, create a perfect home environment, be interesting, have great hair every day (but none anywhere else), wear shoes that make your feet hurt, lacy underwear that cuts your hoo-ha in two, make sure your bedroom antics are porn-star level (even if your husband seems to think the act of getting a hard-on should be enough for his side). She tries to imagine Carl getting his pubic hair lasered to make sure he was attractive enough for her, and it's so unthinkable she laughs out loud. And now, because she is female and did all the things expected of her, she's been discarded for a younger, supposedly sweeter model.

And then, of course, laugh off all this unfairness or be deemed a humourless witch.

These thoughts, which she has suppressed for years (what good would have come from acknowledging them anyway?), are popping up to the surface, like the bubbles in the bath, irrepressible, relentless.

She lies there hearing Grace's insistent music through the closed doors until her fingers and toes wrinkle, the tiny mirror is obscured by steam and the water becomes uncomfortably chilly. She is just emerging from the bathroom when Jasmine returns. The door slams and she is walking up the narrow hallway, unwinding a scarf from her neck when she spies Nisha. She walks straight past her into the kitchen.

'Babe! So where's this surprise? I'm so hungry my mouth was watering the whole way home.'

Nisha stops in her tracks. 'Oh.' She pulls a face. 'Yeah, the thing is I had a problem on the bus. Some stupid woman pretty much sat on my lap and –'

'But what is it? You told me not to eat.' Jasmine is opening the oven door, and lifting the lids on empty pots that sit on the hob.

Nisha's heart sinks. 'Sorry. It – The food thing didn't happen.'

There is a brief silence.

'So – what . . . You made nothing?'

She stares at Nisha, then closes her eyes slowly, as if she is trying hard to quell some imminent eruption. 'I turned down coconut chicken curry for this.'

She takes a deep breath. 'Okay. Well, I guess I'll just have beans on toast. I need to eat fast. My blood sugar is way down.'

Nisha feels a sudden stab of discomfort. 'I – I think I ate the last of the bread.'

'You're joking.'

'I'm sorry.'

'And you . . . didn't think to go out and buy some more?'

'I needed a soak in the tub. I had a really bad day. Look, let me get dressed and I'll get some.'

Jasmine's look could cut glass. 'Well, what did Grace eat?'

'She said she ate at your mom's.'

'Mum told me she ate nothing.'

Jasmine closes her eyes, and lets out a sigh. She opens them, moves past Nisha and opens the airing cupboard to wedge in a pile of freshly laundered sheets. She stops. 'Hang on. Who put the immersion heater on?'

'Me?' says Nisha.

'How long has it been on?'

'I don't know. A couple of hours? I forget.'

Jasmine slams the illuminated switch off. 'Jesus. You know how much that thing costs? Girl, you can't just forget that shit. Oh, my God.' She slams the door shut and turns on her heel. 'No food, no hot water and a whacking great electric bill. You think this is a fricking hotel? You think you're still in the Bentley? Nish, just because you never had to worry about money doesn't mean the rest of us don't! You're just taking the piss now! Jesus!'

She stomps down the corridor to the kitchen, and Nisha is left standing there in the towel.

She dresses, ignoring Grace's pointed sideways glances as she hauls on the awful trousers and a T-shirt. She lets herself out of the apartment, ignoring the sound of slamming kitchen-cupboard doors, and walks quickly to the twenty-four-hour convenience store ten minutes away, too furious with herself to worry about the cold or the catcalling of the youths on the corner or the guys hanging outside the snooker hall. When she lets herself back in twenty minutes later Jasmine is on the sofa in the living room, eating something that looks like packet noodles from a bowl.

'Here,' she says, proffering the grocery bag.

'What?' says Jasmine, hauling her attention from the tele-vision.

'Bread, milk, eggs, some chocolate. Look, I'm – I'm sorry.'

Jasmine glances at it. 'Okay,' she says, and switches her gaze back to the screen.

'And here.'

Jasmine sighs as she is forced to look at her again. She glances down at the wad of notes Nisha is holding out. 'What's that?'

'What I owe you. For staying here. I'd give you more but I need to keep some to get my son back.'

'You owe me what?'

'Whatever it's cost you. This last couple of weeks. I'll pack up and be out of your way in half an hour.' A weird, unfamiliar lump has risen in her throat.

Jasmine looks at her hand again, then up at her face. 'Are you nuts?'

'Well . . . ' Nisha's voice is formal, her neck stiff '. . . it's quite obvious you've had enough of me being here.'

Jasmine stares for a moment longer, then pulls a face. 'Nish. I'm pissed. I was hungry. Yes. But you're my mate. I'm not going to chuck you out on the street because of some hot water.' She shakes her head irritably. 'Sit your arse down, woman. You're making me uncomfortable.'

Nisha remains standing. 'But the bread –'

'Is just bread. You never had nobody get pissed off at you before? It's obvious you've never had to share, okay? You got to think a little before you just do stuff if we're all in the same space, you know? But don't get dramatic about it. My God.'

Jasmine shakes her head. She waits for Nisha to sit tentatively on the other end of the sofa, scrapes out the last noodles from her bowl, and they sit in silence for a few minutes watching the television. Finally she leans over and points at the plastic bag. 'What chocolate did you get me, anyway?'

'Green & Black's. The bitter one.'

'*Yesss!* You *know* me!' Jasmine's smile is sudden and infectious. 'Oh, for God's sake, relax, woman. If I have to tread on eggshells every time I get a mood on we are *not* going to survive your stay here, you know what I'm saying? Go on, go put the kettle on and we'll have this with a cup of tea.'

In her old life, Nisha would rarely have gone to bed before midnight. Carl would be up late answering work calls and checking screens and he didn't like her to be asleep when he came into the bedroom. But these days Nisha is physically exhausted by ten o'clock. And tonight – with all its heightened emotion – has wiped her out. She climbs wearily into the top bunk, her toes making contact with the cold metal bars at the end, and feels every bone in her body sink gratefully into the embrace of the cheap single mattress.

Below her Grace finishes reading and turns out her bedside light, and she is glad suddenly for the sense of another human body nearby, for the laughter at the end of the evening, for Jasmine's incredulous face and hoots of laughter when she told her about Carl and the shoes. *Oh, my God, my darling, how did you survive this man?* 'I guess it's like the frog in boiling water, right?' Nisha says. 'No marriage starts off bad. I guess by the time you realize how weird it's got you're up to your neck.' Jasmine laughs. Jasmine actually laughs at Carl. She has never seen anyone in her life laugh at Carl, or call him ridiculous. It's as if there is not much she could do that would change this woman's feeling that she, Nisha, is fundamentally okay. Out there in the living room right now Jasmine is doing another hour's ironing. Nisha had offered to help but Jasmine had waved her away. *I'm all right, babe. I just watch my programmes. I'm only going to do a little bit.*

'Nish?'

Nisha is pulled from her thoughts.

'Yes?'

She hears Grace shift in her bed.

'I'm sorry.'

'Sorry for what?'

'For being mean about you being here. My mum told me what happened to you. I didn't know. I don't mind you sharing my room. I'm sorry I didn't make you feel welcome.'

A lump rises to Nisha's throat. 'That's . . . that's nice of you, Grace. Thank you.'

In the silence they can hear the thump and hiss of the iron, the distant burble of the television. Grace's voice breaks into the dark. 'My mum is always letting people stay here. I get a bit funny about it. She's too nice to people. Sometimes they just . . . you know, take the p.'

'I know. I'm not one of those people, Grace.'

'That's what my mum says.'

Nisha stares into the dark. She wonders uncomfortably if she actually is one of those people.

'What's your son like?'

'Ray? He's great. Kind. Smart. Funny.'

'How old is he?'

'Um . . . he's sixteen.'

'Where does he live?'

'Well, he's at a – a boarding school. In America.'

'America?' Grace's voice is incredulous. 'You're not even in the same country?'

'Not at the moment, no.'

'Don't you miss him?'

And there it is, that lump again. Nisha feels her eyes prickle with tears and is grateful for the dark, where nobody can see them.

'Very much.'

'Then why do you leave him in a different country from you?'

Nisha hesitates. 'Well . . . Ray had some issues a while back. And his dad . . . well, we didn't think it was a good idea for him to be moving around with us all the time. Ray's dad's work meant that we have . . . we had to travel a lot. We thought he would be more stable, and happier, if he was in a boarding school.' She adds: 'It's a very nice boarding school. I mean he's well looked after. It has a lot of very nice facilities.'

There is a long silence.

'It has a swimming-pool. And the food is really good . . . It has its own dance studio. And he has a very nice room – a big room – with his own television and kitchenette . . .'

Another silence.

'Is he happier, though?'

Nisha stares at the ceiling. In the living room Jasmine starts to hum. In the kitchen the washing-machine moves on to its relentless spin cycle.

'Uh.' She wipes at her eye and swallows. 'That's . . . well . . . you know, I don't think we ever actually asked him that question.'

20

Cat sits in Colleen's bedroom and picks flakes of dark green glittery nail polish off her thumbnail while Colleen tongs her hair. Downstairs Colleen's mum is halfway through her fitness video and they can hear intermittent rhythmic thumps, punctuated by swearing.

'But are you sure it was her? It doesn't sound like your mum.' Colleen winds another long ribbon of hair around the tongs, staring at her reflection in the mirror.

'It was her coat. The one with the furry hood. I saw that and then I looked properly and it was definitely her. Hugging this guy. And why would she be outside a boxing club? Unless it was to meet someone?'

'But are you sure it's an affair, though?'

'Well, put it this way. She was holding this guy really tightly and he had his face sort of buried in her shoulder.'

She can still feel the lurch in her stomach as she rode past on the top deck of the bus, the way she had done a double-take and stood abruptly in her seat to try to see more, even as the woman beside her looked up at her like she was a crazy person.

'My mum hasn't had her hair done since July and I could see her roots. And her handbag. And the worst thing was . . . she was wearing like these high-heeled shoes. Like . . . tarty shoes.'

'Tarty shoes,' Colleen repeats. She releases a long strand of hair, which bounces gently as it drops from the heated tongs.

'You know. Like the kind of shoes you wear if you're trying to look sexy. Red strappy shoes. At least four-inch heels. My mum would never wear those kind of shoes. Not in a million years. Well, not normally.'

Her mum had kind of eased up on her toes when the man hugged her, like she was trying to lean into him as much as possible, so that the heels lifted off the ground. And he had been beaming at her, the kind of smile you do when you have a secret with someone. The shoes had been vivid against the grey of the gym car park. She hadn't seen what happened next because the bus had speeded up and she had been left, shell-shocked, in her seat, her head buzzing with the awfulness of it.

Her mum. Her arms wrapped around a man who wasn't her dad. Looking like someone she didn't even recognize.

Colleen puts the tongs down and turns from the mirror. 'So what are you going to do? Are you going to say something to her?'

And that's the worst bit of it. She doesn't know. Her mum, kind, constant, maybe a little frazzled, has started turning herself into some kind of sex case and she doesn't know how to explain it to herself, let alone her dad. She's always thought of her as a bit of a wimp, a bit downtrodden. She used to feel frustrated that her mum was the kind of woman who just accepted every bit of crap that was dished out to her. Her dad was no better, really. But now she's spent two nights putting it all together: the late evenings home from work, the way Mum's started wearing makeup every day, the way she smelt of perfume the last time Cat hugged her. Feelings of fury and hatred keep rising up like bile in her throat. She's found herself watching her mother all the time. Was she laughing more at the television? Being sweeter to her dad, like she even still cared about him? Why was she using low-fat milk instead of full cream? Was she trying to lose weight? *How could you be so deceitful? How could you just shag someone else and act at home like nothing was even happening?* She hasn't spoken to her since she saw her, pretty much walking out of any room she walks into, or responding to questions with a curt *yes* or *no.* She could feel her mum's confused gaze burning into her back as she left but she didn't care. Why should she even treat her with civility, given what she had done? Everything is wrong, and unbalanced, like the world she knew has somehow tilted on its axis, and Cat is miserable.

She peels off the last of the nail varnish. Underneath, her thumbnail looks pale, shell-like. Vulnerable.

'I don't know. I guess I should tell my dad but he's so depressed. I don't know if it will just make him worse.'

'I would,' says Colleen. 'I mean if it was me I'd want to know.' She turns back to the mirror and picks up the tongs again. 'Jesus. Why are adults so complicated? You'd think you'd have sorted it all out by the time you were in your *forties.*'

Phil sits in the chair and sips from the glass of water that Dr Kovitz always leaves on the side table. For the last three sessions he hasn't touched it but now he finds it's a useful way to gather his thoughts after a question he is not entirely sure how to answer.

'I mean there's definitely something going on with her. She's . . . never home. And a couple of nights this week she's come back late and kind of . . . glowing.'

'Glowing?'

'Like she's . . . really happy. From within.' It hurts him even to say the words out loud.

'Have you asked her where she's been?'

Phil takes a sip of water. 'Um . . . no.'

'Why not? . . . You don't want to know the answer?'

He shakes his head. Not quite a no, more 'I'm not sure'. There is a long silence, in which Phil stares at the carpet, and then Dr Kovitz says, 'I'm struck by your perceived lack of agency, Phil. It's like you feel there's nothing much you can do. Not just about your wife, but about events in general. Is this something you've felt throughout your life?'

Phil thinks. He can remember feeling quite different from this, full of plans, of dynamism. He remembers buying the camper-van, the way he had pictured their future together.

'No.'

'Why do you think you're feeling like this just now?'

Phil takes another sip of water. He cannot think of what else to say so he decides to say nothing. He says nothing for some time.

'I'd like to go back to your father's illness, if I may, Phil. That seems to have had a profound effect on you.'

'I don't really want to talk about that.'

'Well . . . I could just ask you a few general questions then. About him. Was your relationship with him a good one?'

'Of course!' Phil hears his voice, too loud, too emphatic. He knows Dr Kovitz will hear it too. He misses nothing.

'Of course. Did you spend much time together when you were a child?'

'When he was off work, yes. But he worked a lot. He was always working. But, you know, he was a good dad.'

'So he had a strong work ethic.'

'Yes. He used to drum it into us: that we should put everything into our work.'

'And you did?'

'I did. I mean, I was a bit different from him as I think I was more focused on family. Different generations. Men were different then, right? Plus . . . it took me and Sam a while to

206

have Cat, so I felt differently. She had . . . miscarriages, you know. It made her feel . . .'

Dr Kovitz waits.

'Well. She used to say she felt like a failure. I never thought she was. It was just horrible for her. You feel so helpless, you know? She would go through these pregnancies and then just when we'd start to feel like this one was going to stick . . . she'd lose it.'

'And how many times did that happen?'

'Four,' says Phil. 'Four times. The last one at five months.'

'I'm sorry,' says Dr Kovitz. 'That must have been very hard.'

'Well. Hardest on Sam, obviously. She was the one carrying them.'

'Hard on you too, though.'

'You just don't know what to say to them, you know? She'd be crying in the bathroom and she was so sad and after a while you don't know what to do.'

'What did you do?'

'I just told her it would be okay. That we would get there.'

'And you did.'

'We did,' says Phil, smiling suddenly. 'Sam had this procedure. This stitch thing. And then, a few months later, she got pregnant with Cat. And when she was born, she was the most beautiful thing I'd ever seen . . .'

It had been the best few months of his life. All his workmates would moan about sleepless nights, about being ignored by their wives for the baby, or the state of the house, but Phil was always happy to get up and give Sam a rest in the small hours of the night. He loved holding Cat to him, rocking her, breathing in her baby smell, gazing into her eyes. She was so precious, so vulnerable. He felt as if, for the first time in his life, he had achieved something miraculous, something so far beyond his expectations for himself that his eyes would fill with tears when he so much as thought of her. *His child. Their baby.* They didn't try for any more children. They decided to leave it for Nature to decide, and when nothing happened, they decided they were lucky to have their beautiful girl, and that it would be churlish, given what they'd been through, to expect more. Or maybe if they hadn't, they had each decided to keep those thoughts to themselves.

'So . . . that's a lovely thing, Phil. It was understandable that you were a little more focused on your family than your father had been. You had gone through so much to have one.'

'Yes, yes,' says Phil, nodding.

'Family is clearly very important to you. And crucial to your sense of well-being. So if you feel like you've lost one key member, and your mother has changed her role in the family to being someone unexpectedly rather independent, and your wife is no longer seeming to get her happiness from being with you, that's all going to feel quite . . . destabilizing? Would that be a fair summation?'

It is strange hearing it spelled out like that. 'Well. Yeah. I guess.'

'But I'd still like to understand what it is about your father you find so difficult to discuss.'

'He died, didn't he? He died while I was there. Isn't that difficult enough?'

'It can be. But some people consider it a privilege to be at their bedside, to help a person they love enter . . . the next realm.'

Phil feels the familiar knot in his stomach. He can't speak. He wants to leave. He glances around him, wondering if he might just get up and go.

'Phil?'

'It wasn't . . . it wasn't like that for me.'

'Perhaps if you were very reliant on your father's good opinion it felt like there was nothing to aim for when he was gone.'

'No . . . no, it's not that.'

'But he loved you. You've told me in other sessions that he and your mother were very close, and as the only son you were the focus of a lot of attention. That much undiluted attention can be both a good and a bad thing.'

Phil puts his head into his hands. He stays there for a long time, so long that, briefly, he forgets Dr Kovitz is in the room. When he finally speaks, his voice is small, almost unrecognizable to himself.

'He wanted me to end it.'

'What?'

'He wanted me to kill him. To end it. Near the end, day after day, he would lie there in his bed gasping for breath but as soon as my mother left the room he would grab my wrist and tell me to put a pillow over his head. He was in too much pain. He couldn't stand it. He hated being weak in front of my mother, hated her seeing him like that. He didn't want to be there.'

Dr Kovitz is watching him. The intent way he is gazing reminds Phil suddenly of his father's unflinching gaze, the weight of his bony hand on Phil's wrist.

Do IT.

DO IT, PHIL.

'And what happened, Phil?'

'It was . . . awful. I used to dread going. Really dread it. Once I was actually sick before I went in.'

The smell of that little room, disinfectant and something sweet and rotting, the imminence of decay, the hours of stasis with no sound bar his father's rasping breaths, the quiet shuffle of hospital staff's shoes outside the door. 'I would get

Mum to take a break, to go downstairs and get a cup of tea. She was there all the time, you see. She wore herself out.'

'So your mother would leave you in the room alone?'

Phil nods. Wipes at his face. 'Sometimes tears would come from his eyes. And that made him angry. Really angry. I don't think I ever saw him cry in his whole life. He was a strong man, you see. Head of the family. A rock. He didn't want to be . . . weak.'

'How many times did he ask you to do . . . end it?'

'By the last days, every time I turned up. So maybe every day for three weeks? And I lost my job – they said it was "restructuring" but I know it was because I had to keep taking time off. I didn't feel I could leave my mum to deal with it alone.'

Another long silence. Outside a car revs noisily and repeatedly as if someone is no longer convinced by the engine.

'Phil . . . did your father die while you were alone with him?'

Phil nods slowly, not looking at Dr Kovitz.

Dr Kovitz waits before he speaks. When he does, his voice is gentle. 'Phil, if you're going to tell me you helped your father along that pathway I can tell you now I am not obliged legally to report that as a crime, as long as you don't feel you're a threat to others. That's not something you need to be concerned about.'

Phil says nothing.

'Is this . . . is this what has been hanging over you?' Dr Kovitz puts his notepad down. 'I am bound by confidentiality, Phil. You are free to tell me everything. If this is what you're telling me, you have been placed under a huge burden and it may help you to let it out.'

'No.'

Phil looks up. When the words come now, they tumble out of him, unstoppable.

'Mum went for a cup of tea. It was a quarter past five. He told me . . . he told me again to do it. And again. And I – I couldn't. I started to cry. I was so worn down by then, you see. Every day turning up and knowing what was going to happen. The way he would look at me. The sound of him, the way his face was . . . I cried. And then he told me I was useless. He told me I was a worthless piece of shit because I wouldn't do it. I couldn't do it. I know it would have been easier for him if I did but I couldn't. I couldn't kill someone. I'm too weak. He was dying and he was telling me all the ways in which I had disappointed him. That he had always known I was no good. His voice was . . . raspy and so . . . angry. And his hand was gripping my wrist and it was so strong in spite of everything, like I couldn't move. I couldn't move. And he was staring at me with his eyes wide open and just . . . just hatred in them telling me I was useless and that he despised me and I was a stupid, weak little boy and that he had never loved me. I was too weak. Too weak.' Phil is sobbing now. 'And then, suddenly, the machines went and there was all this noise and the nurses came in and he was gone. He was gone.'

Phil doesn't know how long he cries for. He is not sure he has ever cried like this, huge howls erupting out of him, shaking his whole body, his palms wet with his tears. After a couple of minutes he feels Dr Kovitz's hand on his back, becomes aware that the box of tissues is being held in front of him and he wipes and wipes at his face, apologizing because every tissue is immediately damp and discarded and he needs another.

Finally, it subsides, a storm passing. And Phil sits in stunned, exhausted silence, his breath shuddering unevenly in his chest. Dr Kovitz waits, then stands and slowly makes his way back to his seat on the other side of the room.

'Phil,' he says finally. 'I'm going to tell you something. I don't know whether your father meant any of the things he said in his last moments, or whether they were just the flailings of a very ill and frustrated man. But I would like you to consider this. I don't know many people who could have coped with what you went through. Strength – real strength – is not doing what someone asks you, necessarily. Strength is turning up every day to a situation that is intolerable, unbearable even, just to support the people you love. Strength is being in that terrible room hour after hour even though every cell in your body is telling you it's too much for you to cope with.'

Phil is crying hard again now, but over the sound of his own gasping breaths he can just make out the last thing Dr Kovitz says.

'By that measure, Phil, you have done something very brave indeed.'

Something odd has happened to Nisha. She keeps thinking about Aleks. She has become hyper-aware of his presence whenever she goes to get lunch, feels his casual glances like something burning in her back. At night she finds herself thinking about the place where his neck meets his shoulders, the way his eyes narrow when he considers something she's said, as if everything should be given serious weight. He is the most level person she has ever met: no abrupt tantrums or mood switches, like Carl, no bursts of laughter or fits of anger. He smiles the same way when he sees her, hands her food she hasn't known she wanted to eat, lets her go again with a small wave or nod. He is always pleasant, and nice to her, and completely unreadable. It is, frankly, infuriating.

During her lunch break she has started to ask him questions about himself, perching on the surface near him as he works or sharing cigarettes with him out in the alley. He comes from Poland but considers England his home, having been here sixteen years. He is separated, on good terms with his ex, he has always been a chef and, no, never wanted to be anything else. He thinks the management of the hotel is not so great, but he has known worse and he is comfortable here. It is good to work somewhere where you are valued. He would like to own a restaurant one day but is not sure how he would raise the capital. He likes London, owns his small apartment, thanks to his late father, and on 31 December he is going to give up smoking. He says it like it is something he can just decide upon, and Nisha has no doubt it will happen. He has a daughter, eleven, who stays with him when he is off work. His face softens when he talks about her, and his eyes grow distant, as if there is a well of something Nisha has not yet been allowed to see. Everyone likes him in the kitchen, but he doesn't make jokes or hang out in the locker room during his downtime, whingeing about double shifts, or Michel's latest outbursts, like the others. He keeps to himself, apparently content to do his job and then retreat to wherever he goes afterwards. He reads cookery books incessantly. He rarely looks at his phone, and has no apparent interest in sport, or going out drinking. He doesn't try to impress her, or calm her down, or flirt, or ask her questions. She cannot work him out.

'I left your duck on the bus,' she says one day, almost to provoke him.

'Then I will get you another,' he says.

'You never ask me anything about myself,' she says, when he sits opposite her as she eats a sandwich. As they spill from her mouth, the words sound almost like a complaint, which is irritating. He pauses before he answers.

'I think you will probably tell me what you want me to know.'

'How come you never hit on me?' she says, when they walk out one evening at the end of her shift. He has stayed late to deep-clean his station and it is dark, the traffic roaring past them along the Embankment.

'Do you want me to hit on you?' he says, tilting his head towards her.

'No.'

'Then there you go.'

'What does that mean?' She stops, frowning at him.

'It means if you are a man with any sense you can read whether a woman wants you to come on to her.'

'Most men come on to me anyway.'

'I am not surprised. You are very beautiful.'

She gives him a hard look. 'Are you coming on to me now?'

'No. I'm stating a fact.'

He is extremely annoying. And her inability to read him, like she can read almost any man on the planet, makes her feel unbalanced, and cross around him, so that she adopts a weird, challenging tone when she talks to him or, occasionally, avoids him altogether.

And here is the thing: Nisha misses sex. She doesn't miss Carl, exactly. There were times when she would groan inwardly when she caught that look in his eye. But she feels starved of physical contact. She misses being held, touched, desired. She misses the feeling of power she experienced when a man was physically affected by her. She cannot even sort herself out, given that she sleeps on a bunk bed with a fourteen-year-old beneath her.

'You like him,' says Jasmine, who catches her watching him as they eat their sandwiches.

'I do not.'

Jasmine raises an eyebrow. 'Okay.'

'He's a short-order chef with no money and no prospects. Why would I like him?'

Jasmine finishes her mouthful, and dabs at her lips with a

handkerchief before she speaks. 'Girl, if I were you I'd climb that like a tree.'

For almost five months Cat has played a game with herself in the last few steps of her walk home. As she closes the gate behind her and walks up the little path to her front door, she makes a bet with herself as to what position her father will be in when she gets home. Mostly it's lying on the sofa, his head nearest the side table. Occasionally he will be the other way around with his feet nearest the table and his head resting on two sofa cushions. On the few occasions she has guessed right she has awarded herself 'Sloth Bingo'. Now she walks past the rotting camper-van with its massive hippie sunflower, which is, frankly, an embarrassment as well as an ecological disaster, puts her key in the door, and decides it will be a standard day. Her father will have his head by the side table. It's what the bookies call a sure thing. She opens the door, closes it behind her and looks through the living-room door. But the television is off and he is not there.

Cat hangs her coat on the peg and walks through to the kitchen. It's seven fifteen but yet again her mother is not home from work. Cat feels a clench of dismay when she thinks of what life was like here even eighteen months ago: the way she could arrive home and know with some certainty that her mum would be cooking something, Dad leaning against a worktop, chatting away, the radio burbling in the corner. She hadn't understood the deep sense of security that gave her. And now there is no one, just this heavy silence.

She eats a couple of rice cakes from the cupboard (there is barely any food just now) then heads upstairs to her bedroom. And it is then that she sees him: her dad, just lying on the bed, staring at the wall.

She pauses by the open bedroom door.

'. . . Dad?'

He turns his head towards her. He looks exhausted. He always looks exhausted, these days.

'Oh, hi, love.' He raises a small smile.

'What are you doing?'

'I just came up for a rest. Bit . . . tired today.'

'Where's Mum?'

He blinks, as if it has only just occurred to him. 'I don't know. Probably at work?'

'Have you called her?'

'Uh . . . not today. Not now.'

'But it's seven fifteen.' Cat stares at him. At his passivity, his refusal to act even as everything around him is falling apart. And suddenly she cannot bear it any more. 'Jesus, Dad. Wake up!'

He looks startled, and it's weirdly gratifying.

'Where do you think Mum is?'

He shakes his head. 'I – I don't know.'

'She's with a *man*. And you – you're just sitting here like a fucking . . . potato. Just letting her walk away. What do you think is going to happen, Dad? That if you just sit quietly everything will settle back into place? You have to *do* something. You have to get up and see what's going on under your nose!'

'A man?'

'I saw her.' Cat feels tears spring to her eyes now, feels the blood flush to her face, but she doesn't care. 'I saw her from the bus. Hugging him. And every day she puts on makeup and comes home late and you act like nothing is even happening.'

He looks shattered. She doesn't care. She wants him to be shocked. She wants to shake him.

'That's . . . that's not –'

She flings open their wardrobe and begins rifling through the bottom until she comes up with the bag. 'See this?'

216

'A bag?' He looks bewildered.

She unzips it. And there they are, just where she found them two days ago. A stark reminder of everything that is wrong.

She holds up one of the shoes. 'These are Mum's. Your *wife's*. This is what she's wearing to go and meet her lover. And if you took the slightest bit of notice of anything rather than just being stuck in your – your *pit*, then you'd realize you have to do something!'

'Those belong to your mum?' He is staring at the shoes, disbelieving.

'Oh, my God. Do I have to spell it out? Ugh. You guys are meant to be the adults here! And I'm having to literally point out what's wrong with your marriage! Jesus! Dad! Wake up! Wake the fuck up! I hate it here! I hate it!'

Cat cannot bear to look at him any longer. She bursts into tears, hurls the shoe across the room and strides out, slamming the door behind her.

Sam lets herself in through the front door, still warm from the brisk walk home. She seems to walk faster everywhere at the moment, arriving at her destination glowing with effort, as if she is suddenly more purposeful.

Tonight the gym had been amazing. Simon had been in a foul mood all day, picking at her and sending dismissive glances her way whenever he was in sight, and she had felt so anxious and ground down by it that she had nearly decided not to go. But Joel, almost as if he had known, had sent her a text which said: These are the nights you *have* to go. So they had walked there together at six and now, almost two hours later, she feels as if she could conquer the world. The trainer, Sid, had taught her the different ways she could hit someone, how she should tighten her core and jab and swing, the way she could make an impact rather than feebly throwing a punch, limp-wristed and ineffective. By the end he was yelling, *Yes, girl! Yes!* And even as every muscle in her body screamed, she felt her gloves connecting with his pads – *one two, one two* – she was in charge, everything she felt pouring out through the red gloves, her knuckles bruised pleasurably at the end like she was someone much tougher than she was.

'You're nailing it!' Joel had said, as they met outside after the first time she'd gone. She couldn't stop grinning. She was wearing the shoes, because they seemed to just add to that feeling, even though she knew she would change back into her trainers once Joel was out of sight. 'I feel . . . amazing,' she said, and he hugged her tightly and told her she was unstoppable.

She has been four times now, and each time she goes, even though her muscles scream with protest at the unexpected effort, she feels like some piece of her is coming back together. She finds she doesn't mind that it's unglamorous, that she ends each session with sweat dripping into her eyes, her hair scraped back in a greasy ponytail, flushed and makeup free. She watches the other women, from the tiny, sinewy Fatima to Annette, whose backside is barely contained by her enormous tracksuit bottoms, and they are uninterested in how she looks, where she goes on holiday, whether her body fits some prescribed ratio of muscle to body fat. They exchange wry smiles during the punishing warm-up, grin at each other's hooks and jabs, yell encouragement when she lands a good one. Sid treats everyone as if they were a serious athlete, demanding results, issuing joke threats if they don't push themselves hard enough. And through it all, in the corner, if she looks over, she will see Joel, his solid arms a blur as he rains blows on the punchbag, grinning at her as he wipes sweat from his brow with a forearm.

And something is changing. Four sessions in she finds she already stands a little taller at work, walks as if her core is somehow stronger. When Simon starts going on at her about some mistake she has apparently made, she nods and accepts it, but inside she imagines raining a series of lead hooks and uppercuts onto his chin – *three four five six!* – and she is not entirely sure, but she likes to think her failure to crumble makes him irritable and slightly unbalanced.

'Hello?' She opens the front door and takes off her coat. The television is off and she wonders briefly if Phil is even there, then tells herself that of course he is. Where else would he be, these days? She feels a faint drag of resignation and tells herself to stop, to hold on to the high she retains inside her for a few hours after each session. *One two three four. Stay strong. Root yourself through your feet.*

Phil and Cat are in the kitchen. They are sitting at the table, eating a lasagne in silence, and she stops in the doorway.

'Hi!' she says, surprised. They almost never cook without her. 'You've started without me!'

'We didn't know what time you'd be home,' says Cat, without looking up.

'Oh. Sorry. I – I meant to ring but I got caught up. Who bought the lasagne?'

'Me,' says Cat, cutting a small piece and putting it into her mouth.

It takes her a moment to register an odd atmosphere. Phil has not looked up from his food. He is forking it in joylessly, as if he merely needs to add fuel to his body.

'That's kind of you, love. Thank you.' She puts her bag on the worktop. 'Is there a plate for me?'

'In the cupboard,' says Cat, blankly, and Sam gives her a sharp look, but she can detect nothing.

She takes a plate and sits down, helping herself to a slice of the lasagne. She is starving. It makes her happy, thinking of all the calories she must be burning. She grabs some of the vegetables from the serving dish and starts to eat. Phil does not look at her. He just keeps slowly forking food into his mouth. Sam looks around the table.

'So how is everyone? Good day?'

'Fine,' says Cat.

'What did you do?'

'Not much.'

'Phil?' says Sam.

'Fine.'

Sam takes a mouthful. It is delicious. She will focus on this, she decides, rather than the strange atmosphere.

'Well, that's good.' She waits, but nobody says anything. 'This is delicious.'

'It's just Tesco's,' says Cat, and stands abruptly. She takes her empty plate to the dishwasher and slides it in before heading to the door. 'I'm going to Colleen's. I won't be late.'

Sam makes to speak, but her daughter is already gone.

She turns to Phil. 'What's going on with Cat?'

Phil continues chewing.

'She's been odd, the last few days. Don't you think?'

Phil shakes his head, chewing as if he cannot speak.

He probably hasn't even noticed, she thinks. And suppresses a sigh. 'I had some good news today,' she says gamely. 'Well, I don't know if it's actual good news, but Miriam Price, the woman I got a big contract from, has asked to meet me for lunch again later this week. She's got no reason to meet me, given we finished the job, and she was happy. She said there's something she wants to discuss. I mean it might be nothing, right? She might just want advice on something. But it's nice, because she's . . . one of those really impressive people, you know? It just feels good to have someone like that want to take you to lunch.'

Phil nods, putting another forkful into his mouth.

'There's a bit of me that wonders if . . . Well, I know Harlon and Lewis are looking for more account managers. So I was thinking maybe I should bite the bullet and ask her if there are any positions available. It would get me out of Simon's way, you know?'

'Yup,' he says.

'It might be more money,' she says. She hasn't told him about the threat to her job yet. It's another conversation she feels he probably isn't up to.

He doesn't say anything.

'I mean I really love the people I work with.' She feels a slight flush rise to her cheeks as she says this, and hopes it's not as apparent as it feels. 'But if Simon's not going anywhere then maybe I should. It's worth a try anyway, right?'

He looks at her for a moment. His face is blank, unreadable. And then he turns back to his plate.

'Phil? . . . Is everything okay?' she says, finally.

'Fine.' He finishes his meal, and as Sam sits, he raises himself heavily from the table, takes his plate to the dishwasher and heads into the living room. Sam is left eating alone at the table.

For some time now, during the hours that Sam has assumed he was sleeping, Phil has been awake, his eyes closed, wrestling with his father through the small hours, feeling his bony hand gripping his wrist, unable to turn from the intensity and fury of his stare. Sometimes he feels paralysed, lost in the endless repetitive loop of his thoughts: *You are a weak, useless man. Do it! DO IT!* Now, for the first night in months, his father has left him alone, but this has brought no relief. Instead he has been haunted by thoughts of the woman lying beside him, her hands on another man's body, her face lit up by his presence. How long has this been going on? What lies has she told in order to sneak away? In the past couple of weeks she has often returned home flushed and slightly breathless and the thought of what she has been doing with this unknown lover causes a pain in his stomach that pulls his knees to his chest. His Sam. The woman he has laughed with, lain with for more than two decades, who now cares so little for him that he might as well be a piece of discarded furniture. She feels suddenly like someone he has never known. And how could he not have noticed what was happening? Some part of him had known something was different, something off in the air between them. But it had felt like just too much to confront, and he had turned his head away until the fury of his daughter had forced him to see it.

The one thing Phil does not ask himself is why. Because it is obvious why. What can he offer Sam these days? He has been a hollow thing for months, unable to function. Unable to offer her anything. Useless. He should have known she would turn to someone else eventually.

These thoughts whirl and chase each other all night, so that by dawn he is gritty-eyed and overwhelmed. He feels nauseous, restless and exhausted at the same time. He hears her get up, the sound of her showering and getting dressed around him – is she thinking about what to wear for *him*? Some special lingerie, or an outfit this man has told her he particularly likes? – then she's heading lightly downstairs. She no longer reaches across the bed to kiss him before she leaves. He used to think this was her not wanting to disturb him but now he thinks it is probably just that she no longer wants anything to do with him at all. She probably despises him. He hears the front door close and her car starting, and he presses the balls of his hands into his eyes, wanting it all to stop. Wanting to be lifted out of this body, this life, and put somewhere that he doesn't have to deal with any of it.

He has lain there for some unknown length of time – half an hour? Two hours? His hands, his arms, feel odd, his body curiously disconnected from his mind. When he can bear this sensation no longer he gets up and out of bed and walks around the room. He gazes out of the bedroom window at the street, which looks the same but is clearly altered for ever. Then he turns to the wardrobe, opens it, and stares down at the black kitbag his daughter had brandished at him the previous day. He scrutinizes it, his breath coming hard in his chest, as if the thing sitting there is radioactive. And then, slowly, he crouches down and unzips it. There they are, peeping out from the opened zip, the sexy red high-heeled shoes. It's like they belong to someone he doesn't know. He picks one up, staring at it, and then, compelled by some unknown impulse, he presses it to his nose, and as he holds it, he feels his face twisting into a grimace, and then a howl, a silent howl, is emerging from him. She wears these shoes for this man. These shoes are a shared secret between his wife and her lover. He probably fucks her in them. The word hammers its way into his head, even though this is a word he almost never uses out loud. His hands have begun to shake and he stuffs the shoe back into the bag. Phil paces backwards and forwards, letting out low moans of distress. Then he sits again, his head in his hands. Finally he stands up, walks over to the bag, grabs the shoes and stuffs them into the empty plastic bag that sits in the bottom of his wardrobe. He has no idea why the bag is there. It has just been there for no reason for as long as he can remember, like so much in this house. He holds it in front of him, his face contorted, as he walks briskly down the stairs, as someone would if they were disposing of a full nappy or a dog turd. Then he stands in the hallway, unsure what to do with it. He just knows those shoes cannot stay in this house. They cannot be here, their presence contaminating everything he has known and loved. Almost without realizing what he is doing, he opens the front door and walks outside, wrenches open the door of the camper-van (they stopped locking it months ago, when Sam started secretly hoping someone would steal it) and climbs inside, breathing in the mouldering smell of neglect and mild, steady decay. He opens one of the laminated cupboards above the little cushioned sofa bench and shoves in the shoes, slamming it shut. And then he sits down on the bench and breathes hard, trying to clear the red mist that has landed in front of his eyes.

Even if he were the kind of man who was comfortable talking about emotional stuff, there is not a friend in the world Phil can discuss this with, or ask advice from. He thinks about Dr Kovitz: what would he say? He probably wouldn't be surprised, given everything Phil has told him. Would he tell Phil to confront his wife? To get angry with her? Would that be more *manly*? Tell her he knows and she needs to make a choice? But Phil is afraid. Not just because if he confronts Sam he will have to decide what he wants, and he doesn't know what this is yet. But, worse, if he confronts her she may simply pack up the bag with the shoes and everything else and move in with this man, whoever he is.

Phil sits, frozen, staring at his intermittently trembling hands, until he realizes he has grown chilled in his pyjamas and T-shirt. He stands rubbing at his arms and notices the pile of old magazines that someone must have moved in here from the house while waiting for recycling day. Perhaps the bins were full. He can't remember. He stares at the pile, and then, finally, takes a couple of steps across the floor and picks up the top half of it. He adjusts the weight of the magazines against his chest, then pushes open the door with his shoulder and steps out carefully, down the steps, and walks along the short path to the recycling bin, where he dumps them. He returns and takes the other half, gazing at the dusty space that is left. Then he peers inside the bin bag that sits behind them, in which they had left a load of junk items from the old shed at his father's, things his mum couldn't bear to get rid of but nobody actually wanted: blunted tools, old car manuals, light bulbs and keys for long-dead fixings. He had taken the bag to save her feelings. But what for? What was he ever going to do with this junk? He hauls out the bin bag and places it beside the black refuse bin. And then he climbs back into the van and continues going through the contents unthinkingly, on some unknown impulse, methodically working his way through the neglected interior, taking out everything that had been stuffed in there as a temporary measure and carrying it all outside, stacking it in or beside the bins. By the time he has cleared the inside, two hours later, he is sweating, his pyjama bottoms smeared with dust and dirt.

His jaw set, his mouth pressed into a thin line, Phil heads back into the house and goes upstairs, where he casts his gaze around until he sees his hooded sweatshirt, under a pile of his other clothes. He hauls it over his head, then down over his T-shirt, pulls on a pair of socks and boots, and heads back out again. He will be there, wrestling with the innards of the engine, when Sam comes home, and he will not come into the house again until she is sleeping.

21

Nisha has never suffered serious physical violence, but every time she spies Charlotte around the hotel wearing an item of her clothing she feels a sensation that she imagines must be just like being stabbed. Charlotte has worn the Chloé shearling coat in public twice, once the first time in that corridor and again the following Saturday, sashaying through the foyer as if it were hers. Two days later, she wore Nisha's silver Alexander McQueen dress, with the slash at the side, to an evening event – she and Jasmine had spotted her just as they were finishing their shift, heading out from the side-street as she climbed into the waiting car and it was all Nisha could do not to cry out in pain.

But clearly this was not insult enough. On Tuesday lunch-time, as Nisha heads wearily to the sandwich platter, she glances through the open kitchen doors and sees Charlotte about to take a seat in the restaurant. And she is wearing Nisha's pristine white Yves Saint Laurent suit.

'No!' she says, and stops in her tracks, so that a waiter almost collides with her and curses.

Aleks appears at her shoulder. The lunch sitting is nearly over and he is wiping his hands on a cloth. He follows her gaze. 'It is the mistress?'

'She's going to spill something on it.' Nisha is finding it hard to breathe. 'I would never, ever eat in that suit.'

Aleks stares through the door for a moment and sighs. She feels his hand on her shoulder, gently steering her away.

'No no no,' she says, pushing it off. 'You don't understand. You don't *eat* in that suit. It would be like – like eating spaghetti next to the *Mona Lisa*. It's white. Yves. Saint. Laurent. 1971. It's probably the only one left of its kind in the world. I got it from a collector who got it from an exclusive estate sale in Florida. The woman had kept it in a climate-controlled sealed closet and it still had the store tags. The actual *tags*. It had never been worn! You see? That suit is vintage and it is pristine. Completely pristine. She shouldn't be touching it, for God's sake. Not even touching it. But she can't – she can't *eat* in it.' Her voice is anguished. As the doors close, she glimpses Carl sitting down heavily at the table opposite Charlotte, his phone pressed to his ear.

'No,' she says. 'I can't let this happen. I can't – '

'The bodyguard will be nearby,' Aleks murmurs into her ear. 'You cannot go near her. You know this.' She turns and looks at him. His expression is sympathetic, but it says, also, clearly, that it is time for her to walk away.

'How is this fair, Aleks?' she says, as he steers her through to the back of the kitchens. 'How? How can they even get away with this?'

Afterwards she realizes that Aleks's arm is around her shoulders as he offers her a cigarette and waits until she stops hyperventilating. But before she can consider what she thinks about this, he has told her he will fetch Jasmine, she is not to move from that spot, and leaves.

When Jasmine arrives she folds her into her arms and murmurs: *Oh, baby. Oh, my poor baby.* And Nisha doesn't even mind.

She calls Carl that evening from Jasmine's. She has been a ball of barely suppressed rage all day.

'Carl. I –'

'You got them?'

'Got what?' she says.

'The shoes!' he says impatiently.

'The shoes.' Jasmine had sniffed earlier. 'You know the shoes are just a way for him to give you the run-around, right? He probably knows they're the one thing you can't trade so he's making it look like you're the one not meeting your side of the bargain. What man is so attached to a pair of women's shoes?' Nisha had thought about this and it made sense. There is probably some bizarre legal stipulation that insists both sides should comply with requests or something. She would be able to find out, except she *can't get a damn lawyer with no goddamn money.*

'Stop playing games, Carl,' she says. 'Just give me my clothes and the alimony I'm owed, you absolute stinking piece of crap.'

'Ah. The language of the gutter. I wondered how long it would take for you to revert to type.'

She is briefly silenced. She can see Jasmine watching her from across the room as she irons, her face watchful and concerned. She had told Nisha not to call him, to wait it out, make him sweat a little, but Nisha has spent the evening building a froth of fury and cannot hold back.

'You're the one in the gutter, Carl,' she yells. 'I know you're playing games with this stupid shoe thing to avoid paying me what I'm owed. But this is not going to work. No damn judge in the world is going to let you treat me like this.'

'Have fun finding him, darling,' he says coolly, and laughs. He actually laughs.

'Just give me my fair share! Carl, you cannot *do* this! I'm your *wife!*'

'Give me the shoes and we'll talk.'

'You know the shoes were stolen! My God, you probably

228

stole them yourself just to leave me with nothing! What stupid, childish game is this?'

'You're boring me now,' he says coldly. 'No shoes, no money.'

And he puts the phone down on her. She holds hers in her hand, her mouth open.

Jasmine appears in front of her and silently hands her a cushion.

Nisha looks at it. 'What?' she says. 'What's that for?'

'Scream into it, babes. If you make too much noise I'll have the council complaining again.'

Sometimes she thinks about the person who took her shoes, just like she thinks about the duck Aleks gave her, maybe even now travelling in an endless loop around Battersea and Peckham, still swaddled in its muslin wrappings underneath a seat. Her shoes are probably out there, stuffed into the closet of some over-made-up nightclubber, or perhaps packed in tissue by some resale agency, ready to go to an influencer in Dubai. He will probably love it if she cannot get them back. She hates him so much sometimes that it actually hurts.

'I was kind of joking about you missing your clothes more than your old man,' Jasmine says, as she removes the last of Nisha's hair extensions in front of the television. They had started to fall out, matting into lumps where they were attached to her scalp, and Nisha's head feels oddly light and insubstantial without them. 'But you really do? Don't you? I'm serious. You're not crying and weeping and hating this other woman for stealing your man but, boy, are you mad about those clothes.'

It had startled her at first. She looks at Jasmine, considering this for a moment, and takes a tortilla chip from the bowl, waiting for the time it takes her to chew and swallow it. 'I guess they represent something to me. They're the version of me I fought for.'

'A version of you?'

'You don't know what I came from,' she says.

'What did you come from?'

Nisha stares at the television for a while. Then finally she speaks. 'A little town in the Midwest where we used to get our clothes from the DollarSave. And we were lucky if they were new.'

'The what?'

'It's like a discount store. Like your Primark, or whatever it is. But not as classy.'

Jasmine lets out a bark of laughter. 'You're messing with me.'

Nisha shakes her head. She has never told anyone this story. Not since she got on the Greyhound at the age of nineteen and left Anita behind. 'My mom left when I was two. I grew up with my dad and my grandma and they thought that clothes were vanity and that vanity was the Devil's work. At least, they said that. Now I think it was because they'd rather spend any money we managed to get on cheap bourbon. So I had to beg for anything I needed and anything I got came from the DollarSave where everything smelt cheap, and they always bought me everything two sizes too big so that I would grow into it. The two of them were mean and they were tight. If they didn't have it there they bought me second-, third-hand clothes from Goodwill.'

Jasmine is listening intently.

'The ones near us were so nasty even dirt-poor neighbours were too proud to use them. And everyone at school knew you were in Goodwill clothes. They could spot them a mile away and they'd beat you for it. I hated looking like that. I hated everything I ever wore. I would wear my dad's work shirts when I got tall enough because those upset me less than those shitty cheap girls' clothes. They were at least made to last. Heavy-duty. And if you looked like a boy where I lived bad things were less likely to happen to you.' Nisha lights a cigarette, and even though Jasmine doesn't usually allow her to smoke inside the flat, she sees Nisha's trembling hand and doesn't stop her.

She is staring at Nisha now, her eyes wide. 'So how the hell did you end up married to a millionaire?'

Nisha inhales, lets out a long plume of smoke, and shrugs. 'I did what anyone does. Worked at the local bars until I had some money put by. I looked pretty good. Or I had something that made men tip big, anyhow. Worked out I could use that. Got a Greyhound to the big city, did whatever jobs I could, cleaning, housekeeping, working in bars, hustled a little, became Nisha. I saw the name in a magazine and thought it sounded sophisticated. Worked for a guy who knew someone in a gallery, graduated to a better gallery and over a couple of years I remade myself. Learned how to speak without a twang. Dropped the low-cut tops, and dated guys with shelves full of books instead. Turned myself into someone who couldn't be messed with. I met Carl when he came in to buy a painting – a way overpriced Kandinsky, if you want to know – and I liked his confidence. I liked the way he walked into the place like he already owned it. He was charming. He smelt of money. And security. And I liked the way he looked at me. Like I already belonged in his world.'

'He didn't know your past?'

'Oh, I told him some of it. He didn't believe me at first, and then he thought it was funny. Sometimes I thought he was even a little proud of me for it – Carl loves a fighter – but every now and then, if he was pissed, he would use it against me. Call me white trash, or hillbilly, or put me down. But I honestly used to think he would never mess with me, like he messed with other people, because he knew I had already dealt with a life far harder than anything he presented me with. He knew I wasn't afraid of anything.'

She takes a last drag of the cigarette and stubs it out savagely on the edge of her plate. 'I misjudged that one, obviously.'

'Hang on,' says Jasmine. 'So you *had* cleaned toilets before!'

Nisha looks up. '*That*'s what you took from that story?' She laughs wryly. 'Not since I was twenty-two years old. Anita cleaned toilets. Nisha hadn't so much as touched a brush until I came here.'

'Lord. No wonder you hate that man.'

'More than you can possibly imagine.'

She has a sudden memory of Juliana, the two of them sitting out on the fire escape one hot New York evening, months before she had met Carl, sharing a cigarette and laughing, bitching about their boss, catcalling at the construction workers ending their shift. Juliana's throaty giggle breaking through the suffocating heat as the workers called back up to them, her curly brown hair bouncing on her shoulders as she threw her head back. Juliana would have liked Jasmine, she thinks.

Another memory bubbles up, the last day she saw her. Juliana's chin lifted, the catch in her voice as Nisha stood in Carl's vast, ornate apartment and explained what Carl had told her to do, the problems it would cause her if they stayed close. 'So you're choosing *this*? *This* is what's really important to you? I'm your best friend! Your son's godmother, for Chrissakes!' Juliana had backed away from her, her face contorted. 'Who even *are* you, Nisha? Because I tell you, I liked Anita a whole lot better.'

Jasmine's voice drags her back. 'Nish, I knew you were a

fighter, but now I see it. You'll get your stuff back, and then some. I have no doubt about it. We just have to work it out.'

'We?'

Jasmine's eyes open. 'This Carl is an insult to womankind! You didn't think I was going to leave you to handle this one alone? We are sisters now. You know that. Anyway. I have something to tell you.'

'What?'

'Well,' says Jasmine, and then she smiles, 'I was clearing out Grace's old toys – you know we never have enough room here. And I found her practical-joke kit. She used to love that when she was younger. Fart cushions, the fake chewing gum that snaps on your fingers, you know the thing? Anyhow. It had two old packs of itching powder. So . . .' she steeples her fingers together '. . . for the last two days when I've cleaned the penthouse I've left your Carl a little present in his under-pants.'

Nisha stares.

'Nish, I walked behind him down the corridor this morning. Oh, babe, I nearly wet myself. He was *not happy down there.*' She stands up and mimics walking uncomfortably, her butt cheeks rubbing together. She starts to laugh at the memory, her eyes closed, hands pressed against the sides of her nose. When she gets it under control, she looks back at Nisha. 'I got you, babe. We are in this together.'

Nisha blinks. If she was a different kind of woman maybe that would be the point at which she threw her arms around Jasmine, cried and thanked her and said she loved her and they were BFFs for ever. But Nisha is not built that way. Not any more. She studies Jasmine's face for a moment, and then she nods.

'I'll pay you back,' Nisha says. 'For all of it.'

'I know,' says Jasmine.

'Also: I think it's possible you are a genius.'

'I wondered how long it was going to take you to realize,' Jasmine says, and starts to sing to herself as she leaves the room.

22

That night, when Grace is in the bottom bunk with her noise-cancelling earphones on, Nisha climbs up, lies down (the ceiling is too low for her to sit) and dials Ray's number.

'Mom?'

'Hey, baby.' She prompts him to tell her the day's news.

He isn't sleeping and it makes him feel crazy. The dorm manager he liked, Big Mike, had an argument with the administrator and walked out. Now without him or Sasha he feels like there's nobody here he can talk to. A new girl downstairs throws up secretly after every meal and the staff don't know but the downstairs toilets always smell of vomit and he cannot believe like none of their noses even work. 'Mom? When are you coming?'

Nisha closes her eyes and takes a breath. 'Soon.'

'But when? I don't understand why you're still in England.'

'There's something I have to talk to you about, baby. And I wish I could do it in person but it's kind of difficult right now.'

He is silent then and she winces, filled with fear because of what she is about to unleash on him.

'Um . . . well, Daddy and I . . . we're . . . well, the truth is, we're . . . Well, you know things have been a little tricky between us for a while and –'

'Are you leaving him?'

Nisha swallows. 'Kind of. Well, not exactly. He's – he's decided he will be happier with someone else and I – I've agreed that this is probably the best thing for both of us and, well, we're just trying to work out how to do it in the way that will be easiest for you.'

He is silent again.

She puts a hand to her cheek, lowers her voice. 'I'm so sorry, Ray. I really didn't want you to have to deal with any of this. But it will all be okay. I promise. We'll still be a family, just a different sort of family.'

He still doesn't speak. She can just make out the sound of him breathing, so she knows he's still there.

'Ray? . . . Sweetheart? Are you okay?'

'I don't mind if he goes.'

'. . . You don't?'

A pause. 'It's not like he's wanted to spend any time with me the last few years.'

'Oh, he does. He really does, baby. He's just been very busy.'

'Mom, you and I both know that's a lie. Honestly. My therapist has been talking to me about honesty and seeing things as they are. And if Dad wants to go that's okay with me. His loss.'

There is a pause.

'I actually spoke to him two days ago. I told him I wanted to come home, and he said, if that was the case, I shouldn't have been so stupid and that I was . . . he said I was a liability. That I couldn't be trusted.'

'A "liability"?'

'It's fine. I told him to go fuck himself.'

There is a deadness to his voice that makes her stomach constrict. He has been so brave for years but she knows Carl's rejection is a bruise that won't heal. 'Are you really okay, baby?'

A long silence.

'Ray?'

'I've not been doing so great.'

'How not great?'

He doesn't answer.

'Okay. Give me a one to ten on how sad you feel.' That was what the last psychiatrist advised, for when discussions of feelings were too difficult.

There is a short pause and then he says, 'Like, an eight?'

Her stomach flips.

'I didn't want to tell you because I guessed something was going on with you and Dad and . . . I didn't want to bother you.'

'Ray? Ray. I'm totally fine, I promise you. And I'm going to get you out of that school as soon as I can, okay? We'll get a little place together and it'll be just you and me. Wherever you like.'

'Seriously?'

'If you want to.'

'And I don't have to live here any more?'

'No. I've been putting money aside to get us back together. The problem is, honey, I literally have nowhere for you to stay at the moment. I'm with a friend, and it's pretty cramped so I just have to get the financial thing sorted with Dad and then we'll be together.'

'Please, Mom. Just do it quickly. I hate it here. I hate it. Being in this place makes me feel like there's something wrong with me.'

'There's nothing wrong with you.' Her eyes have filled with tears. 'You are absolutely perfect as you are. You always have been.'

She wipes at her cheek with her palm. 'So you're really not upset about Daddy?'

'Why would I be upset? He's an asshole. He's horrible to you and he acts like I don't even exist. You're always on your tippy-toes around him, like he's God or something. If he goes and does that to someone else then, frankly, it's all gravy. He can just leave us alone.'

The pain of hearing her relationship described so brutally makes her feel ill. 'Oh, God, Ray. I'm so sorry you didn't have a better dad.'

'I don't care.' Ray sniffs. 'Like I said. His loss . . . So when are you coming?'

There's the problem. She tells him she's stuck here in England while they sort a financial issue. She figures there's only so much his mind can cope with at once. 'I'm fixing it, but you're just going to have to bear with me. You know he can be a little tricky.'

'What's the financial issue?' Ray's therapist has clearly been working hard.

'Uh . . . uh . . . Well, he . . . wants me to give him something before he will give me the settlement. It's just some kind of game he's playing. I'm working on it.'

'What? What does he want?'

'It's a thing I don't currently have in my possession right now.'

'Mom.'

'It's a pair of shoes.'

'A pair of *shoes?*'

'I know.'

'Why does he want your shoes?'

'Well, my friend Jasmine thinks it's sort of a game. Because he knows they were stolen at the gym. He's just playing for time while he juggles his money or something.'

'Which shoes?'

Typical Ray.

'The handmade Christian Louboutins. The red crocodile-skin ones.'

She waits for his cry of protest. But Ray is silent.

'I will work it out, baby. I promise. I'll get some lookalikes made, if I have to. He's just being a bit of a pain about it all.'

'But *they*'re the lookalikes.'

'What?'

'Those shoes. If they're the ones I'm thinking of . . . I don't think they're real Louboutins.'

'He had them made specially for me, darling. Of course they're real.'

'Back when I was home last March I remember I was in the drawing room next to his study and he was on a call. I heard him saying, "Christian won't do it. You're going to have to get something made up." And then a couple weeks later he gave you the shoes and I remember it because he hadn't bought you anything for ages and I had a look at them afterwards and they did look exactly the same but I just thought there was something off. The signature on the sole wasn't quite right. And I didn't think that was the exact shade of Louboutin red on the sole. It was a little . . . *brash*.'

'What? That's crazy. But why would Daddy buy me fake shoes?'

'I don't know. I remember thinking it was weird. But you really loved them and he liked you wearing them all the time and I didn't want to rain on your parade so I just put it to the back of my mind.'

Suddenly she remembers something odd about when Carl had given her the shoes. They weren't in a box, lined with tissue paper. They weren't in the soft fabric bag that her other Louboutins were. They came in a black silk bag – unmarked. She had assumed it was because they had been made for her.

'None of this makes sense, sweetheart. Why would your father buy me fake Louboutins? He could buy a whole damn store of them, if he wanted to. And why would he want them back?'

'I don't know, Mom. But can you just figure it out and come get me?' His voice grows quieter. 'Please. I really miss you.'

'I miss you too, my darling. I will get this sorted. I promise. Please . . . just look after yourself. I love you so much.'

'Mom . . .'

'Yes?'

A pause.

'Are *you* okay?'

She lets out a muffled sob, clamps her hand over her mouth. She waits a few moments until she's sure her voice is steady. 'Baby, I'm absolutely fine.'

The DollarSave. Half the store devoted to farm feed and maintenance equipment, the aisles lined with hoses, strip lights, rubber matting. The other half stocked with essentials: bulk packets of soup and rice, cartons of sterilized milk, kitchen paper stacked as high as a house. It smelt of petrochemicals and despair. She had been seven years old. It was the first time her dad had made her do it. She walked in wearing the sage green aged-nine-to-eleven padded coat that swamped her, and out again in that same coat but with several sweaters and a bottle of Jim Beam underneath it. Nobody ever suspected a cute kid to be ferrying stolen goods. It was the only time her dad had ever told her she was good at anything.

They had switched their trips between the three Dollar-Saves in the county, once, twice a week for each, and the only time she had been caught – accidentally dropping her haul in the cereals aisle – she had burst into tears and said she had just wanted to get her daddy a surprise birthday present and the security guard had laughed at the little girl and said: *He likes bourbon, huh?* And sent her on her way with a packet of Twinkies and told her to make sure she didn't take anything without passing by the checkout lady in future. Her dad, waiting outside in the truck, had laughed. Especially when she pulled out the other, smaller bottle of bourbon she had tucked into the back of her waistband. 'You see, Anita?' he had said, pulling off the top and taking a swig. 'People only see what they think they see. You keep looking cute enough, people ain't never going to assume you'll do anything bad.'

Nisha lies in the little bunk bed listening to the tinny beat seeping out of Grace's earphones below and even though she has done four shifts and one double since Sunday, she thinks about the shoes and is suddenly wide awake.

The White Horse, if it's possible, looks even more low-rent in daylight, wilted, spindly half-dead plant fronds edging over its hanging baskets, its signage cracked and peeling. She has switched shifts with Jasmine so she can head over when it opens at eleven (who the hell starts drinking alcohol at eleven? What *is* it with these English people?). She pushes her way in even as the barman is unbolting the door and asks immediately to see the CCTV.

'Hold up. I haven't even switched on the till yet.'

'Do I look like I need a drink?'

'Well, why else would you come to a pub?' He is a young hipster type, his dark hair pulled back into a ponytail and his face already masked in irritation.

She switches tack. 'I'm so sorry to bother you.' She smiles. 'I was hoping you could help me with something. I had an item stolen from me a few weeks ago and I was wondering if there was any way I could take a look at your CCTV.'

'You want what?'

She glances up. And notes the domed cameras on the ceiling. 'You have CCTV, right?' She points upwards.

'Yeah,' he says, following the direction of her finger. 'But I don't think I can just let anyone look at –'

'It will literally take you five minutes.' She puts a hand on his arm. Squeezes it lightly. 'You would honestly save my life.'

He gazes at her, briefly wrong-footed, and she smiles, a sweet, hopeful smile. 'Look, I'll explain. I'm in a bit of a spot. It's really hard. I'm a woman on my own in this country and I'm in trouble for reasons I can't fully explain and I need help. I know it's an imposition and, believe me, if it were any other circumstances I wouldn't interrupt your day. I can see you're busy. But I'm really in need of help.'

He's a nice kid. She can see the uncertainty on his face. 'I don't think . . .'

'I can give you the date and time and everything. It will take you five minutes.'

'Yeah, but there's data protection and stuff . . .'

'I'm not asking for names and addresses. I just want to see if something is there.'

'We only keep the tapes for six weeks.'

'That's perfect.'

He frowns, stares at his shoes. When he looks up his expression is suspicious. 'Who are you again? You're not police?'

She laughs prettily. 'Oh, God no. Do I look like police? My name is Anita. I'm just . . . a mom.'

'It's not your bloke cheating and you're going to start some kind of gang war in here?'

'Honey, if my man had been unfaithful I wouldn't need CCTV to deal with it.'

He glances behind him, even though they're apparently the only people in the bar.

'I'd have to show you out here. In the bar. No customers allowed in the office.'

'I get it. You have to be careful.'

When he hesitates again, she looks at his nametag.

'Milo. It's Milo, right? Honestly, you would be saving my life. I just need to locate a personal item. Apparently someone may be on your camera wearing it.'

He glances behind him again.

'And you say you know exactly when and where.'

'Friday the seventh. I just want to see maybe an hour's footage from that evening. Say . . . eight till nine?'

'Stay there,' he says. 'I'll load up the iPad and bring it out.'

'You are a god among men!' she exclaims, and touches his arm again. 'Thank you so, so much.' She sees his expression soften, and thinks, with satisfaction, *Yup, still got it.*

Ten minutes later she is sitting at the bar with a cappuccino as Milo scans through the CCTV images with an expert millennial finger, occasionally peering closer.

'All the images are black-and-white?' she says.

'Yeah. Though we can zoom in if you see anything. It's quite clear. Shoes, you said?'

'About six inches high and strappy. They're Louboutins. Probably better than any other shoes you'll see in here.'

'And you say someone nicked them?'

'And wore them here. Apparently.'

He peers at the screen. 'Shoes are shoes. There are loads of women in heels. How will you know which ones are yours?'

'Oh, I'll know.' She sips at the cappuccino he has made her. So many crappy pairs of cheap, clumpy shoes. So many drunken, lurching girls and bullet-headed men. She feels a sudden stab of anxiety. This is the final White Horse. If this turns up nothing, she has no more leads to go on. And then she sees it.

'There!' she says suddenly, and jabs at the screen. 'Stop! Can you zoom in? That woman there?'

Nine seventeen on the Friday evening. A woman with badly cut hair stumbles from the dance-floor, her legs and feet briefly visible as she walks drunkenly arm in arm with another woman to a bottle-laden table. Milo rewinds a few frames, then moves his fingers around the screen until they zoom in and the woman's feet become clear. She makes him go in as deep as possible until the image starts to blur but they're her shoes. It's as clear as can be. She feels a jolt of recognition.

'That's them! That is definitely them! Can you scroll up? Show me her face?'

There she is, the shoe thief, plain, middle-aged, her eyes half closed and her hair in sweaty wisps around her face. With each frame she wobbles across the screen towards the seat, at one point her ankle buckling slightly.

'That's her. That's the woman who stole my shoes.' She breathes, staring at the pixellated image.

'This is so weird.' Milo shakes his head.

She looks up at him. 'I don't suppose you have any idea who she is?'

He frowns at the image, moves along so that he can see the other people around her. Scans back and forth.

'Uh . . . I think that's the Uberprint lot.'

'The what?'

'The print firm over there. Yeah. Look – I can see Joel there behind her. He's the one with dreadlocks. And Ted. They're always in here on a Friday.'

'Uberprint,' she repeats. 'Can you write that down for me?'

And then, as he hands her the piece of paper, she smiles, an abrupt, genuine, full-wattage smile of joy and gratitude, the kind of smile Nisha rarely bestows in her normal life. And Milo, gratified, smiles right back at her. They gaze at each other for a moment.

'I don't suppose –'

'Don't even think about it,' she says, and hops off the bar stool.

He is alone in the kitchen when she arrives, cleaning his station ready for the evening shift. He is bent over, scrubbing at a mark on the stove.

'Hey! Aleks!' He turns at the sound of his name and she runs up to him. 'I found who stole my shoes!' she says breathlessly. She cannot help herself. She's beaming from ear to ear and she does a little air-punch.

'You're kidding!' he says. 'Now you will get your life back!' He smiles abruptly, his whole face suffused with pleasure, drops his cloth, picks her up and swings her round by her waist so that she squeals and her feet lift from the floor. Suddenly, almost without realizing what she's doing, she's holding his face between her hands and her lips are on his. He hesitates, just a moment, and then his arms surround her, pulling her in, and his mouth lowers onto hers and he is kissing her back, his lips warm and soft, his skin against hers. She is lost in this kiss, consumed by it, the pressure of his mouth on hers, his strong hands pulling her in. He smells of warm bread, of soap and shampoo. He tastes so good she thinks she may actually want to eat him. She bites his lower lip and he lets out a quiet groan of pleasure and it may be the sexiest thing she has ever heard. Her hand clamps around the back of his neck, her body pressed against his. Time stops and swirls. And then they hear the swing door at the far end of the pastry kitchen and they are abruptly disentangling, her hand to her hair, smoothing it awkwardly as she takes a step back.

Minette carries two aluminium trays of dough aloft, humming to herself, her backside pushing the door as she swivels through. Aleks follows her gaze, then looks back at Nisha. He lets out a breath, as if he has been holding it.

'Well,' she says, as Minette disappears into the pastry kitchen.

'Well,' he repeats. He looks at his shoes, a little discombobulated. She feels a faint sense of gratification. When he looks up again, their eyes meet and she guesses there is faint colour in her cheeks.

'You're . . . clearly not a woman to cross.'

Her smile, when it meets his, contains a hint of mischief. 'You'd better believe it,' she says. And then she dusts down the front of her trousers, glances at him again and, because she cannot work out what else to do, walks straight back out of the kitchen door.

23

The car has died. Of course it has. Four times yesterday Simon had informed her that in no way was she to be late today. There was to be a strategy meeting at nine, a sales meeting at ten, planning at eleven and Head Office were going to be at all the meetings. He'd said it like a warning, like this was bad news for her.

'Phil? . . . Phil?' Cat is in the kitchen, staring at her phone as she eats a slice of toast. 'Where's Dad? He's not upstairs.'

Cat shrugs.

'Cat? Where's your father? You must have seen him.'

'Probably in the van.'

She hasn't got time to think about her daughter's coldness, the way she no longer looks her in the eye when she speaks, even though this made her cry the previous evening. She grabs her bag and runs outside. The bonnet of the campervan is up and Phil is underneath it, his upper half obscured.

'The car isn't starting.'

'Probably the battery. It needs replacing.'

Sam waits for him to extract himself from the engine, but he stays there. 'Phil?'

'What?'

'Well, can you help? Do we have any jump leads? I have to be at work for nine or I'm in trouble.'

'Probably best get a cab, then.'

She stands there, staring at her husband's legs. He's been out here at all hours for days. At first she was quietly pleased:

that Phil was doing anything away from the television was a marvel. But there is something determinedly exclusionary about how much time he spends out here now, like he'd do anything rather than spend any time with her.

'You're not even going to help?'

Finally he slides himself out from the bonnet and straightens up. His face, when he looks at her, is curiously blank.

'Well, I can't magic up another battery out of nowhere, can I?'

They lock eyes for a moment and she feels a faint chill at the lack of warmth in his expression. 'Well, thanks,' she says finally. 'Thanks a bunch.'

Without a word, he takes an oily rag from the side of the engine and disappears back inside it.

She is in the cab when her mother calls. She has eighteen minutes left to get into the office, she has worked out, and makes a series of rapid calculations. If she blames car trouble, Simon will find a reason to criticize her for lack of organization, as if anyone could know their battery was about to die. Should she say there was a road accident? He's the kind who would check up, just to prove her wrong. It's best not to lie. Perhaps she could pick up a file on the way in, say she'd gone back for extra figures.

'You didn't come and clean last week. And I need you to look up some socialist hymns for me.'

'What?'

'Socialist hymns,' her mother repeats impatiently. 'Your father is giving a talk about the history of "Jerusalem" at St Mary's and I pointed out that the Bishop of Durham said that "dark satanic mills" actually referred to churches, not flour mills, so it wouldn't be appropriate. You know how easily offended Mrs Palfrey is. She's thick as thieves with the vicar and called poor old Tess Villiers a Maoist for putting ungodly flowers on the altar last week.'

'Ungodly flowers?'

'Arthuriums. Terribly penile. We were all agog. Anyway, your father has done something to the Wi-Fi box thing and we can't get online so we need you to find some more appropriate socialist hymns that he can talk about. Preferably by this afternoon. He's got his eye appointment at teatime.'

Sam rummages in her bag for some makeup. Cat had hogged the bathroom and she had had no time to do her face.

'Oh, and we've decided we're going to take in a refugee. But there's quite a lot of paperwork and we need you to help us fill it all in. We have to get the stuff out of the spare room so that we can put a bed in there. Actually, I think there might be a bed in there. I'm not sure because of all the boxes.'

'A refugee?' Sam cannot keep up.

'It's important to think about people other than ourselves, Samantha. You know Dad and I like to do our bit for the community. And apparently some of them are very nice people. Mrs Rogers has an Afghan and he always takes his shoes off.'

'Mum. I can't do this right now. I'm very busy.'

Her mother's tone manages to convey a precise combination of affront and hurt. 'Oh. Well, it would be nice if you could think of us *occasionally*.'

Sam wedges the phone between ear and shoulder, doing her best to apply a tinted moisturizer. 'I do think of you, Mum. And more than occasionally. Look, if you want to take in a refugee, that's lovely. But I haven't time to clear out your spare room just now, or find socialist hymns. I've got a lot on. I've organized a supermarket delivery for you for Tuesday and I'll come and help when I can.'

'A supermarket delivery.' Her mother's tone is pained.

'Well, I suppose we'll have to tell the poor suffering Afghans our daughter has too much on to find them a bed just now.'

'Mum, nobody's seen the bed in your spare room since 2002, when Dad started piling his eBay train set collection on top of it. I'm not even sure there is a bed. Look, I'll come when I can. I just have a lot on.'

'We all have a lot on, Samantha. You're not the only busy person in this family, you know. Goodness, I hope you don't speak to Phil like this. No wonder he feels so neglected.'

She is four and a half minutes late. For the look Simon gives her as she hurries into the meeting room it might as well be four hours.

'Nice of you to join us,' he says, glancing at his watch, raising his eyebrows, and then looking at his colleagues to make sure they register it.

She thinks about cancelling lunch with Miriam Price all through the second meeting. Simon is relentless, questioning her figures, looking distracted or bored or tapping the end of his engraved biro on his notepad whenever she speaks. Sometimes he even mutters to himself as she's talking. She sees the way the Uberprint managers – who all look like him and dress like him and talk like him – watch this performance and observe her weakness, mark her out as dead meat. When the sales meeting is finished she goes into the Ladies and presses her face hard into her hands so that nobody can hear her crying in the cubicle.

While she is sitting on the loo she texts Phil, who does not reply. He only responds to one in three of her messages at the moment, and she is no longer sure she can blame depression. She texts Cat who answers simply: He's fine. No *x* at the end. No questions about her day. Some days it's hard to feel like anyone even cares if she exists any more.

She makes to text Joel, but it feels somehow too much, an admission of need she doesn't feel comfortable making. Her fingers hover over the keyboard of her phone, and then she hears someone come into the next cubicle and puts it back into her pocket.

By the time she emerges it is already a quarter to twelve: too late to cancel. So she splashes water on her face, reapplies her makeup, and heads out to lunch, ignoring the pointed stare of Simon through the glass of his window as she leaves.

'Sam! How are you?' Miriam is already at the restaurant. She is sitting at a table by the window. As the waiter shows Sam to the table she stands momentarily and gives her a warm smile.

The print job had gone smoothly and Miriam had been satisfied with every aspect, calling her personally afterwards to thank her for her attention to detail. In other times she might have fed this back to her superior, but there was no point with Simon: he would have found something to pick holes in, or asked her why she hadn't charged more.

'Lovely to see you again,' she says, and holds out her hand for a slightly awkward shake. Miriam is dressed in a rainbow-striped jumper and pencil skirt, with heeled ankle boots. Sam would never have felt she could wear an outfit like that to work, yet on Miriam it just looks authoritatively quirky. She has – slightly guiltily – worn the Chanel jacket, given it is Miriam Price and she needed to feel pulled together, instead of the black trousers and grey jumper that is her usual work uniform.

'I wore my Louboutins in your honour!' says Miriam, angling her foot so that Sam can see. She glances down at Sam's feet and Sam thinks she detects a faint flicker of disappointment at her plain black pumps. She immediately wishes she'd worn the shoes too.

'They're gorgeous,' Sam says.

They chat briefly about the weather and their daughters, then compare preferred choices on the menu. Miriam decides on a salad starter and fish, and Sam orders the same salad and a vegetarian tart, which happens to be the cheapest main course. She is slightly worried that she will have to pay for this lunch, as Simon has been clamping down on work lunch claims. She is already calculating what it might come to.

'So tell me about yourself, Sam,' says Miriam, 'and how you ended up at Grayside. Oh, no, I should call it Uberprint now, right?' She has this air of confidence when she speaks, like she knows innately that anything she says will be right.

'I'm not sure there's much to say,' Sam stumbles, and then when Miriam waits, smiling, 'I mean, I didn't intend to work in print. But I got a temporary job as a secretary there when my daughter was small and there was a lovely boss, Henry – he's retired now – and he seemed to think I was good.' Here she gives a nervous little laugh in case she's sounding big-headed. 'After a couple of years he decided to put me in project management. And we sort of built up my role from there. He – he was a very nice man. A good man.'

'Oh, I met Henry a couple of times,' Miriam says. 'I liked him enormously. And what about your family?'

'Husband. A teenage daughter – as you know. And that's it, really. Just us. Plus a couple of needy parents.'

'Oh, we're at that age, aren't we?' Miriam says. 'Mine are in a care home in Solihull. I feel like I spend my life on the motorway or trying to pacify fed-up carers.'

'Really? I'm sorry. I mean, I'm sorry if it's not nice for them. Or you.' Sam backtracks quickly. 'But I don't know, obviously. Maybe it's a very nice place. I'm sure you'd only put them in a nice place.'

'It's nice enough. But I don't think anyone really sets out to end their days in a care home, do they?'

Sam pauses as the waiter puts the water in front of them. 'My parents say they'll die rather than end up in one. Which basically means me doing all their household tasks, cleaning and shopping.'

Miriam nods wryly. There is a shorthand in women this age, Sam realizes. There is none of the sharp elbows of their twenties and thirties, not an ounce of competitiveness. By their late forties and fifties, they're all survivors, of death, divorce, disease, trauma, of *something*.

'That's tough on you,' Miriam begins.

Sam's phone starts to buzz. 'I'm so sorry,' Sam says, cheeks flushing as she reaches into her bag. Miriam waves a hand as if it is of no matter.

Her heart sinks as she sees his name. 'Simon?' she says, trying to muster a smile.

'Where are you?' His voice is terse.

'I'm with Miriam Price. It's in the calendar. I told Genevieve twice.'

'The Dutch job needs to move up four days. They said they've emailed you but had no response.'

'What? Hold on.'

She mouths another *Excuse me* at Miriam and puts him on speaker while she opens her email. There it is, fifteen minutes ago. An email from the Dutch textbook firm asking for the job to be expedited more swiftly.

'Simon – it only came in fifteen minutes ago.'

'And?'

Sam swiftly takes her phone off speaker and holds it to her ear.

'So I hadn't seen it. I'll get on to it obviously. As soon as I'm back.'

'You need to be on top of your email, Sam. I've told you. We at Uberprint have a reputation for swift responses. This isn't good enough.'

'I – I'm sure they'd understand that someone might be getting lunch at one fifteen –'

'This isn't a bloody holiday camp, Sam. I don't know what it's going to require for you to take this job seriously. You'll have to come back. Actually, no, you can't, can you? Not without looking unprofessional to Miriam Price. And we need that job. I'll get Franklin on to it.'

'But that's my project. I brought it in.'

'Irrelevant,' Simon cuts her off. 'It's not enough to just bring jobs in. I need someone who can deliver the whole package. See me when you come back. After your *nice lunch*.' As he says these words, she knows there are people in his office with him, can picture him rolling his eyes at the phone. He ends the call and she is left, stunned, at the table.

'Everything all right?' says Miriam, who has been studying the menu.

'Fine. Fine.' Sam pulls herself together. 'Just work stuff. You . . . know how it is.'

'I know how Simon is.' Miriam lifts her gaze over the top of the menu. 'That's Simon Stockwell, right?'

Sam stares at her.

'Odious little man. He worked for us a few years ago, you know. Back when he was starting out. I had his number straight away. Is he giving you a hard time?'

Sam is frozen. She doesn't know how to answer. 'No! No. Everything's fine. Just fine. There's just a lot going on. I – Well, I – It's just been –' Suddenly, abruptly, she is sobbing, huge, salty, unstoppable tears pouring down her face. Huge gulps hiccup out of her, her shoulders shaking, her palms pressed to her eyes. 'I – I'm so sorry,' she says, mortified, mopping at her face with her napkin. 'I don't know what's happening.'

Oh, God. And now she has ruined the lunch. And Miriam Price will think – will *know* – she is the loser Simon has always had her down as. She glances around desperately trying to locate the Ladies, so that she can escape. But she does not want to have to ask, and she is afraid of getting up and heading in the wrong direction. When she turns back, Miriam is watching her steadily.

'I – I'm so sorry,' she says again, wiping at her eyes.

Miriam's face is serious.

'It's just been a tough time. I'm – I'm mortified. I'm not normally –'

Miriam reaches into her handbag and pulls out a pack of tissues. She passes them across the table. 'Mum's handbag staple,' she says. 'You don't even want to know what else I've got in here. Two sets of car keys, my wife's nasal spray, a prescription for my daughter that she doesn't want to pick up herself, HRT . . . dog treats . . . It's endless, right?'

She smiles, rattling on about nothing, giving Sam the space to mop herself up. Sam scrabbles in her bag for a mirror, but Miriam interrupts. 'You're fine,' she says. 'No smudges.'

'Really?'

The sobs have subsided to sporadic hiccups. Sam feels herself curl over with embarrassment.

'You know,' says Miriam, refilling her water, 'I hope this doesn't sound horribly inappropriate but when you walked in here, I thought the stuffing had been knocked out of you. You looked like a completely different woman from the one I met before.' She hands Sam her glass, waits as she takes a sip. 'And I'm guessing at least fifty per cent of that is Simon Stockwell.' She leans forward. 'You know, the best bit about menopause – just in case you haven't got there yet – is that you genuinely don't give a fuck any more when you're dealing with men like him. And they know it. And when they know you're not intimidated by them, they somehow lose all their power.'

Sam smiles weakly. 'Except when you depend on them for your job.'

'You're very good at your job. Why would it be dependent on him?'

'I – I –' Sam wants to talk, to tell her the myriad ways in which Simon has made her feel useless, redundant, the many times a day in which she feels ignored or undermined. But it seems unprofessional to tell a client about how it has been since Uberprint took over. And what gay black woman wants to hear a middle-aged white woman whingeing about how hard she finds the workplace?

She musters a weak smile. 'Oh, it's not just him. Really. It's been a tricky week.'

Miriam watches her. 'You're being admirably discreet.'

'There's a lot going on.'

'There always is at this age. Oh, good, here's our food. You'll feel better once you've eaten.'

The whole time they eat, Miriam continues a slightly one-sided conversation, drawing Sam out on the capriciousness of teenage girls, the exhaustions of elderly parents, the necessities of treating yourself (she nods here even though she can't remember the last time she treated herself to anything) – and Sam carries on a parallel conversation in her head, in which she tries to analyse how bad this is going to be for her: whether Miriam Price will reveal how this ridiculous woman burst into tears at a client lunch, whether Simon is going to dress her down in front of everyone in the awful glass office when she returns. The thing she feels saddest about is that her memory of her first meeting with Miriam is now spoiled: the woman she had been in the Chanel jacket and heels has evaporated, leaving the real Sam in her place, squashed, defeated, pathetic. She dares not look at her phone, knowing there will be a string of furious texts from Simon about her failings on the Dutch job. So she smiles politely and tries not to sound stupid and picks at her food, some distant part of her observing that remarkably she no longer has any appetite at all.

'Pudding?'

She is dragged back to the table. 'Oh, no, this was lovely. But I think I should probably head back to the office to see what's going on with this job,' she says, declining the menu. 'I'm so sorry again about . . .' She waves a hand vaguely in front of her face, trying to dismiss it.

There is a long silence.

'Sam,' says Miriam. 'This is no way to work.'

'I know,' says Sam, blushing. 'I am going to sort myself out. I am. I promise I'm not normally this –'

'You misunderstand me,' says Miriam. 'I mean, working for a boss who is so clearly grinding you down. You're good at your job. I mentioned you to Ivan over at Drakes and he said you've always been incredibly thorough. And a pleasure to deal with, for that matter.'

Sam lifts her head slowly.

'We're always on the lookout for people and I was very impressed with what you turned around for us. I think you should come in and meet our team.'

' . . . Meet your team?'

'You should be somewhere where you can get your mojo back. Wherever that turns out to be.' Miriam signals to the waiter, and holds out a credit card before Sam can say anything. 'Might you be interested in talking to us?'

Sam is so stunned that she can barely speak. ' . . . Er, yes. Yes – that would be great.'

'Good. I'll email you with a date.' Miriam is standing up. She taps a card on the reader proffered by a waitress, while Sam sits digesting this. Then she tucks her wallet into her bag and leans forward.

'In the meantime, put on some really great shoes with that jacket and a red lipstick and let Simon Stockwell know you're not to be messed with.'

24

The coffee shop gives a clear view of the back of the print-works, a small, litter-strewn yard flanked by a Co-op grocery store, the White Horse pub, and an office block that appears to have been vacated several years ago, judging by the grubby windows and graffiti-strewn walls. Nisha, who was marked off this afternoon at short notice (*zero hours contracts*, Jasmine had sighed) sips a lukewarm cappuccino and watches the battered white vans reverse in and out under the Uberprint sign, the groups of men who gather at the rear entrance, chatting or drinking from mugs of tea between loadings, their laughter sending small puffs of steam into the cold air. She is taut, focused, half waiting for the woman to walk out in her shoes, even though she knows this is unlikely.

She has sat here for almost an hour now, picturing a dozen different outcomes: she follows the thief to her house, con-fronts her, wrestles the shoes from her feet (though that means the woman would have to be wearing them, and she feels icky about touching someone's feet). She calls the cops, though if they're anything like US cops, she might as well whistle. She breaks into the woman's house when the woman is asleep, locates the shoes and escapes. Perhaps wearing a face mask. This is admittedly a risky strategy, especially as she doesn't know who else might be in the house. Plus a face mask will make her itch. There is always the trump card: she could tell Carl and he could send Ari in to get them. But she is not sure she trusts Ari to tell the truth about whether he's got the shoes: he could just as easily spirit them away and leave her in a worse position than before. And there is something about Ari and these shoes that just doesn't sit right.

Nisha sits and considers all these factors, and the dregs of her coffee grow colder. Finally, when the barista comes over for the third time and pointedly asks her if she wants another, she picks up her coat and bag and leaves.

Simon is chatting to colleagues when Sam arrives back. She comes in through the side entrance so that she can go to the Ladies and check her face before anyone spots her. Now she sees a bunch of young men gathered around the desk in his office, looking intently at something on his phone, then bursting out laughing simultaneously. She pictures some gross meme, probably involving a young woman with unfeasibly large breasts. She is relieved that he is not in her cubicle, one buttock resting on the corner of her desk, his head tilted in fake concern. She stands for a moment, watching them, then drops her handbag and places the cream Chanel jacket on the back of her chair. She walks out, through Accounting, past Reception and down the narrow corridor to the loading bay.

The vans are all out and he is seated alone in the little office by the main shutters. He has his back to her when she arrives, his hands linked behind his head as he gazes, apparently deep in thought, out of the window at the yard, his shoulders too broad for his navy blue company sweatshirt. Behind the office, suspended from the rafters, hangs a large black and yellow punchbag. She stops for a moment, gazing at him. She has a sudden memory of them dancing, his hand on her waist, his eyebrows raised in amused appreciation as she strutted in those shoes.

The drivers' office is warm and fuggy, thanks to an ancient bar heater in the corner, and the walls are lined with tacho-graphs and whiteboards detailing the day's jobs, faded birthday cards and new Uberprint memos. She is not sure she has been in here more than a handful of times in all the years she's worked there, and suddenly the office feels smaller than she remembers. Or maybe he is just bigger. He turns in his chair.

'Sam. I didn't know you were –'

'Have you got any gloves?'

He blinks. 'What?'

'Gloves,' she says. 'Boxing gloves. Have you got any here?'

He follows her gaze out to the punchbag. 'Uh . . . I've got mine. But they'll be too big for you.'

'Show me.'

He reaches under his desk and pulls out a kitbag containing two scuffed black gloves, which he holds up to her. She examines them briefly. She pulls them onto her fists, securing the Velcro with her teeth until they are as tight as they can go around her wrists. Then she walks out of the office and over to the punchbag. She stands in front of it for a moment, and takes a breath, tightens her core, allows everything that has been spinning around her head to settle. And then she pulls her arm back from her shoulder and throws everything she has into a right-handed punch. The impact sends the bag wheeling backwards on its ropes. She meets it with her left, rooted through her feet, all her strength coming from her left shoulder so that it spins again. She hits it, again and again, hammering the leather, her hair working loose from its ponytail, her breath coming in short bursts, little gasps emerging from her mouth with each impact. She hits and she hits, not caring who sees her, not worrying if she looks daft attacking a punchbag in her good trousers and a Next blouse.

Joel, who had initially moved back in surprise, walks round to the other side and steadies the punchbag with his arms so that she can hit it harder, and she notes with gratification that increasingly he flinches at each impact, his body leaning in,

261

his left foot sliding forward to give him greater purchase. Sam hits and hits until she feels something in her finally give. And then, abruptly, she stops, her hands dropping to her sides, suddenly aware of her heart racing, the trickle of sweat running down her back into her waistband. There is a silence, broken only by the creak of the punchbag swinging gently on its chain. She looks up at Joel, who is watching her, both hands still resting on the bag, as if he is not sure whether she is about to hit again.

'You okay?' he says.

'Miriam Price wants me to come in and talk to her,' she says, panting.

Joel looks startled.

'About a job,' she adds. They gaze steadily at each other. Sam feels sweat dripping into her eye and attempts to wipe it away with the back of her arm.

Neither of them speaks.

'I don't want you to leave,' Joel says finally, dropping the punchbag.

'I don't want to leave,' she says. They stare at each other. And then, without thinking, she steps forward, takes his face between her boxing gloves, and kisses him.

At the first touch of Joel's mouth, Sam's body goes into a kind of shock. She has kissed nobody but Phil in more than twenty-five years, and she is not sure even they have ever kissed like this. Everything about Joel is alien, and delicious. He smells different, his lips are softer, his body harder, his hands on her hair, the suggestion of overwhelming strength. Joel's arms slide around her, her body melts into his, and the kisses grow deeper, more urgent, her gloved hands at his neck, her breath rapid. Time stalls, everything around her disappears so that it's just his lips, his skin, the heat of his body against hers. Her whole body feels as if it has become molten, melded to his, long-dormant synapses springing to life. She wants to take off the gloves. She wants to feel his skin against hers, smooth and warm. She wants to wrap herself completely around him. She wants to reach into his trousers and – and – She pulls back, her breath hard in her chest, her gloves raised to her face.

And then she sees Ted. He is standing by the loading doors, his mouth slightly open as he sees them, a look of what she can only describe afterwards as horrified disappointment on his kind, fleshy face.

'Joel, I – I –' she stutters. She turns and runs back towards the office, wrestling the gloves off and hurling them behind her as she goes.

Sam walks briskly through the cubicles until she reaches her own, her colour high, her sights fixed in front of her, sure that everyone in there must know what just happened. Her body feels as if it has been ignited, as if she is radiating heat, and her thoughts are churning and jumbled.

She sits down in her chair a little shakily, staring unseeing at the screen. *She has just kissed Joel. She has just kissed Joel. She wanted to do a lot more than just kiss Joel.* She can still feel his mouth on hers, his tough, sinewy body against hers. She thinks of Ted's appalled expression, then abruptly lets out a half-laugh, a strange high-pitched squeal, and puts both hands to her face, immediately mortified. What on earth has she done? Who has she become? She glances guiltily behind her, but nobody seems to have noticed. Heads are bowed. Marina is walking past with a mug of coffee. The photocopier by the fire-exit door appears to be on the blink again. She jumps slightly as her phone buzzes. Joel.

Are you okay?

She stares at it.

I think so, she types, with trembling fingers. Did Ted say anything?

Just that it was none of his business. He went straight out again.

You think I should go after him?

No. No. I don't know. Maybe I should. I don't know what just happened.

She glances up, checking to see if anyone has noticed, if anyone can sense that this is her, Sam Kemp, sneaking around locking lips with a work colleague. Was this almost having an affair? Was this where her life was heading? Did Ted think she was a terrible person? *Help me*, she thinks, not sure who she is actually asking. And then she jumps out of her skin because a dark-haired woman is standing in the doorway to her cubicle glaring at her and saying, in a loud, American voice: 'WHERE ARE MY SHOES, BITCH?'

25

Nisha had walked unchallenged into the offices of Uberprint. The men gathered by the vans glanced at her but nobody seemed to think it unusual that she was walking straight through the back entrance. After a cursory glance at her legs they turned back to their discussion. The offices are drab, the kind of place that might sell pet insurance or drain solutions, and she wrinkled her nose at the smell of stale carpet and machine coffee as she headed down a corridor that looked like it led to the main office. A young woman lifted her head from her phone at the reception desk, but didn't stop her, and Nisha pushed through a set of double doors, finding herself in a large space divided into grey cubicles.

In the corner of the room she saw a big, glass-windowed office containing a gathering of young men in cheap suits, while around her a vague hum of half-hearted industry emanated from the individual desks, people clicking on keyboards, murmuring into phones or sipping tea while chatting at the photocopier. She scanned the room, her bag clamped to her side. Then she spied a woman, hunched in one of the far cubicles as she took her seat, her badly tinted hair visible above the composite partitions. Nisha had stopped and stared.

Nisha had not known what she would do when she finally confronted the woman who had caused so much trouble, a thief who also happens to hold the key to her future. But there was something about the shabbiness of her, the depressed slope of her shoulders that instantly infuriated her.

I have been bested by *this*? she thought, as she strode across the office. Her heartbeat started a loud, insistent thumping in her ears. And suddenly she is in the cubicle, and the woman is spinning in her seat to face her, phone in a limp hand, her features rigid with shock.

'Wh-what?' the woman is stammering. 'What are you talking about?'

She looks, Nisha notes, with some distant sense of gratification, genuinely terrified.

'You stole my shoes! At the gym. You stole my shoes and you've been wearing them. I've got you on CCTV and – and – oh, my God – is that my *Chanel jacket*?'

The woman flushes to the roots of her hair, glances guiltily at the cream bouclé jacket draped on the back of her office chair.

'What the actual –' Nisha wrenches the jacket from the chair and checks the label. 'Where are my shoes? Where is my bag? What have you done with my things? I'm going to call the cops.'

'I didn't steal anything! It was an accident!'

'Oh, an accident! And instead of handing my stuff in you decided to wear my shoes to a bar? And bring my Chanel jacket to work? Sure! That's definitely an accident.'

A small crowd has gathered around the cubicle. The woman is staring at her, her hands waving, palms up, in front of her. 'Look – I can explain – the gym was –'

'You have no idea the trouble you've caused. Bet you thought I'd never find you, right? Well, you have no idea who you're dealing with.'

A man appears at the entrance of the cubicle: gelled hair, cheap suit, bringing with him a slightly self-conscious air of authority.

'What's going on here?'

'What's going on? Ask her, the shoe thief.'

'I told you! I didn't know whose they were! I must have picked up the wrong bag and when I went back to return them they were –'

'I want my shoes.'

The man turns to Sam. 'Sam? What's going on?'

The woman turns to him. 'Simon – I can explain this. When I went to the gym – the day you saw me in the flip-flops – there was a mix-up with the bags and –'

'And you stole them!'

'That's it.'

'That's what?'

'You're fired.'

The room falls silent.

'What?'

'You're fired.' He lifts his voice slightly, as if to make sure everyone in the room can hear his decision. 'With immediate effect. We can't have a thief in the office. You're repeatedly bringing Uberprint into disrepute. You've had plenty of warnings and this is it. Get your things and go.'

He visibly puffs up, glances to his side as if waiting for signs of approval from the people watching. Nisha feels a vague sense of dismay – she hates guys like him – but the woman has brought it on herself.

'Simon. Mate.' A man with dreadlocks has stepped forward. 'You can't fire Sam for a simple mix-up. She told us in the van when we picked her up that she had the wrong bag but we –'

'Not interested,' says Simon, his mouth pressed into a thin line of disapproval and barely suppressed pleasure. 'Not. Interested. This lady here has been quite clear about what actually happened. And this is not the kind of behaviour I'm prepared to tolerate. I've had enough problems with Sam these past weeks and this is the final straw.'

'But –'

'We're done here. Everyone go back to work. The show's over. Sam, gather your belongings and I'll get security to escort you out. HR will sort out your P45.'

Even Nisha is a little taken aback by this. There is a low murmur of unease among the other workers. They hesitate and exchange glances but nobody seems willing to challenge the man's authority and eventually, uncomfortably, they melt away. The dreadlocked man is the last to leave. He murmurs something into the woman's ear but she barely registers it. She looks grey with shock, starts dumbly gathering her things. Nisha will not let her discomfort colour what has just happened. She is in the right! She was not the person who stole someone's belongings. All she has done is try to get her things back.

'I'll be waiting outside,' Nisha says, when the man finally leaves, flanked by several other men in cheap suits. 'I'll need my shoes and bag too. *Sam.*'

Sam collects her framed pictures and puts them into a box that Marina brings over, her fingers slipping so that she drops one on the floor with a clatter that seems to echo around the office. Marina mutters, 'I'm so sorry,' as she puts the cardboard box on the desk but the accusation of 'thief' has clearly done something to the atmosphere and Marina gives her a slightly wary, confused look as she leaves. The cubicles of her co-workers are completely silent around her. Sam cannot bear to look up: she knows Simon and his mates will be watching from his office, muttering to each other, imagines the whispered conversations between her workmates. She is mortified, her ears ringing with that woman's words. She gathers up the last of her things, and Lewis, the security officer from downstairs, appears. He rubs the back of his head and shifts his weight from one foot to the other, as if he is not sure what to do. She glances at him and he pulls an awkward, slightly embarrassed face, then gestures towards the corridor.

It is only when the doors open, when she feels the cold air hit her face and sees the American woman standing there, stubbing out a cigarette that it hits home: *I've lost my job. I have actually lost my job.* And she puts the box on the ground and picks up her phone to call the only person she can think will be able to get her through this.

'Andrea?'

Sam has no car and she does not want to be stuck in a taxi with this crazy woman, who is giving off scary, aggressive vibes. So she begins to walk, the woman maintaining a tail exactly two steps behind her. She is wearing her Chanel jacket, checking the sleeves ostentatiously for signs of dirt or damage.

'I'm not going anywhere, lady. Just so you know.'

'I know,' says Sam, staring straight ahead. 'I'm just walking home.'

Sam puts one foot in front of the other, her head still ringing with Simon's words, the sight of her workmates' faces as everything they thought they knew about her began to slip away. She should have made more of an effort to return the shoes. She should have made it a priority. And now she has lost everything.

'And my stuff had better be at your house.'

'It is at my house. Look, I did try to return your bag. The gym was closed until further notice.'

'I'm not interested.'

'Okay. Well, I'm just telling you. I'm not a thief.'

'Says the woman with my Chanel jacket slung over the back of her chair.'

Sam spins around, tears in her eyes. 'I had an important meeting today, okay? I had a meeting with someone I was trying to impress and I thought it wouldn't hurt if I just wore it once. I'm sorry.'

'Yeah, okay. So you're Mother Teresa. Whatever.'

'What?'

'Just get me my shoes. I don't care what you are. I just go on the evidence.'

The evidence. Sam keeps seeing Simon's face, the way his lip curled with a kind of satisfaction as he called her a thief. She has lost her job. She has actually lost her job. And of course he won't be obliged to give her a reference, she thinks, and her stomach begins to hurt. She will never get another job. Phil and Cat will be out on the streets with her. They will end up in a tiny bed-and-breakfast room, the kind of place the government puts refugees, with one electric ring to cook on and communal toilets. Or they will have to move in with her parents. And everyone will blame her. And they will have every right to. How has she ended up in such a mess?

They walk on in silence for two more streets until Sam turns and stops. 'Can you at least not walk two steps behind me like some kind of security guard? It's unnerving. You really think I'm going to run away? Lugging this bloody box?'

'I don't know you, lady. You could try anything. You could be a top-class sprinter for all I know.'

'Do I look like a top-class sprinter?'

'You don't look like a thief. But somehow *that* happened.'

'Oh, for God's sake.' Sam puts the box down and presses her palms into her eyes for a moment, trying to contain the panic attack that is building in her chest. When she opens them again the woman is staring at her.

After a couple of minutes, however, she does start walking alongside her.

The walk continues like this for some time. Sam is grateful for her sturdy shoes, though the box weighs heavy in her arms with all the photo frames of her family, and she has to keep pausing to adjust the weight. Her elbows hurt, and then her lower back. The American woman strides effortlessly beside her in, Sam realizes, with some surprise, her own flat black shoes. It is a half-hour walk that feels endless. She needs Andrea. She just needs to see Andrea's face and feel her arms around her and know that something in this world is constant and good. That someone knows she is not a bad person. Finally they turn into her street, and she notes that Andrea's little blue Nissan Micra is outside and the relief she feels at the sight of it causes a huge sob to hiccup out of her chest so that the American woman gives her a sharp, quizzical look.

'Here. We're here,' Sam mumbles, and walks past the campervan, where Phil is noisily sanding a bumper on the roadside, wearing a pair of plastic goggles. He does not look up.

Sam wrestles the door open. She drops the box in the hallway and heads straight upstairs, ignoring the dog's delighted welcome. She does not want this woman here a moment longer than is necessary. She pushes open her bedroom door, heads to the wardrobe and hauls out the black Marc Jacobs bag. She hoicks the handles over her shoulder and walks back downstairs. The woman is standing by the front door watching Phil, her arms folded across her chest. She looks up when Sam appears and her eyes switch immediately to the bag.

'At last,' she says, and pulls it from Sam's arm. 'Is everything in there?'

'Of course,' says Sam.

The woman gazes at her for a moment. 'I'm going to check.'

'Fine.' Sam walks away back along the corridor to the

kitchen. And there is Andrea, sitting at the table, her head wrapped in a new bright pink paisley wrap. She climbs heavily to her feet when she sees Sam. 'What's going on, lovely?'

And suddenly Sam is in her arms, her head buried in Andrea's neck, sobbing. And even as she sobs she feels how frail Andrea still is, the boniness of her shoulder, and it makes her even more grief-stricken.

'I lost my job,' she says. Andrea pulls back to look at her.

'You're kidding.'

'He got me out. He finally got me out. It's all because of a stupid misunderstanding. But I don't know what I'm going to do . . . Phil isn't talking to me and I don't know what he's going to say when he finds out.'

Andrea's face is wrinkled with sympathy. She strokes Sam's hair. 'We'll work it out. Don't worry, Sam. We'll work this out. You'll be okay.'

And then Andrea flinches as the American woman strides into the kitchen, rage sparking off her like electricity.

'Where are my fucking *shoes*?'

Sam turns to look at her. 'What?'

'Where are my shoes?'

'They're in the bag. I told you.'

'Who are you?' says Andrea, who suddenly looks a lot less frail.

'I'm the person whose shoes this bitch stole,' says the American woman.

'Don't you dare talk like that in my friend's kitchen. Tone down your language.' Andrea's voice cuts through the air like ice, and Sam notices a faint flicker pass across the American woman's face.

'They must be in there,' Sam says, wiping her eyes.

The woman holds out the gaping bag, unzipped along its length. 'Yeah? Wanna show me?'

Sam blinks. The shoes are gone. She takes a step forward, tentatively moves the T-shirt from the bottom. She's right. The shoes are not there.

Sam's head is racing. 'I don't get it. They've been in there all the time.'

Phil walks in, lifting the goggles from his face. He looks at Sam and doesn't smile. Then he sees the American woman, and Andrea, and perhaps detects some strange vibration in the atmosphere.

'Hello.' He looks at the American woman, waiting for an explanation.

'Phil? Have you seen a pair of red shoes? They were in this bag.'

His face closes over. 'Your new high heels? The tarty ones?'

'*Tarty?* They're Christian Louboutin,' says the American woman. 'And they're mine.'

Phil looks at Sam. 'They weren't *your* shoes?'

'No. Hang on – how did you know about the shoes?'

'Cat saw you wearing them.' He lifts his chin and stares at her. 'When you were out with your lover.'

Sam stares back. The air in the kitchen grows very still. And suddenly Phil's coldness, his determination not to spend any time with her, makes sense. She feels herself flush. 'I – I don't have a lover.'

'She doesn't have a lover. She's been miserable for months because you won't engage with her. Don't be ridiculous, Phil.' Andrea gazes at Sam, and notes the brief silence, the slow flush of colour on Sam's neck. She looks from one to the other. 'Oh. Well, this is interesting.'

'I haven't touched the shoes,' says Phil. 'Well, I did. I took them out to the van because I didn't want them in the house. But then Cat asked where they were. I think maybe she wanted to borrow them.'

'Great,' says Nisha. 'So now my shoes are being passed around from scuzzy foot to scuzzy foot. Perfect.'

Sam is still staring at her husband. 'I'm not having an affair.'

'Aren't you?'

'No! Why would you think that?'

'Well, for one thing, you've changed. You don't have time for me any more.'

'Phil, you've spent months welded to the sofa. You don't notice if I'm alive or dead most of the time.'

'And you've been coming home all glowing and sweaty.'

'I've been boxing! I go boxing three times a week.'

'Boxing? In high heels? Nice try.'

'What?'

'Hello? Can we stay on track, please? I don't care who she's fooling around with. I want my damn shoes.'

Sam turns to Nisha. 'I'll pay you for the shoes. I'm sorry.'

'I don't want your money! Don't you understand? I need those shoes!'

Andrea pulls out her phone. 'Shouldn't we just call Cat?'

Sam stands frozen as Andrea dials her daughter. She cannot stop staring at Phil. His gaze flickers onto and away from her face. She can see the uncertainty as he tries to work out whether she is telling the truth and it feels like a blow.

'Hey, lovey. How are you? . . . Good . . . good. Listen, we've got a bit of an issue at home and I just wanted to ask – where are the red shoes from your mum's wardrobe?'

The room falls silent as Andrea, her voice calm and reassuring, listens to the inaudible voice at the other end. 'I know, lovey. There's been a bit of a misunderstanding. So where did you take them? . . . I know . . . I know . . . You did? Let me just write that down . . . okay.'

She ends the call with more reassurances, a 'Yeah, love you' and a 'See you soon'. Then Andrea lets out a breath, and looks up at the waiting faces. 'She – she thought you were having an affair and she didn't like you wearing them. Plus she says they're a repulsive symbol of patriarchal oppression and she didn't want them in the house.'

'So?' The American woman's voice is brisk.

'So she took them to a charity shop. It's one near her college.'

'She took my shoes to a *goodwill store*?' The American woman throws her hands into the air. 'Oh, this just gets better.'

'When?' says Sam, weakly.

'Yesterday afternoon. Look, don't panic. If we head over now maybe we'll be able to get them back.'

26

Nisha sits in the tiny car, squashed into the back seat, while Sam and her friend drive across London in silence. The friend, whose name is Andrea, is wearing the kind of soft turban and grey pallor that denotes serious illness, but she is oddly cheerful, as if she has been lifted temporarily out of whatever malaise she is in. 'And when are you going to tell me about this "affair"?' Andrea says to Sam.

Sam glances back at Nisha, and says, 'Some other time.'

'So you are having an affair? What the –'

'I am not having an affair.' Sam goes pink. 'I may have kissed someone. That's all.'

'What the fuck, Sam? No bad behaviour, you said.'

'That was before this happened.'

'Don't mind me,' says Nisha, from the back seat. 'You could be getting jiggy with half of London for all I care.'

But she sees Sam's hand creep across and squeeze Andrea's while they sit at traffic-lights, and something in her gives a little at the sight of the tenderness. It is the same gesture she used to make to Ray when they were driving him back to his school, a tiny squeeze intended to convey so much more than words ever could.

Nisha is pissed about the shoes. She is pissed that this Sam clearly thought they were hers to borrow, pissed that the woman's daughter took them to the goodwill store. But as the car navigates its way through the heavy London traffic she is finding it hard to maintain the same degree of blind, righteous fury. This Sam does not seem like a thief – she has none of the feral sense of self-preservation, the ability to lie compulsively and without hesitation. She just looks, Nisha thinks uncomfortably, *sad*.

Maybe it was a mistake. She thinks back to that day in the changing room and has a vague, cloudy memory of shoving another bag onto the floor. It is just possible this thing has been an accident. And then she thinks about that grainy CCTV image of the woman wearing her shoes at the pub. And she thinks of her Chanel jacket hanging casually over the back of that office chair, and her heart hardens again. People are capable of being all sorts of things, regardless of appearances. She knows that better than anyone.

'I think this is it.' Andrea has pulled up on a main road, and is gazing at her phone, then up and out of the driver's window.

Sam reads the sign aloud: 'Global Cat Foundation.'

'You're kidding me,' says Nisha, who has just realized where she is.

'No, that's what she said. Yes, right next to her college.'

Nisha sighs. Of all the goodwill stores in this goddamn city, of course it had to be this one.

'I'll go,' says Sam, climbing wearily out of the car.

'Oooh, no,' says Nisha, wrestling the front seat forward so that she can wriggle out. 'You're not going anywhere by yourself. I'm coming too.'

The stale, fuggy scent of the overheated charity store hits her as Sam opens the door, and Nisha closes her eyes for a second, trying not to feel overwhelmed by the urge to walk straight out again. She takes a breath, braces herself and follows Sam towards the back, where a sad array of crumpled boots sits on dusty shelves, alongside shoes with the maker's name worn off by who knows how many unknown sweaty soles? Sam glances along each shelf, then shakes her head. 'Maybe they haven't put them out yet,' she says. 'My friend works in the Cancer Research Shop in Woking and she says they have bags of people's stuff out the back for weeks before it gets to the actual shop. We could go through those.'

'Today just gets better and better,' Nisha mutters.

They walk around the shop, Nisha peering into corners and examining the shop-window displays – can you call them displays? Mismatched mother-of-the-bride outfits and crockery she wouldn't throw at an enemy. Porcelain cats. Tarnished cruet sets. The shoes are nowhere. When she turns, Sam is standing at the counter. The woman with blue hair looks past her to give Nisha a steady look.

'Hi – I wonder if you can help me?' says Sam. Her voice does a tentative lilt at the end as if she is unsure she should even be speaking. 'It's a bit awkward? I'm sure you must have this happen all the time? My daughter just brought in a pair of shoes and they weren't actually her shoes to give away and we need to get them back so it would be ever so helpful if you could maybe –'

Nisha steps in front of her. 'Oh, for God's sake. We need to see all the shoes that came in yesterday.'

'Do you want your towelling robe back while you're at it?' The blue-haired woman's lips curl a little.

Nisha pulls herself up a little taller. 'Just the shoes. Where are they?'

The woman sniffs. 'Everything that came in yesterday has already been put out.'

Sam and Nisha exchange a glance.

'Out? Where? These are red Christian Louboutins. Six-inch heel. One of a kind.'

'You'll have to look on the shelves.'

'We looked on the shelves.'

The woman glances down at her ledger. 'Then they've gone.' She flicks a page back, runs her finger down the hand-written list. 'Ah. Red Christian Bolton shoes. We sold them this morning.' She leans back on her stool, implacable.

Nisha stares, her heart sinking. 'You can't have sold them already.'

'Are you sure?' says Sam.

'They weren't yours to sell, lady. I need my shoes.'

'We don't accept liability for anything that gets sold. Every-thing that comes in here is assumed to come with the relevant permissions.' She gazes impassively at Nisha. 'It's for a good cause.' She smiles a slow smile. 'If you need another pair of shoes we have a nice selection at the –'

'Jesus Christ!' exclaims Nisha, and stomps outside.

Sam appears a moment later, apologizing repeatedly. 'I'm sure we can work something out,' she keeps saying, but she has the energy of a used tea-bag and Nisha has lost what little patience she had to start.

'Well, that's it,' she says, lighting a cigarette and inhaling angrily. 'You've just cost me several million dollars.'

'We might still be able to find them,' Sam says weakly.

'How? You want to get the CCTV from every local shop and find out who the hell walked into and out of this store? You want to put Betty Blue Hair there in a headlock until she tells you which anonymous person came in and bought a pair of shoes?'

'Look. I – I'll get you another pair of shoes,' says Sam, sit-ting on the kerb. 'Or I'll pay. How much were they?'

'I don't want another pair of shoes,' yells Nisha. 'That was the whole point. I need *those* shoes. How many times do I have to explain this?'

'Hey!' It's quite something to be told off by a woman who looks like she might be about to keel over at any minute, Nisha thinks afterwards. Andrea, all five feet of her, has thrown herself out of the driver's seat and is now pushing at Nisha with a bony palm, getting her to step away from her friend. She pushes her so furiously that her soft wrap dislodges from her head, revealing the vague fluff covering her scalp.

'You don't get to talk to Sam like that, Miss. She told you it was an accident and it was an accident. She's trying to help, and *you* don't get to speak to people like that.'

Nisha takes a step back. Andrea's eyes burn with a clear blue intensity that is a little intimidating. As Andrea straightens the wrap, her eyes not leaving Nisha's, Nisha decides to dial it back a little.

'I just need those shoes, okay? They're really important. My husband – ex-husband is playing a stupid game and without them I can't get a divorce settlement.'

'Well, that's not Sam's fault, is it? They're just a pair of shoes. It's not like anyone could have known.'

'Gift Aid,' says Sam, suddenly. The other two women look at her as she clambers to her feet, like someone waking from a long sleep. 'The woman who bought the shoes. She would have filled out a Gift Aid form. Most people do, right?'

'Genius,' says Andrea, with an abrupt smile. 'Come on!'

Nisha isn't entirely sure what's going on but she follows the two women back into the store and busies herself at the back, listening as Sam explains to the now suspicious woman behind the counter that the shoes really are important and, as they clearly take a note of everyone who buys something, maybe they could tell her who bought them.

'Perhaps she did Gift Aid,' Sam says hopefully.

'Why?'

'Because that means you will have the buyer's name and address. I wouldn't normally ask but we really need those shoes. Sentimental value. It's very important.'

There is a short silence. Nisha edges over to the counter. The woman looks from Sam to Nisha and crosses her arms again.

'I can't give you that information,' she says. 'Data Protection.' She looks at Nisha. 'Besides, you could be anyone. You could be a murderer.'

'Do I look like I'm about to murder somebody?'

'You really want me to answer that?' says the woman.

A few other customers are in the shop now and Nisha sees their eyes flicking towards their end of the store.

'Just give me the information, okay? And we'll be out of your hair. Very . . . nice blue. By the way. Goes well with your British skin tone.'

Sam closes her eyes.

'No,' says the woman. 'And if you can't be polite I suggest you –'

Nisha is just opening her mouth to reply when they are distracted by a sound at the back of the shop, a series of bumps and exclamations. Nisha glances through the clothes rails and sees that Andrea has collapsed, bringing a rail of men's trousers down with her. She can just make out the bright pink wrap of her head, the scattered pile of jigsaw puzzles, surrounded by the anxious faces of the customers nearby.

'Oh, my God. Andrea.' Nisha gazes in horror as Sam bolts towards her, and then, for just a moment, as Andrea is hauled gently upright, she and Nisha lock eyes and Andrea winks.

'Hold on!' The blue-haired woman is bustling round from the counter. 'Get back, please. Get back. I'm a qualified first-aider.' She lunges for a red plastic case under the counter, then pushes past to the end of the shop, where the other customers are gathered around. '*Put her in the recovery position!*' Quickly, Nisha throws her upper body over the desk, and swivels the ledger towards her. She sees the list of items from the previous day and scans them swiftly until she sees it: *Red crocodile-skin Christian Bolton sandals.* And there it is in blue biro beside it – GIFT AID: *Liz Frobisher, 14 Alleyne Road, SE1.*

She rips the page from the ledger and stuffs it into her pocket, just in time to hear Andrea say: 'I'm fine, honestly. I'm just weak from all the chemo. No, no, you don't need to take my temperature. Just get me a sip of water and I'll be right as rain. Thank you so much . . .'

The three women do not speak until Andrea has started the car and pulled out into the road. They drive down two streets and across a set of traffic-lights. Then Nisha leans forward between the front seats.

'Hey, Scarfy. Are you really okay?'

'Of course I am.' Andrea signals left at the roundabout and allows herself a small smile. 'That was actually the most fun I've had in nine months. I hope you both admired my acting skills.'

'You deserve an Oscar,' says Nisha. 'Scared the crap out of me.'

'Seriously, though. The woman was trying to put a plaster on my knee! Like that's what I need to worry about.'

'*You need to be in the recovery position,*' Sam mimics the shop assistant. '*For at least half an hour. My cousin was married to a paramedic.*'

'Because lying between Uncle Fred's nylon long-johns, a framed picture of Brighton Pier and a Teasmade is exactly where I want to spend half my day.'

Nisha cannot help but laugh. 'So where are we going?' she says, composing herself. 'Where is Alleyne Road?'

'Not a clue,' says Andrea. 'But we're on our way.'

Number 14 Alleyne Road sits squat in the middle of a row of identikit houses built sometime in the early seventies and apparently not modernized since. The brief euphoria of getting hold of the address has gradually faded during the car journey, and Sam has found herself preoccupied with what was currently happening a few miles away at home. Did what she had done with Joel qualify as an affair? It was a betrayal of sorts, for sure. Exchanging secret text messages? Sitting in cars? Kissing someone who isn't your husband? She thinks about Joel's lips and feels a flush of heat that might be either pleasure or shame. She doesn't want to interrogate herself as to which. Her daughter had seen it: Cat, who now hates her and thinks of her as some kind of adulterer. She keeps thinking of Phil's aloofness, the way he had looked at her. Even in the depths of his depression he had never regarded her so coldly. She thinks about the conversations that await her at home and her stomach clenches. She has no poker face. Even if she hasn't had an affair they will be able to see guilt written all over her when she discusses it.

'So what do we do now?' says Andrea, turning off the ignition.

'Break in, of course,' says Nisha.

'You can't just break into someone's house,' says Sam.

Nisha considers this. She's probably right. Who knows who else is in that house? Or if the woman is even inside?

'We could just knock on the door and talk to her? Ask to buy them from her?' says Sam.

'What if she says no? Then she knows something is up. Do you understand anything about deals?'

'I know plenty about making deals. That's what I do for a living.'

'Well, if you were any good at it, you'd know you never let your opponent guess that what they have is valuable to you. And, besides, none of us have any cash. No offence,' she adds, as the two women stare at her, 'but you two don't look like you're exactly loaded. I say we break in.'

Nisha leans forward and scans the front of the building, looking for a point of entry. 'And hurt her until she tells us where my shoes are.'

Nisha is a child again, walking the aisles of the DollarSave, trying to work out which bottle of bourbon she can sneak under her coat. Her shoes are in that house, calling to her. She tries to recall how she used to feel, assessing the potential dangers, already preparing her get-out explanation. As she watches, a ginger cat strolls along the wall outside the house and sits, staring at them with greedy yellow eyes.

'The window on the left looks rotten. We could probably force that.'

Sam turns in her seat to stare at Nisha. 'What is *wrong* with you?'

'What do you mean, what is wrong with me?'

'For all we know, this may be a perfectly nice woman who cares deeply about a cat charity and feels delighted to have bought a nice pair of shoes – legally, I might add – and you're talking about going in there and burgling her house or scarring her for life? Seriously? What kind of a person are you?'

Nisha winds down the window and ducks back so that she doesn't need to look at Sam's annoying, anxious face. 'A person who needs her fucking shoes back.'

At that moment the front door opens and a woman emerges from the house. They fall abruptly silent, staring through the windscreen at the figure in a turquoise blouse and jeans. She is around thirty-five, her red hair tonged and styled as if for a day out. She is carrying a black bin bag at arm's length.

Nisha spies them. 'She's wearing my shoes to take out her *trash*? I'm going to decapitate her.'

'Can you not be *quite* so horrible?' Sam puts her head into her hands.

Andrea lifts her phone immediately and starts filming her.

'What are you doing?' says Sam.

'Don't know. We might need . . . evidence?' The instant reflexive reaction to everything these days: if you're not sure, film it.

Nisha's heart has started to thump against her chest at the sight of the Louboutins. Sam is murmuring beside her: 'Look, we'll – we'll have a nice chat with her and explain the situation and I'm sure she'll –'

As they watch, the woman opens the black bin and drops the bag inside. She is so close, thinks Nisha. Six, seven strides and she could be there before the woman realizes what's happening. She could drop her with a Krav Maga move, wrench them off her and be back in the car in seconds. As her hand reaches for the door handle, her breath stalls. At that moment the woman hesitates, then walks up to the cat. She makes as if to stroke it, then, after a surreptitious glance down the street, picks up the cat by the scruff of its neck and dumps it in the brown bin. She closes the lid with a slam, and glances around her. Then she dusts her hands together, walks back inside and shuts the door.

The three women stare from the little car, their mouths open.

'What the hell?' says Nisha, after a moment.

'Did she just . . . put that cat in the *bin*?' Andrea is peering through the windscreen.

'She did,' whispers Sam, almost to herself. 'She put a cat in the bin.'

Then before Nisha can speak, Sam climbs out of the car. She marches a few paces towards the house, then turns to face the car. Her face is flushed. 'You see? This is what we're up against. It was just a cat, minding its own business, probably doing a quite nice job of being a cat. Just leading a quiet cat life. And then some arsehole comes up and, for no reason at all, decides to wreck everything, dumping it for no reason in a bin. An actual bin with all the rubbish, like it didn't even matter.'

She doesn't seem to realize that she's shouting, oblivious to the fact that anyone might hear. Her face is anguished, and she's clearly on the edge of tears. 'That cat wasn't even doing anything bad! It did nothing to that woman! Nothing! It was just living, being a cat! And she tried to ruin its life! Why do people have to be so horrible? Why can't people just *not be so horrible?*'

Nisha turns to Andrea. 'Uh . . . is she okay?'

'*No, I am not okay!*'

Sam turns and runs the few short paces to the bin. As Nisha and Andrea watch in shocked silence, Sam reaches both arms into the bin, struggles to reach down a little further, her feet briefly leaving the ground, then emerges with the cat. It looks a little pissed off, and has a light covering of noodles, but apart from that is pretty much unperturbed. Sam pulls the animal close to her face, flicks off the noodles, strokes it, murmurs something they cannot hear. She closes her eyes and takes a long, deep, shuddery breath. After a moment, she opens them and places the cat carefully on the pavement. It shakes itself, briefly washes a paw, then stalks off slowly along the street without a backward look.

'She's saying she's the cat, right?' Nisha murmurs.

'I think that might be it,' says Andrea.

Sam gazes up to the heavens, then wipes her hands on her trousers. She walks back to the car and climbs in, her eyes burning. There is a short silence before she speaks.

'Fuck her. Do what you want. We're getting those shoes.'

When they arrive Jasmine is in the middle of a batch of ironing. She parks the steaming iron on its rear end without comment and makes tea, listening carefully as Nisha outlines what has happened. Sam stands in the corner of the stranger's kitchen, taking in the piles of laundry, the rigorously clean countertops, and sneaks looks at Andrea beside her, who seems more cheerful and animated than she has been in months. Jasmine, having prepared a tray with four full mugs, shoos them through to the living room, where they sit down.

'So, let me get this straight. You need to get your shoes off this woman. Who bought them from a charity shop. And hasn't actually done anything wrong.'

'She put a cat in a bin.' Sam's face is mulish.

The teenage girl's eyes grow wide. Perhaps detecting some strange shift in the atmosphere, she has hovered in the doorway since they arrived. 'She put a *cat* in a *bin*?'

Andrea holds up the phone, shows her the video. Jasmine's face works its way through several expressions in the few short seconds, ending with bemusement.

She shakes her head. 'Gracie, go do your homework.' The girl tuts under her breath and heads reluctantly out of the room. Jasmine turns to Sam and Andrea. 'And who are you two? In relation to this?'

'I'm Sam. I'm the person who took the shoes in the first place. Accidentally.' Sam glances at Nisha, but for the first time Nisha is not rolling her eyes or looking sceptical.

'Andrea. Sam's friend. Not a clue what I'm doing here to be honest but it's a lot more interesting than being at home.'

Jasmine seems to think these are perfectly reasonable explanations.

'Basically,' Sam says, 'we're trying to work out how to recover the shoes in a way that doesn't involve burglary, or beating anyone up.'

'We haven't ruled them out, though,' says Nisha.

'And you can't just ask this woman for the shoes?'

'She put a cat into a bin,' says Sam, as if explaining something to someone not very bright.

Jasmine nods, a little warily. 'Ohh-*kay*.'

'If we ask her for them and she says no, we're out of options.' Nisha leans forward. 'Jas? I remembered what happened when I took my clothes from the penthouse. How you worked out so quickly how to get them back there. And I thought maybe you could . . .'

Jasmine looks at Nisha. She smooths her hair from her face with a beringed finger. A smile twitches at the corners of her mouth.

'What?' says Nisha.

'Nisha Cantor, are you asking for my help?'

It is the first time Nisha's face loses its hard edges. She stares right back at Jasmine for a moment, and something strange happens to her expression, as if a million tumultuous things are taking place just under the surface. 'Are you going to make a big deal out of this?' she says finally.

Jasmine's expression is incredulous. 'Uh . . . *yes?*'

And Andrea, who has been watching this, puts her mug down on the little coffee-table and rubs her hands together. 'Let's do it.'

*

The four women sit in the little living room until almost ten o'clock that evening, talking, planning, laughing. The planning frequently veers off into anecdotes, hysterical giggles or wry smiles of familiarity. At some point after seven they agree to switch from tea to wine, and Nisha runs to the corner shop to buy snacks and two bottles of the kind of wine she would have considered not worth tipping down a sink a month previously. Emboldened by the cheap alcohol, she tells a couple of stories about Carl – including the one about his rage at having the wrong socks – and the three other women are sympathetic and funny about it in a way that would have made her immediately defensive in her previous life. But now she finds, to her surprise, that she likes the hand that emerges to rub her upper arm in solidarity, the jokes about what she should do in revenge.

When Jasmine tells them about putting itching powder in his pants, Andrea, the sick one, coughs wine all over her lap. She seems to be the most restored by the evening: she becomes raucous and rude, funny about people and their motivations, at odds with the apparent frailty of her body, and Nisha realizes the unusual emotion she is feeling is admiration. Andrea explains her illness in the kind of jokey, detached terms that English people do when they're walking through emotional landmines. Jasmine breaks the brief silence by getting out of her seat and giving Andrea an enormous hug. All she says is 'Mate . . .' and Andrea pats at the arms engulfing her as if this one English word expresses a multitude.

Even Droopy Sam seems to come out of her shell a little, and has stopped looking like someone permanently on the verge of tears. She clearly feels responsible for all of this, and she is the one who tries to keep the conversation – and plans

– on track. At nine Jasmine announces with horror that she has forgotten her ironing, and when she explains her side-hustle to the others, Andrea says they will all do it, that it will take no time at all if they do it together, and the rest of the discussion is spent with Jasmine ironing, Sam and Nisha folding and packing in the corner of the room as they talk, and Andrea parked on the sofa with a needle beside Jasmine's extensive sewing kit, neatly hemming a pair of women's trousers. Jasmine, initially anxious about handing over this job, hugs her and calls her a ninja when she examines the finished stitches.

When Sam and Andrea finally leave, Nisha and Jasmine watch them go, waving from the window. The two women are arm in arm on the walkway, illuminated in orange by the sodium light of the streetlamp. Just as they reach the car, Andrea looks weary and drops her head onto Sam's shoulder. Sam pulls her in close. None of them have mentioned whatever was going on with Sam and her sad husband and her job: sometimes you know when someone needs a break from whatever is dominating their life.

'I like them. We should do that again!' says Jasmine.

And Nisha looks at her. 'Are you kidding me?'

She had half meant it as a joke. But Jasmine puts a hand on Nisha's arm. 'Nisha. Darling. Sometimes you can put that armour down, you know?'

She smiles, not unkindly, and heads off to bed.

Phil is asleep when Sam finally comes up. She tiptoes around the dark bedroom, placing her clothes on the chair in the corner, and sliding into the bed in a way that will hopefully not wake him. She has no idea what to say. She is just glad he is not hiding out in the camper-van again.

She lies under the duvet, listening to the cars navigating the narrow street, the distant bark of a dog, her brain still humming with the strange evening, the strange new world in which she has found herself.

'I'm not ready to talk about all this,' says Phil's voice, into the darkness.

She blinks. 'Okay.'

She reaches out a hand to touch him. It hesitates in mid-air, and then she withdraws it, and settles on her back, gazing up into the darkness, hoping for sleep that she is pretty sure will not come.

27

Sam walks up to the front door with Nisha. She is wearing her best work suit, the one she has just started to fit into again and Nisha is in the Chanel jacket, from whose arms she flicks imaginary lint in a faintly proprietorial manner whenever she catches Sam looking. Across the road and three cars along, Jasmine and Andrea sit in the Nissan Micra, and Sam can feel their eyes trained on her, even at this distance. She takes a deep breath and tries to suppress the bud of fear blossoming in her stomach, unsure whether she is going to be able to carry this off. She has never been any good at lying. But then she glances at the bin, its lid flapping gently against its side because someone has left it open, and her resolve stiffens.

She looks at Nisha who nods. And she knocks on the door.

They wait almost thirty long seconds before a man opens it. He has a neck as wide as his head and is wearing a zip-up hoody and tracksuit bottoms, like someone about to go for a run. It is clearly some time since he has been on a run. He peers at them both, at the clipboard Sam is holding. 'We're not religious,' he says, and makes to close the door.

'We're looking for . . .' Sam scans her clipboard '. . . a Liz Frobisher? Is she here, please?'

'Who are you?'

'We're from the Global Cat Protection Fund,' says Nisha, smoothly.

'We already give to charity,' he says, and makes to shut the door again.

But Nisha's foot is already in the way. 'We don't want any-thing, sir. In fact we're here to tell your wife – you *are* Mr Frobisher? – that she's won a prize.'

The look he gives them is wary.

'What kind of prize?'

'Your wife recently bought something from the Global Cat Protection Fund and it turns out she was the one-millionth customer for the charity. So we would like to award her a prize!'

'Does it involve us paying for something?'

'Not a penny,' says Sam, smiling. 'It's just a lovely prize.'

'What is it?'

'Is your wife here, please, sir? We really need to discuss this with the person who bought the item . . . the shoes. That was it.'

He studies them again for a moment, then turns towards the hallway. 'Liz?'

He calls again, and a voice comes from the bottom of the corridor: 'What?'

'Someone at the door for you. Says you've won a prize.'

A short silence, during which Nisha and Sam smile at the man. Perhaps a little unnervingly brightly, Sam thinks after-wards, when his expression grows visibly uncomfortable. They wait a couple of awkward moments while Liz Frobisher emerges along the passageway. She is wearing a pair of tight jeans, a sweatshirt and a pair of fluffy slippers. Sam catches Nisha staring at her feet and thinks this might not be a bad thing. She arrives in the doorway and stands just behind her husband.

'Liz Frobisher?' says Sam, cheerily.

'Yes?'

'We're delighted to tell you that as the millionth customer of the Global Cats Protection Fund you have won a night for two at the renowned Bentley Hotel in London.'

Liz Frobisher frowns, looks from one to the other. 'What? Really?'

'They say we don't have to pay anything,' says the husband.

'What did you say the prize was?'

Sam explains, a smile plastered on her face: this Sunday, Liz and a guest – she assumes this nice man, ha-ha-ha-ha – will be staying in an executive room at the hotel, as the guests of the charity. The hotel is five-star and known in celebrity circles for its high levels of service and attention to detail.

'You bought a pair of shoes from the Global Cats Protection Fund this week, Mrs Frobisher?'

'Yeah, I did.'

'You didn't tell me,' says the man.

'I don't have to tell you every single thing I buy.'

'You don't even like cats.'

'It was for charity.' Liz Frobisher peers over at the clipboard. 'So what do I have to do?'

'Absolutely nothing,' says Nisha, smiling. 'Except turn up! Oh, hang on . . . There was a request that you bring the shoes you bought at the shop to wear for a publicity photo. This would appear on our Instagram feed and other socials. Might that be possible?'

'A publicity photo.' At the suggestion of imminent fame, Liz Frobisher's face brightens. 'Can I see the Instagram feed?'

'It's actually down for relaunch today. It's all being tied into the one-millionth customer prize,' Nisha says quickly. 'But I think . . . yeah . . . here's a screenshot.' Nisha holds up her phone with the fake Instagram page that Andrea created the previous evening.

The two of them peer at it. 'I . . . I might be able to do that. We can do that, can't we, Darren?'

'I was going to my mum's Sunday.'

'Well, we'll go after your mum's.'

'We told her we were going for our tea.'

'So tell her we'll come for lunch.' Liz Frobisher fixes her smile on Sam. 'Does it have to be this Sunday?'

'I'm afraid so,' says Sam. 'This hotel has a very high occupancy rate and Sunday night is the only night the charity could get this standard of room . . .' she pauses for effect and gazes at her clipboard '. . . or we have to give it to the next customer on the list.'

'Oh, no, we can take it,' says Liz Frobisher, jabbing her husband with her elbow when he starts to protest.

'That's lovely! So if you would like to arrive any time after three and check in, a member of staff will consult with you as to when you're ready for your special photograph.'

'Will there be hair and makeup?' she says.

Sam sees Nisha's eyes start to roll and jumps in. 'I'm not sure, but I can check. Either way it's probably best to turn up camera-ready. It's the kind of place where you never know who is going to be hanging around in the lobby,' she says conspiratorially. 'Paparazzi! You know how terrible they are.'

Terrible, they all agree. Terrible.

'Lovely!' says Sam. 'So we'll see you on Sunday! Here's a card for the hotel. Ask for this person on Reception and we'll look forward to seeing you. Congratulations!'

'And don't forget the shoes!' calls Nisha.

'Okay!' says Liz Frobisher, who is still gazing at the card as her husband closes the door.

The two women begin to walk back down the pathway. Sam lets out a small breath she didn't know she was holding.

Nisha glances behind them, and then says quietly, 'Nice job.'

Sam is so taken aback she forgets to respond. The walk down the path seems to take twice as long as the walk up it, and they can just make out Jasmine and Andrea in the car, their faces visible through the windscreen, their expressions hopeful. And then Sam abruptly ducks back two steps and quickly opens the bin, peering inside. She closes it again and looks up to see all three of the women staring at her.

'What?' she says. 'I'm just checking.'

Nisha and Aleks walk to the bus stop together, as they do several times a week now, somehow accidentally ending their shifts at the same time, or bumping into each other outside the staffroom. They started to walk an extra stop, and then two, three stops, a silent tacit agreement that allows them to keep talking, oblivious to the slate grey rain, the endless stream of traffic that runs along the broiling, muddy river. Occasionally he points things out to her: the old MI5 building, unnoticed fishy gargoyles on the ornate lampposts, and once, a seal, its head just visible above the water, a sight she found oddly magical. This God-awful city does not seem quite as dreary through Aleks's eyes. She finds herself half waiting for this walk all day.

'It sounds like you didn't have many friends in your old life.'

Normally Nisha would read this as a criticism, but she thinks for a moment and then says, 'No. I guess I didn't really like other women. But these guys . . . they're okay.' She shakes her head as if she cannot believe she is saying this. 'Even the one who took my shoes.'

He has listened to her story of the past two days, laughing out loud at Andrea's faked collapse in the charity shop, the vanity of the woman who bought the Louboutins. 'Jasmine is a good woman. She's been through hard times. But she has a big heart. She's always helping someone.'

'Yeah. Me.'

Something in her tone makes him glance sideways at her. His collar is turned up and he is wearing a beanie hat pulled low over his ears, which glistens with tiny drops of rain. Away from the strip lights of the kitchen his skin is less pale and the odd curl of caramel-coloured hair is whipped back on his forehead. 'Why are you so uncomfortable? With someone helping you?'

'I don't know.' She rubs her nose. 'I don't like charity. And it's kind of hard having people do stuff for you when you have nothing to give back.' She steps neatly sideways to avoid a pavement cyclist. 'I guess most of my other friendships were . . . transactional. I get you into this party. You get me onto this list. I get your husband access to my husband. We go on holiday together to your amazing house on Lake Como or at Calabasas or whatever. I buy expensive clothes from you. You make me look great and drop everything to accompany me to events that my husband can't come to.'

'Those aren't friendships.'

'Isn't everything transactional, though, when you think about it?' she wonders aloud. 'Most marriages are, even if it's just "I look after you and bear you children and in return you look after me financially"? Or "I keep myself pretty and give you lots of sex so that you don't look at anyone else"?'

He turns and stops. 'That's how you view marriage?'

She stammers slightly. 'Well – everything's a variation of that, right? All human relationships are transactional in some sense.'

She thinks then of Juliana. Who wasn't transactional. Aleks raises his eyebrows but doesn't say anything and after a moment she finds she is filling the silence.

'I mean, look, even friendship. You listen to my problems, I listen to yours. You are loyal and make me feel good, and

I'm loyal and make you feel good in return. That's a form of transaction, even if it is prettier, right?'

He doesn't seem convinced. 'What about genuine warmth? Love? The desire to do something because you care about someone else?'

'Well, that, too. Of course. I mean . . . I probably wasn't expressing myself very well.' She feels awkward, wrong-footed, as if she has revealed something she didn't mean to expose.

He stops at a crossing. She feels his eyes on her and makes sure she looks straight ahead. She thinks he is about to criticize her, say something else about the way she views relationships, but when the lights change, he says, 'You look different today.'

Her hand goes to her head. 'Ugh. I know. My hair needs cutting and I only have mascara –'

'No. You don't need lots of makeup. You look . . . beautiful. Happier.'

She bristles slightly in her jacket. 'I don't know why. I have absolutely nothing to my name right now.'

'You have self-respect. You have friends. You have satisfaction every day, of a job well done. You have agency over your own life. These are not small things.'

'Do you never give yourself a day off from this Hallmark stuff?'

He grins. 'No.'

She walks for a few strides in silence. Then she says, in a small voice, 'I don't have my son.'

He stops.

'Honestly – I'm happy for around fifteen minutes and then I remember I don't have my son. He's been alone for so long. His dad – his dad thinks he . . .' She swallows and takes a breath. 'The thing is, Ray – my son – he's had some emotional issues – probably because he's spent so much time without his parents being around.'

Her gaze flickers sideways. Aleks's head is dipped, as if he is listening. 'Ray is just . . . he's the greatest kid. Really. If you met him you'd get him, I know it. He's smart, and funny, and gorgeous, and kind . . . He knows things – he knows all sorts of stuff I never knew. He's really good on people. He understands them. But his dad seems to see Ray's sensitivity and – I don't know – his sexual orientation as some kind of negative reflection on him. Carl is, like, a caveman. The kind of guy who believes men can only be straight, tough and macho. He hasn't allowed Ray to travel with us for ages, not for the last couple of years. There was . . . there was an incident a while back. Ray had a bad break-up – first love, you know? – and there was some bullying in his last school and that and all the issues with his dad kind of came to a head. It's hard enough being fifteen at the best of times, right? But Ray, he – he kind of hit rock bottom. And that to Carl was like – well, it was like the final straw. He saw it as weakness. He cannot abide what he sees as weakness.'

She still cannot even say the thing, the *incident*, as they called it, for months afterwards, before Carl stopped allowing any mention of it at all. The trip in the ambulance, the stomach pump, the hushed warnings to keep all sharp objects and medications locked away for the foreseeable future. She cannot look at Aleks's face as she speaks. The words are tumbling out of her now, heedless of the enormous lump in her throat, and they keep coming. She is oblivious to the rain, and the cold, and the stationary cars pumping lead into the air beside the traffic island. For the first time in her life she cannot stop talking. She realizes Aleks has taken her hand.

'It was scary. Really scary. And Ray went to a residential facility – a school for kids who have issues, you know? It's very good. Lots of psychiatrists and special doctors and activities to help kids through it. I mean it comes highly recommended, this place. Super-expensive. Half of Fifth Avenue's kids have been through its gates, the kind of exclusive thing that the families don't admit to but people whisper about. And I didn't want to leave him. I didn't. I agreed because I thought maybe that was going to be the best thing for him. What do I know about good parenting? I come from a long line of fuck-ups. I'm not even very good at friendships. I thought if he went there he wouldn't have to cope with Carl's rejection every day, his moods. I thought maybe I could gradually soften Carl, bring him round, make him see how great his son is. But Carl didn't even want to talk about him once he'd gone. He just wouldn't talk about him. When he realized he wasn't going to be *not* gay, it was like Ray died for him. And then life got really complicated and I guess I took my eye off the ball. I was so busy, and travelling so much, and struggling to keep me and Carl on track.

'I thought we were going through a patch, you know? Maybe a mid-life crisis or something. I've seen so many marriages fall apart and I thought I needed to stick by him, to work through it. I thought that would give Ray stability. I thought it would . . . give . . . Ray . . . stability.'

She stops, as a babbling group of schoolchildren feed past them in a moving snake, the teacher holding a red stick aloft. She watches as they cross the road, then gives a tiny shake of her head.

'You know what? That wasn't it. That was just what I told myself. I'm going to say something terrible to you. So terrible. You probably won't want to hang out with me any more when you hear it.'

He is still holding her hand, but he has now wrapped both of his around it.

'If I'm honest, I guess I didn't want my life as it was to stop. I wanted Ray's problems to just go away. I didn't feel like I could deal with it all. I wanted to live the life I had carved out, you know? It had already cost me so much. I was afraid that if I lost Carl I would end up where I'd started. I'd be that sad, powerless little person again. So I kept hoping they could fix my family. They could fix Ray.

'I called him every day. I mean I always call every day. But I see clearly now – it's Carl who needs to be fixed. And that what Ray really needed . . . was just me. I feel so bad because he just needed me. And now because of all this I can't – I can't even get to him.'

She sees him gazing at her, his eyes soft. 'Pretty crappy mom, huh?'

He shakes his head.

Don't you dare hug me, she thinks. *Don't you dare say something gloopy and sympathetic or go all Hallmark again.* She is already feeling her usual discomfort at having made herself vulnerable, the urge to sprint away from him already creeping over her.

But he doesn't hug her. Or say anything honeyed or saccharine. He keeps her hand in one of his and starts to walk. He says simply, 'You will have your son. Very soon.'

'You think?'

'I know. I think . . .' he frowns as he speaks, as if he is considering his words carefully '. . . I think I have never met a woman who is less afraid of obstacles. I think you will have your son back before too long. And I think he is probably very lucky to have you as his mother.'

It is this last thing that makes her eyes prickle. 'Why are you being so nice to me?' she says. She stops on the island in the middle of the road. 'I'm not going to kiss you again.'

'Why would I say nice things just to kiss you? I'm not . . . How did you say? Transactional.'

He shrugs, tilts his head to one side. 'If I wanted to kiss you I would just kiss you.'

He releases her hand. She stands on the pavement island for several minutes, the traffic surging around her, before she realizes she has absolutely no idea what to say.

28

It was entirely predictable that sleep would not come, so at six, gritty-eyed and faintly nauseous with tiredness, Sam leaves the husband who may no longer be her husband, ignores the work clothes for the job she no longer has, climbs into her trainers and heads to the boxing gym. It is quiet at this time, with only the serious gym addicts locked into their own struggles, their punches and grunts echoing round the near-empty hall. A radio burbles in the corner, unnoticed. Sam warms up on the ancient running machine, feeling her legs begin to protest, her breath shortening in her chest, and then she attempts a few weights, just as Sid had told her, repetitions just to get her muscles moving, the lactic acid flowing, refusing to feel cowed by the inadequate size of her dumbbells. And then she steps off, wraps her hands, places them in the battered and vaguely pungent boxing gloves, tightening the Velcro straps with her teeth, and heads over to the punchbag.

The bag is weighted to the floor so that it does not swing too far, and she starts to punch – *one two, one two* – feeling her muscles start to warm, her core tightening with every impact. She sees one of the men glance over and turn away. She knows that look: it's the dismissive look of a man who thinks she's somewhere she doesn't really belong, the blank stare that disregards a woman no longer considered sexually desirable. She stares at the back of his head for a moment, and then she punches hard, so that the impact hits her all the way back in her shoulder-blade. It feels good. She punches again, hard and deliberate, and she suddenly sees Simon's face, his torso, as her fists connect with the scuffed red leather, and finds she is punching harder, the push from her shoulder, from her feet – *one two*. She jabs and crosses, her face contorted with the effort, sweat dripping into her eyes so that she has to wipe at them with the top of her arm, her breath coming in noisy gasps. She no longer cares if anyone is watching her or judging her crappy technique. She punches everyone who has exploited her kindness, everyone who has looked down on her, laughed at her, ignored her. She punches at the Fates that have left her with no job, the scorn of her daughter, the potential loss of her marriage, and the blows grow harder. She punches the three increasingly passive-aggressive messages her mother has left on her voicemail, the final one stating that her father is attempting to clear the second spare room himself for the Afghans and demanding to know what she is supposed to do if he falls and suffocates under all the stuff. *You've obviously decided to disregard our feelings, just like you disregard Phil's.*

She punches the spectre of Miriam Price, the shame of becoming someone *who was sacked*, and the future job she will no longer be able to look forward to. Even if Miriam had Simon's number, there is no way her company will ignore the reasons for her departure, her lack of a reference. She hits at her own failures and weaknesses, her exhaustion and sadness, embracing the fact that her shoulders are screaming, her heart pumping, that every muscle in her body is begging her to stop. And finally, when she feels the strength ebbing from her, her T-shirt and sports bra dark with sweat, Sam wrestles off the gloves, unwraps her bandages, and throws them all into the basket. Then, gazing at her purpling knuckles with something like satisfaction, she heads to the showers.

Sam takes Andrea to her appointment on Friday. Andrea doesn't protest when she announces that she is coming with her to this one. Sam takes the camper-van, as her car is still not working, but this is, it having been the focus of all Phil's attention for days. She doesn't want to ask Phil to replace the battery on the car. She doesn't want to ask Phil anything just now. She is not ready for his cold stare, the casual shrug that suggests nothing to do with her life is his problem any more.

The two women drive in near silence, and it is not just because Sam has to concentrate harder on navigating the larger, unwieldy camper-van through the narrow streets, nerves fluttering when she tries to ease it into a parking space. Sam doesn't want to be the person who insists that everything is going to be fine, that of course Andrea will be better. *You're a fighter! You can beat this!* She learned pretty early on that this is not the way to talk to someone with a serious illness. More than ever, she knows there are no guarantees.

Andrea is paler than usual, her fingers trembling slightly as she struggles with the seatbelt, and Sam hopes this isn't some terrible harbinger. For months she had found herself scanning Andrea's face whenever she saw her, checking for potential weight loss, a greater frailty to her movements, any sign that *the thing* might be winning.

She sips black coffee in the hospital waiting room, staring unseeing at the pages of a magazine when Andrea's name is called, and when Andrea motions to her to come too, part of her is afraid, and part of her is relieved that this means she doesn't have to be out here alone with her thoughts.

They sit down in the little room without even attempting to smile and Andrea runs through the introductions, reaching for Sam's hand when she's finished. Sam grips it tightly, trying to convey all the love she feels, trying not to think what will happen in the next couple of minutes, how their lives are about to be decided. The consultant, Mr Singh, is the surgeon who treated Andrea. He has been there since Andrea's diagnosis, and his authoritative manner and avuncular, slightly distant charm are that of a man who has defined a thousand futures, and has had to explain the probable outcome of them all. He has an extravagant moustache, a shirt that is impeccably starched and a large ruby ring on his little finger that cuts into the flesh. Sam stares at his face, trying to deduce what he is about to say from the way he is leaning forward in his chair, carefully studying the scans in front of him.

'And how have you been feeling in yourself?' he says, closing the file and leaning back in his chair.

'Not bad, bit tired,' Andrea says. Sam sneaks a look at her. Andrea would say, 'Not bad, bit tired,' if she had had both legs bitten off by a shark.

'Any new pain?'

Andrea shakes her head.

'That's good. That's good.'

Just get on with it, Sam wills him silently. She cannot stop staring at his face. She thinks she may throw up from the tension.

He lowers his chins slightly. 'Well, the scan appears to be clear. The surgery went well, as you know. And there appears to be no spread to the lymph nodes, which is what we were obviously concerned about.'

'What are you saying?' says Sam.

'I do not want to be premature. But these are very good indicators. I think, with the combination of surgery and appropriate chemotherapy, we seem to have had an encouraging result.'

'Encouraging?' says Sam.

He gives her a kindly look. 'This is not an absolute science. We do not like to speak of absolute outcomes. But the cancer appears to have been successfully removed, and there do not appear to be any further signs of it. We will continue to monitor you to make sure, but this is as good a result as we could hope for at this point in time.'

Andrea's voice is tentative. 'So . . . it's really gone?'

Mr Singh clasps his hands together. The ruby ring glints in the sun that streams suddenly through the slatted blinds. 'I very much hope so.'

'Do I . . . do I have to do anything?'

'For now, no. Your treatment has ended. We will monitor you, as I said. And you may want to think about the reconstructive surgery. But for now I would focus on building up your strength and returning to as normal a life as you can.'

Nobody speaks. Then Andrea turns to Sam and suddenly her face is stripped raw, shock and relief etched in deep furrows upon it. Tears are running down her cheeks. The two women stand, almost without knowing what they're doing, and then Sam is holding Andrea to her, gripping her tightly, as if it is only now she has allowed herself to grasp the full horror of what she thought she might face. *Oh, my God*, they are saying over each other, *oh, my God, oh, thank God thank God thank God.*

'I was so afraid of losing you,' she sobs into Andrea's bony shoulder. 'I didn't know how I'd get through everything without you. I don't even know who I'd be without you. And I know that's stupid and selfish for me to be thinking like that because it's you who's been in the shit.'

'You'd be up Shit Creek, no paddle, without me.' Andrea is laughing and crying, clasping Sam to her. Sam can feel Andrea's hot tears on her skin. 'Absolutely useless.'

'I would. I want you to know you're a cow for doing this to me,' she says. 'An absolute cow.'

Andrea is laughing. Her eyes are shining and she wipes at them with a pale hand. 'So selfish. I put you through so much.'

'Honestly. I don't know why we're even friends.'

They hug each other again, laughing and crying, then pull back and look at Mr Singh, who is sitting a few feet away. He's still smiling but with the slightly wary, tremulous expression of someone who is not entirely sure what's going on.

'I *love* you, Mr Singh!' Andrea exclaims, and then they're both hugging him, thanking him, laughing at his muffled protestations when they refuse to let him go.

Sam is so deep in her thoughts when she drives back that she does not see the lights change. She and Andrea had treated themselves to a coffee at a local café, sitting at a rickety table outside where, for the first time in a year, Sam had gazed at her friend and not felt a vague, underlying panic at the possibility that Andrea would catch a chill, that her lack of appetite suggested some sinister development, that she would inhale some random bacterium floating by and be felled by it in her fragile, neutropenic state. They sat and ate a sticky bun in happy silence, enjoying the unseasonal sun on their faces.

They had decided by tacit agreement to put off all the difficult discussions, about Sam's marriage, Andrea's finances, the task ahead of recovering the shoes, and just talk instead in small bursts of the deliciousness of the bun, the glorious strength of the coffee, the simple bliss of the unexpected warmth of the day. Today Andrea is well and everything else has become small and insignificant. It was the best coffee Sam can remember.

And then she runs the red light. She only realizes when she hears the outraged blare of the horn, the sound of the elongated skid as the other driver is forced to brake.

'Jesus,' says Andrea, grabbing at her seatbelt. 'This is not the time to get me killed, Sammy.'

Sam pulls across the junction, her heart thumping, one hand raised in an apology to the other driver.

'I'm so sorry,' she says, her body hot and cold with the shock of what has just happened. 'I just – my mind wasn't –'

'I mean you could give me *one day* of being alive and well.'

They laugh, with terrified eyes.

And then Sam looks in her rear-view mirror and sees the blue light. 'Oh, great.'

She pulls the camper-van over into the nearest space, struggling to steer its bulk in safely, then manoeuvring it back a foot in case the policeman says she has parked unsafely too. She looks in her rear-view mirror and sees the police car pull up behind her, the blue light still flashing. An officer climbs out. The other, whom she cannot see clearly because of the glare on the windscreen, remains in the passenger seat.

Sam lowers her window as the woman approaches. She is fifty-something, stocky, her walk slow and deliberate, and her expression that of someone who has seen seventeen different kinds of bullshit already this morning and is so not ready for yours.

'I'm so sorry,' Sam calls, before she can speak. 'It was entirely my fault.'

'You just ran a red light. You nearly caused quite a pile-up back there.'

'I know. I'm really sorry.'

The officer peers in at Andrea. She turns back to Sam, scanning the interior of the van with a practised eye, then leaning back on her heel to regard the giant sunflower on the side panel. She squints. 'This your vehicle, is it, madam?'

'Yes,' says Sam. 'Well, mine and my husband's.'

'And it's insured? Roadworthy?'

'It was MOTed last week.' Phil hadn't told her. She had only found out because he had left the certificate on the side in the kitchen.

'Brakes work, do they?'

'Yes.'

'And your eyesight is good?'

'It's – it's fine.'

'Then would you like to explain to me why you just ran straight through a red light?'

'No excuse,' says Sam shaking her head. 'But my friend here just got the all-clear from her cancer treatment and I – I hadn't slept last night for worrying about the appointment and I guess I was just so happy and maybe tired, I don't know, that . . . I lost focus for a moment.'

The woman stares at Andrea, taking in the wrapped head, the pale skin.

'It's probably my fault too,' says Andrea. 'I was talking too much. I always talk too much.'

'You know what?' says Sam. 'Just give me the ticket. It's fair enough. I should have been paying better attention. Let's just get this over and done with.'

The officer frowns at her. 'You're *asking* me to give you a ticket?'

Sam doesn't know what has come over her. She lifts her palms and gazes directly at the officer. 'Yes.'

Then, when nobody says anything, she says: 'You know what? I just lost my job because my boss thinks I'm a waste of space. My daughter isn't speaking to me. My husband is leaving me because he thinks I have a lover. Most days I wish I bloody did. And I'm probably menopausal. If I'm not menopausal I'm in real trouble because I cry pretty much every day. I've missed two periods and most mornings I wake up with what feels like a juggernaut pressed on my chest. But right now I can deal with all of it because my best friend here has got through cancer. Everything else is just my own stupid crap. So just give me the ticket. Let's get this over with.'

The officer looks between the two of them. She peers

down at her feet for a moment, thinking, then up again. 'Menopausal, huh?'

'I'm still a safe driver,' Sam says hurriedly. 'I mean, I still drive safely most of the time. You can check my record. I just . . . it's just been a really weird couple of days.'

The officer keeps gazing at her steadily.

'Sorry,' says Sam again.

The woman leans into the window. 'Just wait till you get the night sweats,' she says, her voice lowering. 'They're a *bitch*.'

Sam blinks.

'And those fuckers don't help.' She gestures backwards towards the squad car with her head. She stands back on the kerb. She puts her notepad into her pocket. 'I'm letting you off. This time. Just keep your eyes on the road and pay attention, okay?'

'Really?' says Sam.

The officer is already walking away. She stops and turns for a moment, stooping so she can wave at Andrea. 'And good job. The whole . . . cancer thing,' she says. She pauses, then adds: 'Maybe next time get a taxi home.'

And then she turns and walks slowly back to her squad car, muttering into her radio as she goes.

Kevin has crapped on the hall carpet. He sidles up to her as she opens the front door, his head low, his gait wobbly and the whites of his eyes showing, as if in apology. Phil is not there, and neither is Cat, and she doesn't have the heart to be cross with him. He might have been left alone for hours. 'Don't worry, old man. It's not your fault,' she says, and runs a bowl of detergent and hot water, pulling on her rubber gloves.

She is on her hands and knees when Cat lets herself in. Cat hesitates at the doorway, as if deciding whether to come or go, but perhaps it's hard to walk out on a mother who is scrubbing dog excrement from a beige carpet, so she nods a hello and tiptoes past the affected area, as if this will somehow have an effect on what Sam is doing.

'Is Dad in?'

'No,' says Sam, through gritted teeth. She has run out of the really good carpet shampoo and is now using washing-up liquid. She rocks back on her heels, turning her head away while she tries not to gag. Dog accidents are always her job, and they never get any easier to clean up. She wonders at what point this task was allocated to her. Perhaps she was busy that day and missed the meeting.

And then she becomes aware that Cat is behind her. She twists to see her. Cat's face is solemn.

'You okay?' says Sam, although she thinks she knows the answer.

'I'm sorry about the shoes.'

Sam puts down her sponge. 'Don't be. You weren't to know.'

'I thought you were having an affair.'

'Did you really?'

'You and Dad seemed so unhappy. Like you never did anything together any more. Like . . . you don't get any joy from each other's company.' Her words are a series of little blows. Cat rubs at her nose. Doesn't look Sam in the eye for the next sentence. 'And then I saw you with that man.'

'Joel is just a friend.'

'But the sho—'

'I was wearing those shoes because . . . well, because sometimes you need to feel like a different version of yourself.'

Cat looks at her then, and Sam is unsure whether it's incomprehension or suspicion she can detect in her daughter's face.

'I have been unhappy, Cat. You're right. For a long time. Your dad doesn't see me any more. Most days I've felt like

I don't even exist. It's hard for you to imagine now, while you're young and beautiful and everyone notices every move you make. But I seem to be invisible, these days, and when even the man you love doesn't see you it's . . . well, it's pretty soul-destroying. I needed to feel like a different version of myself – and the shoes, I guess, were a part of that. It's hard to explain. I'm not even sure I can explain it to myself. But I'm sorry you've been caught up in it.'

'Why do you need a man to tell you who you are?'

'What?'

Cat edges around the dark stain on the carpet. 'Why do you need validation from someone else? Dad is down in the dumps, yes, but that doesn't mean you have to fall apart. You're still you. I wouldn't let some man dictate how I felt about myself.'

'Yeah. Well, you always did have it all worked out. I think you knew who you were from the age of three.' She looks at her daughter, whose generation seems to have this all sorted, with their talk of autonomy, of slut-shaming, allyship and body positivity. She feels the reflexive clench of sadness she has started to feel when she remembers that soon this girl will be gone, storming through her own life, no longer clumping through the door in her heavy workmen's boots.

Cat sits down heavily on the bottom step. She reties the laces on one of her boots and waits a moment before she speaks.

'Colleen's mum left her dad last month. She said they were "on different paths".'

Sam is not sure what to say to this, so she organizes her face into a neutral expression.

Cat's face is suddenly vulnerable, like a child's. 'Are you and Dad going to split up?'

Do you have feelings for Joel? he had asked her, the previous evening, as she brushed her teeth. She had struggled with how to respond to him honestly, and continued brushing for an extra few seconds before she spat out the paste. *Not the same as I have for you*, she said. He had gazed at her reflection in the mirror for a moment, then headed off to bed.

'I don't think so,' she says, and hugs her daughter, relishing the brief proximity. She hopes she sounded more convinced than she feels.

Joel has texted her twice. A long, rambling message informed her that he had told everyone in the office what had been going on and they were trying to work out what to do to make things right. Marina felt awful. Franklin had already cocked up on the Dutch order. She shouldn't worry. She should call him if she needed anything, anything at all. He hoped she would soon come back to the gym. She was doing great! The second, sent twenty-four hours later, says simply: I miss you. She stares at it several times a day, when she is alone, and her heart gives an erratic thump every time, like an engine trying to jump-start into life.

29

Phil cannot sit down. Every time he lands on the little couch he springs back up again as if it's electrified, as if there is too much in him to be contained by mere furniture. He paces backwards and forwards around the little room, his words coming in scattergun explosions.

'I mean she pretty much admitted it! Even if it wasn't an affair she had *feelings* for him. What am I supposed to do with that? Can you tell me? Because I don't have an answer. It goes round and round in my head and I don't have an answer.'

Dr Kovitz sits, his notepad on his knee, wearing an expression of eternal patience. It makes Phil want to punch him on the nose.

'She didn't even deny it. She just said her feelings for *him* weren't the same as they were for me.'

'What did you take from that?'

Phil looks at him incredulously. 'What do you think I took from that? My wife has feelings for another man!'

'I have feelings for plenty of people. It doesn't mean I'm going to run off with them.'

'Spare me the word games today, please.'

'They're not word games, Phil. She has told you she isn't having an affair. And, given you say she's an honest person, we have to assume she's telling the truth. She had feelings for another person. You told me in one of our previous sessions that you would actually understand if she went off with someone else.'

'But that was before it was true!'

Phil puts the heels of his hands into his eyes and presses hard so that tiny explosions of dark matter go off behind them, wanting his thoughts to still, wanting it all to stop.

'What has she said to you, Phil? About what she wants to do?'

He sits heavily. 'We haven't talked about it.'

Dr Kovitz's eyebrows are raised.

'I mean, not like this. I just – I don't know what to say to her. I feel like I don't know her any more.'

'Well, it's possible you don't know her any more. We're all changing. All the time. By your own admission you left your wife to cope with everything alone for a long period of time. That's going to alter a person. It's going to alter a marriage.'

Phil crosses his arms around his body and bends over, so that his chest rests on his knees. Some days there is such a pressure in it he feels like he has to suppress it physically.

'Marriage doesn't stay the same year after year, Phil. You've been married a long time. You know this. It's an organic thing. It changes as both parties change. Perhaps sometimes we need to just –'

'She's still hiding things from me,' Phil blurts out.

Dr Kovitz leans back in his chair. 'Okay.'

'I called her company two days ago because the builders wanted to know something about the insurance payment and they said – they said she didn't work there any more.'

There is a long silence.

'She doesn't want to share anything with me, does she?' Phil lets out a long, defeated sigh. 'I count for nothing in her life any more.' Life with Sam was once a reliable thing, the backbone of everything else he ever had to deal with. Now it feels like living with her is a series of small explosions, like he never knows what is coming next.

'Phil,' Dr Kovitz says gently, 'when we're low, it can be easy to see everything through a prism of negativity. Human beings are remarkably bad at understanding other people's motivations, even when they know them terribly well. We write all sorts of inaccurate stories in our heads.' Dr Kovitz steeples his fingers together. 'May I suggest an alternative version?'

Phil waits.

'From what you've said previously, your wife may well have walked out on her job – a job you said she hated. Or she could have been made redundant. We don't know. What if the reason she kept that information to herself was that she was simply worried about telling you? What if she was trying to protect herself from that awful conversation, with all its ramifications for the two of you?'

He pauses. 'You told me Sam has been very much aware of your mental-health struggles for some time. Have you considered the possibility that by not saying anything she was trying to protect *you*?'

Phil remembers that when Sam's phone rang he could always tell if it was her boss from the way she flinched when she saw his name. 'So you basically think I should ignore all this. Just pretend like none of it happened.'

'Not at all. I think it's about time you talked to her.'

30

Nisha is so deep in her thoughts that she jumps when Jasmine approaches. She is standing on the little balcony, looking over the dark and twinkling city, Jasmine's spare dressing-gown wrapped tightly around her against the cold, a cigarette she doesn't even want to smoke between her lips, as if doing something as awful as smoking at 6 a.m. will reaffirm how awful everything is. Some mornings she feels so far from her son it's as if a thread, taut between them, connects her heart to his and causes a constant, only just bearable pain. He had sounded so down again last night, so disbelieving when she said she was going to get the shoes, she *was*, Ray, *really*, that then she could come get him. He had cut her short when she tried to describe the plan to him. He had done badly in a math test, Dad was still cutting off his money, and his friend Zoë was all over Instagram partying with some girls she knew he couldn't stand. He sounded so lonely and flat. Yes, he was still taking his meds. No, he wasn't hungry. No, he wasn't sleeping. Yes, he knew everything was going to be okay. Whatever. 'When are you coming to get me?'

'Soon, baby. I just have to get these shoes to your father and then he'll have to give me the money.'

'I hate him,' he had said vehemently, and when she tried, half-heartedly, to protest that he shouldn't think that, he really shouldn't, he had asked why? In what way did his dad even love him? In what way did Ray owe him anything? And she hadn't been able to come up with a good answer.

They had both been quiet for a few long, anguishing moments and then he had said, in a quiet voice: 'Mom? Remember that song you used to sing me? Would you sing it to me now?'

When she had sung, her voice had trembled.

You are my sunshine, my only sunshine . . .

You make me happy, when skies are grey . . .

'Couldn't sleep either, huh?' Jasmine says, handing her a coffee.

A police helicopter has circled overhead for hours, its vibrations sending shock waves into the night sky, filling the atmosphere with a sense of vague, unspecified threat. Nisha takes the cup and shakes her head.

Jasmine sits down in the little fold-up chair she keeps on the balcony, adjusting her dressing-gown over her knees. 'Me either. I keep asking myself if we're nuts, trying to do this.'

Nisha knows that what Jasmine actually means is that she could lose her job. Every bit of this is a sackable offence. When Jasmine had outlined the plan to the others, Nisha had seen both jaws physically drop, as if they were characters in a cartoon. Nisha has spent hours trying to work out how to protect Jasmine: it will be Nisha who takes the key card, Nisha who removes the shoes, Nisha who, in a worst-case scenario, will hold up her hands and claim it is all down to her, that she bullied Jasmine into collaborating, that she is guilty of all of it. But it still feels like a risk.

'You don't have to do this,' Nisha says, for the fifth time. 'You've done so much for me. I don't want to put you at –'

'Nish. Do I look like someone who does things they don't want to do? No. I've thought about this over and over. What we're doing is righteous. We're getting you what is rightfully yours. We're going to help you. I'm your friend, and I'm going to help you.' She sneaks a sideways look at Nisha. 'Besides, if I don't get you out of my daughter's bunk bed and back into your own place soon Gracie is going to kick my arse.'

They smile. Then Jasmine's smile falls and she takes another sip of her coffee. 'The thing I'm worried about is when you hand the shoes over. If your bloke is going to keep his side of the bargain.'

'Yeah. I've been thinking about that too.'

Carl will do anything to win. If this is just a game to him – and it is entirely possible that it is – he will simply find some other obstacle to place in the way of her settlement. This is her greatest fear: that he will simply have her running in circles endlessly in this strange city, penniless and powerless, while her boy sits alone in that school of his, growing sadder and sadder, thousands of miles away from her. She had thought her position protected her. She had thought the law protected her. And what she had discovered was that everything could be stripped away, and all she had was her own resources, whatever it was that kept her standing.

They drink their coffee in silence, looking at the lights of the city as it slowly comes to life, the red tail-lights of the vehicles making their way into the lead-lined dark.

You'll never know, dear, how much I love you
Please don't take my sunshine away.

Nisha closes her eyes. The thread pulls ever tighter.

'Well, you know what they say? One step at a time.' Jasmine swigs the last of her coffee and pats the wrap on her head that holds her hair in place as she sleeps. 'Come on, babe. We get to work. Then we get your shoes. We'll worry about the rest of it later. And step one is I'm going to put some toast on.'

She disappears inside. Nisha sits and stares at the sky. And then she pulls out her phone and types a message.

JULIANA? Is this still your number?

She hesitates, and then adds: It's Anita.

She waits another moment then presses send, watching the little message wink its way into the ether.

Sam walks the dog in the dark, forgetting for once to be nervous of shadowy strangers on the sodium-lit street. She is thinking about the day ahead, the strange thing she has agreed to. She has never done anything like this in her life. Samantha Kemp: a middle-aged woman, a print manager, married, one kid, still living in the same postcode in which she was raised. She is about to do something completely ridiculous to return shoes to a woman who doesn't even like her. These facts swirl around and around her head. But in truth everything in her life feels so unhinged, so unreal just now, that this day does not feel so far removed. Besides, the worst of everything has already happened: she has lost, or pretty much lost, everything that was important to her, aside from Andrea.

As Kevin sniffs interestedly at the base of every tree and lamppost, she thinks about Jasmine and Andrea, and how they took to each other immediately. Andrea can do that with people: she seems to have a kind of shorthand, a straightforward, open friendliness that cuts through awkwardness and leaves people basking in her glow. When they were younger she could never understand why Andrea was friends with someone like her. Sam had never possessed that charisma, the strange unidentifiable aura that meant people always wanted to be near her. Andrea was not coming today, though – 'Too identifiable,' Jasmine had decreed, and Nisha had said, 'Damn. Scarfy can turn it on when she has to.'

Sam had flinched, but Andrea had just laughed and said she was probably right. 'Yeah, you don't want Gollum in a police line-up. Just wait till my eyebrows grow back, and I'll be like Tom Cruise in *Mission: Impossible*.'

Nisha and Sam still eyed each other warily. There was a kind of boundarylessness around Nisha, a suggestion of fearlessness that made Sam nervous. She had always felt most comfortable around people who followed the rules as she did. She sensed that something about her made Nisha uneasy too. They were perfectly polite, but perhaps the circumstances of their meeting were too weird and too laden with baggage to allow them to be properly warm with each other.

It didn't matter. Sam had lost Nisha's shoes: therefore she had to help her recover them. It's the right thing to do, at a time when nothing else is clear. It is the only thing she can do. Once she's got that out of the way she'll clear the decks, and start worrying about getting another job.

The door is unlocked when she and Kevin arrive home, the roads slowly clogging with traffic, the speculative Sunday shoppers already up and out. She walks into the kitchen and experiences a small jolt when she discovers Phil is up, making a cup of coffee with his back to her, already dressed in a hoody and his old tracksuit bottoms. He turns a fraction and nods as she enters, the most he can bring himself to do in greeting, these days. To hide the stomach-flopping dismay it gives her, she mutters something about taking a shower before he says anything else and leaves him to feed Kevin.

She showers, and dries her hair, conscious, as she moisturizes her face, how the corners of her mouth seem to have settled into tight, downward grooves. She is pretty sure those are new. She stops staring at her face in the magnifying mirror – honestly, they should be banned to all women over the age of thirty – and pulls on a black T-shirt and black jeans, as instructed by Jasmine, then puts a grey jumper and her navy blue parka over the top.

She is just tripping down the last two stairs when he appears in the hallway.

'Can we . . . talk?'

She blinks at him.

'Now?'

'Yes. Now.'

She glances at her watch. 'I – It's not great timing, Phil. I – I have to get to work.'

'Work,' he says. His eyes are dead when he speaks to her. 'On a Sunday.'

'It – it's a special job. I can't really – Look, can we talk when I get back? I'll be a bit late this evening but we can definitely –'

He is staring at her like she's someone he has never met. Just then her mobile phone rings. She glances down, expecting it to be Nisha or Jasmine, but it's Joel. His name flashes, like a grenade going off. She stares at it, colour rising to her cheeks, willing him to go away.

'Take it,' says Phil, who has seen everything.

'I really –'

'Take it.'

She answers the call, looking away from Phil, though she can feel his eyes burning into the back of her head. Her voice, when she speaks, is too high, too false. 'Joel!'

Joel's voice is low, conspiratorial. 'Sorry to bother you on a weekend, Sam. But, look, it's a bit weird but some Israeli guy came to the office on Friday. Asking questions about you.'

'What? . . . Israeli?'

'Yeah. I didn't really get it. He spoke to Martin, who said you'd left and then he was off. I don't know what questions he asked, I just – I got a bad vibe off him. Martin only just told me – I don't want to freak you out – but he says there was something off about it. Just thought you should know.'

'That's odd. Okay. Thanks.'

There is a short silence.

'And I wondered if –'

'Got to go,' she says brightly. 'I'll – see you at work! Thanks for passing that on!'

She rings off before Joel can say anything else. She stuffs her phone into her pocket and tries to rearrange her face into an expression that is not guilty, not slightly flustered.

'So, we'll – we'll talk later?'

Phil looks at her and his whole bearing suggests he is under a weight that is almost unbearable.

'We will, Phil. We'll talk when I'm back. I just – I have to do this.'

'I'm going away,' he says, turns and walks back to the kitchen.

Sam goes very still. 'What?'

'I'm going away. I can't – I can't deal with this any more. I need to get my head straight.'

She walks down the hallway so that she can see him, standing, his back against the worktop. 'What do you – where are you going?'

'I don't know.'

'Phil, this is ridiculous! You can't just walk out. Please don't. We have to – Look, I'll be back later and we'll talk, okay? Just let me get past today and we'll sort this.'

He shakes his head. And when he speaks, he seems genuinely bewildered. 'Twenty-three years, Sam. What is there to talk about?'

Michelle on Reception has always liked Jasmine, so when she offers to look after the front desk for ten minutes, so that Michelle can take a cigarette break, she clearly regards it as just another extension of Jasmine's kindness, her generosity to other members of the Bentley staff. Plus, Michelle happily leaves the desk empty most days while she sneaks a Marlboro Light and this way she's less likely to get into trouble with Frederik. The desk is one of the few areas in the lobby not monitored by CCTV.

Nisha stands a few feet away with Sam, keeping lookout, as Jasmine scans the list of reservations until she finds what she's looking for. She blocks out a room, makes a few quick changes on the screen, whips a key from the board of hooks behind her head, and is standing back from the desk, smiling blandly, when Michelle returns, smelling vaguely of cigarette smoke. She checks her lipstick in a small hand-held mirror and snaps it shut as she slides in.

'You're a lifesaver, Jas. I can't believe Lena didn't turn up for her shift again. Honestly, if they ask me to pull another double I'm going to walk out.'

'Anytime, my darling. Anytime,' says Jasmine, and sweeps out from behind the desk. Michelle looks at her quizzically. 'Funny, I didn't think you were on tod–'

'Perfume. Frederik is going to smell your cigarette.' Jasmine pulls a bottle of unidentified scent from her handbag and squirts two blasts at Michelle, who, distracted, coughs and mutters a weak 'Thank you,' as Jasmine shoves it back into her bag and disappears.

Nisha and Jasmine lead Sam through the side door and down the back staircase to the staff changing room, where they put on their uniform of dark shirts and trousers. Sam has been silent since she arrived, her face pale and drawn, and Nisha wonders if it's nerves. She's going to have to pull it together if she's to get this thing done. She's the kind of woman who might well buckle, suddenly announce that she couldn't tell a lie, or burst into tears. *Please don't let her fuck this up*, she wills some unknown deity. *I need my shoes.*

'You okay?' she says tersely to Sam, as she does up her trousers.

'Fine,' says Sam, who is sitting on the bench, her hands clasped tightly in her lap. Her knuckles are white.

'You're not going to bail on us.'

'I'm not going to bail on you.'

'Why not put on some makeup, babe? You look a little bit pasty.' Jasmine, who clearly needs something to do, is steering Sam to the mirror. She pulls out her oversized makeup bag, then starts to apply blusher and mascara to Sam's face. Sam is completely expressionless, zombified in some private misery. *What is wrong with her?* thinks Nisha. Nisha is the one who will be shouldering this thing, after all. She's the one who has the most to lose.

'There,' says Jasmine, finally. 'Back from the dead!' She laughs kindly and pats Sam's cheek.

Sam gazes at herself in the mirror. 'Thanks,' she says dully. Her eyes have been outlined, her skin glows with bronzer. She wears so little makeup normally that the transformation is almost shocking.

'What's the time?' says Nisha, glancing at her watch. 'Do we need to be at Reception yet?'

'Check-in is at three,' says Jasmine. 'Let's grab some food. You can't fight on an empty stomach, right?'

The three women stand in the corner of the kitchen. Jasmine has eaten her pancakes, but Sam isn't touching her food, which Nisha knows will make Aleks jittery. He gets actual anxiety if he thinks someone isn't enjoying the meal he's made for them. Sometimes she sees him gazing out through the windowed swing doors, silently monitoring who has eaten how much of their omelette, or eggs Benedict and his back will bristle with unhappiness if more than half of it is left.

'You don't like it?' he says, gesturing to Sam's barely touched plate. 'You want me to make you something else?'

'Oh, no. It's lovely,' says Sam, her face creasing into a half-smile. 'I'm just not very hungry.'

'You should eat Aleks's food. He's the best.' Nisha feels vaguely cross at Sam's refusal.

'I said I'm not hungry.' They've snapped at each other all morning, tension bringing to the surface the strange resentments that each has tried to suppress.

Nisha is starving. She had forgotten to eat breakfast, thinking of all the possible angles she needed to cover and distracted by her phone. When Aleks placed a plate of pancakes in front of her, drizzled with maple syrup and ringed with blueberries, she had to fight an almost overwhelming urge to kiss him. She had finished them in a matter of minutes, letting out little moans of pleasure at the perfect fluffiness of them, the sticky syrup and the crisp slivers of bacon.

'You're ready?' he said, tucking his white tea-towel back into his waistband.

'Ready as I'll ever be.' She hands back the plate. 'Thanks for the pancakes.'

'My shift finishes at four. But I will stay. In case you need me.'

'We won't,' she says. And then, because it sounds unfriendly, 'I mean, I hope we won't need you. But it's kind of you.'

He doesn't flinch. He never does.

'I stay here anyway.' He checks with Sam that she really, really doesn't want the pancakes and, with a barely suppressed sigh, takes the plates back to his station.

At a quarter to three, Sam waits in the hotel reception area. She has been sitting for almost half an hour, feeling self-conscious and out of place there, in the marble-clad fortress of imposed serenity. Guests walk by, followed by uniformed porters pushing huge brass trolleys full of luggage, or wheeling one-night cabin bags. Huge bowls of pale orchids punctuate the overstuffed sofas. The smell of vetiver hangs elegantly in the air. Sam cannot remember the last time she was in a hotel, let alone a hotel so grand. Perhaps that night in Formby when she worked for Henry and they went to pitch for a mammoth run of football programmes. She has vague memories of a Travelodge key card that didn't work and a pervasive smell of fish.

She glances up at the ornate clock, then at the door behind which she knows Nisha is waiting, her expression as tense and determined as it has been all morning. She knows Nisha thinks she won't go through with it, and she carries the irritation that comes from Nisha's assumption and also the sneaking suspicion that she may be right. Every cell in her body is telling her to leave. And yet, she realizes, there is nothing for her to go home to. What else is she going to do? Then the glass doors to the street open and Sam sees them: Liz and Darren Frobisher, glancing around in the way that people do when they arrive somewhere they haven't been before. She types HERE into her phone, takes a breath, and she's on her feet, striding over to them before they can reach the reception desk.

'Hello! Mr and Mrs Frobisher! How lovely to see you.'

They had gone over it all multiple times beforehand. Michelle on the front desk wouldn't look twice at a couple being greeted by another guest in the foyer so Sam would be free to shepherd them away and upstairs to the designated room. People used the foyer as an unofficial meeting point even if they weren't staying at the hotel: it's glamorous, and quiet, in the centre of town, and good for Instagram selfies taken by the kind of people who want to suggest they have a posh-hotel kind of lifestyle. Liz Frobisher's endless chatter is briefly quieted by the plush marble interior, and the couple follow Sam obediently to the lifts, where she talks mindlessly at them both, asking them about their journey, what a lovely day it had turned out to be, how very smart they look. Liz Frobisher isn't wearing the shoes, but her husband pulls a cabin bag on wheels and she feels their presence inside it like something radioactive.

The door is unlocked when they reach Room 232 and Jasmine is already inside, pretending to plump pillows.

'Are these our prizewinners?' she says, smiling broadly, and Liz Frobisher offers her a hand, palm down, like a queen greeting a subject. Jasmine manages to restrain herself to only the faintest of eyebrow lifts. The room is a Mid-range Executive Comfort, 42 square metres with a queen-sized bed and a small sofa under the window.

'So,' Sam says. 'Here is the room. One of the hotel's best. We hope you'll be very comfortable.'

Liz Frobisher is walking slowly around the bed, running her fingers over the bedspread and curtains, as if testing its quality. She looks up at the sumptuous décor, an expression of vague disappointment colouring her features. It is possible her status as prizewinner has gone to her head.

'So when do we take the photographs of me?' she says, turning to Sam.

'It would be good if we could do them fairly soon,' says Sam. 'You know, while the light is good.'

'Is this outfit okay?'

Liz Frobisher is wearing a red two-piece fake Chanel suit, with deliberately frayed hems, and a scarf knotted jauntily at her neck. Her red hair, which Sam now sees is dyed, has been sprayed into beach waves, and her makeup suggests upwards of an hour spent at a vanity table.

'Gorgeous,' say Jasmine and Sam in unison, and Liz preens a little, as if this is only to be expected.

'So do we get any free booze?' says Darren.

'Darren, you know we're not drinking,' says Liz, sharply, then adds, 'We wondered . . . you know . . . whether there were any other things included in the evening apart from just the room.' Her *just* hangs in the air like a vague threat.

'I'm sure we can rustle something up for our prizewinners,' says Jasmine, smoothly. Then she writes her number on the notepad by the bed and hands it over. 'Any problems, anything at all, you call this number. I'm your designated senior housekeeper. Just call me direct. I'll be only too happy to help.'

Nisha arrives with a brisk knock, sporting a camera that had been left in Lost Property and not yet disappeared, possibly because none of the staff had been able to make it work. She greets the couple with the kind of practised warmth that seems to come easily to Americans, then waits as Liz opens the suitcase. Sam sees Nisha's eyes widen as she spies her red Christian Louboutin shoes resting neatly on a pale sweater, and watches Liz carefully remove them from the case and strap them on. There they are, Sam thinks, just inches from us, and glances warily at Nisha in case this is the moment Nisha loses the plot and rips them from the woman's feet. But Nisha seems to compose herself, and if her smile is suddenly a little steelier, Sam suspects she is the only person to notice it.

The three of them, Darren, Jasmine and Sam, wait awkwardly as Nisha instructs Liz to pose by the window, seated at the little table, then she and Darren together by the door until Liz insists that Darren shouldn't be in this one as he hadn't shaved that morning, 'And it wasn't him who bought the shoes anyway.' Darren, freed from obligation, starts checking out the television remote control.

'So what are you doing tonight?' says Sam, as Nisha clicks away with the blank camera. 'You'll be eating dinner in the hotel restaurant?'

'Oh, Darren had a look at the menu and doesn't fancy it. He wants to go somewhere else.' Liz lifts her chin and pouts slightly.

'Nothing? Not even a nice burger?' says Sam.

'We're going to get Chinese. I like crispy duck pancakes,' he says.

'I bet you won't be wearing those shoes,' Sam says casually. 'They're very high, aren't they?'

Liz looks down at her feet. 'Oh, I'm used to high heels.'

'But you won't want to walk all the way to Leicester Square in them.'

Liz shrugs. 'I don't know. Depends if it rains, really, doesn't it, Darren?'

'Those are lovely,' says Sam, pointing. 'Those shoes you were wearing when you came in. I'd wear those.'

Nisha is staring silently at Liz's feet. If a look could burn the Louboutins off her, the straps would be giving off a thin plume of smoke just now.

'Oh, those are Russell and Bromley,' says Liz. 'But I'm not sure they really go with this suit.'

'They do! Most definitely. They look lovely,' says Sam.

'The pavements are very uneven around Leicester Square,' says Jasmine, plumping another cushion. 'Be careful you don't turn an ankle if you wear heels. We had a guest who really hurt herself last week.' She nods to herself and adds darkly, 'Really hurt herself.'

Liz sits down on the edge of the bed. 'No. I'll probably

wear these. They're my lucky shoes now, aren't they, Darren?' She swivels an ankle, admiring her foot.

Jasmine and Sam exchange a look of silent dismay.

'Right,' says Sam, backing towards the door. 'Well, then. We'll leave you to it.'

'Don't forget,' says Jasmine. 'Call me direct if you need anything. It'll be much quicker than going through the switchboard.'

'Can I see the pictures?' says Liz, as Nisha walks to the door.

Nisha swings the camera behind her. 'When they're developed. I'll send you a contact sheet.'

The words 'contact sheet' seem to please Liz. The three women stand by the door for a moment.

'Right!' says Jasmine. 'Well, have a wonderful time!'

'It's lovely,' says Sam, suddenly, 'that you came to be here. Just because of your kindness to cats.' She cannot help herself. She swallows a yelp as Nisha jabs her hard in the kidney. And then they're outside in the corridor, Jasmine closing the door behind them.

'Nobody's going to wear open-toe shoes in this weather,' says Jasmine, hopefully. 'Not even her.'

'It is quite chilly,' says Sam.

'She's going to wear her *lucky shoes*,' Nisha spits, 'even if it snows.'

'I can't believe they don't drink.' Jasmine runs her hand around the neck of the redundant bottle of champagne. 'What kind of people don't drink? It would have been so much easier if they were drunk.'

It is a quarter past five, and Jasmine's theory is that the Frobishers will be early eaters. Darren is clearly a man of appetites. They had originally planned to wait until the couple left to go out, then Nisha would run in and get the shoes. Now they sit in the staff changing area, gazing out of the small window, ruminating on whether Liz Frobisher's choice of footwear is going to alter everything.

'Rain, you bastard,' says Nisha, staring out at the grey sky. 'It rains every day in this damn country. Would it hurt so much just to let some down today?'

The text she sent to Juliana has been marked 'Read'. But she hasn't texted back.

31

The Frobishers finally leave Room 232 at a quarter past six, about an hour after the women have decided silently that the plan is not going to work and sunk into despondency. Jasmine has been 'tidying' the office behind the front desk, issuing vague platitudes at Michelle's endless conversations about the unfairness of the rota system while she watches for movement in the foyer. Sam and Nisha wait in silence in the stuffy little changing room, ignoring the incurious glances of the staff coming in to get things from their lockers, or change to go home. They are just anonymous staff to any casual passer-by, neither worth talking to nor acknowledging. The two women sit in silence, each locked in her thoughts. Nisha finds herself irritated by Sam's droopy face, the air she carries of someone defeated by life. And then her phone pings, breaking into her thoughts. She stares at the screen, suddenly alert.

'They're moving.' Nisha stares at her phone as another text comes through. 'Oh, my God,' she says, hardly able to believe what she's reading. 'She's not wearing the shoes.'

'Really?' says Sam, hopefully.

'It's raining,' says Nisha. 'It's actually raining. THANK YOU, LORD.' She is already on her feet. 'Okay. Remember what we said. You follow them out and make sure they're gone, and I'll run up and get the shoes.'

Nisha is wearing a dark shirt and trousers so that she can pass either for hotel staff, if wearing her lanyard, or a particularly boringly dressed guest, if she tucks it into her pocket.

Jasmine has given her a newly programmed guest key, and her heart is thumping against her rib cage. This is it. She is going to have the shoes back. Finally.

She and Sam walk in silence along the corridor until they reach the side entrance and Sam heads out, her phone pressed to her ear as Jasmine instructs her as to which direction they went. *Head right towards Regent Street. She's still in the red suit. No overcoat. Damn fool must be freezing.*

Nisha walks to the elevator, and presses the button for the second floor. She stares at her feet in Sam's flat black shoes as it moves slowly upwards, and turns the key card over and over in her hand. This is it. The elevator arrives at the second floor, the doors open, and she steps out. Her mind is buzzing, a surge of anticipatory triumph pulsing through her veins. Twenty steps, ten steps, and they will be hers.

And there is Ari, talking to two men in suits, halfway down the corridor.

She swivels on her heel, ducks quickly back into the lift and stands with her finger on the 'door open' button, trying to figure out what to do. She moves her head forward tentatively, to check that it really is him, then ducks back. He is showing one of them something on a piece of paper. Just standing there, casually talking, like he has nowhere to go, nowhere else to be. She cannot reach the room without walking past him. But she is not confident she will be invisible a second time.

She exits the lift and sidesteps into the service cupboard, which has been left open by one of the housekeepers. Standing beside the shelves of towels and sheets, she texts Jasmine.

Can't get into room. Ari is there.

Jasmine's reply is immediate. Don't panic. I'll come and get them. Another message follows. We've got this. JUST BREATHE.

There is something unexpectedly soothing about tailing someone through the streets of London, Sam thinks, as she weaves
in and out of the crowds milling down Regent Street. It takes
all of her focus to keep track of the Frobishers, the bright
red of Liz's suit glowing, her pace measured as she pauses
every few feet to point at shop windows. Sam stays thirty feet
behind, the hood of her anorak over her head against the fine
rain, her breath coming in steam puffs in the cold, feeling an
odd sense of gratitude that she is doing something achiev-
able, that the utter concentration it requires means there is no
room in her head for anything else.

And Liz Frobisher is clearly enjoying herself. She walks
with a faint swagger, as if expecting to be admired, *the winner
of the Global Cat Foundation charity-shop award*, reaching up a
hand periodically to smooth her hair or check her makeup
in a window. Darren Frobisher, in contrast, looks sullen and
fed up, surreptitiously checking his phone and visibly sighing
every time she stops.

Sam's phone rings. She answers immediately. 'Well, it's nice
to know you're still *alive*.'

Sam watches as the Frobishers continue up Regent Street,
are briefly lost between a large group of teenagers, then
appear again. 'What is it, Mum?'

'What is it? That's a lovely greeting, I must say. You didn't
find the hymns!'

'What?'

'Your father's now looking at "For Those in Peril on the
Sea". He says all the others are too religious. I said it's awfully
gloomy. It makes me seasick to think about it.'

'I'm kind of in the middle of something right now. Can I
call you back?'

'And it's so patriarchal. All those hymns are!' Her mother

starts to sing. '*Eternal Father, strong to save, Whose arm has bound the restless wave* – I mean honestly. You might as well call on the Incredible Hulk. Though he's gone into a terrible sulk because I said so.'

The couple pauses while they have some kind of conversation, head to head. Darren points eastwards, perhaps towards Chinatown, and pulls a face. Liz holds up a hand, as if she might be noticing the rain.

'Anyway. You're obviously not going to help with the hymns. So I simply want to know when you're coming to help sort the house out. It's really in a terrible state. We have a blockage in the downstairs loo, which has been there for days. Your father feels quite abandoned. I don't know what's going on with you but –'

'I can't do this now, Mum.'

'And I don't like him going in the upstairs loo because he'll probably block that one too. You know what happened after he had those prunes.'

'Mum – I'll call you back.'

'But when –'

Sam ends the call and ducks into a shop entrance, fearful that the couple might see her. Whatever they're talking about has clearly made Darren even less delighted. They stand in heated discussion for a few moments, the crowds of shoppers and commuters surging around them, and then their voices start to lift, so that Sam can hear snatches of it, carried on the breeze in spite of the roar of the traffic.

'Well, I didn't know it would be this cold, did I?'

'I'm starving, Liz. And it's raining. I don't want to walk all the way back to –'

Sam cannot make out the rest of it, but she sees Liz gesticulating, and Darren raising his arms in a gesture of exasperation. As she watches, Liz turns and begins to walk towards her. Sam swivels in the doorway and sees that both are now walking back in the direction of the hotel, still arguing. She glances down at her phone and starts to punch in Nisha's number – just as the phone screen goes dead. Her heart briefly stops. She stares in disbelief. She's out of charge. With everything going on she had forgotten to charge the bloody phone.

Sam looks up. They are already some twenty metres ahead of her, walking back briskly towards the Bentley Hotel, Darren shaking his head at something Liz has said.

Oh, God, oh, God.

They had not planned for this. There is nothing else for it. Sam flips her hood up over her head and begins to run.

Jasmine is just walking towards the lift when she hears Frederik, the hotel manager, behind her, his voice lifting above the low hum of the lobby.

'Ah, Jasmine. Just the person.'

He is standing at the reception desk and beckons her over.

Jasmine curses under her breath and turns around, a smile already plastered across her face.

'Wine spillage in two seventeen. The sheets need replacing. Can you get on to it immediately? They're waiting in the room.'

She opens her mouth to explain that she is not working this shift, but realizes she cannot without explaining what she is doing there. She nods instead, says, 'Of course,' and sets off at a brisk pace to the second floor. She texts Nisha as she walks.

Sorry. Diversion. Give me 5 x

It takes Sam seven minutes to reach the hotel, pushing past people on the busy street, dodging umbrella spokes,

338

apologizing when some curse at her, her chest heaving from the unexpected exercise. She runs into the side entrance, and down the narrow corridor, skidding into the little changing room. A man sits on the bench, polishing a pair of shiny black lace-up shoes.

'Jasmine?' she says breathlessly.

He shakes his head.

She runs along the narrow corridor, yelling Jasmine's name so that a couple of housekeepers turn to look at her, but nobody answers. Swearing under her breath, Sam stops and tries to think clearly. Jasmine could be anywhere in this hotel. It's a rabbit warren. The foyer. Jasmine will be in the foyer. Of course she will. She runs back along the corridor, trying to remember where the service lift is. She spies it at the far end and punches the button, jiggling with anxiety as it makes its way sedately down from the fourth floor. The doors slide open, agonizingly slowly. She jabs the button marked G, once, twice, three times. 'Oh, *come on*,' she says aloud, as the rickety lift thinks about it, then finally acquiesces grudgingly, like a grumpy elderly relative, and judders its way upwards.

Nisha waits in the linen cupboard, listening to Ari still talking in the corridor, his deep, flat voice occasionally lifting as he discusses something she cannot make out. *Oh, but she's so close.* Her whole body is alive with tension, every muscle tensed for the sound of him moving. *It's fine*, she tells herself. *Jasmine will be here in a minute. Just breathe.* And then finally, after several decades have passed, she hears muffled footsteps on the carpet. They come towards her, so she stands very still, huddled against the shelves with her back to the door, some part of her still waiting for it to be thrown open – for him to find her – and then the footsteps recede, and she is holding her breath, turning cautiously to open the door and peer out. There is Ari's back, broad and solid in its dark suit, disappearing down the corridor, Ari apparently deep in conversation with whoever is talking into his earpiece. She looks in the other direction, and the two men he had been speaking to are walking down the corridor the other way, towards the elevator.

Nisha closes her eyes and breathes, trying to ignore the trembling in her fingers, and then, once she is sure of the silence, she straightens her shoulders, walks out of the cupboard and briskly down the corridor to 232, looking like the kind of woman who has every right to be there. She holds her key card against the door, and it clicks with a satisfying sound. Finally she is in.

Sam arrives in the lobby just in time to see Jasmine's back disappearing through the doors at the far end. She slows her pace to a brisk walk as she crosses the expanse of marble, trying to look unobtrusive, then breaks into a run on the other side of the doors. 'Jasmine!' she yells, and Jasmine turns, her hand to her chest. 'Did she get the shoes?'

'I don't know. One of her husband's goons was standing in the corridor. I was meant to go and get them for her but I've got to change some sheets.'

Just then her phone pings.

She looks up at Sam and beams. '*Yesss!* She's in!'

'No, no, no! They're heading back!'

'What?'

'The Frobishers. They had a row and they're coming back for her coat. Tell her to get out of there.'

'Dammit. Stupid woman. It was obvious she'd be too cold in that suit,' Jasmine mutters, then punches out a text to Nisha.

GET OUT! THEY'RE COMING BACK!

*

340

Nisha scans the room, her breath coming in short bursts, Liz Frobisher's pungent, over-sweet perfume still hanging in the air. The shoes are here, dammit. They must be here. She spies the suitcase on the case stand and flings open the top, rifling carefully through it with her fingertips, trying not to consider the ick factor involved in touching someone else's underclothes. Nothing. She opens the wardrobe door. They are not there either. She stands, thinking. Liz Frobisher wasn't wearing the shoes. Jasmine had been certain. And Sam would have messaged them – she was following the couple, after all. Nisha lifts the valance so she can peer under the bed in case they have been kicked underneath. She considers the possibility that Liz Frobisher has taken them with her to put on at her destination and curses. Would anyone take a pair of high heels just to eat Chinese? Finally she ducks her head into the bathroom and lets out a gasp of relief: there they are, lying on the tiled floor, their red soles glowing against the marble. The sight of them causes a bolt of electricity to shoot through her, as if all her nerve endings are suddenly alive. She stoops and grabs the shoes and lets out a breath she hadn't known she has been holding. *Yes!* And then her phone buzzes. She looks down.

GET OUT! THEY'RE COMING BACK!

Nisha does a 360-degree scan of the room, checking that everything is straight, and hurries to the door. She has her hand on the handle when she hears the voices in the corridor.

'That's because I don't go out dressed like I'm going to a summer party in early December. Jesus.'

'Why do you have to be so nasty? Do you actually want me to get a cold?'

'No, Liz, I just want my dinner. You know how I get if I

don't eat. And you could have just brought the coat with you and saved us the bother of coming all the way back.'

The voices stop outside the door. Nisha stares at it in horror. She gazes around the room, and then, with a click, the door begins to open.

'She's not answering.'

'Maybe she's coming back down in the lift. There's no reception in it,' mutters Sam, and Jasmine nods. They stand in the corner of the foyer, two people who apparently don't know each other, their eyes trained dumbly on the lift. Every time it opens it disgorges a handful of guests, but no Nisha. And then her phone buzzes.

I'm in the room. They're back. Get me out.

Jasmine types furiously, Sam gazing over her shoulder.

What do you mean they're in the room? Where are you?

Under the bed. They're having an argument.

'Oh, my days,' murmurs Jasmine, staring in horror at the screen.

'What do we do?' says Sam.

'Stay calm,' says Jasmine. 'If they're coming back for her coat they'll go again in a minute. It's all going to be fine.' She says this twice, as if to reassure herself. 'They're just coming back for her coat, right?'

'Yes,' says Sam. 'Yes. You're right. It's all going to be fine.'

Nisha lies under the queen-sized bed, every cell of her body taut with horror. She and Jasmine always wheel the beds to the side to vacuum underneath, but whoever does the second floor clearly takes no such trouble. There are dust bunnies to each side of her, strands of strangers' hair, skin cells, a whole miasma of disgusting microscopic bodily leftovers *and she is lying right in it*. The thought of it makes her want to sob aloud. She cannot look to the right or left of her, because then she sees what she is lying amid and it makes her want to retch. So she stays very still, eyes screwed shut, hands across her belly so that as little skin as possible is actually touching the floor.

'We're not late for dinner. We didn't have a bloody booking, Darren! Because you couldn't be bothered to make one – as per usual. The only thing we're late for is you wanting to stuff your fat face! Again!'

Footsteps walk around the bed.

'Is this because you wanted to go to your mum's? Jesus.'

'I like going to my mum's on a Sunday! Why is that such a problem for you?'

'You just go there because she runs round after you and doesn't let you lift a finger! No wonder you're so useless at home.'

Just go, thinks Nisha. Just go and have your embarrassing row at a restaurant. Please just get out of this room.

'You know what? I don't feel like going out any more. I'm ordering room service.'

'What?' Liz Frobisher's voice is disbelieving.

'You heard.'

Nisha winces as a weight lands on the bed on top of her. The base of the bed is now less than an inch from her nose. She hears Darren – because it must be Darren – pick up the remote control and switch on the hotel television. Some kind of football match commentary blares into the room.

'So you're just going to stay here? And leave me to eat by myself?'

'You can do what you want. Your idea to come here, you sort yourself out.'

'My sister was right about you.'

'Oh, your sister. Great. Let's bring her into it.'

Something is tickling Nisha's nose. Perhaps some dust particle dislodged by the movement of Darren's bulk. She brings her hand up to her nose and squeezes it tight. She is going to sneeze. Oh, God. She can't stop it. Nisha thinks she may explode. It's unstoppable . . .

At the exact moment she lets out a loud sneeze, the room suddenly erupts in sound.

'*Goal!* A tremendous goal there from Kane. The keeper really didn't stand a chance!' blares the television commentator, and the noise begins to subside. Nisha's eyes are watering. She thinks she may scream. Above her Darren shifts his weight, and she hears the sound of the hotel phone being lifted from the bedside table.

'You're really just going to stay here.'

'Yeah,' says Darren. 'It's too cold out. Let's just eat something.'

'I want to go out. We never go out anywhere nice.'

'We went out last Saturday.'

'Yes, but that was with your brother.'

Nisha tries to separate herself from her body, the way she has heard people talk about. She focuses on her breathing, then realizes that when she breathes deeply she is more likely to be inhaling the detritus under this bed. She screws her eyes shut and clamps a hand over her mouth.

There are footsteps, then nothing but the televised crowd noise of the football.

Nisha opens her eyes and hears muffled sobbing coming from the easy chair in the corner of the room. The bed above her shifts slightly and she sees Darren's feet land on the carpeted floor beside her head. There is a hole in his right sock, which reveals a coin of pale heel.

'Are you crying?'

'Go away.'

A long silence. More muffled sobbing.

'I just wanted this to be my special day. I won a prize, Darren! I was all excited and now you've ruined everything.'

A sigh.

'Nothing's ruined. C'mon. Come here. I'm just hungry.'

Suddenly her phone flashes up a message.

Are you out?

No! she types back.

Are they going out?

I don't know. I am literally going to die under this bed. HELP

There are three pulsing dots, then silence. She imagines Jasmine and Sam downstairs, trying to work out what to do. Jasmine will think of something. She has to.

'All right, babe. We'll go out. Put your coat on.' She hears him climb into his own jacket, the slide of an arm into a sleeve, the rattle of keys. 'Did I put my wallet on the side?'

Go, she thinks. Just go eat. For God's sakes.

And then Liz's sorrowful voice: 'I don't want to go out any more.'

Nisha's eyes widen. *Is this bitch kidding?*

'You've spoiled it.'

Darren's voice bears the conciliatory tone of a man who has dealt with many, many such exchanges. 'Ah, don't cry, babe. You know I can't stand it when you cry.'

Some muffled exchange she can't make out.

'Come here. Come sit on the bed with me. We'll have a cuddle.'

Nisha holds her breath, then winces as the bed creaks slightly under the weight of what may be two people.

'Come here, my little baby boo. Come on.'

The sniffing stops. Is that – Oh, my God. No. The hairs on the back of her neck stand up on end. She hears the sound of kissing.

'You never call me that any more.'

'My baby boo. You look gorgeous in that suit. Really gorgeous.'

'You're just saying that.'

'You look way tastier than a plate of crispy duck.'

There is a reluctant giggle.

Oh, God, please no. NO NO NO.

'Ooh! My favourite bra! You know I like that one.'

The sound of more kissing, more giggling. And then a soft moan. And then a louder, masculine one.

Nisha types again, her fingers jabbing with silent urgency.

JESUS GET ME OUT OF HERE NOW.

Nisha has experienced many states of misery this last month, but all the other things that have happened were merely hors d'oeuvres. She has hit her own personal nadir. It is as if every one of her worst nightmares has been made flesh, in the form of the lumpy couple getting jiggy a matter of inches from her face. She has entered a new mental space, in which it requires every ounce of focus she has just to breathe without screaming, to stay here a second longer without clawing and shrieking her way out across the disgusting carpet. She closes her eyes and tries to think about Ray, but

346

bringing his lovely face into this disgusting farrago is wrong, and she lies there instead, one hand over her mouth, trying to disengage from the noises above her. *This is it*, she thinks. *This is how I die. They will slump into a post-sex coma, I will be stuck here all night, and they will find my tortured corpse the next time one of the second-floor maids decides it's not beneath them to actually move a fucking piece of furniture and vacuum underneath this bed.*

Every time she thinks she cannot bear a moment longer, she forges her way past. One nightmarish second at a time. And then Darren decides to really go for it. The bed starts to move, the slats buckling above her so that they are repeatedly touching her face. The gasps and shrieks of pleasure become louder. Nisha has begun to lose control. She is shaking. Her mind has gone blank. This is too much. It is unbearable. This is –

Sam and Jasmine are at the end of the corridor on the second floor. They are standing a few feet away from each other, Jasmine by the housekeeping trolley, Sam's hood up over her head, and Jasmine is quietly conveying the text messages coming through on her phone, which is resting on a pile of towels.

Jasmine picks up the phone and types, tentatively: R U OK?

NO I AM NOT OKAY THEY ARE ACTUALLY HAVING SEX ON TOP OF ME

Jasmine's eyes widen in horror. She relays this to Sam and lets out a nervous laugh. They lean towards the door of Room 232. And in the silence they can just make out the sounds, the noises that would make a bystander's toes curl at the best of times.

'She will die,' says Jasmine, nodding, as she straightens up. 'She is actually going to die.'

The phone dings again.

ALL THE DUST I'M GOING TO SNEEZE

'No, baby,' Jasmine mutters, typing. Do not sneeze. DO NOT
SNEEZE.

I'M HAVING A PANIC ATTACK

The phone keeps pinging

CAN'T BREATHE HELP ME

'What are we going to do?' Jasmine hisses, anguished.

Sam cannot bear it any longer. She flaps her hands, trying
to think. She closes her eyes, then opens them and scoots
back down the corridor until she spies what she's looking
for. She glances back at Jasmine, slips her Marks & Spencer
navy court shoe from her foot, and whacks the fire alarm button with it – two, three times – until the glass shatters. Then
she slams the button with the heel of her hand. The noise is
immediate and ear-splitting.

'What the hell are you doing?' yells Jasmine.

'Run!' says Sam, and bolts towards the fire escape.

32

The recorded message booms into every one of the Bentley Hotel's 310 bedrooms. *Please do not panic. The fire alarm has been triggered. Please make your way to the nearest fire exit.*

Darren, halted at what might possibly be an inopportune moment, takes a second longer to comprehend what is happening than Liz does. She is already out of bed, her bare feet on the floor.

'Fire? Darren, there's a fire! A fire!'

He says, breathing hard: 'It'll be a false alarm.'

'I can hear people going down the corridor. Darren, get up! We have to go!'

'I don't believe this.' Darren's feet, still in his socks, land on the floor beside Nisha's head. She is frozen, deafened by the noise. She fumbles for the shoes by her right thigh and winds her fingers into the straps. She can hear the Frobishers struggling into their clothes, bickering, gathering their things, the urgent voices and footsteps outside in the corridor. And over it all the piercing, intermittent ring of the fire alarm.

'Bag, where's my handbag?'

'We'll get downstairs and it'll stop, babe.'

'Where are the shoes?'

'Don't worry about the bloody shoes. Just get your –'

'Darren, everyone is leaving the hotel. Come ON.'

She hears the panic in Liz Frobisher's voice. Some distant part of her wonders if this fire is real, whether she will be able to get out in time or burn here, under the bed, and be found in the aftermath, like some human relic from Pompeii.

She hears the click of the hotel door opening, the abrupt noise of a hundred people emerging from their rooms, bleary and confused, a baby crying. Then the door closes and the noise becomes muffled again. There is a brief lull. Nisha waits a moment, then wriggles out from under the bed, coughing and brushing dust from her clothes, her eyes watering as she gags. The photograph. She mustn't forget the photograph. She whips out the printed screenshot, places it on the bedside table, then tiptoes to the door, peers out and, clutching the shoes to her chest, is instantly swept into the moving river of anxious guests heading for the fire-escape stairs, no longer even caring if she is about to be consumed by flames.

It has to be a better fate than remaining in that room.

Sam and Jasmine huddle by the back entrance, where staff are emerging in small clumps, still unsure whether they should be leaving their posts. Some have lit cigarettes, blind to the irony, and a series of white-jacketed chefs stand in a shivering huddle, bemoaning ruined soufflés, burnt fish portions and the wrath of the maître d'.

'She's not answering any texts. Do you think we should call?'

'Maybe give it another five minutes. Just in case.'

'I'll call Aleks. Maybe he knows.'

Sam's heart is beating hard. She feels elated and terrified. She did this. She created this epic state of chaos and havoc. She hears the alarm ringing in the air, the voices of senior managers as they try to establish where the fire is. The hotel is emptying, hundreds of people spilling out of the main entrance onto the pavement, parents trying to shepherd crying children, jet-lagged tourists blinking in the sodium light. Her life has turned to chaos, and now she is creating it herself. She has stopped this enormous machine with one hand. Over the shrill noise, she can see Jasmine talking urgently into the phone, her hand pressed against her other ear. Around her the street is coming to a halt as guests, some in dressing-gowns, some in hastily grabbed coats start to spread into the road, the taxi horns blaring as they navigate in the dark around them.

Sam watches it all, disbelieving, and finds that something strange is happening. A bubble of something unfamiliar is rising in her chest, pushing upwards so that she cannot control it. Sam begins to laugh. She leans her head back against the wall, feeling the cold of the brick against her scalp, the rough texture against her hands, and she starts to laugh at the insane chaos of it all. Sam laughs, and laughs until she's crying, tears leaking from her eyes, clutching her sides. And she sees Jasmine staring at her, frowning in disbelief, and this makes her laugh even more.

'Have you lost your mind?' Jasmine says, shoving her phone into her pocket.

Sam wipes at her eyes, and nods, still laughing. 'Maybe. Yes. Yes, I think maybe I have.'

Nisha makes her way along the corridor in the thick of the throng, slowed at the entrance to the emergency stairs as the crowd begins to bottleneck at the fire door. A large group of young people are laughing and joking, and behind her an elderly couple complain about the noise, holding crêpey hands to their ears. She clasps the shoes to her chest, unable to believe she has made it. She finally has them. She watches the crowd funnel slowly down the narrow stairway, and glances behind her just to see if Jasmine or Sam are nearby. And it is then that she sees him: Ari.

His eyes fix on the shoes in front of her and then his gaze lifts to her face and betrays a flicker of shock when he realizes who he's looking at. Almost immediately he is pushing his way forward through the protesting guests towards her. Nisha's heart stops. She shoves her way through the door into the stairwell, jostling in and out of the people slowly descending the stairs, knowing he will be right behind her.

Watch it! You nearly had me over!

Nisha has no breath to apologize. It is lodged somewhere in her chest. She shoves her way through, stumbles down three steps, hearing the exclamations behind her that mean Ari is doing the same thing. She makes a swift calculation – and ducks out of the exit on the first floor, wincing as someone elbows her hard in the chest. They are packed so closely together that she can smell other people's scents, feel their vague panic. She squeezes between two large men in suits and then she is off, pushing against the current of people forcing their way to the fire escape, and finally running for the service elevator.

The first rule of fire regulations is don't use the elevator, but Nisha nips inside and slams the button to the ground floor, just in time to see Ari's face register hers as the doors close against him. She yells, without knowing what she's yelling, and suddenly the elevator lurches into life, heading slowly downwards. He will be talking to his men. How many will there be? Where will he go? The doors open again on the ground floor and she is running through the packed foyer until she sees the door to the restaurant. She pushes through it, then sprints along the side of the room, which is almost empty, bar a few perturbed guests arguing with the waiting staff about wanting their coats, and then she has reached the kitchens.

Sunday night and normally the kitchens of the Bentley are a world of noise, of clattering pans and steam and things frying at impossible temperatures. Men in whites with harassed expressions yell at each other, wipe smears from plates with linen cloths as the doors open and close with waiters ferrying dishes backwards and forwards. Now there's just a handful of kitchen staff gathering belongings, the smell of food burning as they head to the service door. She spies him: 'Aleks!'

He turns, perhaps sees something in her expression, because he begins to jog towards her.

'He's after me! Help!' she yells, glancing behind her, and without hesitating he grabs her elbow, pushing her along past the prep station.

'In here,' he says, punching a code into the panel beside the metallic door, and then they're in the refrigerator room and he has pulled the heavy door shut behind them, shepherding her through the plastic sheeting towards the back. The lights come on automatically with their movement and she glances around her at the huge trays of meat, the hanging carcasses lining the tiled walls, the shelves of vegetables and industrial cartons of milk.

'Over there,' he points. 'End of the racks.'

She ducks where he says, behind an endless stack of eggs, and they wedge themselves behind a rack of tall stainless-steel canisters, so that they cannot be seen.

It is silent in here, bar the industrial hum of the refrigeration unit. She is breathing hard, and her heartbeat thumps in her ears as the outside din fades. Every time she closes her eyes she sees Ari, the shock and determination on his face as he pursues her.

'You got them,' Aleks says. She looks down, sees she is still holding the shoes, nods silently at him, holding them tighter to her, suddenly realizing that she really does have them. The alarm continues to shriek outside, but in here the siren is muffled, and her nerves slowly stop jangling. He smiles, his face inches from hers, and she smiles back, more nervously. Some part of her still believes Ari will come bursting in and rip the shoes from her.

'He won't get in,' he says, as if reading her mind. 'He would need the code to open the door.'

'Is there really a fire?'

'No. Your friend Sam rang the fire alarm. Jasmine told me.'

'Sam?' She is incredulous. She glances down at her phone, seeing the stream of missed calls and text messages.

'Jasmine says you were having a panic attack and she took an executive decision.' He reaches up to move a lock of hair from her face. 'Are you okay? What happened?'

'You wouldn't believe me if I told you.'

He smiles. His arm is alongside her head, his palm resting on the wall, and she can see the sinews of his forearms, the tiny blond hairs lifting in the cold air. She is suddenly aware of the temperature now she has stopped moving. 'How long do you think we'll have to stay here?'

'Until everyone comes back.'

'You don't think we should sneak out now? While they're all outside?'

He pulls a face. 'It could be a little tricky. This door does not open from inside.'

'What?'

'Faulty mechanism. They never fix anything back of house. It's fine. Everyone will be back in twenty minutes tops. We are not going to freeze to death.'

'I might.' Nisha is already regretting just wearing the black blouse and trousers. There is no protection against the cold in here at all. She wraps her arms around herself, beginning to shiver.

He sees her discomfort and wrestles off his chef's jacket, placing it around her shoulders and buttoning it under her chin. 'Better?'

'A little.'

He is so close to her. She can smell the scent of him, the

354

vague aroma of good things cooking, the citrusy smell of soap underneath. She has a sudden memory of his kiss, the way she had felt like she wanted to melt into him and forget everything around her.

'Here,' he says, and places his arms around her, pulling her into his chest. She can feel the warmth of his body through his T-shirt, and as she rests her head against him, she can just make out the beating of his heart. She closes her eyes, hearing the distant sound of doors, the endless drone of the alarm. He is the calmest person she has ever met . . . and this soothes her. It is all going to be okay. She is safe here. Ari will not find her. She has the shoes.

But.

In the near-silence, above the hum of the refrigerator, she becomes aware of his heartbeat. Surely it's faster than a regular heartbeat. Her hands are cold and he takes one in his own and brings it to his lips, breathing warm air onto it, closing his fingers around it to warm her up. The heartbeat speeds up a little. Nisha slides her other hand under his T-shirt. 'For warmth,' she murmurs, and his heartbeat speeds up a little more. And something in her shifts. She lifts her face and he is looking straight at her, and something has gone a little blurry between them.

'It's so cold in here,' she says quietly. A pause. And then her lips are on his and his hands are in her hair and they are up against the rack, their kisses hot and endless, his hands gripping her to him, and Nisha has forgotten about the temperature completely.

The door is opened twenty-eight minutes later, the alarm silenced and the staff are finally filing back in, muttering and joking, making their way to their stations. Nisha and Aleks are waiting beside the door, she still wearing his chef's white jacket over her shoulders, their expressions suspiciously blank. André opens it and stares at the two people in the doorway.

'I was keeping her warm,' says Aleks, when he keeps staring.

'Right,' says André.

They are halfway down the side alley before they realize Aleks has left his belt and Nisha has the remnants of two broken eggs sliding down her back.

They leave the hotel through a side exit from a large store room for banqueting chairs and tables, somehow emerging onto an alleyway on the other side of the hotel, far from the crowds and chaos. They walk the last half-mile arm in arm to Jasmine's apartment, barely speaking, but the lengthy silences do not make Nisha feel anxious or uneasy. Perhaps for the first time in her life she is experiencing a deep peace, a calm that feels drugged, almost alien to her. Her whole body is charged, hyper-aware of the man walking beside her, but at the same time honeyed, and completely relaxed. Aleks has the shoes stashed safely in his backpack, which is slung over one shoulder; he walks swiftly through the night streets, his stride matching hers, and she speaks only to give him directions. *We need to turn here* or *It's just by that corner* and occasionally he squeezes her slightly to him.

It is a pleasurable thing, that squeeze, not possessive, just comforting, a reminder of his presence. It also sporadically prompts an echo of their half-hour in the refrigeration room and when she thinks of it something at the core of her turns molten and liquid. *So this is what it feels like.* There is something almost sad about it, the revelation of what she has normalized for the last twenty years, the way she had assumed she was in something equal, respectful, when everything Carl had done had actually reinforced his basic disrespect. He had admired her, yes, desired her, often. But loved her? No. She wasn't sure he was capable of that emotion. *Stay with me*, Aleks had murmured, his eyes inches from hers, and in that raw moment she knew she had spent half her life with a man who had failed to connect with her at all. It wasn't even in his vocabulary. I have been a possession, she thinks. I have been an object. A prize, an appendage, then an inconvenience. She closes her eyes, wishing away the shame and sadness that come with understanding.

'She's here!'

Jasmine throws open the door, letting out a warm burst of scented air, and as she steps inside Nisha can see that Sam, Andrea and Grace are waiting in the kitchen, their faces joyful and expectant.

'You did it!' Jasmine is laughing, hugging her emphatically so that Aleks steps obligingly to the side. 'You bloody did it! You rock star! Oh, my God, I do not know how we got through that last half-hour. My heart! Did you know what you were doing to me? I thought I was going to pass out fifty times.' She shepherds them into the kitchen, closing the front door and bolting it. 'Honestly, Nish, when you were sending me those texts I didn't know whether to laugh or have a bloody panic attack with you.'

Nisha has been so locked into the quiet pleasure of her walk with Aleks that it takes her a moment to switch to their frequency.

'We're having champagne,' says Andrea, who is pulling the top from a bottle. 'Well, prosecco – I didn't have the money for champagne – but it's basically the same.' There is a whoop and Jasmine is reaching into one of the cupboards for the glasses, while Grace busies herself emptying a family bag of crisps into a large bowl.

'Do another bowl as well, baby. Those tortilla chips. The cheesy ones. Shall I get dips? Anyone want dips?'

Aleks and Andrea make their introductions over the music Jasmine has put on. Grace hands round the bowl of crisps, sneakily taking some for herself with each one offered. Jasmine hugs Aleks two, three times, quizzes him about where they ended up and her gaze slides sideways knowingly towards Nisha when he tells her. The little room is full of noise and relief and laughter. Nisha takes a sip of the prosecco. It is cheap, too sweet and absolutely delicious. She spies Sam, who is standing as she habitually does, in the corner of any room. She is watching them all with a vague smile, but there is sadness, wariness around her eyes.

Nisha walks through the others, around the table, and up to her. The room falls abruptly silent. She sees Sam stiffen slightly, as if braced for whatever new verbal projectile is going to be hurled at her. They lock eyes.

'Thank you,' Nisha says. 'Thank you for what you did.'

And as the others watch, a little disbelieving, Nisha takes a step forward and hugs Sam, pulling her in tightly, hanging on until she feels the other woman soften and tentatively, but surprisingly tightly, hug her back.

Like the best impromptu parties, this one takes place with minimal effort. The prosecco is drunk, and Aleks nips out for some wine. By nine thirty that evening there is music and conversation and the little flat has become a haven of warmth and laughter. Andrea, whose recovery seems to have gained momentum since her hospital appointment, insists Nisha tell them every second of her time in Room 232 and cries laughing, wiping tears from her eyes and dislodging her head wrap. Jasmine gives a blow-by-blow account of what she was feeling at every point, imitates the managers trying to work out who had set off the fire alarm. It had been put down to a troublemaker coming off the street, just one of those things that happen in a hotel in the centre of the city. She congratulates Sam on wearing her hood inside the hotel, and Sam doesn't have the heart to tell her that she had only done so because she had forgotten it was up. They consider the Frobishers, hauled abruptly from their sexy interlude ('Don't tell that story again, Nish. I will actually wet myself'), who will even now be discovering the printed screenshot Nisha left in their room of Liz Frobisher dumping a cat in a bin. 'They'll think it was cat vigilantes!' Grace is hysterical with laughter.

'And if they do have the brass neck to complain about the missing shoes after that, they're going to find they aren't even registered as guests,' says Jasmine. What hotel is going to take seriously a claim of theft from someone illegally occupying one of their rooms? Someone goes out and gets chips, which they eat from a plastic mixing bowl, dipping them in a pot of tomato ketchup.

Sam, watching from a footstool in the corner, is struck by the change in Nisha – she is altered somehow: softer, more relaxed. She sits beside Aleks on the little sofa, and occasionally, when they think nobody is watching, they link fingers, without looking at each other. It makes Sam sad. I have lost this, she thinks. I had it and I lost it. Now that she has done the thing she had promised to do, her drive and determination have gradually leached out of her. She has helped Nisha recover her shoes, but she has lost everything. The evening swims and blurs. Hours pass in minutes. They are, Sam realizes, all quite drunk and she cannot bring herself to care. Cat is staying at Colleen's, having texted to tell her baldly an hour earlier, and informed her that she has taken the dog 'in case you had forgotten about him'. Phil is gone, and she has nothing to go home for.

She feels Andrea's hand on her arm. 'You okay, my darling?'

'Fine,' she says, trying to muster a smile.

Andrea's eyes search hers. 'We'll talk later,' she says, and pats her reassuringly.

'Can I see the shoes?' says Grace.

'What?'

'I want to see what all the fuss was about,' Grace announces again, over the music.

Aleks smiles and reaches for his bag. 'Sure,' he says. 'Let's celebrate the prize.'

Nisha looks suddenly unsettled. She waits as Aleks extracts each red high heel from his bag and he hands them to her carefully. She places them in a neat pair on the coffee-table in front of her.

'They're really pretty,' says Grace, and Jasmine squeezes her shoulder.

'Mad, isn't it?' says Andrea. 'All that for one pair of shoes.'

It takes Sam a moment to register the way Nisha is staring at them.

'Do you know what's weird?' Nisha says. 'I don't even care.'

'Don't care about what?' Jasmine turns down the music.

'The shoes. Look at them.'

They look at the shoes. And then, with less certainty, at Nisha.

'They're a game to him. A way to keep me running around. I think I actually hate them. They are the perfect summation of our marriage. All show. Me running around after him like a fool, dressed like a fucking show pony. Him pulling the strings. You know my son thinks they're not even real Louboutins?'

'But you've got them now,' says Andrea, reassuringly. 'And that means he has to give you what you've asked for. He has to give you a settlement.'

'No,' says Nisha. 'There's something off here. I don't get why he would be so obsessed with one pair of shoes.'

'It doesn't matter why he wants them,' says Aleks. 'A deal's a deal. You've done your bit.'

Nisha holds one of the shoes, suddenly angry, then puts it down again. 'I mean, what the fuck is this? I was married to him for almost two decades, bore his son, gave my life over to his, gave him everything he wanted. I lost the best friend I ever had because he said I shouldn't be friends with someone like her – and I let him persuade me. I let him tell me who I should be friends with. And after all this he humiliates me by making me run around after a pair of my *own shoes*?'

Sam stares at the glossy shoes, at Nisha's contorted face. The atmosphere in the room has changed suddenly, the joy of the past hours evaporating. Jasmine and Andrea exchange glances. Nobody seems to know what to say.

'They don't even fit her, you know, if that's why he wants them. She has clown feet. Actual clown feet. I hate them,' Nisha says. 'Almost as much as I hate him.'

'Babe. Sit down,' says Jasmine, reaching an arm out. 'You're spinning out. It's okay.'

Nisha looks down at Aleks, who is still sitting. His face is full of sympathy, of understanding.

'The shoes mean nothing,' he says soothingly. 'They are nothing. Just a means to an end. Think about your future. What they will win you. This is all that matters.'

'Get her another drink, Aleks,' Andrea says.

'I don't want another drink.' Nisha stares at the shoes, sitting on the coffee-table. And then almost on impulse she picks one up, turns it over carefully in her hands. She looks at them, her face dark.

'Babe. Seriously . . .' Jasmine begins.

'He said I had to bring him the shoes, right? That was the deal. But he didn't say they had to be in *one piece*.' Before anyone can stop her – amid the shouted protests to *Stop! Stop!*

– she is wrenching at the shoe, pulling at it, bracing it over her knee until with a *crack* the heel comes off in her hand. And out of it spills a glittering shower of diamonds.

The room falls completely silent.

'What the fuck?' says Jasmine. Nisha stares at the hollow heel in shock. And then at the floor.

Aleks is the first on his knees. He carefully scoops up a small handful of the tiny gemstones and deposits them one by one on the coffee-table, where they sit, glinting under the overhead light, dotted with carpet fluff and tortilla crumbs. Nisha makes to speak but no sound comes out.

'Okay,' says Jasmine, tilting her head to one side. 'Well, I guess he really did want the shoes.'

A group of kids are wheelie-ing their bikes up and down the walkways outside Jasmine's apartment, catcalling to each other and dropping firecrackers on the paving. One has a small moped, and occasionally Nisha hears the roar of its engine and the *thunk thunk thunk* of its rider taking it down a small flight of concrete steps, the squeals of occasional girl passengers. Normally this would have left her wild with rage. But tonight she barely registers it. She lies in the narrow bunk bed, her mind humming as she thinks about the ramifications of what was in the shoes, the discussions they had in the last sober hour before everyone left.

Everything has become horribly clear to her now: the way Carl would insist she wear them as they travelled between countries, even though they were frankly uncomfortable for flying; his rage when he discovered they were no longer in her possession. He had used her like a mule. How many times had she unwittingly transported gems for him? They had prised off the other heel and there were more diamonds in the left shoe. None of them knew their value, but she

362

guessed it was in the region of hundreds of thousands of dollars, perhaps more. The diamonds are a good size, beautifully cut; the largest is the width of her thumbnail. They had no magnifying-glass in the tiny apartment but she would bet on superior clarity.

'Oh, my God, babe. There's your settlement.' Jasmine had placed her hands on her knees, leaning forward to gaze at them. 'There. Is. Your. Settlement.'

Andrea had murmured to herself, 'It's like a story. Now you can tell him to get stuffed.'

She thinks of the trips to Africa they had taken over the past few years, other pairs of shoes he has bought her: dark blue Gucci courts, cream Prada platforms. Had any of these been altered in the same way? Had she been an unwitting mule every time? Were these blood diamonds? Stolen? Contraband? And here is the worst of it: she, the ignorant courier, could have been caught at any time. Arrested. She has meant less than nothing to him. How could any husband care about someone he would use in that way?

She climbs out of her bunk, taking care not to wake Grace, and pulls on the old lavender dressing-gown she has become used to wearing. It smells comfortingly of Jasmine's home, her fabric conditioner. It is almost 2 a.m. She makes her way to the living room and quietly opens the door onto the balcony, where she lights a cigarette. She checks the time, then dials a number.

'Ray?'

'Hi, Mom.'

His voice is low, ominously quiet.

'Are you okay?'

There is a short silence. She takes a long, anxious drag on her cigarette. 'Ray? Are you okay?'

He doesn't answer for a moment. 'Yeah.'

'You don't sound good.'

'I don't want to be here any more, Mom.'

'It's not much longer. I promise.'

'Emily and Sasha left and it's just me and the eating disorders. Everyone else is going home at weekends. I just watch TV on my own.'

'I know.'

He gives a long sigh. 'You're going to say you're not coming yet, aren't you?'

She closes her eyes. 'Soon, baby. I have the shoes. I do have the shoes. Things are happening. And I have some things to discuss with your father about . . . about the settlement. Then I will come and get you.'

'I feel like . . .' his voice is soft, resigned '. . . I feel like you're never coming.'

'Why would you say that?'

'When I was ill. That time you said you were going to come, and Dad made you go to Toronto. I was so sad, Mom, and you guys just went to Toronto. You just took his side.'

She remembers the journey, how she had wept on the plane and Carl had become steadily more irritated and said that all teenagers got moody. She and Ray needed to be less sensitive, and the boy was in the best place with the psychiatrists and people who could deal with that stuff. He had already raised two teenage boys with his first wife. He said it had been the same with them, and they'd grown out of it, and the worst thing you could do was keep fussing around them, and she had believed him. Even though his adult sons seemed to despise him, unless they wanted money, she had actually believed him. What had she known about good parenting, after all?

'Ray. Ray. Listen to me. Just give me a couple of days more, okay? I promise. Even if everything goes wrong when I speak to your father, even if I have to go get another passport and borrow money from my workmates for a plane ticket. Even if I have to swim the damn Pacific I will come get you.'

'It's the Atlantic.'

'That too.'

He lets out a reluctant laugh.

'And I'm a fast swimmer. You know it.'

'I hate my life. I hate living like this. It feels like nobody wants me and I've just been dumped here.'

'None of that is true. I am coming, baby.'

A long silence. She closes her eyes and drops her head onto her knees. 'I love you so much, sweetheart. Please hang on in there. I won't let you down again, I promise. It's just going to be you and me together from now on.'

She can hear his breathing, the million unwelcome thoughts whirring around his head.

'Want me to sing for you again?' she says, when she cannot bear the silence any longer. '*You are my sunsh—*'

'Not really,' he says. And ends the call.

And then, before the sense of panic can set in, her phone pings.

Yes this is still my number

Juliana.

33

'Hey.'

'Hey.' Nisha swallows. 'Thank you for picking up.'

'It's fine. I'm just . . . surprised. How are you?'

Juliana's voice is polite, wary. The way she used to speak to their employers, all the Brooklyn girl ironed out for something professional, something *acceptable*. She remembers how Carl used to talk about Juliana, how Nisha shouldn't be hanging out with a maid now they were married, how she was too coarse, too uneducated, a bad influence, his fury when she insisted Juliana was to be Ray's godmother, instead of one of his moneyed friends. What he meant, she understood now, was that Juliana was simply *too poor*.

'I – Listen. I don't know how much credit I have on this phone. But I have a favour to ask.'

Juliana's voice hardens. 'Right.'

'Look, I know I don't deserve to ask you anything, but it's about your godson. It's Ray.'

'Ray? Is he okay?' Juliana's tone switches immediately.

'Not really. I know it's been a long time and it's a big ask but I need someone I trust to check on him. I'm stuck in England – it's a long story – and he's . . . Juliana, he's really low. He's had some big problems and some of them are my fault and I – I need someone I trust to see him. To just – I don't know – tell him I'm coming. Tell him it's going to be okay.'

There is a long pause.

'Tell me where he is.'

'You'll do it?'

'You have to ask?'

And then Nisha is crying. The tears come out of nowhere, tears of relief, of guilt and release. She covers her face with her other hand, trying to wipe them away, to get her voice under control. 'Really? You'd do that? After all this?'

'Text me the address. I'll go straight to him once I've finished work.'

'Thank you. Thank you so much.' Nisha cannot stop. She is shaking.

'Will he know who I am?'

'Yes. We still talk about you.'

'I still think about him. All the time. Sweet boy.'

Nisha screws her eyes shut, her shoulders heaving as she tries to gather herself, to hide the emotion in her voice. They discuss a few details, so that Juliana has an idea of where she's headed, what she might expect. She tells her – in bursts – that she is no longer with Carl. That she is doing everything she can to get back to her son. Juliana tells her in turn that she is married now. Two children, eleven and thirteen. The fact that these seismic things have happened in Juliana's life and Nisha knows nothing of them causes something in her to constrict painfully. And then a recorded message tells her she has almost reached her credit limit.

'I'll text you, okay?' Juliana says. 'Once I've seen him.'

The feeling of relief is overwhelming. Juliana will do what she says she'll do. The most honest, the most straightforward person she has ever met. And then the tears come again.

'I'm so sorry,' Nisha says abruptly. 'You were right. About everything. I've made such a mess. I missed you so much. I just got swept up in everything. I've wanted to call you so many times. I'm so, so sorry.'

There is a long silence. She wonders, briefly, whether she shouldn't have gone there. What right has she to ask anything of Juliana after all? But when Juliana's voice comes back on the line, it is thick with emotion. 'Me too. I'm here, baby. Okay? I'm going to go see your boy.'

Sam leaves Andrea's, where she had ended up sleeping, and walks the short distance home through the quiet morning streets. Her head is still buzzing with the conversations she and Andrea had the previous evening, the shocked acknowledgement of what she had been harbouring under her feet. It made them laugh out loud – the randomness of it – 'Diamonds on the Soles of Her Shoes'! – but every time Sam thinks about the kind of man Nisha had been married to it makes her think of Phil. His kindness. His tenderness towards her. The insane idea that Phil would ever care so little for her that he'd have made her do something like that. She had seen this understanding dawn on Nisha's face while everyone else had been excited about her haul – and what Sam had seen, unnoticed by anyone else, had been sad, and ugly, the final insult on an already steaming pile.

After they left, she and Andrea had sat in Andrea's little front room until the small hours, high on adrenalin and conversation, and she had finally told Andrea about Phil leaving. Andrea had hugged her and said he would be back, of course he would. Sam checks her phone again, wondering whether to text him, but it's early in the morning and she has no idea what to say. Or how honest to be. She wants things to be back to the way they were, when they had felt like a team. When it had felt like she was married to her best friend, before his dad got sick and he lost his job and she developed a crush on the one person who was listening to her. Was that even a reasonable thing to ask? Was it possible to resurrect a marriage when so much damage had been done?

Of course it is, Andrea had said firmly, but she was twice divorced and four glasses of wine in, and Andrea loves her enough to tell her everything will be okay because she so badly wants everything to be okay for her.

Sam turns into her street, noting how different it feels knowing she is walking home to an empty house. She wonders, dully, if this is how it will be from now on. No Phil. Cat increasingly absent until she, too, finally flies the nest completely. Even Kevin will not last for long. He is thirteen, positively geriatric in dog years. It will be just her, alone in that little house, watching the soaps and circling crappy jobs in the classified section of the local paper, being summoned twice a week to clean up for her increasingly crotchety parents.

Stop it, she tells herself firmly. She stands still and breathes – *in for one, hold for four, out for seven.* Was it out for seven? Or should she be holding for seven? She hasn't done it for so long she can't remember. She forces herself to think about her unlikely group of new friends, the warmth of Jasmine, the way even Nisha had held her like she might be someone she actually cared about. She had helped Nisha get the shoes back. She had brought an entire hotel to a shuddering halt, and changed someone's life as a result. She was capable of *something*, even if it was just chaos.

She pauses in front of her house, looking up before she opens the gate, some part of her still hoping that a light might flicker on upstairs, that Phil might have decided to come home. And then she sees it: the faint glow in the upstairs landing. They never leave that light on when they go out. She walks up the pathway, suddenly full of anticipation, wrestles open the front door – and then stands blinking in disbelief at the shimmering fragments of glass, the broken chair and her smashed television on the living-room floor.

34

'Cat?' Sam is shivering in the garden. She had made her way through to the kitchen, her feet crunching on the mounds of upturned cereal and pulses, the smashed crockery, and had turned and walked rapidly back outside, suddenly fearful that the intruder might still be in there. She had waited outside for ten minutes now, nothing stirring in the house, but she didn't feel safe in there.

'Mum?' Cat's voice is bleary, fogged with sleep.

Sam's hand goes to her mouth. 'Oh, thank God.'

'Why are you calling at . . . half past nine in the morning?'

'We've been burgled, love. I just – I just didn't want you to come back here and find it.' She doesn't tell her the truth: that she had suddenly been overwhelmed with fear that Cat might have been here after all, that this had been something so much worse than a burglary.

'What?'

'I know. It's a – a bit of a mess. Don't worry. We'll sort it out. Have you got Kevin?'

'Yep. Ugh. He's just farted. *Kevin.*'

She lets out another breath. She can hear Cat struggling to sit up.

'What did they take? Shall I come back?'

'I don't know. I've called the police. But no. Stay there for now. I don't – I don't want you to see it like this.'

'Have you called Dad?'

Sam stares at the front door, still slightly open. 'I – I don't know if he'd want me to call. It's fine. I'll sort it out.'

370

'Mum –'

'I've got to go, sweetheart. I'll speak to you later. Don't come until I call, okay?'

In the end she sits in the camper-van. It feels less awful than being in the house. She climbs into the passenger seat and stares through the windscreen, unsure what to do next. The police said they would send round an officer – but added that they were very busy and she would probably be wise to get a locksmith in and secure the property. There was no mention of dusting for fingerprints, or even any kind of investigation. 'There's been a spate of them lately in your postcode,' the operator says, in resigned tones.

I wish you were here, she tells Phil silently. She calls Andrea, who says she is on her way. When she tells her friend about the mess, the damage, it hits her that this is real, not some strange fever dream. Her house looks like a war zone and she doesn't know how she's going to afford a new television. Before she hangs up, Andrea says, 'You don't think it's the shoes, do you?'

'What do you mean?'

'The break-in. Could it have been someone looking for the shoes?'

Sam goes cold. She heads back inside, suddenly completely alert. She walks with new eyes through the house, noting now how all the usual targets, televisions, iPads, are still there, albeit broken. But the house has been ransacked ruthlessly, every packet and box overturned and emptied, every drawer tipped out.

When Andrea arrives, she is sitting on the front step, her puffy coat around her shoulders, holding her jewellery box on her knees. Everything is still in it. She knows the little gold trinkets are not valuable – most are gold-plated necklaces, earrings Phil bought her back before Cat was born – but they are also proof that, whoever was in here, they were not opportunists, or junkies trying to get enough for a fix. These intruders were looking for something specific.

'Sammy.' Andrea is out of the car before the engine has stopped ticking, a soft woollen beanie in place of her usual wrap. She half walks, half runs up the path, and as Sam stands up, she embraces her. It is then, for the first time, that Sam feels overwhelmed and tearful. She feels herself giving in to Andrea's tight hug. 'It's so awful in there. It's a complete mess,' she says, into her shoulder. 'I don't even know where to start.'

'Good job we're here, then, isn't it?' Sam glances up and Jasmine is standing behind Andrea on the path, a large bag of cleaning materials in one hand and a roll of black rubbish sacks under her arm. 'No point waiting for the police, babe. You got to be an oligarch or a politician to get police for a break-in these days. Believe me, I *know*.'

Nisha climbs out of the rear car door, bringing with her a mop and bucket, and from the other side of the car Grace emerges, trailing at the rear, carefully holding a cardboard tray of coffees with both hands. 'Andrea called,' Jasmine says. 'We swapped shifts to go in late. We figured this wasn't something you should handle alone.'

She can't even speak. The relief she feels at the sight of them makes her knees go weak. Nisha stops and peers in through the front door. She stands, surveying it for a moment, then turns back to Sam.

'I hate him. I'm really, really sorry.'

Nisha is now an expert at tidying and cleaning messes, but there is something about this particular job that hardens her, tightens a muscle in her jaw as she sweeps and scrubs. She can see past the broken glass and splintered objects to the bones of the little house, a family home, steeped in love; wedding photographs and badly framed family pictures are dotted around like no stylistic note mattered, just the fact of them being together. The worn sofa that speaks of a million comfortably cuddled-up evenings, the faded children's paintings that nobody can face taking down from the hall. Carl has sullied this house. She crouches, sweeping up the tiny fragments of splintered glass, wiping spilled preserves from the kitchen floor, and thinks she has rarely hated Carl more. And she is an Olympic champion at hating Carl. It is one thing for him to punch out at his business foes, at her even. They were opponents who might stand a chance. But to punch down on a little family that clearly has nothing (not even very much taste, she admits guiltily) – it's just mean. She can see from Sam's chalk-white face that she will no longer feel safe in this house, that the things that are broken will not be easily replaced. He has broken the most fragile thing of all: the sense of calm and sanctuary that a home should provide.

'Oh, my God.'

Nisha looks up and Sam, a bin bag in her hand, is staring at her phone. Jasmine and Andrea are working upstairs and she can hear the vacuum cleaner whining as it is dragged backwards and forwards.

'What?'

'Miriam Price – a woman I did some work for – just called. Wanting to know why I hadn't confirmed with her about a job interview.'

'Okay. What did you say?'

'That I didn't feel like I could because I got fired. And because of the whole – you know – theft thing. I didn't think she'd want to speak to me. I mean she'd asked me to come in, but after that happened I just didn't see the point so I didn't bother to –'

'Yeah, but what? What did she say?'

'She wants me to come in for an interview anyway.'

Nisha pulls a face. 'Well, that's good, right? You need a job.'

Sam looks anguished. 'But it's today. Midday today. And look at me! I've been burgled. My house is destroyed. My husband has left me. I've barely slept in two days. How the hell can I do an interview today?'

Nisha wipes at her face with the back of her sleeve. She puts down her mop. 'Call her back. Tell her you'd be delighted.'

Jasmine and Nisha pick out her outfit while she is in the shower. When she emerges, her hair wet and wrapped in a towel, her body draped in a cloud of self-consciousness, Jasmine is walking into her bedroom, bearing a newly ironed pale blue blouse on a hanger.

'Do you fit these?' Nisha is holding up a pair of dark trousers.

'I think so,' she says. She has barely eaten in the last few days.

'Okay. Dark trousers and pale blouse – you can't go wrong. I found this jacket in your daughter's room. I think you'll fit it.'

'But –'

'Your jackets are all awful. No offence. This is Zara but it looks more expensive. No no no no! Put that sweater down. You want to look like you have authority, not like you just escaped from a care facility.'

Nisha holds up a pair of shoes Sam had worn to her cousin's wedding three years ago. 'And these.'

'But they're bright blue. And they're . . . heels.'

'You need something to pop. The outfit is conventional. It shows you mean business first. The shoes suggest there might be something slightly more interesting going on. The shoes say confidence. C'mon, Sam, get with the programme!

These people are going to be judging you from the moment you walk in. This is your armour, your calling card. You have to project.'

When Sam looks hesitant, Nisha seems irritated. She puts the jacket down on the bed and says, 'How did you feel when you wore my shoes?'

Sam wonders if this is a trick question. But Nisha is waiting expectantly. 'Uh . . . a bit awkward?'

'And?'

'And then . . . powerful?'

'Right. Powerful. A force to be reckoned with. And how do you feel now? Look at yourself. Who do you see?'

'Um . . . not me?'

'You see a print sales executive person. Or whatever the hell it is you do. You see a woman who has her shit together. Who has it *going on*.'

Sam sits as Jasmine begins to towel-dry her hair.

'Where's your makeup?'

'Bathroom cabinet. Next door.'

'Yeah, I saw that stuff. No. Your actual makeup bag.'

'That's it.'

Both women stop what they are doing and stare at her.

'Sam.' Nisha is stern. 'That stuff is old enough to walk itself out of your bathroom. Are you an actual savage?'

'Maybe?'

'You have nice skin, though, babe. I can see you look after it.' Jasmine starts combing her hair through, spritzing it with one of Cat's many hair lotions.

'I just use a bit of Nivea.'

Both women laugh. Nisha nudges her. 'Yeah. Right. That's what the supermodels always say.'

'And I stay so slim just by running round after my kids all day.'

They collapse in gales of laughter. Sam, who really does

375

use just a bit of Nivea, raises a weak smile and decides not to say anything else.

Half an hour later, Sam stands in front of the mirror in her now tidy bedroom.

'Shoulders back,' Nisha instructs her.

She stands taller and lifts her chin. Jasmine has blow-dried and tonged her hair so that it is voluminous and vaguely shiny. Her makeup has been done by Nisha, who has magicked away the shadows under her eyes, and done something to her lids so that they seem wider and more defined. She does not look like herself. She looks like someone who might be about to get herself a job. She raises a small smile.

'*Yesss!*' says Nisha. 'There she is. There's our player.'

'Chin up and tits out?' she says, and turns to face them.

'Not too much. That's a terrible bra. What? . . . What?' says Nisha, as Jasmine whacks her.

'Just remember, Sam!' Jasmine says. 'You're the woman who can bring an entire hotel to a halt! Power in those hands!' She points to her palm.

'Yeah. There is,' says Nisha, rubbing her arm ruefully.

'I'm driving you,' says Andrea. 'These guys are going to stay here and finish cleaning up.'

Sam stands in her room, gazing at the three mismatched women. She looks suddenly uncertain again.

'Don't be nervous,' says Andrea. 'It doesn't matter if you don't get this one. Think of it as a practice run so you get used to being in interview situations again.'

But Sam still looks troubled. 'Why would you do this for me?' she blurts out.

Nisha pulls at one of Sam's lapels, straightening it. 'Because . . . because you helped me. And because, you know, you're an okay person. You're okay, Sam.'

376

Sam's eyes have filled with tears. 'But you've done so much. All of you. You've changed everything today. The cleaning up. The clothes. The – I've never had anyone be so – so . . .'

'Nope,' says Nisha, firmly, taking her by the elbow and steering her out of the door. 'You are not getting sentimental. And you are definitely not going to spoil my excellent makeup by crying. Those eyeliner flicks did not get there by accident. Go, Andrea. Go take her. Go get the damn job. We'll be waiting.'

Nisha, Jasmine and Grace listen as Andrea's little car pulls away. When she is sure it has gone, Nisha stoops to pick up the smudged tubes and palettes of makeup that now litter Sam's bed. My God, but that is a terrible duvet cover. What is it with these Englishwomen and their awful florals? She looks up and Jasmine is smiling at her, a knowing smile, hinting at mischief.

'What?'

Jasmine looks at her daughter, then nods to herself. 'You're a nice person.'

'What? No, I'm not. Get out of here.' She gathers up the last of the mucky little tubes, preparing to take them back to Cat's bedroom. Though she could do them both a favour and put the whole lot in the garbage.

'You did a nice thing. There's a heart in there. And you can't help it showing up.'

'Ugh. Just . . . clean up your stuff.'

'*She's a nice person. Nisha's a nice person.*' Grace and Jasmine's voices are singsong and mocking. Over and over she tells them to shut up, but they are still singing it by the time they all go downstairs.

An hour and a half later Sam walks out of the Harlon and Lewis offices. Andrea is waiting in the car park and she walks

377

slowly across the tarmac in the unfamiliar shoes, her bag tucked under her arm. It is possible Andrea may have been dozing: she gives a little start as Sam opens the door of the Micra and climbs in, closing it with a *thunk*.

'Well?'

Sam kicks off the shoes in the footwell. She stares ahead, then turns to her. She looks like someone who has had several electric shocks.

'I got it,' she says, her voice trembling slightly. 'I got the job.'

They stare at each other.

'Working directly to Miriam Price. And it's more money than I was getting at Uberprint. I start in a week.'

Miriam Price leaves the office five minutes later. She walks past the blue Nissan Micra on the way to her car, and sees two middle-aged women bouncing up and down in the front seats, hugging each other and shrieking like teenagers. She pauses to watch, smiles to herself, and turns away to find her car keys.

35

Carl has tried to call Nisha seventeen times, and every time she sees his name she experiences something that may be hot or cold flash through her. She can't quite tell. She lies on the top bunk and stares at the phone buzzing silently and insistently in her hand and waits until it stops. Her not answering him will enrage him. You do not ignore Carl. He will know she has the shoes now, because Ari saw her. Aleks has warned her not to answer it, it may give away her location, but it will only be a matter of time before Ari tracks her down. He had got as far as Sam's house after all.

But she doesn't want to talk to him until she knows what to do. The others have told her she should keep the diamonds, start again somewhere else. *You'll be set for life! I bet they'll be worth loads more than he's offering you!* But she knows Carl. It won't even be about the worth of the gemstones. It's the fact that it will be unbearable to him that she has won any kind of victory over him. And here is her dilemma: if she keeps the diamonds she at least has some kind of financial security. It is still possible he'll try to screw the deal, and avoid paying her. But if she keeps the diamonds he'll never leave her alone. He'll spend the rest of his life looking for payback.

She remembers one of their circle, Rosemary, a furious, steely-eyed betrayed wife who fought back in the courts until she was awarded an alimony settlement of more than seven hundred and fifty thousand dollars a year. Her ex-husband could easily have afforded it; it was basically his lunch budget. But instead, raging at the judge's decision, he refused to pay, circling the globe, shifting his assets, and running up year after year of legal costs challenging the decision until, a decade later, she was exhausted and both of them were broke. Some men couldn't bear to lose at anything. She has walked that afternoon to a place in Hatton Garden where a man suggests they talk in his back office, doesn't ask where the diamonds came from, and says he can take them all off her hands for eighty thousand pounds. From this she deduces they're worth at least ten times as much. She had seen him clocking her cheap jacket, his immediate assumption they were stolen.

'I can take them a couple at a time, if that makes it easier,' he said, as she left.

The phone buzzes again. She stares at it.

And finally she picks up.

'I have the shoes,' she says. 'You'll have them when you show me my settlement.'

'You don't get to dictate terms.'

'Those were your terms, Carl, if you remember.'

He is briefly silent. She can sense his barely suppressed rage at the other end of the line and a faint shiver travels through her.

'Where are you?'

'I'll bring them tomorrow,' she says. 'The hotel. Downstairs in the lobby.'

'Midday. I'm leaving straight after for the airport. So no games. If you don't turn up, you can stay here with no settle-ment and rot.'

He puts the phone down before she can respond.

She still finds herself becoming a little shaky when she hears his voice. She lies there, regulating her breathing for a while then shifts onto her side. She has tried Ray twice this evening and he hasn't picked up. She is just about to send him another text when she notices Grace's collection of costume jewellery on her mirror, the strings of beads and fake crystals hanging from its corner. And Nisha starts to think.

Sam is wiping down the work surfaces in her parents' kitchen. This is not the straightforward job it would be at home, as wiping more than six square inches of the scarred, ancient Formica involves moving jars, piles of paperwork, redundant milk cartons and spare batteries that may or may not have any life left in them but won't be thrown away as 'It's bad for the planet to have them in landfill.' It has taken her four hours so far to haul the house back into something resembling an orderly state, and she hasn't yet finished the kitchen.

'But why is Cat staying with Andrea? Is the house not secure? It's very worrying. I told your father ages ago we should get an alarm.'

His voice echoes from the living room, where he is completing a 2,000-piece jigsaw that may or may not have been contaminated with pieces from the box above it. 'You said not to get an alarm as you didn't want it going off and making a racket.'

'Don't be ridiculous. I wanted an alarm. You were too tight to pay for one.'

Her mother had thrown her hands to her face when Sam told her about the burglary, her apparent delinquency in not cleaning for weeks briefly forgotten while her mother considered this greater transgression. She had wanted to know everything: what they had taken (nothing), whether any of her neighbours' houses had suffered the same fate (no), whether the police were doing anything about it (they still hadn't come) and appeared vaguely disappointed at all the answers.

'But if the house is secure again, why is Cat at Andrea's?'

Sam wrings out the dirty cloth in the sink. 'Because Phil's not at home just now and I didn't want her being alone there

381

while I'm out.' It had actually been Nisha's idea. They should both stay away for now, she said. Ari knew bad people. She had looked vaguely apologetic as she said it.

'Well, where's Phil? Oh, my goodness, they didn't hurt him, did they? Is he in hospital?'

'No, Mum.' She pulls a face when she moves a jar and finds a large lump of mouldering Cheddar behind it. 'He – he's gone away for a bit.'

Even when distracted by the prospect of violent crime her mother possesses the laser instincts of a homing pigeon. 'Are you two still having problems?'

Sam puts the cheese into the bin and washes her hands under the tap, keeping her face turned away. 'He just needs to clear his head.'

'I told you, Tom. Didn't I tell you? This is the problem when a woman works like you do. It is *no good* for a marriage. A man has to have a little pride, and by being the sole breadwinner you have taken it away from him. Look what happened to Judy Garland.'

Sam puts down the cloth. She rests her hands on the edge of the sink. 'You're thinking of *A Star Is Born*. And, actually, Mum, he left because he thought I was having an affair with a work colleague.'

'Don't be ridiculous. Did you just throw that cheese into the bin? That's a waste. We could cut the ends off it.'

Sam stays very still for a moment. Then she opens the bin, pulls it out from the rubbish and places it in her mother's hand.

'Mum,' she says, pulling off her apron. 'This is the last time I am cleaning for you. I love you and Dad very much, but I am about to start a new job, which will be very demanding. In the limited time I have left to myself, I need to focus on my family, or at least what remains of it. Just as you advise. I have called three cleaning agencies, all of which have capacity, and now that the house is straight I'm sure they'll be very happy to help you. Here are the numbers. The second, by the way, is the cheapest. It's possible they use indentured labour. Possibly Afghan. Maybe check with the union. Now if you'll excuse me.'

She kisses her mother's stunned face, squeezes her father's arm, and picks up her coat from the chair, where one of them had dropped it on her arrival.

'Lovely to see you both. Yes, I'm fine, thanks. Still a little shaken, and frankly exhausted. Very, very sad about the end of my marriage. But nothing four hours of unpaid cleaning can't fix. Right! I'm off. I'll let you know how the new job goes.'

She closes the door with a vigorous slam that she knows will annoy them, and doesn't look back as she leaves.

Joel is already waiting in the café when she gets there. She sees his head, dipped over his phone, and when it lifts at the sound of the door opening his smile is tentative and gorgeous. She hesitates for a minute, then walks in and takes a seat at the wooden table opposite him.

'I got you a cappuccino,' he says, pushing it towards her. 'I wasn't sure what you wanted.'

She smiles and takes a sip. Joel watches her and drums his fingers lightly on the table top. He has beautiful nails, even, neat and spotlessly clean. She wonders absently whether he files them. Maybe he gets manicures, like Cat's friend Ben. She knows nothing about him, really. She could have projected all sorts of ideas onto him. For all she knows, he may have a passion for Byzantine lute music, or a collection of antique dolls in his spare room. The thought makes her giggle and it turns into a sort of odd hiccup. What do they know about each other anyway?

'You okay?'

She straightens her face and swallows. 'I think so. You?'

'Fine. Fine.'

She takes another sip.

'So I had a talk with Marina,' he begins. 'And we think we can get you your job back. She got some guidance from a mate in HR and apparently Simon should have given you a formal warning and because we can prove you didn't actually steal those shoes, if we get that woman to write –'

'Joel, I'm not coming back,' she says. And then: 'I got the job. With Miriam Price.'

Joel's eyes widen a fraction. 'Harlon and Lewis. Woah.' He leans back in his chair, taking this in. He is wearing a shirt she hasn't seen before and it stretches over his shoulders as he moves.

'I – I can't come back.' She shakes her head. 'It's not a good place for me any more. Not with . . .' Her voice tails away.

He considers this. His mouth purses at the corners and he nods. 'We can still see each other at boxing, though, right?'

Across the café a couple are dandling a baby on the father's knee. Its head wobbles with mirth as the mother blows raspberries at it.

'I don't know.' She wants so badly to take his hand. She curls her fingers through the handle of the mug, so that she cannot do it without thinking. 'I don't know what's happening with my marriage. But I have to try and I – I can't – this thing –' She holds her coffee mug tighter. 'I don't think I can see you any more. I need to feel like a good person and this . . . this makes me feel good, but it doesn't make me feel like a good person. Does that make sense?'

And it's out there. The thing she has rolled through her head in her sleepless nights. An acknowledgement that there is something between them, and that whatever it is cannot continue. The only thing she has been able to hang on to is the sense that she can somehow be a good person again. She meets his gaze. It is sad and understanding, and makes something in her turn over.

'Are you . . . back together?'

'No. I don't know.' She sighs. 'We've been married a long time. It's hard to just – I mean, he's not a bad man. It's hard to walk away from all that history without a backward look. I don't know. Maybe he already has. Maybe I need to be by myself and work out who I am without him. It's just hard when I've never really been . . . without him.' They sit for a moment. 'It's complicated, isn't it?'

He nods. 'It really is.'

'I thought I'd have it all figured out by this age.'

He lets out a short laugh. And then he looks serious again. 'I hope he appreciates you, Sam. You're . . . you're special.'

'I'm not. Not really. You're probably better off with some-one less . . . complicated. But thank you. For giving me . . .'

He leans forward in his seat then and reaches across the table, his palm resting gently against the side of her face. He kisses her lightly and, just for a moment, lets his forehead rest against hers, so that she can feel the warmth of his skin, their breath mingling in the space between them. They stay like that, oblivious to the gurgle of the coffee machine, the scraping of chairs and the sounds of the baby beside them, and she hears what she thinks might be a sigh.

Sam places her hand over his, and gently brings it down from her face, leaning back slowly in her chair. She gazes at his hand in hers and turns it over, surveying the scarred knuckles, the nails a few shades lighter than his skin. When she looks up, the smile they give each other is sad and true, and filled with the things neither of them can say.

Joel breaks the moment. He squeezes her hand briefly, then stands, releasing it. She is not sure what she can read on his face: pride? Disappointment? Resignation? He turns and, without saying anything else, takes his jacket from the back of the chair, nods to her, and leaves.

Sam drives the camper-van along the narrow street to her house, and parks at the front, noting that the builders have finally finished the adjoining wall. She needs to pick up more clothes for her and Cat, who seems to get through three out-fit changes a day. They will move back in tomorrow once Nisha has sorted things out with Carl. But in the moments she allows herself to think about it, she doesn't know how she will feel about staying in this house. It still holds, in the unmoving air, the echo of the break-in, the occasional tiny crunch of something broken underfoot and lodged deep in the carpet. When she closes her eyes she sees the devastation of her little home; it wakes her up at night. 'At least you have the terrifying guard dog,' Andrea had said, looking at Kevin, legs splayed and snoring on her floor.

Not for the first time, Sam feels the loss of her old life like a wound. The world is full of lasts, she thinks. The last time you pick up your child. The last time you hug a parent. The last time you cook dinner in a house full of the people you love. The last time you make love to the husband you once adored who will walk away from you because you turned into a crazy, resentful hormone-fuelled idiot. And with all these moments you don't know that this will be the last or you would be overwhelmed by the poignancy of them, hang on to them like someone unhinged, bury your face in them, never let them go. Sam thinks about the last time she curled herself around Phil's body. If she had known it would be the last time would she have done things differently? Would she have been more patient? Less angry? If she thinks about the possibility that she will never hold him again, a hole opens up in her middle that leaves her feeling like she might just disintegrate.

In for six, hold for three, out for seven.

Sam steels herself as she reaches the front door. What would Nisha do? She would toughen up, be practical, strategize. So, she will head to John Lewis and replace the broken items tomorrow. At least there will be money coming in again in a month's time. She'll live off credit till then. Perhaps at some point she may even have a little over to help Andrea. She flinches as she hears a sound from inside and stops in her tracks, slowly peers around the door, her heart racing. *Carl Cantor's men.* Her heart thumps all the way up in her throat. She feels a fine sweat break out on her skin.

She creeps around the side of the house to the back door and reaches slowly behind the moss-covered garden gnome for the back-door key. They must have broken in, but she can't see where: there are no obvious signs of forced entry. Of course there aren't. They are professionals, like Nisha said. But that doesn't mean they can just let themselves in. Adrenalin begins to course through her, and as she stands listening to the sounds of movement inside she finds that, instead of fear, she feels only cold fury. There is someone in her house, her home. Treating it like it's theirs to walk all over, to take what they want. Well, they're not going to take anything else. And she's not going to be walked over any more. Sam sees the cat in the bin, Simon's smirk, her kitchen, smashed and desecrated, her beloved family photographs trodden into the floor, the hours it took to get everything straight. Sam Kemp has had enough.

She places her hand quietly on the handle, sees the shadow behind the glass door, and there he is, the man, bending down. To do what? Sift through what he has already wrecked? Finish what he started?

Sam does not have a plan. She knows there are a million reasons why it will be unwise for her to interrupt the intruder who is in her house, but something in her body propels her with a roar that seems to come from somewhere in the pit of her stomach, pulls her right fist back, and with a jab that would have had Sid cheering, punches the intruder full in the face, sending him tumbling backwards onto the floor.

'But what – what were you *doing*?'

'Putting things straight.' Phil's voice is muffled. He is still holding some screws in his left hand and now, as she holds the ice pack against his nose, he drops them gently onto the coffee-table. They leave indents in the skin of his palm where he must have been clutching them too tightly. 'Cat told me what happened. I came to help.'

She'd like to know what else Cat has told him but she doesn't want to ask. She takes the ice pack off for a moment and touches his nose where the bruise is already purpling, the small cut that she has carefully covered in Savlon. His face, so familiar and unfamiliar to her touch. She puts the ice pack back, desperate for something to do with her hands. It is then that she sees the television propped in the corner.

'Oh. Yeah. She told me they'd smashed ours so I rang around the lads and asked if anyone had a television we could borrow. This one's Jim's. He said it lives in his garage because his wife prefers him to watch the racing out there. He's a bit noisy apparently when he has a horse coming in.'

'I thought you didn't like asking your friends for anything.'

'It seemed daft not to. It – it sounded like it was quite a mess.'

'Yes,' she says. 'It was.'

He looks different somehow. Even under the ice pack. She realizes he has shaved. He is wearing jeans instead of jogging bottoms and a fresh shirt. But there is something else: he seems less hunted, like he's more certain of the space he occupies.

'The boxing training's working, then,' he says, and touches his nose gingerly.

'I'm so sorry,' she says. 'If I'd thought for one moment it might be you I wouldn't have –'

'That was quite a punch.'

She feels a little weak as the last of the adrenalin leaches away and she sits heavily back on the sofa. They smile awkwardly. She looks at her knuckles. The middle one has gone a purplish colour and the skin is grazed where it may have made contact with Phil's teeth.

'I – I didn't actually know I could hit that hard.'

He looks at her ruefully. 'Yeah. Well. You always were stronger than you thought.'

They sit for a moment, his words hanging in the air. Phil leans back beside her. He rubs his free hand over the top of his head. Neither of them looks at the other.

'I messed up, Sam,' he begins.

'You didn't mess up. I –'

'Please. Let me just say something. I messed up. I just . . . lost myself for a bit. And I didn't want to admit it. But I've started on anti-depressants – the happy pills. Apparently they should start kicking in soon' – he raises a small smile – 'and I've been talking to someone. A therapist. Yes. Me,' he says, at her shocked expression. 'I should have told you but I knew you were worried about money and, well, I guess I just didn't. I didn't tell you a lot of things.' He sighs. 'I don't know why but I'm doing it now. I'm doing all the things.'

'Phil –'

'Sam. I don't know if I want to talk about what happened yet. I'm not sure I want to know. But – but you and Cat are my life. Spending a few days at my mum's, away from you both, I knew I'd made a terrible mistake. I don't blame you, Sammy. I don't blame you, whatever it was. I just know I want to be better. I want my wife back. I want us back. I want – I want just to feel like I have a home again.' He swallows. 'If . . . if I do still have a home.'

She throws her arms around him then. She had listened to his words, one part of her thinking she should be reserved, maybe argue her case, but he's speaking and there's a sweetness to his face, a hopefulness and openness that makes something in her crack apart. She holds him around his solid waist, feeling his arms slide around her, his lips on her hair, and she thinks, *This is where I need to be.*

'I love you so much, Sammy. I won't lose you again. I promise.' His voice cracks on the words.

'You'd bloody better not,' she says, into his shirt. She cannot let go. She may never let him go. They clutch each other and she is aware suddenly of a rising feeling of gratitude and hope, two sensations that feel utterly, utterly unfamiliar. Maybe sometimes things do work out, she thinks, and it feels like a radical thought.

They are still in this position when the door opens. They hear Kevin's bark before they see Cat, who is standing a little warily in the hall, looking at them through the living-room door. Phil makes as if to move back, but Sam doesn't release him. She thinks she may stay here for the rest of her life.

'I got us another telly,' Phil says, when they cannot think of anything else to say. He gestures towards it.

'Dad is fixing everything,' says Sam, into his shirt.

There is a short silence.

'Oh, no. Does this mean I don't get two Christmases?' says Cat. 'Bummer.' But she's smiling as she strides down the little hallway to the kitchen.

36

Juliana texts her at 1.43 a.m.

He's okay. I've told him you're coming. And I'll go every day until you're here.

Another text follows a couple of minutes later. He reminds me so much of you x

There is something about Aleks's scent that Nisha could inhale for ever. It's not aftershave: Carl used to wear a cologne that was both expensive and intrusive, so that you could tell which room he had been in for half an hour after he had left it. Aleks's scent is indefinable but comforting, and she likes to bury her face in the place where his neck meets his shoulder and just breathe it in.

'Not sleeping?' His voice eases into the dark.

'No.'

'You okay?'

'I think so.'

His hand slides along her side, and she closes her eyes, enjoying the gentle, speculative weight of his warm palm. He lives in a building two streets back from the river, an ex-council block where most of the residents had bought out their leases, so that it carries a sense of pride. His apartment is whitewashed and spare, as if it reflects the aesthetics of its owner. He has installed wooden floors, insulated against noise – he did them himself, he told her with quiet satisfaction

– and aside from his daughter's room, which is rich with colour and shelves of rainbow-coloured tchotchkes, there is little to distract the eye in each room. So little noise seeps in that it is hard to remind herself they are in the centre of London. His bedroom contains simply a low bed with no headboard, an antique chest of drawers, and two large vintage Polish film posters hang on the wall. In the living room there is nothing bar two sofas and a huge built-in shelving unit of books. She had felt infused with its calm, as if it had somehow seeped into her via osmosis as soon as she walked in.

'You don't have much stuff,' she had said.

'I don't need much.'

It is the first time she has slept in another man's bed in almost twenty years. It is the first time she has slept in a double bed in weeks, and the combination of space, fresh cotton sheets and the freedom to wrap herself around Aleks's good hard body have felt like the greatest of luxuries. Aleks doesn't seem to want anything from her, doesn't pepper her with questions or demand responses. He has no expectations as to how she should be when she is with him. He just seems quietly to assess her mood and her wants, then decide where to meet her. She wants him, of course. She can barely look at him without wanting him. It's as if her body is drawn magnetically to his; she needs to feel her skin on his, the warmth of his lips, cannot bear him being close by but physically separate from her. The less he appears to need this from her, the more she wants him. But this changes when he kisses her; it is at this point that she feels something different emerge. He stops being laconic and careful: he drinks her in greedily, his hands stroke and grip, hold her, worship her. His whole self insists she stay connected to him. His eyes are on hers, and there is something raw and deep in this kind of intimacy that feels almost terrifying to her.

'Are you thinking about tomorrow?' he says, pulling her into him.

'Maybe.'

'Your son?'

'Always. But maybe . . . with a little less anxiety.'

'She sounds good, this Juliana. I'm glad you found her again.'

He kisses her forehead, winds his fingers into her hair. If Carl had done this it would have felt like the precursor to an assault. With Aleks it feels delicious, as if they are a knot that cannot be untied. She hooks her leg over his hip, pulling him in further.

'Your head is still whirring,' he says sleepily. 'I can hear it.'

'Really?'

'Like an engine.'

She can hear the smile in his words. She lifts her face to look at him, tilts her hips towards his.

'If you were any kind of gentleman you would find a way to take my mind off it.'

'Oh,' he says, amused. 'I see. You think I am not a gentleman.'

'I'm very much hoping not,' she says. And then he is poised above her, his lips on her skin, and she is breathing him in and a short time later she is not thinking about very much at all.

'So you're just going to hand them all over.'

Andrea shakes her head, her arms crossed over her chest. She reaches for her tea on the table and lets out a low sigh of disapproval.

'I don't have a choice. If I don't he'll come after me – and he might come after you guys too. I don't want you all mixed up in this mess. It's not just about a divorce settlement any more, is it?'

'But what if he doesn't give you a settlement? You'll have nothing. No bargaining chip.'

Nisha pushes her hair back from her face, glances at Aleks beside her. 'I've thought about nothing else for twenty-four hours. He doesn't know I know about the diamonds, and that's the safest place for us to be. I hand back the shoes before he does any more damage, hope he sticks to his word, and then . . . I don't know. I guess I'm free.'

Andrea shrugs. 'Maybe he'll want to marry this other woman. Then it'll be in his interests to get you off the scene as fast and cleanly as possible.'

'I don't know,' says Sam. 'Everything you've said about him? I don't think you can trust him to do the right thing.'

They are in Sam's kitchen, which is almost unrecognizable from the war zone of the weekend, thanks to Phil's efforts, replacing blinds and refixing shelves. He is boiling the kettle to make more tea, and stands with his back resting against the work surface, regarding the little group around the table. She can see he is intrigued by these women, by her sudden place in a story he doesn't recognize. He sees her looking at him and smiles a secret smile, just for the two of them.

'You'll have to make him sign the settlement before you hand over the shoes,' says Andrea. 'It's the only way.'

'Make sure you meet him in a public spot. So he can't snatch them.'

'Where are the shoes, anyway?' says Andrea. It hadn't occurred to her to ask.

'In a safe place,' says Nisha, in a manner that suggests that conversation is over.

'I don't like this,' says Andrea, again. 'I wish Jasmine wasn't working the early shift. I don't like you doing this alone.'

'I'll be in the kitchens,' says Aleks, quietly. 'If you need me. It's not so far away.'

'She won't be alone,' says Sam, and everyone turns to look at her. 'I'll go. I'll go with her.'

*

They drive to the Bentley in silence in the camper-van – Cat has borrowed the car now that Phil has replaced the battery. Sam knows Nisha is nervous as she has failed to complain about the mode of transport once, even when she took a corner too sharply and something fell off a shelf with a crash in the rear. She lets out a sharp exclamation when she sees the menopausal traffic cop at a temporary traffic stop by the hotel and tells Nisha the story of what happened when she ran the red light, but Nisha seems barely to register it. In the end Sam gives up talking completely.

She parks on a meter that seems to charge the GDP of a small country, and they walk the few minutes to the Bentley, going in through the side door so that they can wait undisturbed in the staff changing room.

Nisha has been deep in thought since they left her house, and had insisted on leaving so that they are at the hotel almost an hour early. Jasmine has told Sam a little about Nisha's son, that he is unhappy and alone, so she needs this to work in order to get back to him, and Sam finds herself gazing at her as they sit on the little bench, wondering how it would feel to be a whole continent away from your vulnerable child.

Nisha looks up. 'Are you okay? You're more nervous than I am!'

'I guess it's weird, isn't it? Knowing that this guy was responsible for . . . you know. What happened. And we're just going to sit down with him.'

'I'm pretty sure he's done worse.'

'And this is supposed to make me feel better?'

Half an hour passes. Nisha, checking the time compulsively, decides she needs a cigarette and makes Sam follow her outside. 'Disgusting habit,' she says, standing by the bins and inhaling deeply. 'I'm giving up.'

She keeps glancing down the alley as if she's looking out for Ari. 'I'm just going to have one more.' When she finishes she says: 'Shall we walk through the foyer? Just to work out where to sit?'

There is clearly some huge internal turbulence going on, and Sam has decided the most helpful thing she can do is just go with it. She follows Nisha through the side door into the foyer, only half wondering if someone might recognize her, and there is Michelle, the heavily made-up blonde girl at Reception, chatting on the phone. Jasmine is standing by the concierge. She clocks them and raises an eyebrow. She nods towards the end of the room and Nisha turns to follow her gaze.

'Shit. He's here already.'

Sam feels a shot of adrenalin shoot through her. She glances over to a low table, surrounded by three plush, curved sofas, at which a group of besuited businessmen are drinking coffee. A young blonde woman sits to the side of Carl, taking notes on an iPad. She looks slim, glossy and vaguely proprietorial. Sam looks back at Nisha, who is staring hard, her thoughts clearly somewhere far away.

Sam looks again at the man in the centre. It's clear even at this distance which of the men is Carl: he is bigger, stockier, older than the others, and he gives off a subtle air of authority, a king presiding over a court. The only man larger than he is stands behind him wearing an earpiece.

'I recognize him.'

'Yeah. He's been in a lot of business magazines. He loves being photographed. Hard to believe, right?'

Sam cannot take her eyes from him. The grey-flecked hair, slicked back behind his ears, the oversized belly. And then it hits her. She puts her hand on Nisha's arm. 'Nisha. I have to go.'

'What?'

'I have to get something. I'll be right back.'

Nisha turns to her, disbelieving. 'Are you . . . bailing on me?'

Sam is pushing her way back down to the staff corridor.

'Seriously? You're bailing?'

She can hear Nisha's protest – '*You're just going to leave me to do this by myself?*' – and then she is gone, running as fast as she can towards the van.

'What do you mean she ran off?' Aleks is cooking but turns to face her, one white cloth slung over his shoulder.

Nisha is pacing backwards and forwards in the breakfast station, oblivious to the furious glances of the sous-chefs nearby. 'She took one look at him and his goons and she bailed. Just ran away. Honestly? I should have known. She's too timid. She's too freaked out because of the burglary. I should have asked Andrea.'

Aleks gives his pan a brisk shake. Behind him the kitchens are in full swing, the air filled with the sound of clattering pans and yelled instructions. 'Can you ask Jasmine to be in the foyer? Keep an eye on you? I can't leave my station for at least an hour.'

'I'll be fine,' she says, and reaches up to kiss his cheek. 'Seriously. I'm just . . . mad at her. Just needed to vent. Can I get them?'

He reaches into his pocket with his free hand and pulls out a locker key. She takes it and heads to the staff changing room. In the stale, quiet little room she scans the wall of lockers until she finds 42 and opens the door. Inside are jeans, a clean T-shirt (the chefs always smell of frying when they're done).

She lifts his T-shirt out carefully and inhales the scent of his washing powder, briefly taken back to the previous evening, and as she puts it back, she notices the picture on the door: a small, battered image of him with his arm around a young blonde girl, who is gazing at him adoringly. She stares at it for a minute, and thinks of Ray at the same age. *I'm coming for you, baby*, she tells him silently. And then she reaches into the back, where the shoes are secured in a black plastic bag, and closes the locker again.

'I'll be right here, Nisha,' he says, when she hands back the key. 'Call me when you're done.' He puts his pan down, places his arms around her and kisses her, not even caring if the other kitchen staff see. 'You're going to be fine. You're going to get what you want. Because you are a magnificent, magnificent woman.'

She closes her eyes for a moment, letting him murmur the words into her ear.

'Thank you,' she says, and straightens her Chanel jacket.

She smokes two more cigarettes out by the bins, goes to the staff toilet twice (what is it with nerves and bladders?), then brushes her teeth and rearranges her hair, putting it up and taking it down again just three or four times. She checks her phone, and takes several deep breaths. It is five minutes to twelve.

37

The businessmen are just leaving when Nisha approaches
the little table. She waits a few feet away until she's sure he's
seen her, and he takes an extra long time over his goodbyes.
A power move. She's watched him do it a million times: make
someone wait and they are already somehow less important
than you. The anger that had fuelled her through their last
meeting seems to have dissipated and now Nisha feels the
butterflies trembling in her stomach, the slight shakiness in
her legs. She remains visibly emotionless, conscious of the
men looking at her curiously, at the proximity of Charlotte,
who shifts just an inch closer to Carl, either to display her
own power, or perhaps because she is a little nervous about
Nisha too. Finally, after an interminable wait, he acknowledges her.

'Ah. Nisha,' he says, and motions at her to sit down. He
does not stand up.

'Not with her,' she says.

He holds her gaze, as if trying to assess whether this is an
argument he wants to pursue. But then he turns to Charlotte.
'Give us a minute, darling. Perhaps you can make sure everything is cleared from the room.'

'But not my clothes,' says Nisha. And then adds, mischiev-
ously, 'Darling.'

Charlotte, perhaps aggrieved at being denied her moment
of triumph, gives Nisha a sharp, resentful look as she stands.
She stalks off towards the elevators with a toss of her hair.

'Where's Ari?' Nisha says, sitting down.

'Why do you want to know?'

'Just wanted to make sure he's not breaking into anybody else's house. A public service, if you like.'

'I can't think what you're talking about,' he says, and smiles blankly. He spies the carrier-bag by her shoes.

'So now you're carrying plastic bags instead of Chanel handbags. Classy.'

'I didn't think the moment deserved much more.'

He laughs then. 'Nisha, Nisha. I always enjoyed your sharp tongue. So – are they in there?'

He reaches forward, but she scoots the bag back under her feet.

'I want to see the settlement. I'm assuming it's all drawn up.'

'I want the shoes first.'

'Why would I be here if I wasn't bringing the shoes?'

'I don't know, darling. Your behaviour has always been a mystery to me.'

'You'll get them when I see the settlement.'

He sighs, shakes his head. He motions to a bespectacled man in a suit she hasn't noticed before, but who has clearly been waiting at a nearby table. The man hurries over and presents Nisha with a sheaf of papers. She looks down. A typewritten agreement of several pages, the first headed *Separation Agreement.*

'Well?' he says.

'I need to read it,' she says. She looks up, and sees Ari in the corner, watching her. She scans the room. Frederik the manager is by the desk talking to one of the receptionists, a man she does not recognize. As he talks he glances over twice. He will have been briefed too. She cannot see Jasmine. She sits up straight, determined not to let him see how alone she feels.

This document states according to the law of the state of New York that the petitioner and the respondent's relationship has broken down for a minimum of six months and that the petitioner has so stated under oath.

'Hang on,' she says, suddenly. 'This document is dated six months ago.'

'Yes. That's when you signed it.'

She flicks through the pages until she sees it: her signature, a little unsteady but it definitely resembles hers. 'What? I never signed this. This says we have been separated for months. This has already worked out all the financial stuff. This says we are practically divorced.'

'I thought it was best to get the ball rolling. Alistair prepared a document for us in advance.'

She scans the financial settlement. A sum to pay for a two-bedroom apartment in the city of her choice, up to a value of one point five million dollars. Ray's college fees. A monthly settlement of ten thousand dollars until he leaves college.

'I didn't agree to this. You've – you've forged my signature.'

'No, darling. You just don't remember signing it. You always did have your head full of nonsense.'

She looks at Alistair, who turns away, a little awkwardly.

'But this is not even five per cent of what you would owe me in a proper settlement.'

'It's perfectly fair. If you look at the company accounts you'll see we've had a very tough few years. We've had to sell all sorts of property to pay our debts. This – it's half of what I have left. The judge apparently thought it was perfectly equitable.'

She thinks of what the lawyer had told her, that Carl would have been busy hiding his assets in all sorts of secretive offshore places. She thinks of the house in London he had sold without telling her. He has been planning this for months.

'This is not a fair settlement, Carl, and you know it.'

'It's a hundred per cent more than you'd have got in Hicksville, Ohio.'

He leans back against the sofa cushions. 'Anyway. You seemed perfectly happy signing it all when we were in St Tropez.'

She thinks back suddenly, to a night at the Hôtel du Cap. He had insisted they drink cocktails, even though he knew she couldn't hold her spirits. That evening, just when she had said she really needed to go to bed, her head spinning, he had told her he needed her to sign a pile of papers, had stood over her as she worked her way through them without looking. This was not unusual: she was used to signing documents that helped him with his business. She had been a director, a spouse, a company secretary, a tax dodge. Roles that came and went according to what his accountant said was needed at the time. It was what she did. The perfect company wife.

'You tricked me into signing my own divorce papers?'

He checks his watch. 'The offer is on the table for ten minutes. After that you can fight me for whatever you think you'll get. I'm going to take a piss.'

He gets up heavily, and Ari appears suddenly at his side, walking him the twenty yards to the foyer lavatories. Jasmine, who has clearly been waiting while slowly dusting the surfaces in the lobby, rushes around the sofa and sits down beside her.

'What's happening?' She picks up the sheaves of paper, ignoring the mild protestations of Alistair, who cannot work out why a maid has just grabbed his highly confidential financial document.

'Nope,' says Jasmine, scanning it and putting it down. 'No, babe. That's not even what he pays in retainers to this place to keep the penthouse. I saw the figures once.' She shrugs when Nisha stares up at her. 'You can't let him fob you off with this.'

'But if I don't I might end up with nothing. He's clearly planned it all.'

'You can't sign these. That's it. Right?' Jasmine turns to Alistair. 'If she signs the rest of the papers she can't claim for anything else?'

Alistair blinks. 'Ah, yes. That would be correct. They will be technically divorced from that point.'

Jasmine and Nisha stare at each other. Nisha sits, her thoughts whirring.

Jasmine puts a hand on her arm. 'Babe. You can't do this.'

'He's done me up like a kipper,' Nisha says quietly.

Carl is making his way back from the Gents, listening to something Ari is saying. He starts laughing, looking as relaxed and cheerful as if he had just come back from a good lunch. Charlotte emerges from the lift and skips after him. She says something urgently to him and he lets his hand rest briefly on her belly and nods. As Nisha stares, registering this, Charlotte follows him back to the table, a smile already on her lips.

He has outmanoeuvred her again, Nisha realizes. In so many ways. She never stood a chance. She lifts her chin and remains composed as Charlotte arranges her extravagantly long legs alongside Carl's.

Just then, her attention is drawn to a faint commotion in the foyer. She glances to her right and there is Sam, running towards her, slipping slightly on the marble floor.

'Nisha! Nisha!' She is holding up her hand. As she sees Carl, she stops, and motions frantically.

Carl looks at Sam, at her anorak, her mom jeans and scuffed trainers. He smirks at Nisha. *This is who you mix with now?*

'Nisha. *Please.* I need to speak to you.'

Nisha looks at Sam's pleading expression. 'Give me a minute.'

'We're leaving in five,' Carl says, and sits down, waving to Ari to fetch him some water. Charlotte runs a manicured hand over his thigh, letting it rest there.

'I recognized him,' Sam says breathlessly, dragging Nisha to the side of the foyer. 'I recognized him. Your husband. I've put the original in a safe place, but I got Phil to download it onto my phone.'

Nisha stares at her, trying to work out what Sam is telling her. She looks down at Sam's phone as Sam, fingers stumbling on the keys, clicks a little video into stuttering life. And there he is: Carl, stark naked in black and white in a tiny pixellated form, Charlotte crouched over him.

'What's this?' says Jasmine, peering over her shoulder.

'Oh – *oh.*' Nisha is briefly transfixed. '*Ohhh. Oh, no.*' She blinks, then pulls a face. Then looks up at Sam, who is watching her intently.

'The night I wore the shoes. This man just handed it to me in the pub. I had a quick look with Andrea and we just . . . well, we just thought, *Eurgh* . . . like it was some kind of prank. Sorry, no offence.'

'Totally fair,' says Jasmine.

'And I just stuffed it into a drawer and forgot about it. And then I realized when we walked in. That's your husband, isn't it? Him! In the video.'

Nisha looks at Sam. 'My insurance,' she murmurs. 'I'd forgotten.'

'I already texted it to you. Figured you'd need copies.'

Nisha looks at her phone. Sees the notification that says the video is there, waiting.

'Okay,' she says, breathing hard. 'Okay.'

'Now you can roast that pitiful excuse for a man,' says Jasmine. '*Yesss!*'

Sam smiles then, a huge abrupt smile of happiness and pride. 'You can. There's your bargaining chip. There's your new settlement.' She cannot resist a further comment. 'See? I told you I knew about deals.'

Carl looks briefly perplexed when the two women sit down on the sofa. He regards, with barely disguised disgust, Sam's dishevelled appearance, her slightly jiggly air of anticipation. And then he becomes almost theatrically bored. He sighs, checks his watch, and drawls, 'Are you done?'

Nisha leans forward and studies the document. 'So, according to this document we separated six months ago. Even though you and I know that's not true.'

'That's right.' He takes a sip of his water and leans back in the chair.

'And you will transfer that settlement . . . when? Now?'

'Nish – hang on!' Sam begins, but Nisha holds up a hand.

Carl nods. 'Alistair will do it. But I want to see the shoes first.'

Nisha reaches down. She pulls the bag onto her lap and removes one of the crocodile-skin high heels. She had glued the heels back on carefully with Grace's craft gun the previous evening. She turns it left and right, then pulls out the other, so that he can see both, then puts them back into the bag.

'So . . . making me run around trying to find my own shoes was just a joke. A way of keeping me at bay while you fixed this up.'

Carl's expression doesn't flicker. 'Maybe. Does it matter?'

'You know her feet are too big for them? She does have very large feet.' She nods towards Charlotte, who opens her mouth, and then smiles sweetly at Carl. 'Are you *really* sure you want these shoes?'

They hold each other's gaze, and suddenly there it is. They despise each other. Nisha cannot believe she ever shared her life with this man.

'Give me the shoes,' he says, his voice low and dangerous.

'Sam – give me your bank details,' Nisha says.

'What?'

'I don't have access to a bank account here. As he well knows. Give me your bank details.'

Sam slowly taps her phone, then hands it over. Nisha hands the phone to Alistair.

'Nisha –' Sam protests. But Nisha stays her with a raised palm.

'I want to see the money arrive in that account. Oh, for God's sake, Carl,' she says, when he hesitates. 'I'm hardly about to run away now. I know Ari will have people at every entrance. I'm not stupid.'

'This is a bad idea,' Sam whispers urgently. 'Nisha. Don't do this.'

'Do it,' says Carl. They wait as the transaction is completed online. Sam reluctantly shows Nisha the figure in her bank account. Nisha motions to Jasmine, who is hovering nearby.

'Can you collect my things from the penthouse, please? And bring them to the front entrance?'

'Your belongings, madam. Certainly!' Jasmine says, and hurries off towards the elevators. Nisha waits until Jasmine is in the elevator. And then she holds out her hand for a pen.

'Okay, I'll sign.'

'Nisha,' Sam grabs Nisha's arm, '*you don't have to do this. You have the thing. You can get what's owed to you!*'

But Nisha shakes her off. She signs each document carefully, hands them back and waits as Alistair witnesses each one. He hands her a finished copy. Nisha takes it and folds it neatly, tucking it into her jacket. Then she lets out a long breath.

'So that's it. All over. We're signed and done.'

'We're done,' says Carl.

She stands then, and holds out the bag with the shoes. She can see Carl does not want to hold a plastic bag – it is clearly beneath him – so he nods at Ari, who takes it from her and peers into it. Beside her Sam is staring at Nisha open-mouthed, her expression one of barely suppressed anguish.

Ari nods. Carl turns back to her. 'Well, darling. You were as cheap at the end as you were at the beginning.'

'Nice, Carl,' says Nisha. She begins to make her way out from behind the table. She waits until she is a few feet away, then stops.

'Oh. I nearly forgot. I've just sent you something,' she says, with a small smile. 'A little parting gift.'

Carl is standing, straightening his jacket. She waits as he looks down at his phone, hears the little *ping* that sounds its arrival.

'From now on we're strangers. You leave us alone. If you or your goons come after me or Ray, or anything more happens to any of my friends, this will be uploaded onto the internet. Or maybe sent to the tabloid press. Whichever is more . . . appropriate. There are several copies, so don't get any silly ideas.'

'What are you talking about?'

'Just a little something for you two lovebirds to watch on your ride home,' she says. 'Also? Charlotte? A word of advice: some women really can't wear Yves Saint Laurent. You make it look like . . . What is it?' She turns to Sam and spits the words. 'Oh, yes, *Primark*.'

And with that, Nisha strides across the foyer and into the watery winter sunshine, just catching his muffled yell of outrage as the main doors are opened in front of her.

Nisha is walking so fast that Sam has to jog to keep up with her. Her head is spinning, and the words come tumbling out of her now that they are away from the table.

'What the hell did you just *do*? You could have got a proper settlement out of him. You could have been set up for life. I gave you what you needed!'

'I don't care,' Nisha says, striding away from the hotel. 'I don't want it. Where's the RV?' She turns, distracted, looking towards the back entrance.

Sam pulls her round to face her. 'But you had everything in place. Everything! You could have got him to agree to anything with that video.'

'And then I would have been just as disgusting a human being as he is. Where the hell is Jasmine?' Nisha lifts her head, scanning the entrance.

It takes a moment before they spot her emerging from the side entrance. She is pushing a huge brass suitcase trolley alongside Viktor, laden with all of Nisha's clothes. When she sees them, she and Viktor change tack, pushing it towards them.

'Can you bring it to the RV?' Sam calls. 'It's only around the corner.'

'What is going on, babe?' Jasmine is slightly out of breath. She swings the strap of her handbag onto her shoulder as Nisha grabs the other corner of the trolley.

'I don't understand,' Sam exclaims. But Nisha doesn't appear to be paying attention. She is apparently focused only on getting to the camper-van, and doesn't look back. Sam exchanges a glance with Jasmine, who shakes her head like she doesn't get it either.

By the time they reach the van they are all out of breath.

Viktor helps them load the clothes into the back, and gives Nisha a handshake when she hands him a ten-pound note. 'Right,' she says, as they watch him pushing the empty trolley back towards the hotel. 'Let's go.'

Sam finally erupts. 'You're insane!' she yells. 'You've spent all this time going on about how you have to have what you're owed, making us believe it too. You go on and on about people standing up for themselves. And then, when it comes to it, you just – you just fold and give it away! Jesus, Nisha. You've made me feel like an absolute limp lettuce for weeks. Why should I have listened to a word you said?'

She climbs into the front. Jasmine takes the place between them on the bench seat and Nisha climbs in last, pulling the door shut behind her.

'Please – just tell me you've got the diamonds hidden somewhere,' says Sam.

'Nope. They're in the heels of those shoes.'

'You could have kept them!'

'And then I would have been no better than him.'

'That man destroyed my house. He put the fear of God into all of us. He took twenty years from you and brought your son to his knees. And you're just going to give him what he wants and walk away? And you made me watch while you did it? I don't understand you, Nisha. I really don't.'

'Girl's found her voice,' says Jasmine.

'I have enough,' Nisha says calmly. 'If I have a roof over my head, my son with me and my friends, then I have enough. I'm happier. Okay? I'm happier this way.'

Sam wrenches the camper-van out into the traffic. The two other women have fallen silent, Nisha apparently deep in thought and Jasmine briefly silenced by this turn of events. Sam, trying to focus on driving the unwieldy vehicle, decides she cannot think about this just now. She cannot feel so angry.

The whole few days have been too discombobulating. She just wants to go home and be with Phil. She wants to be with people she understands.

'Where's the traffic cop?' says Nisha.

'What?'

'The cop you pointed out on the way here. Where is she?'

Sam glances at Jasmine, who gives the universal subtle facial arrangement that says, *No, me either.*

'I'm not going to run another red light,' she says, irritated. 'I'm going to drive back very carefully. Okay?'

'Go past the traffic cop. There. There she is.'

Sam indicates left, even though that way is longer, and drives at a precise 20 m.p.h. until she sees the policewoman.

'Slow down,' says Nisha. 'Now pull in.'

Sam, confused, stops the camper-van, ignoring the blast of the horn behind her. Nisha waves vigorously out of the window. The traffic officer looks up, then tilts her head to one side as if she's unsure what she's seeing. She begins to walk over to the van, clocking the huge sunflower on the side.

'Not you again,' she says, when she sees Sam.

'I'm so sorry,' Sam begins. 'I'm not sure why my friend is –'

Nisha is leaning out of the passenger window.

'I have a tip for you that is going to change your life. Take down this registration: PYF 483 V. In this car there will be a man with a pair of fake Christian Louboutin shoes. In the heels there are more than a million dollars' worth of uncertified diamonds that have been imported illegally into this country. It's not the first time he's done it.'

The cop looks at Nisha, then at Sam. 'Is this a joke?'

'No,' says Nisha. 'I am so far from joking.'

'And why should I believe you?'

'Do I look like I'm kidding?'

The two women stare at each other for a minute. Some

peculiar understanding that only occurs between one woman of a certain age and another seems to take place.

'Illegal diamonds.'

'If this doesn't get you a massive promotion I will come back here and you can arrest my ass.'

Jasmine and Sam say nothing. The traffic officer studies Nisha's face. 'What was that registration again?'

'PYF 483 V. The car will be leaving the Bentley Hotel and headed towards London City Airport. In about five minutes.'

The woman narrows her eyes.

'It's true,' says Sam.

'How's your friend?' says the officer, suddenly.

'Really good, thanks,' says Sam. 'Her hair's growing back.'

'Oh. Nice.' The officer nods, satisfied.

'Five minutes,' says Nisha. 'Tops.'

She looks at each of them in turn, still thinking. As they wait, she slowly lifts her radio to her mouth, her eyes never leaving Nisha's.

'Control? Yeah, I need eyes on a vehicle possibly containing smuggled diamonds. Registration PYF 483 V. Yes. ASAP. Leaving the Bentley Hotel and headed for City Airport. Yes, large quantity of illegal diamonds on board.'

She lowers her radio.

'And this tip comes from?'

'Oh, just an anonymous member of the public.'

The officer gazes at Nisha's left hand. 'An anonymous pissed-off ex-wife member of the public?'

'I like you, PC 43555. You should have been a detective.'

'Marjorie,' says the officer. 'And I've been bypassed for promotion four times in five years.'

'Not after this one. You have a great day, Marjorie,' says Nisha, and as the officer turns back to her radio, Sam pulls into the road.

Sam drives for a few minutes, her mind racing. She keeps glancing at Nisha, who is sitting beside her, eyes closed, hands resting on her knees, as if some huge turmoil is finally easing. 'I've just worked it out. You were ahead of him the whole time.'

'He wouldn't have left me alone. Or you. Or Ray,' Nisha says, opening her eyes and staring straight ahead through the windscreen. 'But he thinks we know nothing about the diamonds. So he won't associate us with what is about to happen to him.'

She lights a cigarette. 'Only useful thing my daddy ever gave me,' she says, inhaling. 'People decide what they think you're capable of based on how you look, doubly so if you're a woman. And if you're a woman of a certain age, that boils down to pretty much nothing. In my case Carl thinks I'm just an angry desperate has-been who cares about nothing but her wardrobe.'

Sam shakes her head. 'Oh, you're good,' she says.

Nisha lets out a long plume of smoke. 'Also, as I am now apparently divorced, there appears to be nothing in law to stop me testifying against him.'

There is a brief silence. Then Jasmine lets out a whoop. Sam starts to laugh. She cannot help herself. She laughs so much that she crunches the gears and has to swerve to avoid a bollard.

Nisha smooths imaginary lint from her trousers. 'See?' she says, smiling sweetly at Jasmine. 'I told you I wasn't nice.'

38

A strike by airline staff at Terminal 5 means that bad-tempered queues are backed up almost to the doors of Heathrow airport. Nisha doesn't mind, even when the son of the family behind keeps wheeling his suitcase into the backs of her legs as the security queue inches forward. She stands beside Aleks, who periodically places his hand on the small of her back, or shifts her oversized Prada handbag into his other hand. The first time he had offered to take it for her she had laughed incredulously: Carl would have died rather than hold a woman's handbag, but Aleks seems to find the offer unremarkable. 'It looks heavy. I can carry it for you.'

She is wearing her Chloé shearling coat, ready for the winter weather Stateside, and although she tries to imagine she is not a shallow person, these days, every time she feels the luxurious softness of the high collar something in her just melts with pleasure. You can change a person, but probably only so much.

She thinks back to the previous evening at Sam's. Sam had cooked for everyone – roast chicken and all the trimmings, a proper send-off, she said. They had sat around the little kitchen table until the small hours, talking and drinking and laughing. Sam had glowed. She was wearing makeup like Nisha had shown her – even if Nisha thought privately she hadn't quite mastered her eye flicks – and she smiled and laughed easily and glanced at her husband often. She was excited to start her new job. Miriam had called her twice just checking she had all the information she needed, suggesting they go for a drink after her first day so she could debrief. She had fixed her up her own parking space in the car park. 'It's going to have my name on it! My name on a parking space!' Nisha thought that twelve inches of plastic lettering in a car park in White City might not be the zenith of her own ambition but, hell, it made Sam happy, so she smiled and said it sounded amazing.

Andrea left her head bare for the entire evening. She wore big earrings and a soft red scarf, which disguised the pronounced slenderness of her neck and said she would have two portions of chicken as she seemed to be getting her appetite back. She did not have a job. Or a partner. 'But I'm okay for now,' she said philosophically. 'That's all we can ever be, right? Okay for now.' They had toasted this wisdom, which had seemed infinitely wiser three bottles of wine in.

Grace had sat at the end of the table near Cat. They had talked in the tentative way that teenagers who don't know each other but are in a crowd of adults do. Sometimes Nisha would watch them and wonder what it would be like to have Ray among them. He would like Cat, who was sassy and interesting-looking. She would not be a pushover, like her mother had been. But it's Grace, she thinks, who would *get* him. Grace with her watchful nature and faint hint of mischief.

'Are you excited?' Aleks says, breaking into her thoughts.

She cannot speak then, thinking of her son. She looks up at him and smiles and he gives her a gentle squeeze.

Aleks had not left her side the entire evening. He is the easiest of company, engaging Phil in conversation about his job applications, discussing literature with Grace, who wants to do an English degree, offering to help with sauces and complimenting Sam extravagantly on her cooking. He feels new and old at once, so effortless to be with that she sometimes wonders if this can be real at all. That night, as they lay together in the near-dark, her head a little woozy with the amount of wine she had drunk, he had taken her hand in his and kissed each knuckle, one at a time, and told her with great solemnity that she was extraordinary and beautiful and brave and funny, and that when he closed his eyes she had somehow taken up residence in every part of him so that he felt entirely altered by her in the best possible way. She had stared at him. 'I think those may be the nicest words anyone has ever spoken to me,' she had said, her voice stumbling uncharacteristically.

'Oh, no,' he said. And kissed the knuckle of her thumb. 'There will be many more.'

'This could just be a sex thing,' she said cautiously. 'I mean, I've been in a relationship a long time. I don't really know . . . who I am outside of it yet. I mean, I might just be using you for sexual gratification.'

'And what a terrible thing that would be for me,' he said, and his eyes slid towards hers, narrowed with amusement.

They do not talk about the future. Nisha understands now that whatever you plan will probably be blown out of the water anyway.

Jasmine had cried for half an hour on the doorstep of Sam's house, refusing to let Nisha go. 'You're going to come back, right? I mean we'll stay in touch? You're not going to just forget us?'

'I will call you the moment I land.'

'You're not going to get all hoity-toity and leave us behind now you've got money?'

Nisha had tilted her head and given her the same kind of look Jasmine would have given her for leaving the immersion switch on, so that Jasmine started waving her hands.

'I know, babe. I know. I'm just really going to miss you.'

They had hugged tightly, and Nisha had whispered, 'Don't go all sentimental on me. This is just a short break, okay? We have a whole bunch of things to do together. I need to see you opening up that dressmaking business for a start.'

'Passport.' The security officer holds out a bored hand. She hands it over while he checks her ticket, and then, as she takes it back, stamped and readied, she steps to the side of the queue. Aleks passes her the handbag, his face grave.

'So,' he says.

'I'll call you when I land.'

He nods.

'Oh,' she says. 'I nearly forgot. Will you do something for me? Drop these in? I don't want to put them in the post.'

He looks down at the addresses on the small brown Jiffy bags and says, 'Sure. Did you forget to do it last night?'

'Something like that.'

He pulls her to him then and embraces her tightly, silently, oblivious to the mutterings of the crowd, the jostling of the hundreds of people around them. She presses her face against his chest, her eyes closed, and above the noise she can just detect the beat of his heart.

'Call anytime,' he murmurs into her hair. 'I'll be waiting.'

I think he actually will, Nisha thinks. And this thought finally gives her the resolve it takes for her to extract herself from him. She gathers her bags and is waved forward by the airport personnel, fed into the stream of passengers through the opaque glass doors and into the security area.

Nine hours later Nisha is in a yellow taxi cab, speeding through the watery December sunshine towards Westchester County, the suspension bumping and rattling as it flies over the neglected freeway. There are many things that Nisha has become accustomed to in her new straitened circumstances, but flying cattle class is not one of them. She rubs her neck as she straightens up in the back seat from her short nap, and lets out an involuntary *ow* as her thumb finds a particularly unhappy tendon. The aircraft had been packed, and turbulent, and the endless adjustments of the seat in front of her and the muttered argument between the two passengers on her right has meant that she has arrived exhausted, crumpled and tetchy, not refreshed and glowing, as she had assumed she would.

'This one, lady?' The driver raps on the glass between them with a fat knuckle.

She looks over and sees the sign. 'That's it. Are you still happy to wait?'

'You're paying, I'm waiting,' he says, without a smile, and turns up the long driveway, accelerating a little.

She is a quarter-mile from the building when she spies the figures on the steps. She leans forward in the rear seat, trying to see better through the windscreen, and as the taxi makes its way up the sweeping drive, the thinner figure stands. Against the elegant white brickwork of the school building, she sees the shock of dark hair, the gawky limbs, even at this distance. And something starts to pump through her, an energy she has not been aware of these last years, a thread pulled so tight that she feels it must surely snap. Beside him, Juliana stands and says something into his ear, then puts a hand on his shoulder. Nisha is out of the taxi even before it has stopped moving in the parking circle, ignoring the shouted warning of the driver, the fact that she has twisted her ankle in her high-heeled shoes, the way her handbag has dropped onto the drive, its contents spraying over the pale gravel.

And there he is, his ungainly teenage body unfolding, stepping at first tentatively, and then his limbs falling over each other as he jogs down the steps, and then he is running and she is running and they reach each other by the large stone lions and she wraps her boy in her arms, her beautiful, clever,

417

kind boy, and feels his arms around her and suddenly, Nisha Cantor, who rarely cries, is sobbing, her fingers clutching his head, her face pressed against his as she lets herself acknowledge what she has missed.

'Mom,' he says, and he is crying too, holding her so tightly she can barely breathe.

And she screws her eyes closed, just breathing him in, joyous and finally, finally home. 'Baby. *I'm here.*'

Epilogue

The case of *HMRC Customs* v. *Mr Carl Cantor* is surprisingly straightforward, despite the battalion of lawyers he employs to obstruct and combat the legal process prompted by the discovery of £21 million worth of uncertified stones in his possession. Records obtained after his security adviser Mr Ari Peretz decides to turn Queen's evidence against him show that this is the fourteenth such smuggling operation Mr Cantor has completed in five years, moving uncut, uncertified diamonds into the UK where they are polished, then returned to the US and sold on via contacts in the South African and Russian diamond trade. Despite Mr Cantor's protestations of innocence, he is found guilty and sentenced to be incarcerated in the US under an extradition agreement, the length of sentence to be decided.

Tabloid newspapers take a special, somewhat triumphant interest in the judge's observation that Mr Cantor appears to have been duped by his own contacts. The records of the smuggling operation that caused his downfall appear to be misleading. Discovered among the large, cushion-cut gems removed from the insides of a pair of specially adapted women's shoes, many worth several million pounds each, are three basic paste stones of the kind one might find in a child's necklace. The journalists note that Mr Cantor appears to be as angered by this apparent deception as he is by the prospect of a lengthy spell in prison (a possibility he steadfastly refuses to accept, despite the best efforts of his counsel).

Andrea wakes with a hangover, and observes dully that feeling like death when you have sunk the best part of a bottle of wine each with your friends is not that much better than actually feeling like death. She smiles wryly at the thought as she moves slowly down the stairs of the cottage to make what she promises herself is going to be a large mug of her very good coffee, the final capsule before she will finally have to admit financial defeat and switch to the supermarket own-brand instant variety. She feeds the cat that winds itself around her legs and, while the machine is brewing, reaches over to the cupboard to get her favourite striped cup. It is then that she notices the envelope on her doormat. It is several hours before the post usually arrives (if it arrives at all), and as she steps closer she notes that the envelope has no stamp.

Briefly comforted by the fact that this, at least, is unlikely to be another final demand, she checks the handwriting, which she does not recognize, and then, taking a sip of her coffee, opens the Jiffy bag carefully, squinting at the writing as her eyes are still a little blurry.

It takes her two attempts to read the note inside.

Take this to the address below at Hatton Garden. He will give you less than it's worth, but it should be enough to keep you going until you're back on your feet.
N x
PS Do not tell Sam or Jasmine. They'll just get weird about it.

Underneath the address, secured to the note-card with a piece of sticky tape, is what appears to be a large, glittering, cushion-cut diamond.

It will be three weeks before Nisha returns with her son,

ready for the introductions and joyful reunions that will herald this next stage of their lives. It will be three months and eleven nights out – the last to celebrate the opening of Jasmine's new business – before Sam, Jasmine and Andrea discover during a tentative and then increasingly animated conversation that each of them received exactly the same note.

*

'Nice jacket.' Miriam has arrived late, and is slightly breathless as she enters the boardroom. She has called Sam to declare a hamster emergency: she needed to take her daughter's pet to the good small-animal vet on the other side of town. Miriam is big on flexible working, for whatever reasons. If you do the work, she says, and get the results, then you can work in the small hours for all she cares. Sam takes her seat at the boardroom table. She has bought Miriam a coffee and Miriam accepts it gratefully, sitting down.

'Thanks. It's just Zara,' says Sam, 'but I think it looks good.'

'It does. You should wear more bright colours. Hey, do you and Phil fancy lunch this Sunday? We want to christen the new extension. There'll be some people there I think you'll like. I promise we won't talk work.'

'That would be really nice. Thank you!'

Phil and Sam are trying to do something new every weekend. It's a thing Sam read in a magazine, an article about how to inject fun back into your marriage. She thinks she might enjoy lunch with Miriam and Irena more than the indoor climbing wall Phil had insisted on the previous week. They had agreed, ruefully, as they rubbed their aching, middle-aged limbs afterwards, that rock-climbing might not be their thing.

'Ah. And here they are,' says Miriam, shuffling the papers in front of her into a neat pile. She looks up and smiles at

Sam. 'So this is the company we're taking over. I couldn't really talk about it until the legals were done. But I thought you might like to lead this one. We're going to have to make some personnel cuts, to start. I think you'll have no problem working out where that should happen. My feeling is that it needs someone like you to be in charge.'

'In charge?'

'Yes. The board would like you to consider heading up this company. Or should we say, this new division of Harlon and Lewis?'

Sam looks through the doorway where Emma, the receptionist, is just showing in two young men, both carrying folders. Sam blinks at the familiar slightly pointed shoes, and then registers the shiny suit, the sudden unease visible in their owner as Simon recognizes her.

She looks at Miriam, her jaw dropping slightly.

Miriam raises her eyebrows. Smiles. 'Like I said, I thought you'd like to take this initial meeting. We can discuss your more formal change of position later.'

Sam lets her hands rest on the table for a moment. Then she picks up her pen and takes a deep breath.

'Well,' she says, beckoning them in, 'this is going to be fun.'

Acknowledgements

All books are a collaborative endeavour and so thank you, as ever, to my wonderful editors: Louise Moore and Maxine Hitchcock at Penguin Michael Joseph; Pamela Dorman at Pamela Dorman Books, Penguin Random House, in the US; Katharina Dornhofer at Rowohlt Germany; and the other editors across the globe who have continued to support, help and guide me. It is such a privilege to be published by such excellent publishing houses, and I never forget it.

Thank you to my tireless agent Sheila Crowley at Curtis Brown; the translation rights team present and past, including Katie McGowan, Grace Robinson and Claire Nozieres; and thanks Jonny Geller, Nick Marston and everyone else at the agency. Thanks across the pond to Bob Bookman of Bob Bookman Management for his endless energy and support and giving me tastes for wine some way beyond my budget.

Thanks again to Clare Parker, Liz Smith and Marie Michels and all the teams on each side of the Atlantic for your awesome skills in helping me get my stories in front of people. On a wider scale, thanks to Tom Weldon and Brian Tart and in Germany to Anoukh Ferg.

Huge thanks to Catherine Bedford of Harbottle and Lewis, who has been invaluable in explaining the divorcing behaviour of the super-rich (all stories discreet and anonymized, of course). I still think – with horror – about some of the things you told me. Any deviations from normal legal practice have been for the somewhat intricate plot requirements of the story, and any mistakes are entirely my own.

More personally during these strange few years, thank you yet again to Jackie Tearne for administrative help and friendship, Sarah Phelps for storyboarding over yard coffees, Emily White for back-up, Cathy Runciman, Alice Ross, my Litmix pals Maddy Wickham, Jenny Colgan and Lisa Jewell, Glenys Plummer, Lydia Thomson for keeping me afloat, Lee Child and Ol Parker for invaluable advice when I needed it most, Becky McGrath and, last but not least, John Hopkins for cheerleading me through the tougher parts of writing this and so much more.

Endless gratitude to my family – Jim Moyes, Brian Sanders, and most of all Saskia, Harry and Lu for always being so understanding about the weirder parts of this job.

I love you all very much.